D1468986

Also by Sue Grafton

C is for Corpse
&
D is for Deadbeat

Two Novels in One

Sue Grafton

St. Martin's Paperbacks

This is a work of fiction. All of the characters, organizations, and events portrayed in this book are either products of the author's imagination or are used fictitiously.

Published in the United States by St. Martin's Paperbacks, an imprint of St. Martin's Publishing Group

For information, address St. Martin's Publishing Group, 120 Broadway, New York, NY 10271.

www.stmartins.com

ISBN: 978-1-250- 80097-8

Our books may be purchased in bulk for promotional, educational, or business use. Please contact your local bookseller or the Macmillan Corporate and Premium Sales Department at 1-800-221-7945, ext. 5442, or by email at MacmillanSpecialMarkets@macmillan.com.

Printed in the United States of America

St. Martin's Paperbacks edition / March 2022

10 9 8 7 6 5 4 3 2 1

C is for Corpse

For the children who chose me:
Leslie, Jay, and Jamie

The author wishes to acknowledge the invaluable assistance of the following people: Steven Humphrey; Sam Chirman, M.D., and Betty Johnson of the Rehabilitation Group of Santa Barbara; David Dallmeyer, R.P.T.; Deputies Tom Nelson and Juan Tejeda of the Santa Barbara County Sheriff's Department; C. Robert Dambacher, Chief of Investigations, Los Angeles County Medical Examiner–Coroner; Andrew H. Bliss, Director of Medical Records, LAC-USC Medical Center; Delbert Dickson, M.D.; R. W. Olson, M.D.; Peg Ortigiesen; Barbara Stephans; Billie Moore Squires; H. F. Richards; Michael Burridge; Midge Hayes and Adelaide Gest of the Santa Barbara Public Library; and Michael Fitzmorris of Security Services Unlimited, Inc.

1

I met Bobby Callahan on Monday of that week. By Thursday, he was dead. He was convinced someone was trying to kill him and it turned out to be true, but none of us figured it out in time to save him. I've never worked for a dead man before and I hope I won't have to do it again. This report is for him, for whatever it's worth.

My name is Kinsey Millhone. I'm a licensed private investigator, doing business in Santa Teresa, California, which is ninety-five miles north of Los Angeles. I'm thirty-two years old, twice divorced. I like being alone and I suspect my independence suits me better than it should. Bobby challenged that. I don't know quite how or why. He was only twenty-three years old. I wasn't romantically involved with him in any sense of the word, but I did care and his death served to remind me, like a custard pie in the face, that life is sometimes one big savage joke. Not funny "ha ha," but cruel, like those gags sixth-graders have been telling since the world began.

It was August and I'd been working out at Santa Teresa Fitness, trying to remedy the residual effects of a broken left arm. The days were hot, filled with relentless sunshine and clear skies. I was feeling cranky and bored, doing push-downs and curls and wrist rolls. I'd just worked two cases back-to-back and I'd sustained more damage than a fractured humerus. I was feeling emotionally battered and I needed a rest. Fortunately, my bank account was fat and I knew I could afford to take two months off. At the same time, the idleness was making me restless and the physical-therapy regimen was driving me nuts.

Santa Teresa Fitness is a real no-nonsense place: the brand X of health clubs. No Jacuzzi, no sauna, no music piped in. Just mirrored walls, body-building equipment, and industrial-grade carpeting the color of asphalt. The whole twenty-eight-hundred square feet of space smells like men's jockstraps.

I'd arrive at eight in the morning, three days a week, and warm up for fifteen minutes, then launch into a series of exercises designed to strengthen and condition my left deltoid, pectoralis major, biceps, triceps, and anything else that had gone awry since I'd had the snot beaten out of me and had intersected the flight path of a .22 slug. The orthopedist had prescribed six weeks of physical therapy and so far, I'd done three. There was nothing for it but to work my way patiently from one machine to the next. I was usually the only woman in the place at that hour and I tended to distract myself from the pain, sweat, and nausea by checking out men's bodies while they were checking out mine.

Bobby Callahan came in at the same time I did. I wasn't sure what had happened to him, but whatever it was, it had hurt. He was probably just short of six feet tall, with a football player's physique: big head, thick neck, brawny shoulders, heavy legs. Now the shaggy blond head was held to one side, the left half of his face pulled down in a permanent grimace. His mouth leaked saliva as though he'd just been shot up with Novocain and couldn't quite feel his own lips. He tended to hold his left arm up against his waist and he usually carried a folded white handkerchief that he used to mop up his chin. There was a terrible welt of dark red across the bridge of his nose, a second across his chest, and his knees were crisscrossed with scars as though a swordsman had slashed at him. He walked with a lilting gait, his left Achilles tendon apparently shortened, pulling his left heel up. Working out must have cost him everything he had, yet he never failed to appear. There was a doggedness about him that I admired. I watched him with interest, ashamed of my own interior complaints. Clearly, I could recover from my injuries while he could not. I didn't feel sorry for him, but I did feel curious.

That Monday morning was the first time we'd been alone together in the gym. He was doing leg curls, facedown on the bench next to mine, his attention turned inward. I had shifted over to the leg-press machine, just for variety. I weigh 118 and I only have so much upper body I can rehabilitate. I hadn't gotten back into jogging since the injury, so I figured a few leg presses would serve me right. I was only doing 120 pounds, but it hurt anyway. To distract myself, I was playing a little game wherein I tried to determine which apparatus I hated most. The leg-curl machine he was using was a good candidate. I watched him do a set of twelve repetitions and then start all over again.

"I hear you're a private detective," he said without missing a beat. "That true?" There was a slight drag to his voice, but he covered it pretty well.

"Yes. Are you in the market for one?"

"Matter of fact, I am. Somebody tried to kill me."

"Looks like they didn't miss by much. When was this?"

"Nine months ago."

"Why you?"

"Don't know."

The backs of his thighs were bulging, his hamstrings taut as guy wires. Sweat poured off his face. Without even thinking about it, I counted reps with him. Six, seven, eight.

"I hate that machine," I remarked.

He smiled. "Hurts like a son of a bitch, doesn't it?"

"How'd it happen?"

"I was driving up the pass with a buddy of mine late at night. Some car came up and started ramming us from behind. When we got to the bridge just over the crest of the hill, I lost it and we went off. Rick was killed. He bailed out and the car rolled over on him. I should have been killed too. Longest ten seconds of my life, you know?"

"I bet." The bridge he'd soared off spanned a rocky, scrub-choked canyon, four hundred feet deep, a favorite jumping-off spot for suicide attempts. Actually, I'd never heard of anyone surviving that drop. "You're doing great," I said. "You've been working your butt off."

"What else can I do? Just after the accident, they told me I'd never walk. Said I'd never do anything."

"Who said?"

"Family doctor. Some old hack. My mom fired him on the spot and called in an orthopedic specialist. He brought me back. I was out at Rehab for eight months and now I'm doing this. What happened to you?"

"Some asshole shot me in the arm."

Bobby laughed. It was a wonderful snuffling sound. He finished the last rep and propped himself up on his elbows.

He said, "I got four machines to go and then let's bug out. By the way, I'm Bobby Callahan."

"Kinsey Millhone."

He held his hand out and we shook, sealing an unspoken bargain. I knew even then I'd work for him whatever the circumstances.

We ate lunch in a health-food café, one of those places specializing in cunning imitation meat patties that never fool anyone. I don't understand the point myself. It seems to me a vegetarian would be just as repelled by something that *looked* like minced cow parts. Bobby ordered a bean-and-cheese burrito the size of a rolled-up gym towel, smothered in guacamole and sour cream. I opted for stir-fried veggies and brown rice with a glass of white wine of some indeterminate jug sort.

Eating, for Bobby, was the same laborious process as working out, but his single-minded attention to the task allowed me to study him at close range. His hair was sun-bleached and coarse, his eyes brown with the kind of lashes most women have to buy in a box. The left half of his face was inanimate, but he had a strong chin, accentuated by a scar like a rising moon. My guess was that his teeth had been driven through his lower lip at some point during the punishing descent into that ravine. How he'd lived through it all was anybody's guess.

He glanced up. He knew I'd been staring, but he didn't object.

"You're lucky to be alive," I said.

"I'll tell you the worst of it. Big hunks of my brain are gone, you know?" The drag in his speech was back, as though the very subject affected his voice. "I was in a coma for two weeks, and when I came out, I didn't know what the fuck was going on. I still don't. But I can remember how I used to be and that's what hurts. I was smart, Kinsey. I knew a lot. I could concentrate and I used to have ideas. My mind would make these magic little leaps. You know what I mean?"

I nodded. I knew about minds making magic little leaps.

He went on. "Now I got gaps and spaces. Holes. I've lost big pieces of my past. They don't exist anymore." He paused to dab impatiently at his chin, then shot a bitter glance at the handkerchief. "Jesus, bad enough that I drool. If I'd always been like this, I wouldn't know the difference and it wouldn't bug me so much. I'd assume everybody had a brain that felt like mine. But I was quick once. I know that. I was an A student, on my way to medical school. Now all I do is work out. I'm just trying to regain enough coordination so I can go to the fuckin' toilet by myself. When I'm not in the gym, I see this shrink named Kleinert and try to come to terms with the rest of it."

There were sudden tears in his eyes and he paused, fighting for control. He took a deep breath and shook his head abruptly. When he spoke again, his voice was full of self-loathing.

"So. That's how I spent my summer vacation. How about you?"

"You're convinced it was a murder attempt? Why couldn't it have been some prankster or a drunk?"

He thought for a moment. "I knew the car. At least I think I did. Obviously, I don't anymore, but it seems like . . . at the time, I recognized the vehicle."

"But not the driver?"

He shook his head. "Couldn't tell you now. Maybe I knew then, maybe not."

"Male? Female?" I asked.

"Nuh-un. That's gone too."

"How do you know Rick wasn't meant to be the victim instead of you?"

He pushed his plate away and signaled for coffee. He was struggling. "I knew something. Something had happened and I figured it out. I remember that much. I can even remember knowing I was in trouble. I was scared. I just don't remember why."

"What about Rick? Was he part of it?"

"I don't think it had anything to do with him. I couldn't swear to it, but I'm almost positive."

"What about your destination that night? Does that tie in somehow?"

Bobby glanced up. The waitress was standing at his elbow with a coffeepot. He waited until she'd poured coffee for both of us. She departed and he smiled uneasily. "I don't know who my enemies are, you know? I don't know if people around me know this 'thing' I've forgotten about. I don't want anyone to overhear what I say . . . just in case. I know I'm paranoid, but I can't help it."

His gaze followed the waitress as she moved back toward the kitchen. She put the coffeepot back on the unit and picked up an order at the window, glancing back at him. She was young and she seemed to know we were talking about her. Bobby dabbed at his chin again as an afterthought. "We were on our way up to Stage Coach Tavern. There's usually a bluegrass band up there and Rick and I wanted to hear them." He shrugged. "There might have been more to it, but I don't think so."

"What was going on in your life at that point?"

"I'd just graduated from UC Santa Teresa. I had this part-time job at St. Terry's, waiting to hear if I was accepted for med school."

Santa Teresa Hospital had been called St. Terry's ever since I could remember. "Wasn't it late in the year for that? I thought med-school candidates applied during the winter and got replies back by spring."

"Well, actually I *had* applied and didn't get in, so I was trying again."

"What kind of work were you doing at St. Terry's?"

"I was a 'floater,' really. I did all kinds of things. For a while, I worked Admissions, typing up papers before patients came in. I'd call and get preliminary data, insurance coverage, stuff like that. Then for a while, I worked in Medical Records filing charts until I got bored. Last job I had was clerk-typist in Pathology. Worked for Dr. Fraker. He was neat. He let me do lab tests sometimes. You know, just simple stuff."

"It doesn't sound like hazardous work," I said. "What about the university? Could the jeopardy you were in be traced back to the school somehow? Faculty? Studies? Some kind of extracurricular activity you'd been involved in?"

He was shaking his head, apparently drawing a blank. "I don't see how. I'd been out since June. Accident was November."

"But your feeling is that you were the only one who knew this piece of information, whatever it was."

His gaze traveled around the café and then came back to me. "I guess. Me and whoever tried to kill me to shut me up."

I sat and stared at him for a while, trying to get a fix on the situation. I stirred what was probably raw milk into my coffee. Health-food enthusiasts like eating microbes and things like that. "Do you have any sense at all of how long you'd known this thing? Because I'm wondering . . . if it was potentially so dangerous . . . why you didn't spill the beans right away."

He was looking at me with interest. "Like what? To the cops or something like that?"

"Sure. If you stumbled across a theft of some kind, or you found out someone was a Russian spy . . ." I was rattling off possibilities as they occurred to me. "Or you uncovered a plot to assassinate the President . . ."

"Why wouldn't I have picked up the first telephone I came to and called for help?"

"Right."

He was quiet. "Maybe I did that. Maybe . . . shit, Kinsey, I don't know. You don't know how frustrated I get. Early on, those first two, three months in the hospital, all I could think about was the pain. It took everything I had to stay alive. I didn't think about the accident at all. But little by little, as I got better, I started going back to it, trying to remember what happened. Especially when they told me Rick was dead. I didn't find out about that for weeks. I guess they were worried I'd blame myself and it would slow my recovery. I did feel sick about it once I heard. What if I was drunk and just ran us off the road? I had to find out what went on or I knew I'd go crazy on top of everything else. Anyway, that's when I began to piece together this other stuff."

"Maybe the rest of it will come back to you if you've remembered this much."

"But that's just it," he said. "What if it does come back? I figure the only thing keeping me alive right now is the fact that I can't remember any more of it."

His voice had risen and he paused, gaze flicking off to one side. His anxiety was infectious and I felt myself glancing around as he had, wanting to keep my voice low so our conversation couldn't be overheard.

"Have you actually been threatened since this whole thing came up?" I asked.

"No. Un-un."

"No anonymous letters or strange phone calls?"

He was shaking his head. "But I *am* in danger. I know I am. I've been feeling this way for weeks. I need help."

"Have you tried the cops?"

"Sure, I've tried. As far as they're concerned, it was an accident. They have no evidence a crime was committed. Well, hit-and-run. They know somebody rear-ended me and forced me off the bridge, but premeditated murder? Come on. And even if they believed me, they don't have manpower to assign. I'm just an ordinary citizen. I'm not entitled to police protection twenty-four hours a day."

"Maybe you should hire a bodyguard—"

"Screw that! It's you I want."

"Bobby, I'm not saying I won't help you. Of course I will. I'm just talking about your options. It sounds like you need more than me."

He leaned forward, his manner intense. "Just get to the bottom of this. Tell me what's going on. I want to know why somebody's after me and I want them stopped. Then I won't need the cops or a bodyguard or anything else." He clamped his mouth shut, agitated. He rocked back.

"Fuck it," he said. He shifted restlessly and got up. He pulled a twenty out of his wallet and tossed it on the table. He started for the door with that lilting gait, his limp more pronounced than I'd seen it. I grabbed my handbag and caught up with him.

"God, slow down. Let's go back to my office and we'll type up a contract."

He held the door open for me and I went out.

"I hope you can afford my services," I said back over my shoulder.

He smiled faintly. "Don't sweat it."

We turned left, moving toward the parking lot.

"Sorry I lost my temper," he murmured.

"Quit that. I don't give a shit."

"I wasn't sure you'd take me seriously," he said.

"Why wouldn't I?"

"My family thinks I've got a screw loose."

"Yeah, well that's why you hired me instead of them."

"Thanks," he whispered. He tucked his hand through my arm and I glanced over at him. His face was suffused with pink and there were tears in his eyes. He dashed at them carelessly, not looking at me. For the first time, I realized how young he was. God, he was just a kid, banged up, bewildered, scared to death.

We walked back to my car slowly and I was conscious of the stares of the curious, faces averted with pity and uneasiness. It made me want to punch somebody out.

2

By two o'clock that afternoon, the contract was signed, Bobby had given me a two-thousand-dollar advance against fees, and I was dropping him off outside the gym, where he'd left his BMW before lunch. His disability entitled him to the handicapped slot, but I noticed he hadn't used it. Maybe someone else was parked there when he arrived, or maybe, obstinately, he preferred to walk the extra twenty yards.

I leaned across the front seat as he got out. "Who's your attorney?" I asked. He held the door open on the passenger side, his head tilted so he could look in at me.

"Varden Talbot of Talbot and Smith. Why? You want to talk to him?"

"Ask him if he'd have copies of the police reports released to me. It would save me a lot of time."

"O.K. I'll do that."

"Oh, and I should probably start with your immediate family. They might have a theory or two about what's going on. Why don't I give you a call later and find out when people are free?"

Bobby made a face. On the way to my office, he'd told me his disabilities had forced him to move back into the family home temporarily, which didn't sit well with him. His parents had divorced some years ago and his mother had remarried, in fact, this was marriage number three. Apparently, Bobby didn't get along with his current stepfather, but he had a seventeen-year-old stepsister named Kitty whom he seemed to like. I wanted to talk to all three. Most of my investigations start with paperwork, but this one felt different from the outset.

"I have a better idea," Bobby said. "Stop by the house this afternoon. Mom's having some people in for drinks around five. My stepfather's birthday. It'll give you a chance to meet everyone."

I hesitated. "You sure it'll be all right? She might not want me barging in on a special occasion like that."

"It's fine. I'll tell her you're coming. She won't care. Got a pencil? I'll give you directions."

I rooted through my handbag for a pen and my notebook and jotted down the details. "I'll be there about six," I said.

"Great." He slammed the car door and moved off.

I watched him hobble as far as his car and then I headed for home.

I live in what was once a single-car garage, converted now to a two-hundred-dollar-a-month studio apartment maybe fifteen feet square, which serves as living room, bedroom, kitchen, bathroom, closet, and laundry room. All of my possessions are multipurpose and petite. I have a combination refrigerator, sink, and stovette, a doll-sized stacking washer/dryer unit, a sofa that becomes a bed (though I seldom bother to unfold it), and a desk that I sometimes use as a dining-room table. I tend to be work-oriented and my living quarters seem to have shrunk, year by year, to this miniature state. For a while, I lived in a trailer, but that began to feel too opulent. I'm often out of town and I object to spending money for space I don't use. It's possible that one day I'll reduce my personal requirements to a sleeping bag that I can toss in the backseat of my car, thus eliminating altogether the need for paying rent. As it is, my wants are few. I don't have pets or houseplants. I do have friends, but I don't entertain. If I have any hobbies at all, they consist of cleaning my little semi-automatic and reading up on evidential documents. I'm not exactly a bundle of laughs, but I do pay my bills, keep a little money tucked away, and provide myself with medical insurance to cover the hazards of my trade. I like my life as it is, though I try not to boast overmuch about the fact. About every six or eight months, I run into a man who astounds me sexually, but between escapades, I'm celibate, which I don't think is any big deal. After two unsuccessful marriages, I find myself keeping my guard up, along with my underpants.

My apartment is located on a modest palm-lined street a block from the beach and it's owned by a man named Henry Pitts, who lives in the main house on the property. Henry is eighty-one years old, a retired baker who supplements his income now by turning out breads and pastries that he trades with local merchants for goods and services. He caters tea parties for the little old ladies in the neighborhood, and in his spare time, he writes crossword puzzles that are a bitch to figure out. He's a very handsome man: tall, lean, and tanned, with shocking-white hair that looks as soft as baby fuzz, a thin aristocratic face. His eyes are a violet-blue, the color of ground morning glories, and they radiate intelligence. He's caring, compassionate, and sweet. It shouldn't have surprised me, therefore, to find him in the company of the "babe" who was having mint juleps with him in the garden when I got home.

I had parked my car out front as usual, and I was heading around to the back, where my entrance is located. My apartment faces the rear and looks out onto a picturesque little bit of scenery. Henry has a patch of grass back there, a weeping willow, rosebushes, two dwarf citrus trees, and a small flagstone patio. He was just coming out of his own back door with a serving tray when he caught sight of me.

"Oh, Kinsey. Well, good. Come on over here. There's someone I want you to meet," he said.

My glance followed his and I saw a woman stretched out on one of the lounge chairs. She must have been in her sixties, plump, with a crown of dyed brown curls. Her face was as lined as soft leather and she used makeup skillfully. It was her eyes that bothered me: a velvety brown, quite large, and, just for a moment, poisonous.

Henry set the tray down on a round metal table between the chairs. "This is Lila Sams," he said, then nodded at me. "My tenant, Kinsey Millhone. Lila's just moved to Santa Teresa. She's renting a room from Mrs. Lowenstein down the street."

She held out a hand with a clatter of red plastic bracelets, moving as though she meant to struggle to her feet.

I crossed the patio. "Don't get up," I said. "Welcome to the neighborhood." I shook hands with her, smiling sociably. Her return smile erased the chill from her gaze and I found myself doing a mental doubletake, wondering if I'd misinterpreted. "What part of the country are you from?"

"Here, there, and everywhere," she said, glancing slyly at Henry. "I wasn't sure how long I'd stay, but Henry makes it seem veerry niiice."

She wore a low-cut cotton sundress, a bright green-and-yellow geometric print on a white background. Her breasts looked like two five-pound flour sacks from which some of the contents had spilled. Her excess weight was carried in her chest and waist, her hefty hips and thighs tapering to a decent set of calves and quite dainty feet. She wore red canvas wedgies and fat red plastic button earrings. As with a painting, I found my gaze traveling right back around to the place where it began. I wanted to make eye contact again, but she was surveying the tray Henry held out to her.

"Oh my. Well, what's all this? Aren't you a sweetie pie!"

Henry had prepared a plate of canapés. He's one of those people who can whip into the kitchen and create a gourmet snack out of canned goods from the back of the cupboard. All I have at the back of my kitchen cupboard is an old box of cornmeal with bugs.

Lila's red fingernails formed a tiny crane. She lifted a canapé and conveyed it to her mouth. It looked like a toast round with a bite of smoked salmon and a dab of dilled mayonnaise. "Mmm, that's *wonderful*," she said, mouth full, and then licked her fingertips, one by one. She wore several crusty diamond rings, the stones clotted together with rubies, and a square-cut emerald the size of a postage stamp, with diamonds on either side. Henry offered me the plate of canapés. "Why don't you try one of these while I fix you a mint julep?"

I shook my head. "I better not. I may try to jog and then I have work to do."

"Kinsey's a private detective," he said to her.

Lila's eyes got big and she blinked in wonderment. "Oh my goodness. Well, how interesting!" She spoke effusively, implying more enthusiasm than etiquette required. I wasn't nearly that thrilled with her and I'm sure she sensed it. I like older women as a rule. I like almost all women, as a matter of fact. I find them open and confiding by nature, amusingly candid when it comes to talk of men. This one was of the old school: giddy and flirtatious. She'd despised me on sight.

She looked at Henry and patted the chaise pad. "Now, you sit down here, you bad boy. I won't have you waiting on me hand and foot. Can you believe it, Kinsey? All he's done this afternoon is fetch me this, fetch me that." She bent over the canapé plate, enthralled. "Now, what is this one?"

I glanced at Henry, half expecting him to shoot me a

pained look, but he had settled on the chaise as commanded, peering over at the plate. "That's smoked oyster. And that's a little cream cheese and chutney. You'll like that one. Here."

He was apparently about to hand-feed her, but she smacked at him ineffectually.

"Quit that. You take one for yourself. You are spoiling the life out of me, and what's more, you're going to make me get fat!"

I could feel my face set with discomfort, watching their two heads bent together. Henry is fifty years older than I am and our relationship has always been completely decorous, but I wondered if this was how he felt on those rare occasions in the past when he'd spotted some guy rolling out of my place at six A.M.

"Talk to you later, Henry," I said, moving toward my front door. I don't even think he heard me.

I changed into a tank top and a pair of cutoffs, laced up my running shoes, and then slipped out again without calling attention to myself. I walked briskly one block over to Cabana, the wide boulevard that parallels the beach, and broke into a trot. The day was hot and there was no cloud cover at all. It was now three o'clock and even the surf seemed sluggish. The breeze fanning in off the ocean was dense with brine and the beach was littered with debris. I don't even know why I was bothering to run. I was out of shape, huffing and puffing, my lungs on fire within the first quarter-mile. My left arm ached and my legs felt like wood. I always run when I'm working and I guess that's why I did it that day. I ran because it was time to run and because I needed to shake the rust and stiffness from my joints. As dutiful as I am about jogging, I've never been a big fan of exercise. I just can't think of any other way to feel good.

The first mile was pure pain and I hated every minute of it. Mile two, I could feel the endorphins kick in, and by mile three, I'd found my pace and might have gone on forever. I checked my running watch. It was 3:33. I never said I was swift. I slowed to a walk, pouring sweat. I would pay for this on the morrow, I was relatively sure, but for the moment, I felt loose, my muscles soft and warm. I used the walk home to cool down.

By the time I reached my place again, evaporating sweat had left me chilled and I was looking forward to a hot shower. The patio was deserted, empty mint-julep glasses sitting side by side. Henry's back door was closed and the window shades were drawn. I let myself into my place with the key I carry tied to my shoelace.

I washed my hair and shaved my legs, slipped into a robe, and puttered around for a while, tidying up the kitchen, cleaning off my desk. Finally, I donned a pair of pants, tunic top, sandals, and cologne. At 5:45, I grabbed my big leather handbag and went out again, locking up.

I checked the directions to Bobby's house and turned left on Cabana toward the bird refuge, following the road as it wound into Montebello, which is rumored to have more millionaires per square mile than any other community in the country. I don't know if that's true or not. The residents of Montebello are a mixed lot. Though the big estates are interspersed now with middle-class homes, the overall impression is of money, carefully cultivated and preserved, vintage elegance harking back to a time when wealth was handled with discretion and material display reserved for one's financial peers. The rich, these days, are merely gaudy imitators of their early California counterparts. Montebello does have its "slums," a curious string of clapboard shacks that sell for $140,000 apiece.

The address Bobby'd given me was off West Glen, a narrow road shaded by eucalyptus and sycamore, lined with low walls of hand-hewn stone that curve back toward mansions too remote to be seen by passing motorists. An occasional gatehouse hints at the stately digs beyond, but for the most part West Glen seems to wander through groves of live oak with nothing more on its mind than dappled sunshine, the scent of French lavender, and bumblebees droning among hot-pink geraniums. It was six now and wouldn't get dark for another two hours or so.

I spotted the number I was looking for and turned into a driveway, slowing. To my right were three white stucco cottages, looking like something the three little pigs might have built. I peered through the windshield, but couldn't see a parking place. I rolled forward, hoping there would be a parking pad somewhere around the bend coming up. I glanced back over my shoulder, wondering why there weren't any other cars in sight, and wondering which of the little bungalows belonged to Bobby's folks. I felt a brief moment of uneasiness. He *had* said this afternoon, hadn't he? I could just picture myself arriving on the wrong day. I shrugged. Oh, well. I'd suffered worse embarrassments in my life, though for the moment, I couldn't think of one. I rounded the curve, looking for a place to pull in. Involuntarily, I slammed on the brakes, skidding to a stop. "Holy shit!" I whispered.

The lane had opened out into a large paved courtyard. Just ahead I saw a house. Somehow, in my gut, I knew Bobby Callahan lived here, not in one of those homey little snuggeries up front. Those were probably servants' quarters. This was the real thing.

The house was the size of the junior high school I'd attended and had probably been designed by the same architect, a man named Dwight Costigan, dead now, who had revitalized Santa Teresa single-handedly during the forty-odd years he worked. The style, if I'm not mistaken, is Spanish Revival. I have tended, I confess, to sneer at white stucco walls and red tile roofs. I've been contemptuous of arches and bougainvillea, distressed beams and balconies, but I had never seen them put together quite like this.

The central portion of the house was two stories high, flanked by two cloistered arcades. Arch after arch after arch, supported by graceful columns. There were clusters of airy palms, sculptured portals, tracery windows. There was even a bell tower, like an old mission church. Hadn't Kim Novak been pushed out of something similar? The place looked like a cross between a monastery and a movie set. Four Mercedes were parked in the courtyard like a glossy ad campaign, and a fountain in the center shot a stream of water fifteen feet high.

I pulled in as far to the right as I could get and parked, then looked down at what I had on. The pants, I saw now, had a stain on one knee that I could only conceal if I held myself in a continual crouch so the tunic would hang down that far. The tunic itself wasn't bad: black gauzy stuff with a low square neck, long sleeves, and a matching tie belt. For a moment, I considered driving home again to change clothes. Then, it occurred to me that I didn't have anything at home that looked any better than this. I torqued myself around to the backseat, sorting through the incredible collection of odds and ends I keep back there. I drive a VW, one of those nondescript beige sedans, great for surveillance work in most neighborhoods. Around here, I could see I'd need to hire a stretch limo. The gardeners probably drove Volvos.

I pushed aside the law books, file boxes, tool kit, the briefcase where I keep my gun locked. Ah, just what I was looking for: an old pair of pantyhose, useful as a filter in an emergency. On the floor, I found a pair of black spike heels I'd bought when I'd intended to pass myself off as a hooker in a tacky part of Los Angeles. When I'd gotten there, of course, I'd discovered that all the whores looked like college girls, so I'd abandoned the disguise.

I tossed the sandals I was wearing into the backseat and hunched my long pants off. I wiggled into the pantyhose, did a spit polish on the pumps, and slipped into those. I took the self-belt off the tunic and tied it around my neck in an exotic knot. In the bottom of my handbag, I found an eyeliner pencil and some blusher and I did a quick makeover, tilting the rearview mirror so I could see myself. I thought I looked weird, but how would they know? Except for Bobby, none of them had ever seen me before. I hoped.

I got out of the car and steadied myself. I hadn't worn heels this high since I'd played dress-up in my aunt's castoffs when I was in first grade. Beltless, the tunic hit me midthigh, the lightweight fabric clinging to my hips. If I walked in front of a light, they'd see my bikini underpants, but so what? If I couldn't afford to dress well, at least I could provide a distraction from the fact. I took a deep breath and clattered my way toward the door.

3

I rang the bell. I could hear it echo through the house. In due course, the door was opened by a black maid in a white uniform like a nurse's aide's. I wanted to fall into her arms and be dragged off to the infirmary, my feet hurt so bad, but I mentioned my name instead and murmured that Bobby Callahan expected me.

"Yes, Miss Millhone. Won't you come in, please?"

She stepped aside and I moved into the hallway. The ceiling in the entryway was two stories high, light filtering down through a series of windows that followed the line of the wide stone stairs curving up to the left. The floor was tile, a soft red, polished to a satiny sheen. There were runners of Persian carpeting in faded patterns. Tapestries hung from ornamental wrought-iron rods that looked like antique weaponry. The air temperature was perfect, cool and still, scented by a massive floral arrangement on a heavy side table to my right. I felt like I was in a museum.

The maid led me down the hallway to a living room so large the group of people at the far end seemed constructed on a smaller scale than I. The stone fireplace must have been ten feet wide and a good twelve feet high, with an opening big enough to roast an ox in. The furniture looked comfortable; nothing fussy or small. The couches, four of them, seemed substantial, and the chairs were large and overstuffed, with wide arms, reminding me somehow of first-class seats on an airplane. There was no particular color scheme and I wondered if it was only the middle class that ran out and hired someone to make everything match.

I caught sight of Bobby and, mercifully, he lumbered in my direction. He had apparently divined from my expression that I was ill-prepared for this whole pageant.

"I should have warned you. I'm sorry," he said. "Let me get you a drink. What would you like? We've got white wine, but if I tell you what it is, you'll think we're showing off."

"Wine is perfect," I said. "I'm crazy about the show-off kind."

Another maid, not the one who opened the door, but one especially trained for living rooms, anticipated Bobby's needs, approaching with glasses of wine already poured. I was really hoping I wouldn't disgrace myself by spilling a drink down my front or catching a heel on the rug. He handed me a glass of wine and I took a sip.

"Did you grow up in this place?" I asked. It was difficult to picture binkies, Johnny-Jump-Ups, and Tonka trucks in a room that looked like the nave of a church. I suddenly tuned in to what was happening in my mouth. This wine was going to ruin me for the stuff in a cardboard box, which is what I usually drink.

"Actually, I did," he said, looking around with interest now, as though the incongruity had just occurred to him. "I had a nanny, of course."

"Oh sure, why not? What do your parents do? Or should I guess."

Bobby gave me a lopsided smile and dabbed at his chin, almost sheepishly, I thought. "My grandfather, my mother's father, founded a big chemical company at the turn of the century. I guess they ended up patenting half the products essential to civilization. Douches and mouthwashes and birth-control devices. A lot of over-the-counter drugs, too. Solvents, alloys, industrial products. The list goes on for a bit."

"Brothers? Sisters?"

"Just me."

"Where's your father at this point?"

"Tibet. He's taken to mountain climbing of late. Last year, he lived in an ashram in India. His soul is evolving at a pace with his VISA bill."

I cupped a hand to my ear. "Do I detect some hostility?"

Bobby shrugged. "He can afford to dabble in the Great Mysteries because of the settlement he got from my mother when they divorced. He pretends it's a great spiritual journey when he's really just indulging himself. Actually, I felt O.K. about him until he came back just after the accident. He used to sit by my bedside and smile at me benevolently, explaining that being crippled must be something I was having to sort through in this life." He looked at me with an odd smile. "Know what he said when he heard Rick was dead? 'That's nice. That means he's finished his work.' I got so upset Dr. Kleinert refused to let him visit anymore, so he went off to hike the Himalayas. We don't hear from him much, but it's just as well, I guess."

Bobby broke off. For a moment, tears swam in his eyes and he fought for control. He stared off toward a cluster of people near the fireplace and I followed his gaze. There were only ten or so on a quick count.

"Which one is your mother?"

"The woman in the cream-colored outfit. The guy standing just behind her is my stepfather, Derek. They've been married three years, but I don't think it's working out."

"How come?"

Bobby seemed to consider several replies, but he finally settled for a slight head shake and silence. He looked back at me. "You ready to meet them?"

"Tell me about the other people first." I was stalling, but I couldn't help myself.

He surveyed the group. "Some, I forget. That woman in blue I don't know at all. The tall fellow with gray hair is Dr. Fraker. He's the pathologist I was working for before the accident. He's married to the redhead talking to my mom. My mother's on the board of trustees for St. Terry's so she knows all these medical types. The balding, heavyset man is Dr. Metcalf and the guy he's talking to is Dr. Kleinert."

"Your psychiatrist?"

"Right. He thinks I'm crazy, but that's all right because he thinks he can fix me." Bitterness had crept into his voice and I was acutely aware of the level of rage he must be dealing with day by day.

As though on cue, Dr. Kleinert turned and stared at us and then his eyes slid away. He looked like he was in his early forties with thin, wavy gray hair and a sorrowful expression.

Bobby smirked. "I told him I was hiring a private detective, but I don't think he's figured out yet that it's you or he'd have come down here to have a little chat to straighten us out."

"What about your stepsister? Where is she?"

"Probably in her room. She's not very sociable."

"And who's the little blonde?"

"My mother's best friend. She's a surgical nurse. Come on," he said impatiently. "You might as well take the plunge."

I followed Bobby, keeping pace with him as he hobbled down the room toward the fireplace, where people had congregated. His mother watched us approach, the two women with her pausing in the middle of their conversation to see what had engaged her attention.

She looked young to be the mother of a twenty-three-year-old, lean, with narrow hips and long legs. Her hair was a thick glossy bush of pale fawn brown, not quite shoulder-length. Her eyes were small and deep-set, her face narrow, mouth wide. Her hands were elegant, her fingers long and thin. She wore a cream-colored silk blouse and a full linen skirt nipped in at the waist. Her jewelry was gold, delicate chains at her wrist and throat. The gaze she turned on Bobby was intense and I thought I could feel the pain with which she regarded his crippled form. She looked from him to me, smiling politely.

She moved forward, holding out her hand. "I'm Glen Callahan. You must be Kinsey Millhone. Bobby said you'd be stopping by." Her voice was low and throaty. "I'll give you a chance to enjoy yourself. We'll talk in a bit."

I shook hands with her, startled how bony and warm her hand felt in mine. Her grip was iron.

She glanced at the woman to her right, introducing me. "This is Nola Fraker."

"Hi, how are you?" I said as we shook hands.

"And Sufi Daniels."

Murmured pleasantries were exchanged. Nola was a redhead, with clear, fine-textured skin, and luminous blue eyes, wearing a dark red jumpsuit that left her arms bare and a deep V of naked flesh visible from throat to waist. Already, I didn't want her to bend down or make any sudden moves. I had the feeling I knew her from somewhere. Possibly I'd seen her picture in the society section or something of that sort. Reminder bells went off, at any rate, and I wondered what the story was.

The other woman, Sufi, was small and somewhat misshapen, thick through the trunk, her back hunched. She wore a mauve velour sweatsuit that looked like she'd never sweated in it. Her blond hair was thin and fine, worn too long, I thought, to be flattering.

After a decent interval, the three of them resumed their conversation, much to my relief. I hadn't the faintest idea what to say to them. Nola was talking about a thirty-dollar fabric remnant she was whipping up to wear to a wine-tasting down in Los Angeles. "I checked all the shops in Montebello, but it was ridiculous! I wouldn't pay four bills for an outfit. I wouldn't even pay *two*," she said with energy.

That surprised me. She looked like a woman who enjoyed extravagance. Unless I just make up things like that. My notion of women with money is that they drive to Beverly Hills to have their legs waxed, charge a bauble or two on Rodeo Drive, and then go to charity luncheons at $1,500 a plate. I couldn't picture Nola Fraker pawing through the bargain bin at our local Stretch N' Sew. Maybe she'd been poor as a young girl and couldn't get used to being a doctor's wife.

Bobby took my arm and steered me toward the men. He introduced me to his stepfather, Derek Wenner, and then in quick succession to Drs. Fraker, Metcalf, and Kleinert. Before I knew what to think, he was hustling me toward the hallway. "Let's go upstairs. We'll find Kitty and then I'll show you the rest of the house."

"Bobby, I want to talk to those people!" I said.

"No, you don't. They're dull and they don't know anything."

As we passed a side table, I started to set my wineglass down, but he shook his head. "Bring it with you."

He grabbed a full bottle of wine out of a silver cooler and tucked it under his arm. He was really moving at a fair clip, limp and all, and I could hear my high heels clip-clopping along inelegantly as we moved toward the foyer. I paused for a moment to slip my shoes off, and then I caught up with him. Something about Bobby's attitude made me want to laugh. He was accustomed to doing exactly as he pleased among people I'd been taught to respect. My aunt would have been impressed by the company, but Bobby didn't seem to be.

We went up the stairs, Bobby pulling himself along by the smooth stone banister.

"Your mother doesn't use the name Wenner?" I asked, as I followed him.

"Nope. Callahan is her maiden name as a matter of fact. I changed mine to Callahan when she and my father divorced."

"That's unusual, isn't it?"

"Doesn't seem that way to me. He's a jerk. This way, I don't have to be connected to him any more than she does."

The gallery at the top formed a semicircle with wings branching out on either side. We passed through an archway to the right and into a wide corridor with rooms opening off at intervals. Most of the doors were closed. Daylight was beginning to fade and the upstairs was gloomy. I once conducted a homicide investigation at an exclusive girls' school that had this same air to it. The house felt as if it had been converted to institutional use, someplace impersonal and chill. Bobby knocked at the third door down on the right.

"Kitty?"

"Just a minute," she called.

He flashed me a smile. "She'll be stoned."

Hey, why not? I thought with a shrug. Seventeen.

The door opened and she looked out, gaze shifting from Bobby to me with suspicion. "Who's this?"

"Come on, Kitty. Would you knock that shit off?"

She moved away from the door indifferently. Bobby and I went in and he closed the door behind us. She was anoretic; tall and painfully thin, with knees and elbow joints standing out like Tinkertoys. Her face was gaunt. She was barefoot, wearing shorts and a white tube top that looked about as big as a man's crew sock, one size fits all.

"What are *you* looking at?" she said. She didn't seem to expect an answer so I didn't bother with one. She flopped down on an unmade king-sized bed, staring at me as she took up a cigarette and lit it. Her nails were bitten to the quick. The room had been painted black and looked like a parody of an adolescent girl's room. There were lots of posters and stuffed animals but all of them had a nightmare quality. The posters were of rock groups in tartish makeup, sinister and sneering, depicted in vignettes largely hostile toward women. The stuffed animals ran more to satyrs than Winnie-the-Pooh. The air was scented with eau de dope and my guess was she'd smoked so much grass in there, you could bury your nose in the bedcovers and get high.

Bobby apparently enjoyed her antagonism. He pulled a chair over for me, dumping clothes on the floor unceremoniously. I sat down and he stretched out on the foot of the bed, circling her left ankle with one hand. His fingers overlapped as if he were holding her wrist instead. It reminded me of Hansel and Gretel. Maybe Kitty was worried that if she got fat, they'd put her in the cooking pot. I thought they'd put her in a grave long before that point and it was frightening. She leaned back on both elbows, smiling at me faintly down the length of her long, frail legs. All the veins were visible, like an anatomical diagram with a celluloid overlay. I could see how the bones were strung together in her feet, her toes looking almost prehensile.

"So what's going on downstairs?" she said to Bobby, her gaze still pinned on me. Her speech was ever so slightly slurred and her eyes seemed to swim in and out of focus. I wondered if she was drunk or had just popped some pills.

"They're standing around sucking up booze as usual. Speaking of which, I brought us wine," he said. "Got a glass?"

She leaned over to her bed-table and sorted through the mess, coming up with a tumbler with something sticky and green in the bottom: absinthe or crème de menthe. She held the glass out to him. The wine he poured into it became tainted with the remnants of liqueur.

"So, who's the chick?"

I loathe being called a chick.

Bobby laughed. "Oh God, I'm sorry. This is Kinsey. She's the private detective I told you about."

"I should've figured as much." Her eyes came back to mine, her pupils so dilated I couldn't tell what color the irises were. "So how do you like our little sideshow? Bobby and I are the family freaks. What a pair, right?"

This child was getting on my nerves. She wasn't smart enough or quick enough to pull off the tough air she was affecting, and the strain was evident, like watching a stand-up comic with second-rate gags.

Bobby cut in smoothly. "Dr. Kleinert's downstairs."

"Ah, Dr. Destructo. What did you think of him?" She took a drag of her cigarette, feigning nonchalance, but I sensed that she was genuinely curious about my response.

"I didn't talk to him," I said. "Bobby wanted me to meet you first."

She stared at me and I stared back. I remembered doing this sort of stuff in sixth grade with my mortal enemy, Tommy Jancko. I forget now why we disliked each other, but stare contests were definitely the weapons of choice.

She looked back at Bobby. "He wants me hospitalized. D'I tell you that?"

"You going?"

"Hey, no *way*! Get all those needles stuck in me? Uh-un, no thanks. I'm not interested." She swung her long legs over the side of the bed and got up. She crossed the room to a low dressing table with a gilt-edged mirror above it. She studied her face, glancing back at me. "You think I look thin?"

"Very."

"Really?" She seemed fascinated by the notion, turning slightly so she could see her own flat behind. She studied her face again, watching herself take a drag of her cigarette. She did a quick shrug. Everything looked fine to her.

"Could we talk about this murder attempt?" I said.

She padded back to the bed and flopped down again.

"Somebody's after him. Definitely," she said. She stubbed out her cigarette, with a yawn.

"What makes you say that?"

"The vibes."

"Aside from the vibes," I said.

"Oh balls, you don't believe us either," she said. She turned sideways and settled against the pillows, folding an arm under her head.

"Is someone after you too?"

"Nun-un. I don't think so. Just him."

"But why would someone do that? I'm not saying I don't believe you. I'm looking for a place to start and I want to hear what you have to say."

"I'd have to think about it some," she said and then she was quiet.

It took me a few minutes to realize she'd passed out. Jesus, what was she on?

4

I waited in the hallway, shoes in hand, while Bobby covered her with a blanket and tiptoed out of the room, closing the door gently.

"What's the story?" I said.

"She's O.K. She was just up late last night."

"What are you talking about? She's half dead!"

He shifted uneasily. "You really think so?"

"Bobby, would you *look* at her? She's a skeleton. She's doing drugs, alcohol, cigarettes. You know she's smoking dope on top of that. How's she going to survive?"

"I don't know. I guess I didn't think she was that bad off," he said. He was not only young, he was *naïve*, or maybe she'd been going under so gradually that he couldn't see the shape she was in.

"How long has she been anoretic?"

"Since Rick died, I guess. Maybe some before that. He was her boyfriend and she took it pretty hard."

"Is that what Kleinert's seeing her for? The anorexia?"

"I guess. I never really asked. She was a patient of his before I started seeing him."

A voice cut in. "Is there some problem?"

Derek Wenner was approaching from the gallery, highball in hand. He was a man who'd been good-looking once. Of medium height, fair-haired, his gray eyes magnified by glasses with steel-blue frames. He was in his late forties now, by a charitable estimate, a solid thirty pounds overweight. He had the puffy, florid complexion of a man who drinks too much and his hairline had receded in a wide U that left a runner of thinning hair down the center, clipped short and brushed to one side. The excess pounds had given him a double chin and a wide neck that made the collar of his dress shirt seem tight. His pleated gabardine pants looked expensive and so did his loafers, which were tan and white, with vents cut into the leather. He'd been wearing a sport coat earlier, but he'd taken it off, along with his tie. He unbuttoned his collar with relief.

"What's going on? Where's Kitty? Your mother wants to know why she hasn't joined us."

Bobby seemed embarrassed. "I don't know. She was talking to us and she fell asleep."

"Fell asleep" seemed a bit understated to me. Kitty's face had been the color of a plastic ring I sent away for once as a kid. The ring was white, but if you held it to the light for a while and then cupped your hand over it, it glowed faintly green. This, to me, did not connote good health.

"Hell, I better talk to her," he said. I had to guess

he'd had his hands full with her. He opened the door and went into Kitty's room.

Bobby gave me a look that was part dismay and part anxiety. I glanced in through the open door. Derek put his drink on the table and sat down on Kitty's bed.

"Kitty?"

He put a hand on her shoulder and shook her gently. There was no response. "Hey, come on, honey. Wake up."

He shot me a worried look.

He gave Kitty a rough shake. "Hey, come on. Wake up."

"You want me to get one of the doctors from downstairs?" I said. He shook her again. I didn't wait for a response.

I slipped my shoes on and left my handbag by the door, heading for the stairs.

When I reached the living room, Glen Callahan glanced over at me, apparently sensing that something was wrong.

She moved forward. "Where's Bobby?"

"Upstairs with Kitty. I think it might be smart to have somebody take a look at her. She passed out and your husband's having trouble rousing her."

"I'll get Leo."

I watched while she approached Dr. Kleinert, murmuring to him. He glanced over at me and then he excused himself from his conversation. The three of us went upstairs.

Bobby had joined Derek at Kitty's bedside, his face

creased with concern. Derek was trying to pull Kitty into a sitting position, but she slumped to one side. Dr. Kleinert moved forward swiftly and pushed both men out of the way. He did a quick check of her vital signs, pulling a penlight out of the inside breast pocket of his suit. Her pupils had contracted down to pinpoints, and from where I stood, the green eyes looked milky and lifeless, apparently responding little to the light he flashed first in one, then the other. Her breathing was slow and shallow, her muscles flaccid. Dr. Kleinert reached for the telephone, which was sitting on the floor near the bed, and dialed 911.

Glen remained in the doorway. "What is it?"

Kleinert ignored her, apparently talking to the emergency dispatcher.

"This is Dr. Leo Kleinert. I'm going to need an ambulance out on West Glen Road in Montebello. I've got a patient suffering from barbiturate poisoning." He gave the address and a brief set of instructions about how to reach the place. He hung up and looked at Bobby. "You have any idea what she took?"

Bobby shook his head.

Derek responded, addressing the remark to Glen. "She was fine half an hour ago. I talked to her myself."

"Oh Derek. For God's sake," she said with annoyance.

Kleinert reached over and opened the bed-table drawer. He sorted through some junk and then hesitated, pulling out a stash of pills that would have felled an elephant. They were in a Ziploc bag, maybe two hundred capsules: Nembutals, Seconals, blue-and-orange Tuinals, Placidyls, Quaaludes, like colorful supplies for some exotic cottage industry.

Kleinert's expression was despairing. He looked up at Derek, holding the bag by one corner. Exhibit A in a trial that had been going on for some time by my guess.

"What are those things?" Derek said. "How'd she get them?"

Kleinert shook her head. "Let's get people out of here and then we'll worry about that."

Glen Callahan had already turned and left the room and I could hear her heels clipping purposefully toward the stairs. Bobby took my arm and the two of us moved out into the hallway.

Derek was apparently still having trouble believing this was happening. "Is she going to be O.K.?"

Dr. Kleinert murmured a reply, but I couldn't hear what it was.

Bobby steered me into a room across the hall and closed the door. "Let's stay out of the way. We'll go downstairs in a bit." He rubbed at the fingers of his bad hand as if it were a talisman. The drag in his voice was back.

The room was large, with deep-set windows looking out onto the rear of the property. The wall-to-wall carpeting was white, a dense cut-pile so recently vacuumed that I could see Bobby's footprints in places. His double bed seemed diminutive in a room that was probably thirty feet square, with a large dressing room opening off to the left and what was apparently a bathroom beyond that. A television set rested on an antique pine blanket-chest at the foot of the bed. On the wall to my right was a long built-in desk with a white Formica surface. An IBM Selectric II and the keyboard, monitor, and printer for a home computer were lined up along its length. The bookshelves were white Formica too, filled almost exclusively with medical texts. There was a sitting area in the far corner: two overstuffed chairs and an ottoman covered in a plaid fabric of rust, white, and slate blue. The coffee table, reading lamp, books and magazines stacked nearby suggested that this was where Bobby spent his leisure time.

He went to an intercom on the wall and pressed a button.

"Callie, we're starving up here. Could you send us a tray? There are two of us and we'll need some white wine too."

I could hear a hollow clattering in the background: dishes being loaded into the dishwasher. "Yes, Mr. Bobby. I'll have Alicia bring something up."

"Thank you."

He limped over to one of the chairs and sat down. "I eat when I'm anxious. I've always done that. Come sit down. Shit, I hate this house. I used to love it. When I was a kid, it was great. Places to run. Places to hide. A yard that went on forever. Now it feels like a cocoon. Insulated. But it doesn't keep bad stuff out. It feels cold. Are you cold?"

"I'm fine," I said.

I sat down in the other chair. He pushed the ottoman over and I put my feet up. I wondered what it must be like to live in a house like this where all of your needs were tended to, where someone else was responsible for grocery shopping and food preparation, cleaning, trash removal, landscape maintenance. What did it leave you free to do?

"What's it like coming from money like this? I can't even imagine it."

He hesitated, lifting his head.

In the distance, we could hear the ambulance approach, the siren reaching a crescendo and then winding down abruptly with a whine of regret. He glanced at me, dabbing self-consciously at his chin. "You think we're spoiled?" The two halves of his face seemed to give contradictory messages: one animated, one dead.

"How do I know? You live a lot better than most," I said.

"Hey, we do our share. My mother does a lot of fund-raising for local charities and she's on the board for the art museum and the historical society. I don't know about Derek. He plays golf and hangs out at the club. Well, that's not fair. He has some investments he looks after, which is how they met. He was the executor for the trust my grandfather left me. Once he and Mom got married, he left the bank. Anyway, they support a lot of causes so it's not like they're just self-indulgent, grinding the poor underfoot. My mother launched the Santa Teresa Girls' Club just about single-handedly. The Rape Crisis Center too."

"What about Kitty? What does she do with herself besides get loaded?"

He looked at me carefully. "Don't make judgments. You don't know what any of us has been through."

"You're right. I'm sorry. I didn't mean to sound quite so righteous. Is she in private school?"

He shook his head. "Not anymore. They moved her over to Santa Teresa High School this year. Anything to try to get her straightened out."

He stared at the door uneasily. The house was so solidly constructed there was no way to tell if the paramedics had come upstairs yet.

I crossed the room and opened the door a crack. They were just coming out of Kitty's room with the portable gurney, its wheels swiveling like a grocery cart's as they angled her into the hall. She was covered with a blanket, so frail that she scarcely formed a mound. One thin arm was extended outside the covers. They'd started an I.V., a plastic bag of some clear solution held aloft by one of the paramedics. Oxygen was being administered through a nose cone. Dr. Kleinert moved toward the stairs ahead of them and Derek brought up the rear, hands shoved awkwardly in his pockets, his face pale. He seemed out of place and ineffectual, pausing when he caught sight of me.

"I'm going to follow in my car," he said, though no one had asked. "Tell Bobby we'll be at St. Terry's."

I felt sorry for him. The scene was like something out of a TV series, the medical personnel very deadpan and businesslike. This was his daughter being taken away and she might actually die, but no one seemed to be addressing the possibility. There was no sign of Bobby's mother, no sign of the people who'd come for drinks. Everything felt ill-planned somehow, like an elaborate entertainment that was falling flat. "You want us to come, too?" I asked.

Derek shook his head. "Let my wife know where I am," he said. "I'll call as soon as I know what's going on."

"Good luck," I said, and he flashed me a weak smile as if good luck was not something he'd had much experience with.

I watched the procession disappear down the stairs. I closed the door to Bobby's room. I started to say something, but Bobby cut me off.

"I heard," he said.

"Why isn't your mother involved in this? Are she and Kitty on the outs or what?"

"Jesus, it's all too complicated to explain. Mom washed her hands of Kitty after the last incident, which isn't as heartless as it sounds. Early on, she did what she could, but I guess it was just one crisis after another. That's part of the reason she and Derek are having such a tough time."

"What's the other part?"

His look was bleak. Clearly, he felt he was equally to blame.

There was a tap at the door and a Chicano woman with her hair in a braid appeared with a tray. Her face was expressionless and she made no eye contact. If she knew what was happening, she gave no indication of it. She fussed around for a bit with cloth napkins and cutlery. I almost expected her to present a room-service check to be signed off with a tip added in.

"Thanks, Alicia," Bobby said.

She murmured something and departed. I felt uncomfortable that it was all so impersonal. I wanted to ask her if her feet hurt like mine, or if she had a family we could talk about. I wanted her to voice curiosity or dismay about the people she worked for, carted away on stretchers at odd hours of the day. Instead, Bobby poured the wine and we ate.

The meal was like something out of a magazine. Plump quartered chicken served cold with a mustard sauce, tiny flaky tarts filled with spinach and a smoky cheddar cheese, clusters of grapes and sprigs of parsley tucked here and there. Two small china bowls with lids held an icy tomato soup with fresh dill clipped across the surface and a little dollop of crème fraîche. We finished with a plate of tiny decorated cookies. Did these people eat like this every day? Bobby never batted an eye. I don't know what I expected him to do. He couldn't squeal with excitement every time a supper tray showed up, but I was impressed and I guess I wanted him to marvel, as I did, so I wouldn't feel like such a rube.

By the time we went downstairs, it was nearly eight and the guests were gone. The house seemed deserted, except for the two maids who were tidying up the living room in silence as we passed. Bobby led us to a heavy oak-paneled door across the wide hall. He knocked and there was a murmured response. We went into a small den, where Glen Callahan was seated with a book, a wineglass on the end table at her right hand. She'd changed into chocolate-brown wool slacks and a matching cashmere pullover. A fire burned in a copper grate. The walls were painted tomato red, with matching red drapes drawn against the chill dusk. In Santa Teresa, most nights are cold regardless of the month. This room felt cozy, an intimate retreat from the rest of the house with its high ceilings and chalk-white stucco walls.

Bobby sat down in the chair across from his mother. "Has Derek called yet?"

She closed her book and set it aside. "A few minutes ago. She's pulled out of it. She had her stomach pumped and they'll be admitting her as soon as she's out of emergency. Derek will stay until the papers have been signed."

I glanced at Bobby. He lowered his face into his hands and sighed once with relief, a sound like a low note on a bagpipe. He shook his head, staring down at the floor.

Glen studied him. "You're exhausted. Why don't you go on to bed? I'll want to talk to Kinsey alone anyway."

"All right. I might as well," he said. The slur in his voice had become pronounced and I could see now that the fine muscles near his eyes were being tugged, as though stimulated electrically. Fatigue apparently exacerbated his disability. He got up and crossed to her chair. Glen took his face in her hands and stared at him intently.

"I'll let you know if there's any change in Kitty's condition," she murmured. "I don't want you to worry. Sleep well."

He nodded, laying the good side of his face near

hers. He moved toward the door. "I'll call you in the morning," he said to me, then let himself out. I could hear his dragging gait for a moment in the hallway and then it faded from hearing.

5

I sat in the chair Bobby had vacated. The down-filled cushion was still warm, contoured to the shape of his body. Glen was watching me, formulating, I gathered, an opinion of me. By lamplight, I could see that her hair color was the handiwork of an expert who'd matched it almost exactly to the mild brown of her eyes. Everything about her was beautifully coordinated: makeup, clothing, accessories. She was apparently a person who paid attention to detail and her taste was impeccable.

"I'm sorry you had to see us like this."

"I'm not sure I ever see people at their best," I said. "It gives me a rather skewed impression of humankind. Will he be paying my bills or will you?"

The question caused her to focus on me with interest and I guessed that she brought a considerable intelligence to any matter involving money. She raised an eyebrow ever so slightly.

"He will. He came into his trust when he was twenty-one. Why do you ask?"

"I like to know who I'm reporting to," I said. "What's your feeling about his claim that someone's trying to kill him?"

She took a moment to respond, shrugging delicately. "It's possible. The police seem convinced that someone forced him off that bridge. Whether it was premeditated, I have no idea." Her voice was distinct, low, and intense.

"From what Bobby says, it's been a long nine months."

She ran a thumbnail along her pantleg, directing her comments to the crease. "I don't know how we survived it. He's my only child, the light of my life."

She paused, smiling slightly to herself, and then looked up at me with an unexpected shyness. "I know all mothers must talk like this, but he was special. He really was. Even from infancy. Smart, alert, sociable, quick. And gorgeous. Such a beautiful little boy, easygoing and affectionate, funny. He was magical.

"The night of the accident, the police came to the house. They weren't able to notify us until four in the morning because the car wasn't discovered for a while and then it took hours to get the two boys up the side of the mountain. Rick died instantly, of course."

She broke off and I thought at first she'd lost her train of thought. "Anyway. The doorbell rang. Derek went down, and when he didn't come back, I grabbed a robe and went down myself. I saw two policemen in the foyer. I thought they'd come to tell us there was a burglary in the neighborhood or an accident on the road out front. Derek turned around and he had this awful look on his face. He said, 'Glen, it's Bobby.' I thought my heart had stopped."

She looked up at me and her eyes were luminous with tears. She laced her fingers together, making a steeple of her two index fingers, which she rested against her lips. "I thought he was dead. I thought they'd come to tell me he'd died. I felt a spurt of ice, like I'd been stabbed. It started in my heart and spread through my body 'til my teeth chattered. He was at St. Terry's by then. All we knew at that point was he was still alive, but barely. When we got to the hospital, the doctor didn't give us any hope at all. None. They told us there were extensive injuries. Brain damage and so many broken bones. They said he'd never recover, that he'd be a vegetable if he survived. I was dying. I died because Bobby was dying and it went on for days. I never left his side. I was crazy, screaming at everyone, nurses, doctors . . ."

Her gaze flattened and she lifted an index finger, like a teacher who wants to make a point very clear. "I'll tell you what I learned," she said carefully. "I understood I couldn't buy Bobby's life. Money can't buy life, but it can buy anything else you want. I'd never used money that way, which seems odd to me now. My parents had money. My parents' parents had money. I've always understood the power of money, but I'd never wielded it with quite such effect. He had the best of everything. The best! Nothing was spared. And he pulled out of it. Having endured so much, I'd hate to think someone did it deliberately. To all intents and purposes, Bobby's life is ruined. He'll be all right and we'll find a way for him to live productively, but only because we're in a position to make that happen. The losses are incalculable. It's miraculous he's come this far."

"You have any theories about why someone might try to kill him?"

She shook her head.

"You said Bobby has his own money. Who benefits if he dies?"

"You'd have to ask him that. He has a will, I'm sure, and we've discussed his leaving his money to various charities . . . unless of course, he marries and has legitimate heirs of his own. You think money might be the motive?"

I shrugged. "I tend to look at that first, especially in a situation like this when it sounds like there's a lot."

"What else could it be? What could anyone have against him?"

"People murder for absurd reasons. Someone gets into a rage over something and retaliates. People get jealous or want to defend themselves from a real or imagined attack. Or they've done something wrong and they kill to cover it up. Sometimes it doesn't even make that much sense. Maybe Bobby cut someone off in a lane change that night and the driver followed him all the way up the pass. People go nuts in cars. I take it he wasn't in the middle of a hassle with anyone?"

"Not that I was aware of."

"Nobody mad at him? A girl friend maybe?"

"I doubt it. He was going with someone at the time, but it was a fairly casual relationship from what I could tell. Once this happened, we didn't see much of her. Of course, Bobby changed. You don't come that close to death without paying a penalty. Violent death is like a monster. The closer you get to it, the more damage you sustain . . . if you survive at all. Bobby's had to pull himself out of the grave, step by step. He's different now. He's looked into the monster's face. You can see the claw marks on his body everywhere."

I glanced away from her. It was true. Bobby looked like he had been attacked: torn and broken and mauled. Violent death leaves an aura, like an energy field that repels the observer. I've never looked at a homicide victim yet without a quick recoil. Even photographs of the dead chill and repulse me.

I shifted back to the matter at hand. "Bobby said he was working for Dr. Fraker at the time."

"That's right. Jim Fraker's been a friend of mine for years. That's why Bobby was hired at St. Terry's, as a matter of fact. As a favor to me."

"How long had he worked there?"

"At the hospital itself, maybe four months. He'd been working for Jim in Pathology for two months, I think."

"And what did he actually do?"

"Cleaned equipment, ran errands, answered the phone. It was all routine. They'd taught him to do a few lab tests and sometimes he monitored machinery, but I can't imagine his job entailed anything that would endanger his life."

"He had his degree from UCST by then, I gather," I said, repeating what Bobby'd told me.

"That's right. He was working temporarily, hoping to get accepted to med school. His first applications had been turned down."

"How come?"

"Oh, he got cocky and only applied to about five schools. He'd always been an excellent student and he'd never failed at anything in his life. He miscalculated. Med schools are ferociously competitive and he simply didn't get accepted to the ones he tried for. It set him back on his heels for a time, but he'd rallied, I think. I know he felt the job with Dr. Fraker was valuable, because it gave him some exposure to disciplines he wouldn't otherwise have known about until much later in the game."

"What else was going on in his life at that point?"

"Not a lot. He went to work. He dated. He did some weight lifting, surfed now and then. He went to movies, went out to dinner with us. It all seemed very ordinary at the time and it seems very ordinary looking back."

There was another avenue I needed to explore and I wondered how she would react. "Were he and Kitty involved with one another sexually?"

"Ah. Well, I can't really answer that. I have no idea."

"But it's possible."

"I suppose so, though I don't think it's likely. Derek and I have been together since she was thirteen. Bobby was eighteen, nineteen, something like that. Out of the house at any rate. I do think Kitty was smitten with him. I don't know how he felt about her, but I can't believe a thirteen-year-old would interest him in the least."

"She's grown up pretty fast from what I've seen."

She crossed her legs restlessly, wrapping one around the other. "I don't understand why you're pursuing this point."

"I need to know what was going on. He was anxious about her tonight and more than relieved when he found out she was all right. I wondered how deep the connections ran."

"Oh. I see. A lot of his emotionalism is the aftermath of the accident. From what I'm told, it's not uncommon for people who've suffered head injury. He's moody now. Impatient. And he overreacts. He weeps easily and he gets very frustrated with himself."

"Is part of that the memory loss?"

"Yes," she said. "What makes it hard is he can never predict where the losses will occur. Sometimes he can remember the most inconsequential things, then he'll turn around and forget his own birthdate. Or he'll blank out on someone altogether, maybe someone he's known all his life. That's one of the reasons he's seeing Leo Kleinert. To help him cope with the personality changes."

"He told me Kitty was seeing Dr. Kleinert, too. Was that for the anorexia?"

"Kitty's been impossible from the first."

"Well, I gathered that much. What was it about?"

"Ask Derek. I'm the wrong person to consult about her. I did try, but I don't give a damn anymore. Even this business tonight. I know it sounds cruel, but I can't take it seriously. She does it to herself. It's her life. Let her do anything she wants as long as it doesn't affect the rest of us. She can drop dead for all I care."

"It looks like her behavior affects you whether you like it or not," I ventured carefully. This was clearly touchy stuff and I didn't want to antagonize her.

"I'm afraid that's true, but I've had it. Something's got to change. I'm tired of playing games and I'm sick of watching her manipulate Derek."

I shifted the subject slightly, probing a question I'd been curious about. "You think the drugs were actually hers?"

"Of course. She's been stoned since she walked in my front door. It's been such a bone of contention between Derek and me I can hardly speak of it. She's ruining our relationship." She closed her mouth and composed herself, then said, "What makes you put it that way?"

"About the drugs? It seems odd to me, that's all," I said. "I can't believe she'd leave them in her bed-table drawer in a Ziploc bag for starters and I can't believe she'd have pills in that quantity. Do you know what that stuff is worth?"

"She has an allowance of two hundred dollars a month," Glen said crisply. "I've argued and cajoled until I'm blue in the face, but what's the point? Derek insists. The money comes out of his own account."

"Even so, it's pretty high-level stuff. She'd have to have an incredible connection somewhere."

"I'm sure Kitty has her little ways."

I let the subject pass and made a mental note for myself. I'd recently made the acquaintance of one of Santa Teresa High School's more enterprising drug dealers and he might be able to identify her source. He might even *be* her source, for all I knew. He'd promised me he'd shut down his operation, but that was like a wino promising to buy a sandwich with the dollar you'd donated in good faith. Who were we trying to kid here?

"Maybe we should let it go for now," I said. "I'm sure this day has seemed long enough. I'd like to have the name and telephone number of Bobby's old girl friend if you have it, and I'll probably want to talk to Rick's parents too. Can you tell me how to get in touch with them?"

"I'll give you both numbers," she said. She got up and crossed to a little antique rosewood desk with pigeonholes and tiny drawers along the top. She opened one of the large drawers below and took out a monogrammed leather address book.

"Beautiful desk," I murmured. This was like telling the Queen of England she has nice jewels.

"Thank you," Glen said idly, while she leafed through the address book. "I bought it at an auction in London last year. I'd hesitate to tell you how much I paid for it."

"Oh, give it a whirl," I said, fascinated. I was getting giddy hanging out with these people.

"Twenty-six thousand dollars," she murmured, running a finger down the page.

I could feel myself shrug philosophically. Hey, big deal. Twenty-six grand was as nothing to her. I wondered what she paid for underwear. I wondered what she paid for *cars*.

"Here it is." She scribbled the information on a scratch pad and tore off a leaf, which she passed to me.

"You'll find Rick's parents rather difficult, I suspect," she said.

"How so?"

"Because they blame Bobby for his death."

"How does he handle that?"

"Not well. Sometimes I think he believes it himself, which is all the more reason to get to the bottom of this."

"Can I ask you one more thing?"

"Of course."

"Is it 'Glen' as in 'West Glen'?"

"The other way around," she said. "I wasn't named for the road. The road was named for me."

By the time I got back in my car, I had a lot of information to digest. It was 9:30, fully dark, and too chilly for a black gauze tunic that ended six inches above my knees. I took a few minutes to wiggle out of my pantyhose and hunch into my long pants. I dropped the high heels into the backseat and pulled on my sandals again, then started the car and put it in reverse. I backed around in a semicircle, looking for a way out. I spotted the second arm of the drive and followed it, catching a glimpse of the rear of the house. There were four illuminated terraces, each with a reflecting pool, shimmering black by night, probably giving back sequential images of the mountains by day, like a series of over-lapping photographs.

I reached West Glen and turned left, heading toward town. There'd been no indication that Derek had gotten home and I thought I'd try to catch him at St. Terry's before he left. Idly, I wondered what it'd be like to have a city street named after me. Kinsey Avenue. Kinsey Road. Not bad. I figured I could learn to live with the tribute if it came my way.

6

Santa Teresa Hospital, by night, looks like an enormous art deco wedding cake, iced with exterior lights: three tiers of creamy white, with a square piece missing in front where the entranceway has been cut out. Visiting hours must have been over because I found a parking space right across the street. I locked my car, crossed, and headed up the circular driveway. There was a large portico and covered walk leading up to double doors that shushed open as I approached. Inside, the lobby lights had been dimmed like the interior of an airplane on a night flight. To my left was the deserted coffee shop, one waitress still at work, dressed in a white uniform almost like a nurse's. To my right was the gift shop with a window display done up with the hospital equivalent of naughty lingerie. The whole place smelled like cold carnations in a florist's refrigerated case.

The decor had been designed to soothe and pacify, especially over in the area marked "cashier." I moved to the information desk, where a woman who resembled my old third-grade teacher sat in a pink-striped pinafore with an expectant look on her face.

"Hi," said I. "Can you tell me if Kitty Wenner's been admitted? She was brought into the emergency room a little while ago."

"Well, now let me just check," she said.

I noticed that her name tag read "Roberta Choat, Volunteer." It sounded like one of a series of novels for young girls that was now sorely out of date. Roberta must have been in her sixties and she had all sorts of good-conduct medals pinned to her bib.

"Here it is. That's Katherine Wenner. She's on Three South. You just walk down this corridor and around these elevators to the bank on the far side. Third floor, and you'll be turning to your left. But now, that's a locked psychiatric ward and I don't know that you'll be able to see her. Visiting hours are over, you know. Are you family?"

"I'm her sister," I said easily.

"Well now, dear, why don't you repeat that to the charge nurse up on the floor and maybe she'll believe you," Roberta Choat said just as easily.

"I hope so," I said. It was actually Derek I wanted to see.

I moved down the corridor, as instructed, and rounded the elevators to the bank on the far side. Sure enough, there was a sign that read SOUTH WING, which I found reassuring. I punched the "up" button and the doors opened instantly. A man entered the elevator behind me and then hesitated, eyeing me as if I were the kind of person he'd read about in a rape-prevention pamphlet. He punched "2" and then stayed close to the control panel until he reached his floor and exited.

The south wing looked better than most of the hotels where I've stayed. Of course, it was also more expensive and offered many personal services that didn't interest me, autopsy being one. The lights were all on and the carpet was a blaze of burnt orange, the walls hung with Van Gogh reproductions; a curious choice for the psycho ward, if you ask me.

Derek Wenner was sitting in a visitors' lounge just outside a set of double doors that had small windows embedded with chicken wire and a sign reading PLEASE RING FOR ADMITTANCE with a buzzer underneath.

He was smoking a cigarette, an issue of *National Geographic* open on his lap. He glanced at me blankly when I sat down next to him.

"How's Kitty?" I said.

He started slightly. "Oh. Sorry. I didn't recognize you when you came around the corner. She's better. They just brought her up and they're getting her settled. I'll have a chance to see her in a bit." His glance strayed toward the elevators. "Glen didn't come down with you by any chance, did she?"

I shook my head, watching a mixture of relief and momentary hope fade out of his face.

"Don't tell her you caught me with a cigarette," he said, sheepishly. "She made me quit last March. I'll toss these out before I go home tonight. It's just with Kitty so sick and then all this stuff—" He broke off with a shrug.

I didn't have the heart to tell him he reeked of tobacco. Glen would have to be comatose not to notice it.

"What brings you down here?" he asked.

"I don't know. Bobby went off to bed and I talked to Glen for a while. I just thought I'd stop by and see what was happening with Kitty."

He smiled, not quite sure what to make of it. "I was just sitting here thinking how much this felt like the night she was born. Waiting out in the lounge for hours, wondering how it was all going to come out. They didn't let fathers in the delivery room in those days, you know. Now, I understand, they practically insist."

"What happened to her mother?"

"She drank herself to death when Kitty was five."

He lapsed into silence. I couldn't think of a comment that didn't seem either trivial or beside the point. I watched him put out his cigarette. He worked the hot ember loose, leaving an empty socket like a pulled tooth.

Finally, I said, "Is she being admitted to Detox?"

"Actually, this is the psychiatric ward, I think the detoxification unit is separate. Leo wants to get her stabilized and then do an evaluation before he does anything. Right now, she's a little bit out of control."

He shook his head, pulling at his double chin. "God, I don't know what to do with her. Glen's probably told you what a source of friction it's been."

"Her drug use?"

"Oh, that and her grades, her hours, the drop in her

weight. That's been a nightmare. I think she's down to ninety-seven pounds at this point."

"So maybe this is where she needs to be," I said.

One of the double doors opened and a nurse peered out. She wore jeans and a T-shirt. No cap, but she did wear a nursing pin and a name tag that I couldn't read from where I sat. Her hair was ill-dyed, a shade of orange I'd only seen before in marigolds, but her smile was quick and pleasant.

"Mr. Wenner? Would you like to follow me, please?"

Derek got up with a glance at me. "You want to wait? It won't be long. Leo said five minutes was all he'd permit, given the shape she's in. I could buy you a cup of coffee or a drink as soon as I'm done."

"All right. That's nice. I'll be out here."

He nodded and moved off with the nurse. For one brief moment, as they passed into the ward, I could hear Kitty delivering some high-decibel curses of a quite imaginative sort. Then the door closed and the key turned resoundingly in the lock. No one on 3 South was going to sleep tonight. I picked up the *National Geographic* magazine and stared at a series of time-lapse photographs of a blowhole in Yosemite.

Fifteen minutes later, Derek and I were seated in a motel bar half a block away from the hospital. The Plantación is a rogue of a drinking establishment that looks as if it's crept to its present location from some other part of town. The motel itself was apparently built with an eye to sheltering the relatives of the ill and infirm who come to St. Terry's for treatment from small towns nearby. The bar was added as an afterthought, in violation of God knows what city codes, as it is smack in the middle of the residential neighborhood. Of course, the area by now has been infiltrated by medical buildings, clinics, convalescent homes, pharmacies, and various other suppliers to the health-care industry, including a mortuary two blocks away to service folk when all else fails. Maybe the city planning commission decided, at some point, to help ease the pain by making eighty-six-proof alcohol available along with the other kind.

The interior is narrow and dark, with a diorama of a banana plantation that extends behind the bar in the space that usually supports a long mirror, liquor bottles, and a neon beer sign. Instead, arranged as though on a small lighted stage, scale-model banana palms are laid out in orderly rows and tiny mechanized laborers go about the business of harvesting fruit in a series of vignettes. All of the workers appear to be Mexican, including the tiny carved woman who arrives with a water barrel and a dipper just as the noon whistle blows. One man waves from a treetop while a wee wooden dog barks and wags its tail.

Derek and I sat at the bar for a while, scarcely speaking, we were so taken by the scene. Even the bartender, who must have seen it hundreds of times, paused to watch while the mechanical mule pulled a load of bananas around the bend and another cart took its place. Not surprisingly, the house specialties run to cuba libres and banana daiquiris, but no one cares if you or-der something adult. Derek had a Beefeater martini and I had a glass of white wine that made my lips pull together like a drawstring purse. I'd watched the bar-tender pour it from a gallon jug that ran about three bucks at any Stop N' Go. The label was from one of those wineries the grape pickers are always striking and I pondered the possibility that they'd peed on the crop to retaliate for unfair labor practices.

"What do you think about this business with Bobby?" I said to Derek when I finally got my mouth unpuckered.

"His claim about a murder attempt? God, I don't know. It sounds pretty farfetched to me. He and his mother seem to believe it, but I can't figure out why anybody'd do such a thing."

"What about money?"

"Money?"

"I've been wondering who benefits financially if Bobby dies. I asked Glen the same thing."

Derek began to stroke his double chin. The excess weight made him look as if he had one normal-sized face superimposed on a much larger one. The jowls were just leftover flesh hanging out the sides. "It'd be a fairly conspicuous motive, I should think," he said. He wore the skeptical look of a man in a stage play: an ex-aggerated effect for the audience twenty-five rows back.

"Yeah, well forcing him off the bridge was conspic-uous too. Of course, if he'd died in the wreck, nobody would have known the difference," I said. "Cars go off the pass every six months or so anyway because people take the curves too fast, so it could have been passed off as a single-car accident. There might have been some damage to the rear bumper where the other driver made contact, but by the time they'd hauled Bobby's car up the mountain, I don't think anybody would have suspected what really occurred. I take it there weren't any witnesses."

"No, and I'm not sure you can count on what Bobby says."

"Meaning what?"

"Well, he obviously has a vested interest in having someone else to blame. The kid doesn't want to own up to the fact that he'd been drinking. He always drove too fast anyway. His best friend gets killed. Rick was Kitty's boyfriend, you know, and his death threw her for a loop. I don't mean to cast doubt on Bobby's version of the story, but it's always struck me as self-serving to some extent."

I studied Derek's face, wondering at the change in his tone of voice. It was an interesting theory and I got the impression that he'd been thinking about it for some time. He seemed uncomfortable, though, pretending to be casual and objective when, in fact, he was undermining Bobby's credibility. I was sure he hadn't dared mention his idea to Glen. "You're saying Bobby made it up?"

"I didn't say *that*," he replied evasively. "I think *he* believes it, but then it gets him off the hook, doesn't it?" His eyes slid away from mine and he signaled to the bartender for a repeat, then glanced back at me. "You ready for another one?"

"Sure, why not?" I hadn't actually finished the wine I had, but I hoped he'd be more at ease if he thought I was matching him drink for drink. Martinis will make you say anything and I was curious what might come out once his tongue was loosened. I could already see that look in his eyes, something slithery and pink that hints of alcoholic tendencies. He fumbled in his shirt pocket and took out the pack of cigarettes, his gaze riveted to the diorama. A tiny mechanical Mexican with a machete was climbing up the tree again. Derek lit a cigarette without looking at it and the gesture took on a curious air, as if it couldn't count against him if he ignored it himself. He was probably the kind of person who eats while watching TV and tops off his Scotch so it will always look as though he is only having one.

"How was Kitty when you saw her? You haven't said."

"She was . . . you know, she was upset, I guess, to find herself hospitalized, but I told her . . . I said, 'Now look, kid. You're just going to have to shape up.'" Derek had shifted into his parental persona and he seemed uncomfortable with that too. I could just imagine how effective he'd been to date.

"Glen didn't seem very sympathetic," I said.

"Well, no. I can't blame her for that, but then Kitty's had it rough and I don't think Glen understands the toll it can take on a kid like her. Bobby's had every advantage money could buy. Why shouldn't he have it made? I tell you what bothers me. I mean, anything Bobby does is excused. Anything Kitty does is the crime of the century. Bobby's screwed up. Don't kid yourself. But when he fouls up, Glen can always find a way to rationalize what he's done. Know what I mean?"

I shrugged noncommittally. "I don't know what he's done."

The drinks arrived and Derek took a sip from his as though he tasted martinis for a living. He nodded judiciously and set the glass down with care in the center of his cocktail napkin. He touched a knuckle to the corners of his mouth. His movements were becoming liquid and his eyes were beginning to slide around in their sockets like marbles in oil. Kitty had apparently gotten crocked in exactly the same way, only on downers instead of gin.

The bartender took a couple of beers out of the cooler and moved down to the other end of the bar to serve a customer.

Derek's voice dropped. "This is just between you and me and the lamppost," he said. "But the kid's been cited twice on drunk-driving raps and he got some little gal knocked up over a year ago. Glen wants to treat it like youthful hijinks—boys will be boys and all that sort of crap—but let Kitty cross the line once and all hell breaks loose."

I was beginning to see why Bobby thought their marriage wouldn't last. We were playing hardball here, parent vs. parent in the semifinals. Derek tried on a smile that was meant to charm, shifting over to neutral ground.

"So where do you start on a thing like this?" he asked.

"I don't know yet. Usually I nose around, do a background check, uncover a thread, and follow where it leads." I looked at him, watching while he nodded as though I'd actually said something significant.

"Well, I wish you luck. Bobby's a good kid, but there's a lot going on. More to that kid than meets the eye," he said with a knowing look. His speech wasn't slurred, but the consonants were getting soft. The winsome smile flickered back with its sly message. His whole manner implied that he could have said plenty, but discretion held him back. I didn't take him seriously. He was doing some kind of maneuvering, apparently unaware of how transparent he was. I took a sip of wine, wondering if there was anything else I might learn from him.

Derek glanced at his watch. "I better get home. Face the music." He tossed the rest of his martini back and eased himself off the barstool. He pulled out his wallet and sorted through several layers of bills until he found a five and a ten, which he placed on the bar.

"Will Glen be mad?"

He smiled to himself as if he were considering a number of replies. "Glen is always mad these days. It's been a hell of a birthday, I can tell you that."

"Maybe next year will be better. Thanks for the drinks."

"Thanks for coming down here. I appreciate your concern. If I can do anything to help you, you just let me know."

We walked the half-block to my car and then parted company. I watched him in my rearview mirror as he ambled toward the visitors' parking lot on the far side of the hospital. I suspected he was pretending more motor control than he actually had. We'd only been in the Plantación for thirty minutes and I'd watched him down two martinis. I started my car and did a U-turn, pulling up next to him. I leaned across the seat and opened the door on the passenger side. "Why don't I give you a lift?"

"Oh no, I'm fine," he said. He stood for a moment, his body swaying slightly. I could see the message being relayed through his central nervous system. He cocked his head, frowning, and then he got into my car and pulled the door shut. "I got problems enough, right?"

"Right," I said.

7

By the time I got into the office the next morning at nine, Bobby's attorney had forwarded copies of the initial accident report, along with notes from the follow-up investigation and numerous eight-by-ten color photographs that showed in glossy detail just how thoroughly demolished Bobby's car had been and just how dead Rick Bergen had become as a result. His body had been found, crushed and mangled, halfway down the slope. I recoiled from the sight as though a bright light had been flashed in my face, a shock of revulsion running down my frame. I had to steel myself to look again so that I could study the details dispassionately. There was something about the way the police photographer's lights had been rigged against the harsh dark of night that made the death seem garish, like a low-budget horror move that was real short on plot. I shuffled through the series until I found photographs of the accident scene itself.

Bobby's Porsche had taken out a big section of guardrail, had sheared off a scrub oak at its base, scarred boulders, and dug a long trench through the underbrush, apparently flipping over five or six times before it came to rest at the bottom of the ravine in a crumpled mass of twisted metal and shattered glass. There were several views of the car, front and rear, showing its position relative to various landmarks in the terrain and then the close-ups of Bobby before the ambulance crew had removed him from the wreckage. "Oh shit," I breathed. I put the whole stack down for a moment and put a hand across my eyes. I hadn't even had my coffee yet and there I was looking at human bodies turned inside out on impact.

I opened the French doors and went out on the balcony and sucked in some fresh air. Below me, State Street was orderly and quiet. Traffic was light and pedestrians obeyed the signals as if they were appearing in an educational film instructing grade-school kids how to conduct themselves on city streets. I watched all the healthy people walk up and down with their limbs intact and the flesh still covering their bones. The sun was shining and the palm trees weren't even stirred by a breeze. Everything looked so ordinary, but only for the moment and only as far as I could see. Death could pop up anytime, a jarring jack-in-the-box with a fixed, bloody grin.

I went back inside and made a pot of coffee and then sat down at my desk, going through the photographs again and taking time now to study the police reports. A copy of the postmortem examination on Rick Bergen had been included and I noticed that it had been conducted by Jim Fraker, whose responsibilities at St.

Terry's apparently extended to such services. Santa Teresa is too small a town to pay for its own police morgue and its own medical examiner, so the work is contracted out.

The report Dr. Fraker had dictated effectively reduced Rick's death to observations about the craniocerebral trauma he'd sustained, with a catalogue of abrasions, contusions, small-intestine avulsions, mesenteric lacerations, and sufficient skeletal damage to certify Rick's crossing of the River Styx.

I hauled out my typewriter and opened a file for Bobby Callahan, feeling soothed and comforted as I translated all the unsettling facts into a terse account of events to date. I logged in his check, made a note of the receipt number, and filed the copy of the contract he'd signed. I typed in the names and addresses of Rick Bergen's parents and Bobby's ex–girl friend, along with a list of those present at Glen Callahan's house the night before. I didn't speculate. I didn't editorialize. I just typed it all out and used my two-hole punch at the top of the paper, which I then clamped into a folder and placed in my file cabinet.

That done, I glanced at my watch, Ten-twenty. Bobby's physical-therapy regimen was parceled out into daily stints, while mine was set up for Mondays, Wednesdays, and Fridays. It was possible he was still at the gym. I closed up the office and went down the back steps to the lot, where I keep my car parked. I headed toward Santa Teresa Fitness, gassing up on the way, and caught Bobby just as he was coming out of the building. His hair was still damp from the shower and the scent of Coast soap radiated from his skin. Despite the facial paralysis, the crippled left arm, and the limp, something of the original Bobby Callahan shone through, young and strong, with the blond good looks of a California surfer. I'd seen pictures of him broken, and by comparison, he now seemed miraculously whole, even with the scars still etched on his face like tattoos done by an amateur. When he saw me, he smiled crookedly, dabbing automatically at his chin. "I didn't expect to see you here this morning," he said.

"How was your workout?"

He tilted from side to side, indicating so-so. I tucked my arm through his.

"I have a request, but you don't have to agree," I said.

"What's that?"

I hesitated for a moment. "I want you to go up the pass with me and show me where the car went off."

The smile faded. He glanced away from me and launched into motion again, moving toward his car with that lilting gait. "All right, but I want to stop by and see Kitty first."

"Is she allowed to have visitors?"

"I can talk my way in," he said. "People don't like to deal with cripples, so I can usually get anything I want."

"Spoiled," I said.

"Take any advantage you can," he replied sheepishly.

"You want to drive?"

He shook his head. "Let's drop my car off at the house and take yours."

I parked in the visitor's lot at St. Terry's and waited in the car while he went in to see Kitty. I imagined she'd be back on her feet by now, still pissed off, and raising hell on the ward. Not anything I wanted to face. I hoped to talk to her again in a couple of days, but I preferred to give her time to settle down. I flipped on the car radio, tapping on the steering wheel in time to the music. Two nurses passed through the parking lot in white uniforms, white shoes and hose, with dark blue capes that looked like something left over from World War I. In due course, Bobby emerged from the building and hobbled across the parking lot, his expression preoccupied. He got into the car. I flipped the radio off and started the engine, backing out of the slot.

"Everything okay?"

"Yeah, sure."

He was quiet as I headed across town and turned left onto the secondary road that cuts along the back side of Santa Teresa at the base of the foothills. The sky was a flat blue and cloudless, looking like semigloss paint that had been applied with a roller. It was hot, and the hills were brown and dry, laid out like a pile of kindling. The long grasses near the road had bleached out to a pale gold, and once in a while, I caught sight of lizards perched up on big rocks, looking as gray and still as twigs.

The road twisted, two lanes of blacktop angling back and forth up the side of the mountain. I downshifted twice and my little VW still complained of the climb.

"I thought I remembered something," Bobby said after a while. "But I can't seem to pin it down. That's why I had to see Kitty."

"What kind of thing?"

"I had an address book. One of those small leather-bound types about the size of a playing card. Cheap. Red. I gave it to someone for safekeeping and now I have no idea who." He paused, shaking his head with puzzlement.

"You don't remember why it was important?"

"No. I remember feeling anxious about it, thinking I better not have it in my possession because it was dangerous to me, so I passed it on. At the time—and I remember this part clearly—I figured I could retrieve it later." He shrugged, snorting derisively. "So much for that."

"Was this before the accident or afterward?"

"Don't know. I just remember giving it to someone."

"Wouldn't it be dangerous to whoever you gave it to?"

"I don't think so. God." He slid down on his spine so he could rest his head on the back of the seat. He peered through the windshield, following the line of gray hills up to the left where the pass cuts through at the crest. "I *hate* this feeling. I hate knowing I once knew something and having no access to it. It's just an image with nothing attached to it. There aren't any memory cues so I have no way to place it in time. It's like pieces of a jigsaw puzzle with a whole hunk knocked off on the floor."

"But how does it work when you forget like that? Is there any retrieving the information or is it just gone?"

"Oh, sometimes it'll come back, but usually it's blank . . . like a hole in the bottom of a box. Whatever used to be there has spilled out along the way."

"What made you think of it in the first place?"

"I don't know. I was looking through a desk drawer and came across the red leather memo pad that was part of the same set. Suddenly, I got this flash." He fell silent. I glanced over at him and realized how tense he was. He was massaging his bad hand, milking the fingers as if they were long rubber teats.

"Kitty didn't know anything about it?"

He shook his head.

"How's she doing?"

"She's up and around. I guess Derek's going over to see her later on. . . ." He paused. We were reaching the crest of the hill and a muscle near his left eye had started to jump.

"Are you going to be all right with this?" I asked.

He was staring intently at the side of the road. "Just up here. Slow down and pull over if you can."

I checked my rearview mirror. There were three cars behind me, but the road was narrowing from three lanes to two. I eased over to the right and found a gravel shoulder where I could park. The bridge, with its low concrete guardrails, was about ten yards ahead. Bobby sat there, staring to his right.

Where the road descends from the summit, the whole valley opens out, hills sweeping back as far as the eye can see to a range of lavender mountains pasted against the rim of the sky. The August heat shimmered in silence. The land seemed vast and primitive, looking as it must have looked for thousands of years. In the distance, live oaks dotted the landscape, as shaggy and dark and hunched as buffalo. There'd been no rain for months and the vista seemed chalky and pale, the color washed out.

Closer to us, the roadside dropped away into the treacherous canyon that had nearly marked Bobby's death nine months ago. A length of metal railing had been replaced, but where the bridge began, there was still a chunk of concrete missing.

"The other car started ramming us from behind just as we came over the rim of the hill," he said. I thought he meant to continue, so I waited.

He walked forward a few feet, gravel crunching under his shoes. He was clearly uneasy as he peered down the rocky slope. I looked back over my shoulder at the few cars passing. No one paid the slightest attention to us.

I studied the scene, picking out one of the scarred boulders I'd seen in the photograph, and farther down, the raw, jagged stump where a scrub oak had been snapped off at the base. I knew the Santa Teresa police had swept the area clean of debris from the accident, so there was no need to whip out a magnifying glass or creep around picking fibers from the underbrush.

Bobby turned to me. "Have you ever been close to death?"

"Yes."

"I remember thinking, 'This is it. I'm gone.' I disconnected. I felt like a plant ripped up by the roots. Airborne." He stopped. "And then I was cold and everything hurt and people were talking to me and I couldn't understand a word they said. That was in the hospital and two weeks had passed. I've wondered since then if that's how newborn babies feel. Bewildered like that and disoriented. Helpless. It was such a struggle to stay in touch with the world. Sending down new roots. I knew I could choose. I was barely attached, barely tethered, and I could feel how easy it'd be just to let go like a balloon and sail away."

"But you hung on."

"Hey, my mother willed it. Every time I opened my eyes, I saw her face. And when I closed my eyes, I heard her voice. She'd say, 'We're going to make it, Bobby. We're going to do this, you and I.'"

He was silent again. I thought, Jesus, what must it be like to have a mother who could love you that way? My parents had died when I was five, in a freak car accident. We'd been on a Sunday outing, driving up to Lompoc, when a huge boulder tumbled down the mountain and smashed through the windshield. My father had died instantly and we'd crashed. I'd been in the backseat, thrust down against the floorboards on impact, wedged in by the crushed frame. My mother had lingered, moaning and crying, sinking into a silence finally that I sensed was ominous and forever. It had taken them hours to extract me from the wreckage, trapped there with the dead whom I loved who had left me for all time. After that, I was raised by a no-nonsense aunt who had done her best, who had loved me deeply, but with a matter-of-factness that had failed to nourish some part of me.

Bobby had been infused with a love of such magnitude that it had brought him back from the grave. It was odd, when he was so broken, that I experienced an envy that made tears well up in my eyes. I felt a laugh burble and he turned a puzzled glance on me.

I took out a Kleenex and blew my nose. "I just realized how much I envy you," I said.

He smiled ruefully. "That's a first."

We got back in the car. There'd been no blinding recall, no sudden recollection of forgotten facts, but I'd seen the miry pit into which he had been flung and I'd felt the bond between us strengthened.

"Have you been up here since the accident?"

"No. I never had the nerve and no one ever suggested it. Made me sweat."

I started the car. "How about a beer?"

"How about a bourbon on the rocks?"

We went to the Stage Coach Tavern, just off the main road, and talked for the rest of the afternoon.

8

When I dropped him off at his house at five, he hesitated as he got out of the car, pausing as he'd done before with his hand on the door, peering back in at me.

"Know what I like about you?" he said.

"What," I said.

"When I'm with you, I don't feel self-conscious or like I'm crippled or ugly. I don't know how you do that, but it's nice."

I looked at him for a moment, feeling oddly self-conscious myself. "I'll tell you. You remind me of a birthday present somebody's sent through the mail. The paper's torn and the box is damaged, but there's still something terrific in there. I enjoy your company."

A half-smile formed and disappeared. He glanced over at the house and then back to me. He had something else on his mind, but he seemed embarrassed to admit to it.

"What," I coaxed.

He tilted his head and the look in his eyes was one I knew. "If I were O.K. . . . if I'd been whole, would you have thought about having a relationship with me? I mean, boy-girl type?"

"You want the truth?"

"Only if it's flattering."

I laughed. "The truth is if I'd run into you before the accident, I'd have been intimidated. You're too good-looking, too rich, and too young. So I gotta say no. If you were 'whole,' as you put it, I probably wouldn't have known you at all. You're really not my type, you know?"

"What is your type?"

"I haven't figured that out yet."

He looked at me for a minute with a quizzical smile forming.

"Would you just say what's on your mind?" I said.

"How can you turn it around and make me feel good that I'm deformed?"

"Oh God, you're not deformed. Now, quit that! I'll talk to you later."

He smiled and slammed the car door, moving back then so I could make the turn-around and head out the far side of the driveway.

I drove back to my place. It was only 5:15. I still had time to get a run in, though I wondered at the wisdom of it. Bobby and I had spent the better part of the day drinking beer and bourbon and bad Chablis, gnawing barbecued spareribs and sourdough bread tough enough to tug your dentures out. I was really more in the mood for a nap than a run, but I thought the self-discipline would serve me right.

I changed into my running clothes and did three

miles while I went through the mental gymnastics of getting the case organized. It felt like iffy stuff and I wasn't quite sure where to start. I thought I better check with Dr. Fraker in the Pathology Department at St. Terry's first, maybe pop in and see Kitty at the same time, and then try the newspaper morgue and go through the tedious business of checking back through local news prior to the accident just to see what was going on at the time. Maybe some event then current would shed light on Bobby's claim that someone had tried to murder him.

I went over to Rosie's at seven for a glass of wine. I was feeling restless and I wondered if Bobby hadn't set something in motion somehow. It was nice having someone to pal around with, nice to while away an afternoon in good company, nice to have someone whose face I looked forward to seeing. I wasn't sure how to categorize our relationship. My affection for him wasn't maternal in any way. Sisterly, perhaps. He seemed like a good friend and I felt for him all the admiration one feels for a good friend. He was fun, and being with him was peaceful. I'd been alone for so long that a relationship of any kind seemed like seductive stuff.

I snagged a glass of wine at the bar and then I sat in the back booth and surveyed the place. For a Tuesday night, there was a lively crowd, which is to say, two guys arguing nasally at the bar, and an old couple from the neighborhood sharing a big plate of pancakes layered with ham. Rosie remained at the bar with a cigarette, smoke drifting up around her head in a halo of nicotine and hair spray. She's in her sixties, Hungarian and bossy, a creature of muumuus and dyed auburn tresses, which she wears parted down the center and plastered into place with sprays that have sat on the grocery-store shelves since the beehive hairdo bumbled out of fashion in 1966. Rosie has a long nose, a short upper lip, eyes that she pencils into narrow, suspicious-looking slits. She's short, top-heavy, and opinionated. Also she pouts, which in a woman her age is ludicrous, but effective. Half the time, I don't like her much, but she never ceases to fascinate.

Her establishment has the same crude but cranky appeal. The bar extends along the left wall with a stuffed marlin arched above it that I suspect was never really alive. A big color TV sits on the far end of the bar, sound off, images dancing about like transmissions from another planet where life is vibrant and lunatic. The place always smells of beer, cigarette smoke, and cooking grease that should have been thrown out last week. There are six or seven tables in the center of the room surrounded by chrome-and-plastic chairs out of somebody's 1940s dinette set. The eight booths along the right wall have been fashioned out of plywood and stained the color of walnut, complete with tasteless suggestions carved in by ruffians who apparently had had a go at the ladies' room too. It's possible that Rosie doesn't read English well enough to divine the true meaning of these primitive slogans. It's also possible that they express her sentiments exactly. Hard to know with her.

I glanced over at her and discovered that she was sitting bolt upright and very still, squinting narrowly at the front door. I followed her gaze. Henry had just come in with his new lady friend, Lila Sams. Rosie's antennae had apparently gone up automatically, like My Favorite Martian in drag. Henry found a table that seemed reasonably clean and pulled out a chair. Lila sat down and settled her big plastic bag on her lap like a small dog. She was wearing a bright cotton dress in a snazzy print, bold red poppies on a ground of blue, and her hair looked as if it had been poufed at the beauty parlor that very afternoon. Henry sat down, glancing back at the booth, where he knows I usually sit. I gave a little finger wave and he waved back. Lila's head swiveled in my direction and her smile took on a look of false delight.

Rosie, meanwhile, had set her evening paper aside and had left her stool, gliding through the bar like a shark. I could only surmise that she and Lila had met before. I looked on with interest. This might be almost as entertaining as *Godzilla Meets Bambi*, at my local cinema. From my vantage point, of course, the whole encounter took place in pantomime.

Rosie had her order pad out. She stood and stared at Henry, behaving as though he were alone, which is exactly how she treats me when I come in with a friend. Rosie doesn't speak to strangers. She doesn't make eye contact with anyone she hasn't known for some time. This is especially true when the "anyones" are women. Lila was all aflutter. Henry conferred with her and ordered for them both. Much discussion ensued. I gathered that Lila had made some request that didn't suit

Rosie's notion of gourmet Hungarian cuisine. Maybe Lila wanted the peppers left out or something roasted instead of fried. Lila looked like the sort of woman who'd have lots of dietary taboos. Rosie only had the one. You ate it the way she served it or you went somewhere else. Lila apparently couldn't believe that she couldn't be catered to. Shrill and quarrelsome noises arose, all Lila's. Rosie didn't say a word. It was her place. She could do anything she wanted to. The two men at the bar who'd been arguing about politics turned to watch the show. The couple eating the sonkás palacsinta paused simultaneously, forks in midair.

Lila flounced her chair back. I thought for a minute she meant to hit Rosie with her purse. Instead, she delivered what looked like a scathing remark and marched toward the door with Henry scrambling after her. Rosie remained unruffled, smiling secretly as cats do in the midst of mouse dreams. The customers in the place, all five of us, got very quiet, tending studiously to our own private thoughts lest Rosie turn on us inexplicably and eighty-six us for life.

Twenty minutes passed before Rosie found an excuse to head my way. My wineglass was empty and she was bringing me a refill with unheard-of good grace. She set the second glass on the table and then folded her hands in front of her, wiggling slightly in place. She does this when she wants your attention or feels you haven't lauded her with quite enough praise for some culinary accomplishment.

"Looks like you took care of *her*," I remarked.

"Is vulgar woman. Terrible creature. She was in once before and I don't like her a bit. Henry must be crazy nuts to come in my place with a hussy like that. Who is she?"

I shrugged. "Listen, all I know is her name is Lila Sams. She's renting a room from Mrs. Lowenstein and Henry seems to be smitten."

"I'm gonna smitten her if she comes in here again! She got something funny with her eyes." Rosie screwed her face up and did an imitation of Lila that made me laugh. Rosie's generally a humorless person and I had no idea her powers of observation were so keen, let alone her ability to mimic. She was dead serious, of course. She drew herself together. "What's she want with him anyway?"

"What makes you think she wants anything? Maybe the two of them are just interested in a little companionship. Henry's very handsome, if you ask me."

"I didn't ask you! He's very handsome. He's good fellow too. So why does he need companionship with that little snake?"

"Like they say, Rosie, there's no accounting for taste. Maybe she has redeeming qualities that aren't immediately evident."

"Oh no. Not her. She's up to something no good. I'm gonna talk to Mrs. Lowenstein. What's the matter with her, renting to a woman like that?"

I rather wondered about that myself, walking the half-block home. Mrs. Lowenstein is a widow who owns considerable property in the neighborhood. I couldn't believe she needed the money and I was curious how Lila Sams had arrived at her doorstep.

When I got back to my place, Henry's kitchen light was on and I could hear the muffled sounds of Lila's voice, shrill and inconsolable. The encounter with Rosie had apparently upset her thoroughly and all of Henry's murmured reassurances were doing no good. I unlocked my door and let myself in, effectively shutting out the noise.

I read for an hour—six thrilling chapters from a book on burglary and theft—and went to bed early, wrapping myself up in my quilt. I turned off the light and lay there for a while in the dark. I could have sworn I still heard the faint rise and fall of Lila's whine, circling my ear like a mosquito. I couldn't distinguish the words, but the tone was clear . . . contentious and ill-humored. Maybe Henry would realize she was not as nice as she pretended to be. Maybe not, though. I'm always startled at what fools men and women make of themselves in the pursuit of sex.

I woke at seven, had a cup of coffee while I read the paper, and then headed over to Santa Teresa Fitness for my Wednesday workout. I was feeling stronger and the two days of jogging had left my legs aching pleasantly. The morning was clear, not yet hot, the sky was blank as a canvas being prepared for paint. The parking lot at the gym was almost full and I snagged the one empty space. I spotted Bobby's car two slots over and I smiled, looking forward to seeing him.

The gym was surprisingly populated for the middle

of the week, with five or six two-hundred-and-eighty-pound guys lifting weights, two women in tights on the Nautilus equipment, and a trainer supervising the workout of a young actress whose rear end was spreading out like slowly melting candle wax. I caught sight of Bobby doing bench presses on a Universal machine near the far wall. He'd apparently been there for a while because his T-shirt was ringed with sweat and his blond hair had separated into damp strands. I didn't want to interrupt him so I simply stashed my gym bag and got down to business myself.

I started my workout with some bicep curls, using dumbbells with hardly any weight, beginning to concentrate as I warmed up. By now, I knew my routine and I had to fight a certain mounting impatience. I'm not a process person. I like goals and closure, the arrival instead of the journey itself. Repetition makes me rebellious. How I manage to jog from day to day I'm never sure. I proceeded to wrist curls, mentally leaping ahead through my routine, wishing I was at the end of it instead of two exercises in. Maybe Bobby and I could have lunch again if he was free.

I heard a clatter and then a thump and looked up in time to see that he'd lost his balance and stumbled against a stack of five-pound plates. It was clear he hadn't hurt himself, but he seemed to catch sight of me for the first time and his embarrassment was acute. He flushed, trying to scramble to his feet again. One of the guys at the next machine leaned over casually and gave him an assist. He steadied himself self-consciously, waving aside any further help. He limped over to the leg-press machine, his air brusque and withdrawn. I went on working out as though I hadn't seen anything, but I kept a discreet eye on him. Even at that distance, I could see that his mood was dark, his face tense. A couple of people sent looks in his direction that spoke of pity, veiled as concern. He mopped at his chin, his attention turned inward. His left leg was going into muscle spasms of some sort and he clutched at his knee with frustration. The leg was like a separate creature, jumping fitfully, defying containment or control. Bobby groaned, pounding angrily at his own flesh as though he might subdue it with his fist. I struggled with an impulse to cross the room, but I knew it would only make things worse. He'd been pushing himself and his body was vibrating with fatigue. Just as suddenly as it had begun, the spasm seemed to fade. He dashed at his eyes, keeping his head low. As soon as he was able to walk again, he snatched up a towel and headed for the locker room, abandoning the rest of his regimen.

I hurried through the rest of my workout and showered as quickly as I could. I expected to find his car gone, but it was still parked in the slot where I'd seen it. Bobby sat with his arms encircling the steering wheel, his head resting on his arms, his shoulders convulsing with dry, hacking sobs. I hesitated for a moment and then approached the car on the passenger side. I got in and closed the door and sat there with him until he was done. I didn't have any comfort for him. There wasn't anything I could do. I had no way to address his pain or his despair and my only hope was to let him know by my presence that I did feel for him and I did care.

It passed by degrees, and when it was over, he dried his eyes with a towel and blew his nose, keeping his face averted.

"You want to go have some coffee?"

He shook his head. "Just leave me alone, O.K.?" he said.

"I got time," I said.

"Maybe I'll call you later."

"All right. I'll go ahead and take care of some business and maybe we can connect up this afternoon. You need anything in the meantime?"

"No." The tone was dull, his manner listless now.

"Bobby—"

"No! Just get the fuck away from me and leave me alone. I don't need your help."

I opened the car door. "I'll check back with you," I said. "Take care."

He reached over and grabbed the door handle, slamming it shut. He started the engine with a roar, and I stepped aside, as he backed out of the slot with a squeal of tires and shot out of the parking lot without a backward glance.

That was the last I ever saw of him.

9

The Pathology Department at St. Terry's is located below ground in the heart of a maze of small offices. Miles of corridors branch out in all directions, connecting the non-medical departments charged with the actual running of the facility: maintenance, housekeeping, engineering, plant operations. Where the floors above are renovated and tastefully done, the decor down here runs to brown vinyl tile and glossy paint the color of vanished bones. The air smells hot and dry and certain open doorways reveal glimpses of ominous machinery and electrical ducts as big as sewer pipes.

There was a steady flow of pedestrian traffic that day, people in hospital uniforms, as pale and expressionless as residents of an underground city, starved for sunlight. The Pathology Department itself was a pleasant contrast: spacious, well lighted, handsomely appointed in royal blue and gray, with fifty to sixty lab technicians working to accommodate the blood, bone, and tissue specimens that filtered down from above.

The computerized equipment seemed to click, hum, and whir: efficiency augmented by an army of experts. Noise was muted, telephones pinging daintily against the artificial air. Even the typewriters seemed to be muffled, recording discreetly the secrets of the human condition. There was order, proficiency, and calm, the sense that here, at least, the pain and indignation of illness was under control. Death was being held at bay, measured, calibrated, and analyzed. Where it had claimed a victory, the same crew of specialists dissected the results and fed them into the machinery. Paper poured out in a long road, paved with hieroglyphics. I stood in the doorway for a moment, struck by the scene. These were microscope detectives, pursuing killers of another order than those I hunted down.

"May I help you?"

I glanced over at the receptionist, who was watching me.

"I'm looking for Dr. Fraker. Do you know if he's here?"

"Should be. Down this aisle to the first left, then left again and you can ask somebody back there."

I found him in a modular compartment lined with bookshelves, furnished with a desk, a swivel chair, plants, and graphic art. He was tipped back in his chair, his feet propped up on the edge of his deck, leafing through a medical book the size of the *Oxford English Dictionary*. He had a pair of rimless bifocals in one hand, chewing on one of the stems as he read. He was substantially built—wide shoulders, heavy thighs. His hair was a thick, silvery white, his skin the warm tone of a flesh-colored crayon. Age had given his face a softly crumpled look, like a freshly laundered cotton sheet that needs to be starched and ironed. He wore surgical greens with matching booties.

"Dr. Fraker?"

He glanced up at me and his gray eyes registered recognition. He pointed a finger. "Bobby Callahan's friend."

"That's right. I wondered if I could talk to you."

"Sure, absolutely. Come on in."

He got to his feet and we shook hands. He indicated the chair near his desk and I sat down.

"We can make an appointment to talk later if I've caught you at a bad time," I said.

"Not at all. What can I do for you? Glen told me Bobby hired someone to look into the accident."

"He's convinced it was a murder attempt. Hit and run. Has he talked to you about that?"

Dr. Fraker shook his head. "I haven't seen him for months except for Monday night. Murder. Do the police agree?"

"I don't know yet. I've got a copy of the accident report and as nearly as I can tell, they don't have much to go on. There weren't any witnesses and I don't think they found much evidence at the scene."

"That's unusual, isn't it?"

"Well, there's usually *something* to go on. Broken glass, skid marks, transfer traces on the victim's vehicle. Maybe the guy jumped out of his car and swept up all the soil and paint flecks, I don't know. I do trust

Bobby's intuition on this. He says he was in danger. He just can't remember why."

Dr. Fraker seemed to consider that briefly and then shifted in his seat. "I'd be inclined to believe him myself. He's a bright boy. He was a gifted student too. It's a damn shame there's so little left of that. What's he think is going on?"

"He hasn't any idea and, as he points out, the minute he remembers, he's in more trouble than he is now. He suspects somebody's still after him."

He cleaned his glasses with a handkerchief, contemplating the matter. He was a man apparently accustomed to dealing with puzzles, but I imagined his solutions were derived from symptoms instead of circumstances. Diseases don't require an underlying motivation in the same way homicide does.

He shook his head slightly, his eyes meeting mine. "Odd. The whole thing's a little bit out of my range." He put his glasses on, turning businesslike. "Well. We better figure out what's going on, then. What do you need from me?"

I shrugged. "All I know to do is start back at square one and see if I can determine what kind of trouble he was in. He'd worked for you for what? Two months?"

"About that. He started in September, I believe. I can have Marcy look that up if you want exact dates."

"I gather he was hired here because of your relationship with his mother."

"Well, yes and no. We generally have a slot available for a premed student. It just happened that Bobby filled the bill in this case. Glen Callahan's a very big cheese around here, but we wouldn't have hired him if he'd been a dud. Can I get you some coffee? I'm about to have some."

"All right, sure."

He leaned sideways slightly, calling to the secretary, whose desk was in his line of sight. "Marcy? Can we get some coffee in here, please?"

To me, he said, "You take cream and sugar?"

"Black is fine."

"Both black," he called out.

There was no reply, but I assumed it was being taken care of. He turned his attention back to me. "Sorry to interrupt."

"That's all right. Did he have desk space down here?"

"He had a desk up front, but that was cleared out, oh, I'd say within a day of the accident. Nobody thought he'd survive, you know, and we had to bring somebody else in pretty quickly. This place is a madhouse most of the time."

"What happened to his things?"

"I dropped them by the house myself. There wasn't much, but we put what we came across in a cardboard box and I passed it on to Derek. I don't know what he did with it, if anything. Glen was at the hospital twenty-four hours a day at that point."

"Do you remember what was in it?"

"His desk? Odds and ends. Office things."

I made a note to myself to check for the box. I supposed there was a chance it was still at the house somewhere. "Can you walk me through Bobby's day and show me what sorts of things he did?"

"Sure. Actually, he divided his time between the lab and the morgue out in the old county medical facility on Frontage Road. I've got to make a run out there anyway and you can ride along if you like, or follow in your car if that's easier."

"I thought the morgue was here."

"We've got a small one here, just off the autopsy room. We've got another morgue out there."

"I didn't realize there was more than one."

"We needed the added space for the contract work we do. St. Terry's maintains a few offices out there too."

"Really. I didn't think that old county building was still in use."

"Oh yes. There's a private radiology group that works out there, and we've got storage rooms for medical records. It's a bit of a hodgepodge, but I don't know what we'd do without it."

He glanced over as Marcy came in with two mugs, her gaze carefully affixed to the surface of the coffee, which was threatening to slop over the sides. She was young, dark-haired, no makeup. She looked like the sort of person you'd want holding your hand if the lab techs did something excruciating.

"Thank you, Marcy. Just on the edge of the desk here is fine."

She set the mugs down and gave me a quick smile on her way out.

Dr. Fraker and I discussed the office procedures while we drank the coffee and then he took me on a tour of the lab, explaining Bobby's various responsibilities, all of which seemed routine and not very important at that. I made a note of the names of a couple of his coworkers, thinking I might talk to them at a later date.

I waited while he took care of a few details and signed out, telling Marcy where he'd be.

I followed him to the freeway in my car, heading toward the former county hospital. The complex was visible from the highway: a sprawling labyrinth of yellowing stucco and red tile roofs that had turned nearly rust-brown with age. We passed it, took the next off-ramp, and circled back along Frontage Road, turning left into the main driveway.

County General had once been a flourishing medical facility, designed to serve the entire Santa Teresa community. It was secondarily earmarked as the treatment center for the indigent, funded through various social-service agencies. As the years passed, it came to be associated with the underprivileged: welfare recipients, illegal aliens, and all the unfortunate victims of Saturday-night crime sprees. Gradually, County General was shunned by both the middle class and the well-to-do. Once MediCal and Medicare came into effect, even the poor opted for St. Terry's and other local private hospitals, turning this place into a ghost town.

There was a sprinkling of cars in the parking lot. Temporary wooden signs shaped like arrows directed the visitor to Medical Records, nursing offices, Radiology, the morgue, and departments representing obscure branches of medicine.

Dr. Fraker parked his car and I pulled into the slot

next to his. He got out, locked up, and waited while I did the same. A modest attempt was being made to maintain the grounds, but the driveway itself was cracked, coarse weeds beginning to sprout through the asphalt. The two of us headed toward the main entrance without saying much. He seemed to take the place for granted, but I found it all vaguely unsettling. The architecture was, of coarse, of the usual Spanish styling: wide porches along the front, deeply recessed windows faced with wrought-iron bars.

We went in, pausing in a spacious lobby. It was clear that over the years some attempt had been made to "modernize" the place. Fluorescent lighting was now tucked up against the high ceilings, throwing down illumination too diffuse to satisfy. Once-grand anterooms had been partitioned off. Counters had been built across two of the interior arches but there was no furniture in the reception area and no one awaiting admission. The very air was permeated with the smell of abandonment and neglect. From the far end of the dim hallway to our right, I could hear a typewriter clacking, but it sounded like an old manual, operated by an amateur. There was no other indication of occupancy.

Dr. Fraker gave me a perfunctory tour. According to him, Bobby had made the round-trip as needed between this place and St. Terry's, picking up inactive files for patients readmitted to the hospital after an interval of years, hand-delivering X rays and autopsy reports. Old charts were automatically retired to the storage facilities out here. Of course, most data was kept on computer now, but there was still a backlog of paper that had to be warehoused somewhere. Bobby apparently also did some moonlighting out here, taking the graveyard shift for morgue attendants who were out sick or on vacation. Dr. Fraker indicated that this was largely a babysitting function, but that Bobby had put in a considerable number of hours during the two months he was on the job.

We were on our way downstairs by then, descending a wide staircase of red Spanish tile, our footsteps resounding at a hollow, mismatched pace. Because the hospital is constructed against a hillside, the rear of the building is below ground, while the front portion looks out onto paths partially overgrown with shrubs. It was darker down here, as though the utilities had been cut back for the sake of economy. The temperature was cool and the air was scented with formaldehyde, that acrid deodorant for the deceased. An arrow on the wall pointed us to Autopsy. I began to armor myself against the images my senses were conjuring up.

Dr. Fraker opened the door with its frosted-glass panel. I didn't actually hesitate before entering, but I did do a quick visual scan to assure myself that we weren't interrupting some guy with a boning knife filleting a corpse. Dr. Fraker seemed to sense my apprehension and he touched at my elbow briefly.

"There's nothing scheduled," he said and led the way.

I smiled uneasily and followed. At first glance, the place seemed deserted. I noted walls of apple-green ceramic tile, long stainless-steel counters with lots of drawer space. This was like a high-tech kitchen in a decorator magazine, complete with a stainless-steel island in the middle that sported its own wide sink, tall crook-necked faucets, a hanging scale, and drainboard. I felt my mouth set in distaste. I knew what was prepared here and it wasn't food.

A swinging door on the far side of the room was pushed open and a young man in surgical greens backed in, pulling a gurney after him. The body on the cart was wrapped in a dense, tawny plastic that obscured age and sex. A toe tag was visible and I could see a portion of the dark head, blank face swaddled in plastic like a mummy's. It reminded me vaguely of the caution spelled out now on dry cleaners' bags: "WARNING: To avoid danger of suffocation, keep away from babies and children. Do not use in cribs, beds, carriages, or playpens. This bag is not a toy." I averted my gaze, taking in a deep breath then just to prove I could.

Dr. Fraker introduced me to the attendant, whose name was Kelly Borden. He was in his thirties, big and soft-bodied, with fuzzy, prematurely graying hair pulled back in a fat braid that extended halfway down his back. He had a beard, a handlebar mustache, mild eyes, and a wristwatch that looked like it would keep time on the ocean floor.

"Kinsey's a private investigator looking into Bobby Callahan's accident," Dr. Fraker said.

Kelly nodded, his expression neutral. He rolled the gurney over to what looked like a big refrigerator case and eased it in beside a second gurney, also occupied. Roommates, I guessed.

Dr. Fraker looked back at me. "I've got some things

to take care of upstairs. Why don't I leave you two alone and you can ask him anything you want. Kelly worked with him. Maybe he can fill you in and then we can talk again, when you see what's what."

"Great," I said.

10

Once Dr. Fraker left, Kelly Borden got out a spray bottle of disinfectant that he began to squirt on the stainless-steel counters, wiping everything down methodically. I wasn't sure he really needed to do it, but it allowed him to keep his eyes averted. It was a polite way of ignoring me, but I didn't object. I used the time to circle the room, peering into glass-fronted cabinets filled with scalpels, forceps, and grim little hacksaws.

"I thought there'd be more bodies," I said.

"In there."

I glanced over at the door he'd come through. "Can I look?"

He shrugged.

I crossed and opened the door, which had a temperature gauge beside it reading forty degrees. The room, about the size of my apartment, was lined with fiberglass pallets arranged in tiers like bizarre bunk beds. There were eight bodies in evidence, most wrapped in the same yellowing plastic, through which I could discern, in some cases, arms and legs and seeping injuries, blood and body fluids condensing on the surface of the plastic wrap. Two bodies were covered with sheets. An old woman, lying on the pallet nearest me, was naked, as still as wood and looking faintly dehydrated. A dramatic Y-shaped cut had been made down the middle of her body, sewn back in big clumsy stitches, like a chicken, stuffed and trussed. Her breasts were splayed outward like old beanbags and her pubic area was almost as hairless as a young girl's. I wanted to cover her, but what was the point? She was beyond cold, beyond pain, modesty, or sex. I watched her chest, but there was no reassuring rise and fall. Death was beginning to seem like a parlor trick—how long can you hold your breath? I felt myself breathing deeply again, not wanting to participate. I closed the door, stepping back into the warmth of the autopsy room. "How many can you accommodate?"

"Fifty, maybe, in a pinch. I've never seen more than eight or so."

"I thought most people went straight to a mortuary."

"They do if they've died of natural causes. We get everything else. Homicide victims, suicides, accidents, any death of a suspicious or unusual nature. Most of those are autopsied and then released to a mortuary in a relatively short period of time. Of the ten we have on hand, some are indigents. A couple of 'em are John Does we're holding in hopes we'll get a positive I.D. Sometimes burial arrangements are pending so we hold a body for the next of kin. Two we've had around for years. Franklin and Eleanor. Like mascots."

I crossed my arms, feeling chilled, shifting the subject back to the living. "Do you know Bobby very well?" I asked. I turned and leaned against the wall, watching him polish the faucet handles on the stainless-steel sink.

"I hardly know him at all. We worked different shifts."

"How long have you worked out here?"

"Five years."

"What else do you do with your time?"

He paused, looking up at me. He didn't seem to like the personal questions, but he was too polite to say so. "I'm a musician. I play jazz guitar."

I stared at him for a minute, hesitating. "Have you ever heard of Daniel Wade?"

"Sure. He was a local jazz pianist. Everybody's heard of him. He hasn't been around town in years, though. He a friend of yours?"

I moved away from the wall, taking up my rounds. "I was married to him once."

"*Married* to him?"

"That's right." There were some jars filled with a brackish liquid in which body parts were marinating. I wondered if there might be a pickled heart tucked in among all the livers, kidneys, and spleens.

Kelly went back to his work. "Incredible musician," he remarked in a tone of voice that was part caution, part respect.

"That he is," I said, smiling at the irony. I never

talked about this stuff and it seemed odd to be doing it in an autopsy room to a morgue attendant in surgical greens.

"What happened to him?" Kelly asked.

"Nothing. He was in New York last I heard. Still playing his music, still on drugs."

He shook his head. "God, the talent that guy has. I never really knew him, but I used to see him every chance I got. I can't understand why he never got anywhere."

"The world is full of talented people."

"Yeah, but he's smarter than most. At least from what I heard."

"Too bad I wasn't as smart as he was. I could have saved myself a lot of grief," I said. Actually, the marriage, though brief, had been the best few months of my life. Daniel had the face of an angel back then . . . clear blue eyes, a cloud of yellow curls. He always reminded me of some artist's rendering of a Catholic saint—lean and beautiful, ascetic-looking, with elegant hands and an unassuming air. He exuded innocence. He just couldn't be faithful, couldn't lay off the drugs, couldn't stay in one place. He was wild and funny and corrupt, and if he came back today, I can't swear I'd turn him down, whatever he asked.

I let the conversation lapse and Kelly, prompted by the silence, finally spoke up.

"What's Bobby doing these days?"

I glanced back at him. He had perched himself on a tall wooden stool, the rag and disinfectant on the counter to his left.

"He's still trying to get his life back together," I said. "He works out every day. I don't know what else he does with his time. I don't suppose you have any idea what was going on back then, do you?"

"What difference does it make at this point?"

"He says he was in some kind of danger, but his memory's shot. Until I fill in the gaps, he's probably still in trouble."

"How come?"

"If somebody tried to kill him once, they may try again."

"Why haven't they done that so far?"

"I don't know. Maybe they think they're safe."

He looked at me. "That's weird."

"He never confided in you?"

Kelly shrugged, his manner ever so slightly guarded again. "We only worked together a couple of times. I was off on vacation for part of the time he was here, and the rest of it, I was on days while he did graveyard shift."

"Is there any chance he might have left a small red leather address book out here?"

"I doubt it. None of us even have lockers for our stuff."

I took a business card out of my wallet. "Will you give me a call if you have any ideas? I'd like to know what was going on back then and I know Bobby'd appreciate some help."

"Sure."

I went in search of Dr. Fraker, passing Nuclear Medicine, the nursing offices, and the offices of a group of local radiologists, all in the basement. I ran into Fraker just as he was coming downstairs again.

"All through?" he said.

"Yes, are you?"

"I've got a 'post' at noon, but we can find an empty office and talk if you like."

I shook my head. "I don't have any other questions for the moment. I may want to check back with you at some point."

"Absolutely. Just give me a call."

"Thanks. I'll do that."

I sat in my car in the parking lot, making notes on some three-by-five index cards I keep in the glove compartment: date, time, and names of the two people I'd talked to. I thought Dr. Fraker was a good resource, even though the interview with him hadn't yielded much. Kelly Borden hadn't been much help either, but at least it was an avenue I'd explored. Sometimes the noes are just as important as the yeses because they represent cul-de-sacs, allowing you to narrow your field of inquiry until you stumble into the heart of the maze. In this case, I had no idea where that might lie or what might be hidden there. I checked my watch. It was 11:45 and I thought about lunch. I have a hard time eating meals when I should. Either I'm not hungry when I'm supposed to be or I'm hungry and not in a place where I can stop and eat. It becomes a weight-control maneuver, but I'm not sure it's good for my health. I started my car and headed toward town.

I went back to the health-food restaurant where Bobby and I had eaten lunch on Monday. I was really hoping to run into him, but he was nowhere in sight. I ordered a longevity salad that was supposed to take care of 100 percent of my nutritional needs for life. What the waitress brought me was a plate piled with weeds and seeds, topped with a zesty pink dressing with specks. It didn't taste nearly as yummy as a Quarter Pounder with cheese, but I did feel virtuous, knowing I had all that chlorophyll coursing through my veins.

When I got back in my car, I checked my teeth in the rearview mirror to make sure they weren't flecked with alfalfa sprouts. I prefer not to interview people looking like I've just been grazing out in some field. I leafed through my notebook for Rick Bergen's parents' address and then I hauled out a city map. I had no idea where Turquesa Road was. I finally spotted it, a street about the size of an ingrown hair, off an equally obscure lane in the foothills that stretch across the back of town.

The house was staunch and plain, all upright lines, with a driveway so steep that I avoided it altogether and squeezed my car in along the ice plant growing below. A bald cinderblock wall prevented the hillside from tumbling into the road and gave the impression of a series of barricades as it zigzagged up to the front. Once I reached the porch, the view was spectacular, a wide-angle shot of Santa Teresa from end to end with the ocean beyond. A hang-glider hovered high up to my right, sailing in lazy circles toward the beach. The day was full of hard sunlight, meager clouds looking like white foam just beginning to evaporate. It was dead quiet. No traffic, no sense of neighbors nearby. I could see a rooftop or two but there was no feeling of people. The landscaping was sparse, composed of drought-tolerant plants: pyracantha, wisteria, and succulents.

I rang the bell. The man who came to the door was short, tense, unshaven.

"Mr. Bergen?"

"That's right."

I handed him my business card. "I'm Kinsey Millhone. Bobby Callahan hired me to look into the accident last—"

"What for?"

I made eye contact. His were small and blue, red-rimmed. His cheeks were prickly with a two-day growth of beard that made him look like a cactus. He was a man in his fifties, radiating the smell of beer and sweat. His hair was thinning and combed straight back from his face. He wore pants that looked like he'd retrieved them from a Salvation Army box and a T-shirt that read "Life's a bitch. Then you die." His arms were soft and shapeless, but his gut protruded like a basketball pumped to maximum pressure per square inch. I wanted to respond in the same rude tone he was using with me, but I curbed my tongue. This man had lost a son. Nobody said he had to be polite.

"He thinks the accident was an attempt on his life," I said.

"Bullshit. I don't mean to be rude to you, lady, but let me fill you in. Bobby Callahan is a rich kid. He's spoiled, irresponsible, and self-indulgent. He fuckin' drank too much and he ran off the road, killing my son, who was incidentally his best friend. Anything else you've heard is horseshit."

"I'm not so sure of that," I said.

"Well, I am and I'm telling you straight. Check the police reports. It's all there. Have you seen 'em?"

"I got copies yesterday from Bobby's attorney," I said.

"No physical evidence, right? You got Bobby's claim someone ran him off the road, but you got nothing to substantiate a word he says, which in my mind makes his story pure crap."

"The police seem to believe him."

"You think they can't be bought off? You think the cops can't be persuaded by a few bucks?"

"Not in this town," I said. This man had really put me on the defensive and I didn't like the way I was handling myself.

"Says who?"

"Mr. Bergen, I know a lot of the local police. I've worked with them—" It sounded lame, but I was sincere.

He interrupted again, saying, "Nuts!" He made a dismissive gesture, turning his head with disgust. "I got no time for this. Maybe my wife'll talk to you."

"I'd rather talk to you," I said. He seemed surprised by that, as though no one ever preferred to talk to him.

"Forget it. Ricky's dead. It's all over with."

"Suppose it's not? What if Bobby's really telling the truth and it wasn't his fault?"

"What's it to me in any event? I don't give a good goddamn about him."

I nearly replied, but I shut my mouth instead, trusting some other instinct. I didn't want to get caught up in endless petty arguments that would only serve to keep this man inflamed. His agitation was profound, but I suspected that there was an ebb and flow to it. "May I have ten minutes of your time?"

He thought about it for a moment and then agreed with an air of annoyance. "Christ, come on in. I'm havin' my lunch. Reva's gone anyway."

He walked away from the door, leaving it up to me to close it after us and follow him through the house, which was drably carpeted and smelled as if it had been closed up. Window shades were drawn against the afternoon sun and the light in the house had an amber cast. I received a brief impression of overscaled furniture: two matching recliners covered in green plastic, and an eight-foot sectional sofa with an afghan on one end, occupied by a big black dog.

The kitchen was done in thirty-year-old linoleum with cabinets painted an intense shade of pink. The appliances made the room look like an illustration from an old issue of *Ladies' Home Journal*. There was a small built-in breakfast nook with newspapers piled up on one bench, and a narrow wooden table with a permanent centerpiece composed of sugar bowl, paper-napkin dispenser, salt and pepper shakers shaped like ducks, a mustard jar, ketchup bottle, and a bottle of A-1 Sauce. I could see his sandwich preparations laid out too: an assortment of processed cheese slices and a lunchmeat laced with olives and ominous chunks of animal snout.

He sat down and motioned me into the bench across from him. I shoved aside some of the newspapers and took a seat. He was already slathering Miracle Whip on that brand of soft white bread that can double as a foam sponge. I kept my eyes discreetly averted as if he were engaged in pornographic practices. He laid a thin slice of onion on the bread and then peeled the cellophane wrap from the cheese, finishing with layers of lettuce, dill pickles, mustard, and meat. He looked up at me belatedly. "You hungry?"

"Starved," I said. I'd eaten a mere thirty minutes before and it wasn't my fault if I was hungry again. The way I looked at it, the sandwich was filled with preservatives, which might be just what I needed to keep my body from going bad. He cut the first masterpiece diagonally, passing half to me, and then he made a second sandwich more lavish than the first and cut that one, too. I watched him patiently, like a well-trained dog, until he gave the signal to eat.

For three minutes, we sat in silence, wolfing down lunch. He popped open a beer for me and a second one for himself. I despise Miracle Whip but, in this instance, it seemed like a gourmet sauce. The bread was so soft our fingertips left dents near the crust.

Between bites, I dabbed the corners of my mouth with a paper napkin. "I don't know your first name," I said.

"Phil. What kind of name is Kinsey?"

"My mother's maiden name."

And that was the extent of the social niceties until we'd both pushed our plates back with a sigh of relief.

11

After lunch, we sat out on the deck in painted metal porch chairs pockmarked with rust. The deck was actually a shelf of poured concrete, forming the roof of the garage, which had been carved into the hillside. Wooden planters filled with annuals formed a low protective barrier around the perimeter. A mild breeze was picking up, offsetting the heavy blanket of sunshine that settled on my arms. Phil's belligerence was gone. He'd been pacified perhaps by the many chemicals in his lunch, but more likely by the two beers and the prospect of the cigar he was clipping with a pocket guillotine. He plucked a big wooden kitchen match from a can next to his chair and bent down, using the surface of the deck to scratch it into life. He puffed on the cigar until it drew fully, then shook the match out and dropped it in a flat tin ashtray. For a moment, we both sat and stared out at the ocean.

The view was like a mural painted on a blue backdrop. The islands in the channel looked grim and deserted, twenty-six miles out. On the mainland, the small beaches were faintly visible, the surf like a tiny ruffle of white lace. The palm trees looked no bigger than fledgling asparagus. I could pick out a few landmarks: the courthouse, the high school, a big Catholic church, a theater, the one office building downtown over three stories high. From this vantage point, there was no evidence of the Victorian influence or any of the later architectural styles that blended now with the Spanish.

This house, he told me, had been finished in the summer of 1950. He and his wife, Reva, had just bought the place when the Korean War broke out. He'd been drafted and had gone off two days after they moved in, leaving Reva with stacks of cardboard boxes to unpack, returning fourteen months later with a service-related disability. He didn't specify what it was and I didn't ask, but he had apparently only worked sporadically since his medical discharge. They'd had five children and Rick had been the youngest. The others were scattered now through the Southwest.

"What was he like?" I asked. I wasn't sure he'd answer. The silence stretched on and I wondered if perhaps it might have been the wrong question. I hated to spoil whatever sense of camaraderie we'd established.

He shook his head finally. "I don't know how to answer that," he said. "He was one of those kids you think you're never going to have a minute's trouble with. Always sunny, did things without being told, good grades in school. Then when he was sixteen or so—his last year in high school—he seemed to lose his footing. He graduated all right, but he didn't seem to know what to do with himself. He was drifting. Had the grades for college and God knows I'd have found the money someplace, but it didn't interest him. Nothing did. Oh, he worked, but it never amounted to a hill of beans."

"Was he doing drugs?"

"I don't think so. At least there was never any sign of it that I could see. The kid drank a lot. Reva thought it was that, but I don't know. He did like to party. He was out 'til all hours, slept the weekends away, hung out with kids like Bobby Callahan, way above us socially. Then he started dating Bobby's stepsister, Kitty. Christ, that girl was trouble the day she was born. By then, I was sick of putting up with him. If he didn't want to be part of the family, fine. Go somewhere else, though, earn your own keep. Don't think you can use this place to get meals and laundry done." He paused, looking over at me. "Was I wrong? I'm asking you."

"I don't know," I said. "How can you answer a question like that anyway? Kids get off-course and then they straighten out. Half the time, it doesn't have anything to do with parents. Who knows what it is?"

He was silent, staring out at the horizon, his lips encircling the cigar like a hose coupling. He sucked in some nicotine, then blew out a cloud of smoke. "Sometimes I wonder how bright he was. Maybe he should have seen a therapist, but how did I know? That's what Reva says now. What's a psychiatrist going to do with a kid who has no ambition?"

I didn't have a response to any of this so I made sympathetic sounds and let it go at that.

Brief silence. He said, "I hear Bobby's all messed up."

His tone was hesitant, a guarded inquiry about a hated rival. He must have wished Bobby dead a hundred times, cursing his good fortune at having survived.

"I'm not sure he wouldn't trade places with Rick if he could," I said, feeling my way. I didn't want to set off a fresh surge of agitation, but I didn't want him harboring the notion that Bobby was somehow "luckier" than Rick. Bobby was working his ass off to make life all right, but it was a struggle.

Below us, an old pale blue Ford rattled into view, spewing exhaust. The driver swung wide around my car and paused, apparently activating an automatic garage door. The car nosed out of sight beneath us and, moments later, I heard the muffled sound of the car door slamming.

"That's my wife," Phil said, as the garage-door mechanism ground under our feet.

Reva Bergen trudged up the steep walk, burdened with grocery sacks. I noted with curiosity that Phil made no move to assist her. She caught sight of us as she reached the porch. She hesitated, her face a perfect blank. Even at that distance, her gaze had an unfocused quality that seemed more pronounced when she finally came out of the back door, moments later, to join us. She was a dishwater blonde with that washed-out look women sometimes acquire in their fifties. Her eyes were small, nearly lashless. Pale eyebrows, pale skin. She was frail and bony, her hands looking as clumsy as gardening gloves on her narrow wrists. The two of them seemed so entirely unsuited to each other that I quickly discarded the unbidden image of their marital bed.

Phil explained who I was and the fact that I was investigating the accident in which Rick had been killed.

Her smile was mean. "Bobby's conscience bothering him?"

Phil interceded before I could frame a response. "Come on, Reva. What harm can it do? You said yourself the police—"

She turned abruptly and went back inside. Phil shoved his hands down in his pockets with embarrassment. "Nuts. She's been like that ever since it happened. Things set her off. I haven't been a joy to live with myself, but this thing has torn her heart out."

"I should be on my way," I said. "But I would like for you to do one thing if you would. I've been trying to figure out what could possibly have been going on back then and I'm not having much luck so far. Did Rick give you any indication that Bobby was in trouble or upset? Or that he might have had some kind of problem himself?"

He shook his head. "Rick's whole life was a problem to me, but it didn't have anything to do with the accident. I'll ask Reva, though, and see if she knows anything."

"Thanks," I said. I shook his hand and then fished a

card out of my bag so he'd know how to get in touch with me.

He walked me down to the road and I thanked him again for lunch. As I got in my car, I glanced up. Reva was standing on the porch, staring down at us.

I headed back into town. I stopped by the office to check my answering machine for messages (none) and my mail, which was all junk. I made a fresh pot of coffee and hauled out my portable typewriter, detailing the notes on my investigation to that point. It was painstaking stuff, given the fact that I'd turned up absolutely nothing. Still, Bobby was entitled to know how I'd spent my time and at thirty bucks an hour, he was entitled to know where the money went.

At three o'clock, I locked the office and walked over to the public library, which was two blocks over and two blocks up. I went downstairs to the periodicals room and asked for the previous September's newspapers, now consigned to microfilm. I found a machine and sat down, threading in the first reel. The print was white on black, all of the photographs looking like negatives. I had no idea what I might spot so I was forced to skim every page. Current events, national news, local political issues, fire, crime, storm systems, folks being born and dying and getting divorced. I read the lost-and-found column, the personals, society, sports. The mechanism for advancing the film was somehow out of whack, so that paragraphs jerked onto the nine-by-twelve screen with the focus slightly skewed, generating a motion sickness of sorts. Around me, people were browsing among the magazines or were seated in low chairs, reading newspapers attached to upright wooden lances. The only sounds in the room were the drone of the machine I was using, an occasional cough, and the rustle of newsprint.

I managed to check the papers for the first six days of September before my resolve faltered. I'd have to do this in small doses. My neck felt stiff and my head was starting to ache. A glance at my watch showed that it was nearly five and I was bored to death. I made a note of the last date I'd scanned and then I fled into the late-afternoon sunshine. I walked back to my office building and retrieved my car from the parking lot without going upstairs.

On the way home, I stopped off at the supermarket for milk, bread, and toilet paper, doing a quick tour with my cart. There was so much lyrical music playing overhead, I felt like the heroine in a romantic comedy. Once I'd found what I needed, I moved to the express lane, twelve items or less. There were five of us in line, all surreptitiously counting the contents of each other's carts. The man in front of me had a head too small for the size of his face, like an underinflated balloon. He had a little girl with him, maybe four years old, wearing a brand-new dress several sizes too big. Something about it spelled "poor," but I don't know why. It made her look like a midget; waistline at her hips, the hem down around her ankles. She held the man's hand with perfect trust, giving me a shy smile so filled with pride that I found myself smiling back.

I was tired by the time I got home and my left arm ached. There are days when I scarcely remember the injury, other days when I feel drained by a constant dull pain. I decided to skip my run. To hell with it. I took a couple of Tylenol with codeine, kicked my shoes off, and crawled into the folds of my quilt. I was still there when the phone rang. I awoke with a start, reaching automatically for the receiver. My apartment was dark. The unexpected shrill blast of sound had sent a jolt of adrenaline through me and my heart was pounding. I glanced at the clock with uneasiness. Eleven-fifteen.

I mumbled hello, rubbing a hand across my face and through my hair.

"Kinsey, it's Derek Wenner. Have you heard?"

"Derek, I'm sound asleep."

"Bobby's dead."

"What?"

"I guess he'd been drinking, though we're not even sure of that at this point. His car went off the road and smashed into a tree on West Glen. I thought you'd want to know."

"What?" I knew I was repeating myself, but I couldn't understand what he was talking about.

"Bobby's been killed in a car accident."

"But when?" I don't know why it mattered. I was just asking questions because I couldn't cope with the information any other way.

"A little after ten. He was dead by the time they got him to St. Terry's. I have to go down and identify him, but there doesn't seem to be any doubt."

"Can I do anything?"

He seemed to hesitate. "Well, actually, maybe you

could. I tried to reach Sufi, but I guess she's out. Dr. Metcalf's service is tracking him down, so he'll probably be here in a bit. I wonder if you could sit with Glen in the meantime. That way, I can head on over to the hospital and see what's going on."

"I'll be right there," I said and hung up.

I washed my face and brushed my teeth. I was talking to myself the whole time, but I didn't feel anything. All my inner processes seemed to be suspended temporarily while my brain struggled with the facts. The information kept bounding back. No way. Nuh-un. How could Bobby be gone? Not true.

I grabbed a jacket, my handbag, and my keys. I locked up, got in my car, started the engine, pulled out. I felt like a well-programmed robot. When I turned onto West Glen Road, I saw the emergency vehicles and I could feel a chill tickle at the base of my spine. It was just at the big bend, a blind corner near the "slums." The ambulance was already gone, but patrol cars were still there, radios squawking in the night air. Bystanders stood on the side of the road in the dark while the tree he'd hit was washed with high-intensity floodlights, the raw gash in the trunk looking like a fatal wound in itself. His BMW was just being removed by a tow truck. The scene looked, oddly, like a location for a movie being shot. I slowed, turning to peer at the site with an eerie feeling of detachment. I didn't want to add to the confusion and I was worried about Glen, so I drove on. A little voice murmured, "Bobby's dead." A second voice said, "Oh no, let's don't do that. I don't want that to be true, O.K.?"

I pulled into the narrow drive, following it until it opened out into the empty courtyard. The entire house was blazing with lights as if a massive party were in progress, but there was no sound and not a soul in sight, no cars visible. I parked and moved toward the entrance. One of the maids, like an electronic sensing device, opened the door as I approached. She stepped back, admitting me without comment.

"Where's Mrs. Callahan?"

She closed the door and started down the hall. I followed. She tapped at the door to Glen's study and then turned the knob and stepped back again, letting me pass into the room.

Glen was dressed in a pale pink robe, huddled in one of the wing-back chairs, knees drawn up. She raised her face, which was swollen and waterlogged. It looked as if all of her emotional pipes had burst, eyes spilling over, cheeks washed with tears, her nose running. Even her hair was damp. For a moment, still in disbelief, I stood there and looked at her and she looked at me and then she lowered her face again, extending her hand. I crossed and knelt by her chair. I took her hand—small and cold—and pressed it against my cheek.

"Oh Glen, I'm sorry. I'm so sorry," I whispered.

She was nodding acknowledgment, making a low sound in her throat, not even a clearly articulated cry. It was a sound more primitive than that. She started to speak, but she could only manage a sort of dragged-out, stuttering phrase, sub-English, devoid of sense. What difference did it make what she said? It was done and nothing could change it. She began to cry as children cry, deep, shuddering sobs that went on and on. I clung to her hand, offering her a mooring line in that churning sea of grief.

Finally, I could feel the turbulence pass like a battering rain cloud moving on. The spasms subsided. She let go of me and leaned back, taking in a deep breath. She took out a handkerchief and pressed it against her eyes, then blew her nose. She paused, apparently looking inward, much in the way one does at the end of an attack of hiccups.

She sighed. "Oh *God*, how will I get through this?" she said, and the tears welled up again, splashing down her face. She regained control after a moment and went through the mop-up process again, shaking her head. "Jesus. Shit. I don't think I can do this, Kinsey. You know? It's just too hard and I don't have that kind of strength."

"You want me to call anyone?"

"No, not now. It's too late and what's the point? In the morning, I'll have Derek get in touch with Sufi. She'll come."

"What about Kleinert? You want me to let him know?"

She shook her head. "Bobby couldn't stand him. Just let it be. He'll find out soon enough. Is Derek back?" Her tone was anxious now, her face tense.

"I don't think so. You want a drink?"

"No, but help yourself if you like. The liquor's in there."

"Maybe later." I wanted something, but I wasn't sure what it was. Not a drink. I was afraid alcohol would eat through the thin veneer of self-control. The last thing in the world she needed was to have to turn around and comfort me. I sat down in the chair across from her and an image flashed into my mind. I remembered Bobby bending down to say good night to her just two nights ago. He had turned automatically so he could offer her the good side of his face. It had been one of his last night's sleep on this earth, but neither of them had known that, nor had I. I glanced up at her and she was looking at me as if she knew what was going on in my head. I glanced away, but not quickly enough. Something in her face spilled over me like light through a swinging door. Sorrow shot through the gap, catching me off-guard, and I burst into tears.

12

Everything happens for a reason, but that doesn't mean there's a point. The next few days were a nightmare, the more so as mine was only a peripheral role in the pageantry of Bobby's death. Because I'd appeared in the first moments of her grief, Glen Callahan seemed to fix on me, as though I might provide a solace for her pain.

Dr. Kleinert agreed to release Kitty until after the burial, and an attempt was made to reach Bobby's natural father overseas, but he never responded and nobody seemed to care. Meanwhile, hundreds of people streamed through the funeral home: Bobby's friends, old high-school classmates, family friends and business associates, all the town dignitaries, members of the various boards Glen served on. The Who's Who of Santa Teresa. After that first night, Glen was totally composed—calm, gracious, tending to every detail of Bobby's funeral. It would be done properly. It would be done in the best of taste. I would be on hand throughout.

I had thought Derek and Kitty would resent my constant presence, but both seemed relieved. Glen's single-mindedness must have been a frightening prospect to them.

Glen ordered Bobby's casket closed, but I saw him for a moment at the funeral home after his body had been "prepared." In some ways, I needed that glimpse to convince myself that he was really dead. God, the stillness of the flesh when life has gone. Glen stood there beside me, her gaze fixed on Bobby's face, her own expression as blank and inanimate as his. Something had left her with his death. She was unflinching, but her grip on my arm tightened as the lid to the casket was closed.

"Good-bye, baby," she whispered. "I love you."

I turned away quickly.

Derek approached from behind and I saw him move as though to touch her. She didn't turn her head, but she radiated a rage so limitless that he kept his distance, intimidated by the force of it. Kitty stood against the back wall, stony, her face blotchy from tears wept in solitude. Somehow I suspected that she and her father wouldn't remain in Glen's life for long. Bobby's death had accelerated the household decay. Glen seemed impatient to be alone, intolerant of the requirements of ordinary intercourse. They were takers. She had nothing left to give. I scarcely knew the woman, but it seemed clear to me that she was suddenly operating by another set of premises. Derek watched her uneasily, sensing, perhaps, that he wasn't part of this new scheme, whatever it was.

Bobby was buried on Saturday. The church services were mercifully short. Glen had selected the music and a few passages from various non-Biblical sources. I took my cue from her, surviving the eulogy by neatly disconnecting myself from what was said. I wasn't going to deal with Bobby's death today. I wasn't going to lose control in a public setting like this. Even so, there were moments when I could feel my face heat up and my eyes blur with tears. It was more than this loss. It was all death, every loss—my parents, my aunt.

The funeral cortege must have been ten blocks long, cruising across the city at a measured pace. At every intersection, traffic had been forced to stop as we rolled by, and I could see the comments in the faces we passed. "Ooo, a funeral. Wonder whose." "Gorgeous day for it." "God, look at all the cars." "Come on, come on. Get out of the way."

We wound into the cemetery, as green and carefully landscaped as a housing tract. Headstones stretched out in all directions, a varied display, like a stonecutter's yard filled with samples of his work. There were intermittent evergreens, clusters of eucalyptus and sycamore. The cemetery parcels were sectioned off by low walls of shrubbery and on a plot map probably had names like Serenity and Heavenly Meadows.

We parked and everyone trooped across the newly trimmed grass. It felt like an elementary-school outing: everyone on their best behavior, nobody quite sure what to do next. There were occasional murmured conversations, but for the most part, we were silent. Mortuary personnel, in dark suits, escorted us to our seats like ushers at a wedding.

The day was hot, the afternoon sunlight intense. There was a breeze that rustled the treetops and lifted the canvas tent flaps flirtatiously. We sat dutifully while the minister conducted the final rites. I felt better out here and I realized it was the absence of organ music that made the graveside ceremony less potent. Even the most banal of church hymns can rip your heart out at times like this. I preferred the sound of wind.

Bobby's casket was a massive affair of glossy walnut and brass, like an oversized blanket chest too large for the space allotted. Apparently, the casket would fit down into the vault especially purchased to house it underground. There was some kind of complex mechanism set up above the grave site that would eventually be used to lower the casket into the hole, but I gathered that was done at some later time.

Funeral styles had evolved since my parents were buried and I wondered, idly, what had dictated the change. Technology, no doubt. Maybe death was tidier these days and easier to regulate. Graves were dug by machinery, which carved out a neat pit surmounted now by this low-slung contraption on which the casket rested. No more of this horseshit with the loved ones flinging themselves into the grave. With this new apparatus in place, you'd have to get down on your belly and leopard-crawl into the hole, which robbed the gesture of its theatrical effect.

Off to one side among the mourners, I saw Phil and

Reva Bergen. He seemed upset, but she was impassive. Her gaze drifted from the minister's face to mine and she stared at me flatly. Behind them, I thought I saw Kelly Borden, but I couldn't be sure. I shifted in my chair, hoping to make eye contact, but the face was gone. The crowd began to disperse and I was startled to realize it was over. The minister, in his black robes, gave Glen a solemn look, but she ignored him and moved toward the limousine. Derek, in a show of good manners, lingered long enough to exchange a few remarks.

Kitty was already in the backseat when we reached the limo. I would have bet money she was high on something. Her cheeks were flushed and her eyes were feverishly bright, her hands restless in her lap, plucking at her black cotton skirt. The outfit she'd elected to wear had an outlandish gypsy air to it, the black cotton top composed of tiers of ruffles, embroidered in garish shades of turquoise and red. Glen had blinked lazily when she'd first set eyes on Kitty and an almost imperceptible smile had hovered on her lips before she turned her attention to something else. She'd apparently decided not to make an issue of it. Kitty's manner had been defiant, but with no resistance on Glen's part the juice had drained out of the drama before she'd even launched into the first act.

I was standing by the limo when I saw Derek approach. He climbed into the backseat and pulled down one of the collapsible camp stools, reaching to pull the door shut.

"Leave it open," Glen murmured.

The limo driver was still nowhere in sight. There was a delay while people took their places in the vehicles parked along the road. Others were milling around on the grass to no apparent purpose.

Derek tried to catch Glen's eye. "Well, I thought that went very well."

Glen turned pointedly and peered out of the far window. When your only child has been killed, who really gives a shit?

Kitty took out a cigarette and lit it. Her hands looked like birds' claws, the skin almost scaly. The elasticized neckline of her blouse revealed a chest so thin that her sternum and costal cartilages were outlined like one of those joke T-shirts.

Derek made a face as the smell of smoke filled the back-seat. "Jesus, Kitty, put that out. For Christ's sake!"

"Oh, leave her alone," Glen said, dully. Kitty seemed surprised by the unexpected support, but she stubbed out the cigarette anyway.

The driver appeared and closed the door on Derek's side, then moved around the rear of the limousine and slid in under the steering wheel. I moved on toward my car as he pulled away.

The mood was much lighter once we got to the house. People seemed to shrug death aside, comforted by good wine and lavish hors d'oeuvres. I don't know why death still generates these little têtes-à-têtes. Everything else has been modernized, but some vestige of the wake remains. There must have been two hundred people crowded into the living room and hall, but it all seemed O.K. It was filler, just something to smooth the awkward transition from the funeral to the bone-crushing sleep that was bound to come afterward.

I recognized most of the people who'd been at Derek's birthday gathering that past Monday night: Dr. Fraker and his wife, Nola; Dr. Kleinert and a rather plain woman whom I assumed was Mrs. K.; the other doctor who'd been present, Metcalf, in conversation with Marcy, who had worked with Bobby briefly in the Pathology Department. I snagged a glass of wine and inched my way across the room to Fraker's side. He and Kleinert had their heads bent together and they paused as I approached.

"Hi," I said, suddenly self-conscious. Maybe this wasn't such a hot idea. I took a sip of wine, noting the look that passed between them. I guess they decided I could be privy to their discussion, because Fraker picked up where he'd left off.

"Anyway, I won't be doing the microscopic until Monday, but from the gross, it looks like the immediate cause of death was a ruptured aortic valve."

Kleinert said, "From impact with the steering wheel."

Fraker nodded, taking a sip of wine. The explanation of his findings continued almost as though he were dictating it all over again. "The sternum and multiple ribs were fractured and the ascending aorta was incompletely torn just above the superior border of the valve cusps. Additionally, there was a left hemothorax of eight hundred cc and a massive aortic adventitial hemorrhage."

Kleinert's expression indicated that he was following. The whole thing sounded sickening to me and I didn't even know what it meant.

"What about the blood alcohol?" Kleinert asked.

Fraker shrugged. "That was negative. He wasn't drunk. We should have the rest of the results this afternoon, but I don't think we're going to find anything. I could be surprised, of course."

"Well, if you're right about the CSF blockage, a seizure was probably inevitable. Bernie warned him to watch for the symptoms," Kleinert said. His face was long and etched with a look of permanent sorrow. If I had emotional problems and needed a shrink, I didn't think it would help me to look at a face like that week after week. I'd want somebody with some energy, pizzazz, somebody with a little hope.

"Bobby had a seizure?" I asked. It was clear by now that they were discussing his autopsy results. Fraker must have realized I didn't have any idea what they were actually saying, because he offered a translation.

"We think Bobby may have been suffering from a complication of the original head injury. Sometimes, a blockage develops in the normal flow of cerebrospinal fluid. Intracranial pressure builds up and part of the brain starts to atrophy, resulting in posttraumatic epilepsy."

"And that's why he ran off the road?"

"In my opinion, yes," Fraker said. "I can't state this categorically, but he'd probably been experiencing headaches, anxiety, irritability perhaps."

Kleinert cut in again. "I saw him at seven, seven fifteen, something like that. He was terribly depressed."

"Maybe he suspected what was going on," Fraker was saying.

"Too bad he didn't speak up then, if that's the case."

The murmuring between them continued while I tried to take in the implications.

"Is there any way a seizure like that could have been drug-induced?" I asked.

"Sure, it's possible. Toxicology reports aren't comprehensive and the analyses' results depend on what's asked for. There are several hundred drugs which could affect a person with a predisposition to seizures. Realistically, it isn't possible to screen for all of them," Fraker said.

Kleinert shifted restlessly. "Actually, after what he went through, it's a wonder he survived as long as he did. We tried to spare Glen, but I think we've all been worried that something like this might occur."

There didn't seem to be anything left to say on the subject.

Kleinert finally turned to Fraker. "Have you eaten yet? Ann and I are going out for supper if you and Nola want to join us."

Fraker declined the invitation, but he did need his wine-glass filled and I could see him eyeing the crowd for some sign of his wife. Both doctors excused themselves.

I stood there, unsettled, reviewing the facts. Theoretically, Bobby Callahan had died of natural causes, but in fact, he'd died as a consequence of injuries received in the accident nine months ago, which he, at least, believed was a murder attempt. As nearly as I could remember, California law provides that "a killing is murder or manslaughter if the party dies within three years and a day after the stroke is received or the cause of death is administered." So the truth was, he was murdered and it didn't make any difference at all if he died that night or last week. At the moment, of course, I didn't have any proof. I did still have the bulk of the money Bobby had paid me and a clear set of instructions from him, so I was still in business if I wanted to be.

Mentally, I got up and dusted myself off. It was time to put grief aside and get back to work. I set my wineglass down and had a brief word with Glen to let her know where I'd be and then I went upstairs and systematically searched Bobby's room. I wanted that little red book.

13

I was operating, of course, on the hope that Bobby had hidden the address book somewhere on the premises. He said he remembered giving the book to someone, but that might not be true. There was no way I could search the entire house, but I could certainly comb a couple of places. Glen's study, maybe Kitty's room. It was quiet upstairs and I was glad to be alone for a while. I searched for an hour and a half and came up with nothing. I wasn't discouraged. In some odd way, I was heartened. Maybe Bobby's memory had served him correctly.

At six, I wandered out into the corridor. I leaned my elbows on the balustrade that circled the landing and listened for sounds filtering up from below. Apparently, the crowd had diminished considerably. I heard smatterings of laughter, an occasional light conversational swell, but it sounded like most of the guests had departed. I retraced my steps and tapped on Kitty's door.

Muffled response. "Who is it?"

"It's me. Kinsey," I said to the blank door. After a moment, I heard the lock retracted, but she didn't actually let me in.

Instead, she hollered, "Enter!"

Lord, she was tedious. I entered.

The room had been tidied and the bed was made, I'm sure through no effort of hers. She looked as if she'd been crying. Her nose was reddened, her makeup smeared. She was, of course, doing drugs. She had gotten out a mirror and a razor blade and was laying out a couple of lines of coke. There was a half-filled wineglass on the bed table.

"I feel like shit," she said. She had exchanged her gypsy outfit for a raw silk kimono in a lush shade of green with butterflies embroidered on the back and sleeves. Her arms were so thin she looked like a praying mantis, her green eyes aglitter.

"When are you due back at St. Terry's?" I asked.

She paused to blow her nose, not wanting to screw up her high. "Who knows?" she said, glumly. "Tonight, I guess. At least I'll have a chance to pack some of my own clothes to take with me. Shit, I ended up on the psycho ward with *nothing*."

"Why do you do this stuff, Kitty? You're playing right into Kleinert's hands."

"Terrific. I didn't know you came up here to lecture me."

"I came up to search Bobby's room. I'm looking for the little red address book he asked you about last Tuesday. I don't suppose you have any idea where it might be."

"Nope." She bent over, using a rolled-up dollar bill like a straw, her nostril forming a little vacuum cleaner. I watched the coke fly up her nose, like a magic trick.

"Can you think who he might have given it to?"

"Nuh-un." She sat back on the bed, pinching her nose shut. She wet her index finger and cleaned the surface of the mirror, running her fingertip across her gums then, like a remedy for teething pains. She reached for her wineglass and settled back against the bed pillows, lighting a cigarette.

"God, that's great," I said. "You're tagging all the bases today. Do a little coke, knock back some wine, cigarettes. They're going to have to run you through Detox before you hit Three South again." I knew I was baiting her, but she got on my nerves and I was spoiling for a fight, which I suspected would feel better than grief.

"Fuck you," she said, bored.

"Mind if I sit down?" I asked.

She gestured permission and I perched on the edge of the bed, looking around with interest.

"What happened to your stash?" I asked.

"What stash?"

"The one you kept in there," I said, indicating the bed table drawer.

She stared. "I never kept a *stash* in there."

I loved the little note of righteous indignation. "That's funny," I said. "I saw Dr. Kleinert pull a whole Ziploc bag full of pills out of there."

"When?" she said in disbelief.

"Monday night when they carted you away. Quaaludes, Placidyls, Tuinals, the works." Actually, I didn't really believe the pills were hers, but I was curious to hear what she had to say.

She stared at me for a moment more, then eased out a mouthful of smoke, which she neatly channeled up her nose. "I don't do any of those," she said.

"What'd you take Monday night?"

"Valium. Prescription."

"Dr. Kleinert gave you a prescription for Valium?" I asked.

She got up with annoyance and started pacing the room. "I don't need your bullshit, Kinsey. My step-brother was buried today in case your memory's short. I got other things on my mind."

"Were you involved with Bobby?"

"No, I wasn't 'involved' with Bobby. What do you mean, like some kind of sexual thing? Like was I having an *affair*?"

"Yeah, like that."

"God, you are so imaginative. For your information, I didn't even think about him that way."

"Maybe he thought about you that way."

She stopped pacing. "Says who?"

"Just a theory of mine. You know he loved you. Why wouldn't he have sexual feelings as well?"

"Oh come on. Did Bobby say that?"

"No, but I saw his reaction the night you were hospitalized. I didn't think it was strictly brotherly love I was looking at. In fact, I asked Glen about it at the time, but she said she didn't think there was anything going on."

"Well, there wasn't."

"Too bad. Maybe you could have saved each other."

She rolled her eyes, giving me a look—God, adults are such geeks!—but she was restless and distracted. She located an ashtray on the chest of drawers and stubbed out her cigarette. She lifted the lid to a music box and let a few notes of "Lara's Theme" escape before she snapped it shut again. When she looked at me again, she had tears in her eyes and she seemed embarrassed by that.

She pushed away from the chest of drawers. "I gotta pack my stuff."

She went into the closet and hauled out a canvas duffel. She opened her top dresser drawer and snatched up a stack of underpants, which she shoved into the duffel. She bumped the drawer shut and opened the next one, grabbing T-shirts, jeans, socks.

I got up and moved to the door, turning back with my hand on the knob. "Nothing lasts, you know. Not even misery."

"Yeah, sure. Especially not mine. What do you think I do drugs for, my health?"

"You're tough, right?"

"Shit, why don't you go work in a rescue mission? You got the line down pat."

"One day some happiness is going to come into your life in spite of you. You ought to keep yourself alive so you can enjoy it."

"Sorry. No sale. I'm not interested."

I shrugged. "So die. It won't be that big a deal. It

sure won't be the loss that Bobby's death was. So far, you haven't given the world a thing."

I opened the door.

I heard her bump a drawer shut. "Hey, Kinsey?"

I looked back at her. Her smirk was almost self-mocking, but not quite.

"Want to do a line of coke? My treat."

I left the room, closing the door quietly. I felt like slamming it, but what would be the point?

I went down to the living room. I was hungry and I needed a glass of wine. There were only five or six people left. Sufi sat next to Glen on one of the sofas. I didn't recognize anybody else. I crossed to the buffet table that had been set up on the far side of the room. The Chicano maid, Alicia, was rearranging a platter of shrimp, consolidating hors d'oeuvres so the plates wouldn't look all ratty and half eaten. God, there was a lot to this business of being rich. It had never occurred to me. I thought you just invited people over and turned 'em loose, but I could see now that entertaining requires all kinds of subtle monitoring.

I filled a plate and picked up a fresh glass of wine. I chose a seat close enough to the others so I wouldn't seem rude, but far enough away so I wouldn't have to talk to anyone. I have a shy streak that surfaces in situations like this. I'd rather have chatted with some hooker down on lower State Street than try to exchange pleasantries with this crew. What could we possibly have discussed? They were talking about long-term paper. I took a bite of salmon mousse and tried to keep an interested look on my face, like maybe I had a lot of long-term paper I was hoping to unload. Such a nuisance, that shit, isn't it?

I felt a light touch on my arm and glanced over to see Sufi Daniels easing into the chair next to mine.

"Glen tells me Bobby was very fond of you," she said.

"I hope so. I liked him."

Sufi stared at me. I kept eating because I couldn't think what else to say. She was wearing an odd outfit: a long black dress of some silky material with a matching jacket over it. I assumed it was meant to disguise her misshapen form with its slightly hunched back, but it made her look as if she were about to perform with some big philharmonic orchestra. Her hair was the same lank, pale mess it had been when I met her the first time and her makeup was inexpert. She couldn't have been more different from Glen Callahan. Her manner was faintly patronizing, like she was just on the verge of slipping me a couple of bucks for my services. I might have been short with her, but there was always the chance that she had Bobby's little red book.

"How do you know Glen?" I asked, taking a sip of wine. I set the glass down on the floor near my chair and forked up some cold shrimp in a spicy sauce. Sufi's gaze flickered over to Glen and then back.

"We met in school."

"You've been friends a long time."

"Yes, we have."

I nodded, swallowing. "You must have been around

when Bobby was born," I remarked, just to keep things going.

"Yes."

Shit, this is fun, I thought. "Were you close to him?"

"I liked him, but I can't say we were close. Why?"

I retrieved my wine and took a sip. "He gave someone a little red book. I'm trying to figure out who."

"What sort of book?"

I shrugged. "Addresses, telephone numbers. Small, bound in red leather, from what he said."

She suddenly began to blink at me. "You're not still investigating," she said. It wasn't a question. It was a statement tinged with disbelief.

"Why not?"

"Well, the boy is dead. What difference could any of it possibly make?"

"If he was murdered, it makes a difference to me," I said.

"If he was murdered, it's a matter for the police."

I smiled. "The cops around here love my help."

Sufi looked over at Glen, lowering her voice. "I'm sure she wouldn't want this pursued."

"She didn't hire me. Bobby did. Anyway, why do you care?"

She seemed to catch the danger in my tone, but it didn't worry her much. She smiled thinly, still superior.

"Of course. I didn't mean to interfere," she murmured. "I just wasn't sure what your plans were and I didn't want Glen upset."

I was supposed to make comforting noises back to her, but I just sat there and stared. A bit of color rose in her cheeks.

"Well. It's been nice seeing you again." She got up and wandered over to one of the remaining guests, engaging in conversation with a pointed turning of her back. I shrugged to myself. I wasn't sure what she'd been up to. I didn't care either, unless it pertained to the case. I glanced over at her, speculating.

Soon after, almost at a signal, people started getting into their good-bye behavior. Glen stood by the archway to the living room, being hugged, having her hands pressed in sympathy. Everyone said the same thing. "You know we love you, sweetie. Now you let us know if we can do anything."

She said "I will" and got hugged again.

Sufi was the one who actually walked them to the door.

I was on the verge of following when Glen caught my eye. "I'd like to talk to you if you can stay on for a while."

"Sure," I said. I realized for the first time that I hadn't seen Derek for hours. "Where's Derek?"

"Taking Kitty back to St. Terry's." She sank into one of the couches, slouching down so she could rest her head on the back. "Would you like a drink?"

"Actually, I could use one. Shall I fix you one while I'm at it?"

"God, I'd love it. There's a liquor cabinet in my den if we're low out here. Make it Scotch. Lots of ice, please."

I crossed the hall and went into the den, fetching an old-fashioned glass and the bottle of Cutty Sark. When I reached the living room again, Sufi was back and the house was mantled in that dull quiet that follows too much noise.

There was an ice bucket on the end of the buffet table and I plopped a couple of cubes into the glass with a set of those sterling-silver ice tongs that look somehow like dinosaur claws. It made me feel sophisticated, like I was in a 1940s movie wearing a suit with shoulder pads and stockings with a line up the back.

"You must be exhausted," Sufi was murmuring. "Why don't I get you into bed before I take off?"

Glen smiled wearily. "No, that's all right. You go ahead."

Sufi had no other choice but to bend down and give Glen a buss and then find her purse. I handed Glen the glass with ice, pouring Scotch into it. Sufi made her final farewells and then left the room with a cautionary look at me. A few moments later, I heard the front door shut.

I pulled a chair over and sat down, propping my feet up on the couch, cataloguing my current state. The small of my back ached, my left arm ached. I finished off the wine in my glass and added Cutty Sark.

Glen took a long swallow of hers. "I saw you talking to Jim. What did he have to say?"

"He thinks Bobby had a seizure and that's why he ran off the road. Some kind of epilepsy from his head injuries in the first accident."

"Meaning what?"

"Well, as far as I'm concerned, it means if *that* accident was really a murder attempt, it finally paid dividends."

Her face was blank. She dropped her gaze. "What will you do now?"

"Hey, listen. I still have money left from the retainer Bobby gave me. I'll work 'til I find out who killed him."

She met my eyes and the look she gave me was curious. "Why would you do that?"

"To settle accounts. I believe in clearing the ledger, don't you?"

"Oh yes," she said.

We stared at each other for a moment and then she raised her glass. I lifted mine and we drank.

When Derek came in, the two of them went upstairs and, with Glen's permission, I spent the next three hours in a fruitless search of her den and Kitty's room. Then I let myself out and went home.

14

By Monday morning at eight o'clock I was in the gym again, working out. I felt like I'd been to the moon and back. Without even thinking about it, I looked for Bobby, realizing a millisecond later that he was gone and wasn't ever going to be there again. It didn't sit well with me. Missing someone is a vague, unpleasant sensation, like gnawing anxiety. It isn't as concrete as grief, but it's just as pervasive and there's no escaping it. I kept moving, working out hard, as though physical pain might blot out its emotional counterpart. I filled every minute with activity and I suppose it worked. In some ways, it's like rubbing Ben-Gay on a sore back. You want to believe it's doing you some good, but you can't think why it would. It's better than nothing, but it's no cure.

I showered, got dressed, and headed over to the office. I hadn't been there since Wednesday afternoon. There was several days' mail piled up and I tossed it on the desk. The message light on my answering machine was blinking, but I had other things to attend to first. I opened the French doors and let some fresh air circulate, then made a pot of coffee for myself. I checked the half-and-half in my little refrigerator, sniffing at the carton spout. Borderline. I'd have to replace that soon. When the coffee was done, I found a clean mug and filled it. The half-and-half formed an ominous pattern on the surface, but it tasted O.K. Some days I drink my coffee black, some days with cream for the comfort of it. I sat down in my swivel chair and propped my feet up, punching the replay button on the answering machine.

The tape rewound itself and Bobby came on. I felt a chilly finger touch the nape of my neck when I realized who it was.

"Hi, Kinsey. This is Bobby. I'm sorry I was such a jerk a little while ago. I know you were just trying to cheer me up. One thing came to me. I know this doesn't make much sense, but I thought I'd pass it on anyway. I think the name Blackman ties into this. Somebody Blackman. I don't know if that's who I gave the little red book to or the guy who's after me. Could be it's nothing the way my brain scrambles things. Anyway, we can put our heads together later and see if it means anything. I've got some stuff to do and then I have to see Kleinert. I'll try to get back to you. Maybe we can have a drink or something later tonight. Bye for now, kid. Watch your backside."

I flipped the machine off and stared at it.

I reached in my top drawer for the telephone book and hauled it out. There was one Blackman listed, an S. No address. Probably a woman trying to avoid obscene phone calls. I believe in trying for the obvious first. I mean, why not? Maybe Sarah, or Susan, or Sandra Blackman knew Bobby and had his little red book, or maybe he'd told her exactly what was going on and I could wrap the whole thing up with one phone call. The number was a disconnect. I tried it again, just to double-check. The same recording clicked in again. I made a note. The number might still pertain. Maybe S. Blackman had left town or died mysteriously.

I punched the replay button, just to hear Bobby's voice again. I was feeling restless, wondering how to get down to brass tacks on this thing. I checked back through Bobby's file. I hadn't yet talked to his former girl friend, Carrie St. Cloud, and that seemed like a reasonable possibility. Glen had told me she dropped out of the picture after the accident, but she might remember something from that period. I tried the number Glen had given me and had a brief chat with Carrie's mother, explaining who I was and why I wanted to get in touch with her. Carrie had apparently moved out of the family home a year ago and into a little apartment of her own that she shared with a roommate. She was working full-time now as an aerobics instructor at a studio on Chapel. I made a note of the two addresses, her work and home, and thanked the woman. I set my mug aside, unplugged the coffeepot, locked the office, and trotted down the back stairs.

The day was overcast, the sky a low ceiling of white. A pale gray haze seemed to permeate the streets with chill air. After the insufferable heat of the last few weeks, it seemed odd. The weather in Santa Teresa has been straying from the norm of late. It used to be that you could count on clear sunny skies and a tamed and temperate sea, with maybe a few clouds massing behind the mountains more for the visual effect than anything else. The rains came dutifully in January, two weeks of constant downpour, after which the countryside turned emerald green, bougainvillea and cape honeysuckle exploding across the face of the town like gaudy makeup. Nowadays, there are enexplicable rains in April and October, chilly days like this in August when the temperature should be eighty-five degrees. The shift is baffling, the sort of climatic alteration associated with the eruption of South Sea volcanoes and rumors about the ozone being penetrated by hair sprays.

The studio was only half a block away, housed in a former racquetball club that had gone belly-up once the passion for racquetball had passed. With aerobics coming in, it made perfect sense to convert all those plain narrow rooms with hardwood floors into little fat-burning ovens for women who yearned to be lean and fit. I asked if Carrie was teaching and the woman at the desk pointed mutely toward the source of the deafening music that made further conversation unlikely at best. I followed the end of her finger and rounded the corner. On my right, there was a waist-high wall overlooking an aerobics class in full swing one floor below.

The acoustics were grim. I watched from the observer's gallery while the music blasted. Carrie hollered out encouragement and fifteen of the best-looking female bodies in town exercised with a fanaticism I'd seldom seen. Apparently, I'd caught the class at its apex. They were doing buttocks lifts that looked obscene: women groaning on the floor in frosted, skintight leotards, doing hip thrusts and bun squeezes as if unseen partners were grinding away at them in unison.

Carrie St. Cloud was a surprise. Her name suggested a second runner-up for a Junior Miss pageant, or maybe a budding actress whose real name is Wanda Maxine Smith. I had pictured run-of-the-mill California good looks, the trim surfer's body, blond hair, dazzling white teeth, maybe a little tendency to tap dance. She was none of these things.

She couldn't have been more than twenty-two with a body builder's musculature and dark hair to her waist. Her face was strong, like Greek statuary, with a full mouth, rounded chin. The leotard she wore was a pale yellow Spandex, defining the wide shoulders and lean hips of a gymnast. If she had an ounce of fat on her, I didn't spy it anyplace. She had no breasts to speak of but the effect was intensely female anyway. This was no beach bunny. She took herself seriously, and she knew what fitness was about, breezing through the exercises without even breathing hard. Every other woman in the place was in pain. It made me grateful that all I have to do is jog three miles a day. I'm never going to look as good as she, but it didn't seem like a bad trade.

Carrie took the class through cool-down, a slow

stretch, and a couple of yoga moves and then let them sprawl on the floor like casualties on a battle-field. She turned the music off, grabbed a towel, and buried her face in it, moving out of the room through a doorway just below me. I found the stairs and headed down, catching her at the water fountain just outside the locker rooms. Her hair fell across her shoulders like a nun's veil and she had to gather it in a knot and hold it to one side so she could drink without getting it wet.

"Carrie?"

She straightened up, blotting a trickle of sweat with the sleeve of her leotard, the towel around her neck now, like a fighter just out of the ring. "That's right."

I told her who I was and what I was doing and then asked her if we could talk about Bobby Callahan.

"All right, but we'll have to do it while I clean up. I have to be somewhere at noon."

I followed her through a door and into the locker room. The floor plan was open, with a counter on the right that circled the perimeter about halfway, banks of metal lockers, a line of hair dryers mounted on the wall. The tile was a pristine white and the place was spotless, with benches anchored to the floor, mirrors everywhere. I could hear showers running somewhere out of sight to my left. Women were beginning to straggle in from the class and the level of laughter, I knew, would rise as the room filled.

Carrie kicked off her shoes and peeled her leotard down like a banana skin. I busied myself looking for a place to perch. As a rule, I don't interview naked ladies in a roomful of chattering strippers. I noticed that they smelled just like the guys at Santa Teresa Fitness and I thought that was nice.

I waited while she tucked her hair up under a plastic cap and went into the showers. In the meantime, women paraded back and forth in various stages of undress. It was a comforting sight. So many versions of the female breast, of buttocks and bellies and pubic nests, endless repetitions of the same forms. These women seemed to feel good about themselves and there was a camaraderie among them that I enjoyed.

Carrie returned from showering, wrapped in a towel. She pulled her shower cap off and gave her dark mane a toss. She began to dry herself off, talking to me over her shoulder.

"I thought about coming to the funeral, but I just couldn't handle it. Did you go?"

"Yeah, I went. I hadn't known Bobby long, but it was tough. You were dating him when he had the accident, weren't you?"

"Actually, we'd just broken up. We dated two years and then things went sour. I got pregnant, among other things, and that was the end of it. He paid for the abortion, but we weren't seeing much of each other by then. I did feel terrible when he got hurt, but I stayed away. I know people thought I was a real cold fish, but what could I do? It was over. I couldn't see hovering around him loyally just so I'd look good."

"Did you hear any talk about the accident?"

"Just that someone ran him off the road."

"You have any idea who it might have been or why?"

She sat down on a bench and hauled a foot up, drying carefully between her toes. "Well, yes and no. Not who really, but I know something was going on with him. He didn't confide much by then, but he did go with me when I had the abortion and he stayed real close for a couple of days." She switched feet, bending to inspect her toes. "I worry about athlete's foot," she murmured. "Sorry."

She tossed the towel aside and got up, crossing to a locker, taking out clothes. She glanced at me. "I'm just trying to say this right because I don't really have any facts. Just an impression. I remember him saying some friend of his was in trouble and I had the feeling it was blackmail."

"Blackmail?"

"Well, yes, but not in any ordinary sense. I mean, I don't think there was money changing hands or anything like that. It wasn't sinister cloak-and-dagger stuff. Somebody had something on somebody else and it was pretty serious. I gathered he'd been trying to help and he'd just figured out how to do it. . . ." She pulled on her underpants and then an undershirt. I guess she figured her breasts weren't big enough to worry with a bra.

"When was this?" I asked. "Do you remember the date?"

"Well, I know I had the abortion on November sixteenth and he stayed with me that night. The accident was the day after that, I think, the night of the seventeenth, so it was all in that same week."

"I've been going through the newspaper starting in

September, thinking maybe he was caught up in something public. Did you get *any* impression of the arena where all this was taking place? I mean, I don't even know what to look for."

She shook her head. "I have no idea. Really. I'm sorry, but I couldn't even make a guess."

"You think Rick Bergen was the friend in trouble?"

"I doubt it. I knew Rick. I think Bobby would have told me if it had been Rick."

"Somebody at work?"

"Look, I just can't help you with that," she said impatiently. "He was being very tight-lipped and I wasn't in a mood to pry. I was just glad the abortion was over with. I was taking pain-killers anyway so I slept a lot and the rest was a blur. He was just talking for the sake of it, to take my mind off things and maybe a little bit from nerves."

"Does the name Blackman mean anything to you?"

"I don't think so."

She pulled on a pair of sweatpants and slipped her feet into some thongs. She bent at the waist, flipped her hair across one shoulder, and gave it a couple of whacks with a hairbrush, then grabbed up her shoulder bag, moving toward the door. I had to do a quick two-step to catch up with her. I didn't think she'd finished dressing but I could see now that this was all she intended to wear. Sweatpants and an undershirt? She was going to freeze once she got outside. I scurried after her, catching the door as she passed into the corridor.

"Who else was he hanging out with back then?" I asked, trotting up the stairs to the main entrance with her. "Just give me a couple of names. I gotta have something to go on."

She paused, glancing back at me. "Try a kid named Gus. I don't know his last name, but he works at that skate-rental place down at the beach. He's an old high-school buddy and I think Bobby trusted him. Maybe he'll know what it's about."

"What were the other things? You said you got pregnant 'among other things.'"

Her smile was tense. "God, you are so persistent. He was in love with someone else. I have no idea who, so don't bother to ask. If I'd known about the other woman I'd have broken off our relationship long before. As it was, I didn't hear about her until I told him I was pregnant. I thought at first he might marry me, but when he told me he was seriously involved with someone else, I knew what I had to do. To his credit, he did feel terrible about the bind I was in and he did as much as he could. There was nothing cheap about Bobby and he really was a sweet guy at heart."

She started to move away and I caught her by the arm, thinking rapidly. "Carrie, is there a chance that the friend in trouble and the woman he was involved with were one and the same person?"

"How do I know?"

"I don't suppose he gave you a little red address book, did he?"

"All he gave me was heartache," she said and walked off without looking back.

15

The skate-rental shack is a dark green box just off a parking lot near the wharf. For three bucks, you can rent roller skates for an hour, with kneepads, elbow pads, and wrist braces thrown in without charge so you won't sue them later for the harm you might do yourself.

Bobby's taste in friends was hard to predict. Gus looked like the sort of fellow if you saw on a street corner, you'd reach over casually and make sure your car doors were locked. He must have been Bobby's age, but he was sunken-chested and frail, and his color was bad. His hair was dark brown and he was struggling to grow a mustache that only made him look like a fugitive. I'd seen mug shots of felons I'd trust before him.

I had introduced myself and ascertained that this was indeed Bobby's friend, when a blonde with flyaway hair and long tanned legs came up to turn in a pair of skates. I watched their interchange. Despite my first impression, Gus had a nice way about him. His manner was mildly flirtatious and he had a tendency to glance in my direction, showing off, I suspect. I waited, looking on while he calculated how much she owed him. He returned her street shoes and I.D. and she hopped over to a bench to put on her tennies. Gus waited until she was gone before he spoke.

"I saw you at the funeral," he said shyly when he turned back to me. "You were sitting near Mrs. Callahan."

"I don't remember seeing you," I said. "Did you come to the house afterward?"

He shook his head, coloring. "I wasn't feeling too good."

"I don't think there's any way to feel good about that."

"Not when your buddy dies," he said. His voice carried a barely perceptible quaver. He turned away, making a big display of shoving the shoe skates back into the proper slot on the shelf.

"Have you been sick?" I asked.

He seemed to debate for just an instant and then said, "I got Crohn's disease. You know what that is?"

"No."

"Inflammatory bowel disease. Everything goes right through me. I can't keep weight on. Run a fever half the time. Stomach hurts. 'Etiology unknown,' which means they don't know what causes it or where it comes from. I've had it almost two years and it's got me down. I can't keep a real job, so I do this."

"Is that something you recover from?"

"I guess so. In time. That's what they say, at any rate."

"Well, I'm sorry you're suffering. It sounds grim."

"You don't know the half of it. Anyway, Bobby cheered me up. He was in such bad shape himself, we'd get laughin' sometimes. I miss him. When I heard he died, I almost gave up, but then this little voice said, 'Aw Gus, get up off your dead ass and get on with it . . . this isn't the end of the world, so don't be a jerk.'" He shook his head. "It was Bobby, I swear. Sounded just like him. So I got up off my dead ass. Are you looking into his death?"

I nodded, glancing over as a couple of kids approached to rent skates.

Gus conducted some business and came back to me, apologizing for the interruption. It was summer and despite the uncharacteristic chill in the air, the tourists were swarming the beaches. I asked him if he had any idea what Bobby was involved in. He moved uneasily, glancing off across the street.

"I got an idea, but I don't know what to say. I mean, if Bobby didn't tell you, why should I?"

"He couldn't remember. That's what he hired me for. He thought he was in danger and he wanted me to find out what was going on."

"So maybe it's best to just leave it be."

"Leave what be?"

"Look, I don't know anything for sure. Just what Bobby said."

"What are you worried about?"

He shifted his gaze. "I don't know. Let me think about it some. Honest, I don't know much, but I don't want to talk about it unless it feels right. You know what I mean?"

I conceded the point. You can always push people around, but it's not a good idea. Better to let them volunteer information for reasons of their own. You get more that way.

"I hope you'll give me a call," I said. "If I don't hear from you, I might have to come back and make a pest of myself." I took a card out and laid it on the counter.

He smiled, apparently feeling guilty for holding out. "You can skate for nothing if you want. It's good exercise."

"Some other time," I said. "Thanks."

He watched me until I pulled out of the parking lot, turning left. In the rearview mirror, I could see him scratching at his mustache with the corner of my business card. I hoped I'd hear from him.

In the meantime, I decided to see if I could lay my hands on the cardboard box the lab had packed up after Bobby's accident. I drove over to the house. Glen had apparently flown up to San Francisco for the day, but Derek was home and I told him what I needed.

His look was skeptical. "I remember the box, but I'm not sure where it went. Probably out in the garage, if you want to have a look."

He closed the front door behind him and the two of us crossed the courtyard to the three-car garage that stretched out at one end of the house. There were storage bins built into the back wall. None of them was locked, but most were stacked top to bottom with boxes that looked as if they'd been on the premises since the year oughty-ought.

I spotted a carton that seemed to be a good bet. It was shoved against the back wall under a workbench, marked "disposable syringes" with the name of the medical supplier and a torn shipping label addressed to Santa Teresa Hospital Pathology Department. We hauled it out and opened it. The contents looked like Bobby's, but were disappointing nevertheless. No little red book, no reference to anybody named Blackman, no clippings, no cryptic notes, no personal correspondence. There were some medical books, two technical manuals for radiology equipment, and office supplies of the most benign sort. What was I going to do with a box of paper clips and two ballpoint pens?

"It doesn't look like much," Derek remarked.

"It doesn't look like *anything*," I replied. "You mind if I take it with me anyway? I may want to check through it again."

"No, go right ahead. Here let me get that." I stepped back obligingly and let him heft the box up off the floor and carry it to my car. I could have done it, but it seemed important to him, so why hassle? He shoved some stuff aside and we wrestled the box into the backseat. I told him I'd be in touch and then I took off.

I went back to my place and changed into my running clothes. I was just locking up when Henry came around the corner with Lila Sams. They were walking hip to hip, arms entwined. He was a good foot taller than she and lean in all the places she was plump. He looked flushed with happiness, that special aura people take on when they've just fallen in love. He was wearing pale blue brushed denim pants and a pale blue shirt that made his blue eyes look nearly luminous. His hair looked freshly cut and my guess was he'd actually had someone "style" it this time. Lila's smile tensed somewhat when she caught sight of me, but she recovered her composure, laughing girlishly.

"Oh Kinsey, now look what he's gone and done," she said and held her hand out. She was sporting a big square-cut diamond that I hoped was some gaudy fake.

"God, it's gorgeous. What's the occasion?" I asked, heart sinking. Surely, they weren't engaged. She was so wrong for him, so giddy and false, while he was genuine.

"Just celebrating the fact that we met," Henry said with a glance at her. "What was it, a month ago? Six weeks?"

"Well, naughty you," she said with a playful stamp of her little foot. "I have half a mind to make you take this right back. We met June twelfth. It was Moza's birthday and I'd just moved in. You catered that tea she gave and you've spoiled me rotten ever since." She lowered her voice then to its most confidential pitch. "Isn't he awful?"

I don't know how to talk to people this way, exchanging pointless banter. I could feel my smile becoming self-conscious but I couldn't make it go away.

"I think he's great," I said, sounding somehow lame and inept.

"Well, of course he's great," she said in a flash. "Why wouldn't he be? He's such an innocent, anyone can take advantage of him."

Her tone was suddenly quarrelsome, as though I'd insulted him. I could feel the warning signals clanging away like crazy, but I still couldn't guess what was coming. She was wagging a finger at me, red painted nails piercing the air near my face. "You, for one, you bad girl. I told Henry and I'll say it right to your face, the rent you pay is a scandal and you know perfectly well you've been robbing him blind."

"What?"

She narrowed her eyes, pushing her face toward mine. "Now don't you play dumb with me. Two hundred dollars a month! My stars. Do you know what studio apartments are renting for in this neighborhood? Three hundred. That's a hundred dollars you take away from him every time you write him a check. Disgraceful. It's just a disgrace!"

"Oh now, Lila," Henry broke in. He seemed nonplussed that she'd launched into this, but it was clearly something they'd discussed. "Let's don't get into this now. She's on her way out."

"You can spare a few minutes, I'm sure," she said with a glittering look at me.

"Sure," I said faintly and then glanced at him. "Have you been unhappy with me?" I felt the same sick combination of heat and cold that Chinese-food syndrome produces. Did he really feel I'd been cheating him?

Lila cut in again, answering before he could even open his mouth. "Let's not put Henry on the spot," she said. "He thinks the world of you, which is why he hasn't had the heart to speak up. You're the one I'd like to spank. How could you take an old softie like Henry and twist him around your finger that way? You should be ashamed."

"I wouldn't take advantage of Henry."

"But you already have. How long have you been living here at that same ridiculous rent? A year? Fifteen months? Don't tell me it never occurred to you that you were getting this place dirt-cheap! Because if you say that, I'll have to call you a liar right to your face and embarrass us both."

I could feel my mouth open, but I couldn't say a word.

"We can talk about this later," Henry murmured, taking her by the arm. He was steering her around me, but her eyes were still fixed on mine and her neck and cheeks were now blotchy with rage. I turned and stared as he moved her toward his back stairs. She was already starting to protest in the same irrational tone I'd heard the other night. Was the woman nuts?

When the door closed behind them, my heart began to thump and I realized I was damp with sweat. I tied my door key to my shoelace and then I took off, breaking into a trot long before I'd had a chance to warm up. I ran, putting distance between us.

I did three miles and then walked back to my place,

letting myself in. Henry's back shades were down and his windows were shut. The rear of his house looked blank and uninviting, like a beachfront park after closing time.

I showered and threw some clothes on, and then took off, fleeing the premises. I still felt stung, but I was getting in touch with some anger too. What business was it of hers anyway? And why hadn't Henry leapt to my defense?

When I pushed into Rosie's, it was late afternoon and there wasn't a soul in sight. The restaurant was gloomy and smelled of last night's cigarette smoke. The TV set on the bar was turned off and the chairs were still upside down on the tabletops, like a troupe of acrobats doing tricks. I crossed to the rear and opened the swinging door to the kitchen. Rosie glanced up at me, startled. She was sitting on a tall wooden stool with a cleaver in her hand, chopping leeks. She hated anyone intruding on her kitchen, probably because she violated health codes.

"What happened?" she said when she saw my face.

"I had an encounter with Henry's lady friend," I replied.

"Ah," she said. She whacked a leek with the cleaver, sending hunks flying. "She don't come in here. She knows better."

"Rosie, the woman is crazy as a loon. You should have heard her the other night after you tangled with her. She ranted and raved for hours. Now she's accusing me of cheating Henry on the rent."

"Take a seat. I got some vodka somewhere." She

crossed to the cabinet above the sink and stood on tip-pytoe, tilting a vodka bottle into reach. She broke the seal and poured me a hit in a coffee cup. She shrugged then poured herself one too. We drank and I could feel the blood rush back to my face.

I said, "Woo!" involuntarily. My esophagus felt scorched and I could sense the contours of my stomach outlined in alcohol. I always pictured my stomach much lower down than that. Weird. Rosie placed the chopped leeks in a bowl and rinsed the cleaver at the sink before she turned back to me.

"You got twenty cents? Give me two dimes," she said, holding a hand out. I fished around in my handbag, coming up with some loose change. Rosie took it and crossed to the pay phone on the wall. Everybody has to use that pay phone, even her.

"Who are you calling? You're not calling Henry," I said, with alarm.

"Ssss!" She held a hand up, shushing me, her eyes focusing in the way people do when someone picks up the phone on the other end. Her voice got musical and syrupy.

"Hello, dear. This is Rosie. What are you doing right this minute. Uh-hun, well I think you better get over here. We have a little matter to discuss."

She clunked the receiver down without waiting for a response and then she fixed me with a satisfied look. "Mrs. Lowenstein is coming over for a chat."

Moza Lowenstein sat on the chrome-and-plastic chair that I'd brought in from the bar. She is a large woman with hair the color of a cast-iron skillet, worn in braids wrapped around her head. There are strands of silver threaded through like tinsel, and her face, with its pale powder, has the soft look of a marshmallow. Generally, she likes to hold on to something when she talks to Rosie: a bouquet of pencils, a wooden spoon, any talisman to ward off attack. Today, it was the dish towel she'd brought with her. Apparently, Rosie had interrupted her in the middle of some chore and she'd hurried right over, as bid. She's afraid of Rosie, as anyone with good sense would be. Rosie launched right in, skipping all the niceties.

"Who is this Lila Sams?" Rosie said. She took up her cleaver and began to pound on some veal, making Moza flinch.

Her voice, when she found it, was trembly and soft. "I don't really know. She came to my door, she said in response to an ad in the paper, but it was all a mistake. I didn't have a room for rent and I told her as much. Well, the poor thing burst into tears and what was I to do? I had to ask her in for a cup of tea."

Rosie paused to stare in disbelief. "And then you rented her a room?"

Moza folded the towel, forming a lobster shape like a napkin in a fancy restaurant. "Well, no. I told her she could stay with me until she found a place, but she insisted that she pay her own way. She didn't want to be indebted, she said."

"That's called room rent. That's what that is," Rosie snapped.

"Well, yes. If you want to *put* it that way."

"Where does this woman come from?"

Moza flapped the towel out and dabbed it against her upper lip, blotting sweat. She laid it out on her lap and pressed it with her hand, keeping her fingers together in a wedge like an iron. I saw Rosie's flinty gaze follow every movement and I thought she might give Moza's hand a smack with the cleaver. Moza must have thought so too because she quit fiddling with the towel and looked up at Rosie with guilt. "What?"

Rosie enunciated carefully, as though speaking to an alien. "Where does Lila Sams come from?"

"A little town in Idaho."

"*What* little town?"

"Well, I don't know," Moza said defensively.

"You have a woman living in your house and you don't know what town she comes from?"

"What difference does it make?"

"And you don't know what difference it makes?" Rosie stared at her with exaggerated astonishment. Moza broke eye contact and folded the towel into a bishop's miter.

"You do me a favor and you find out," Rosie said. "Can you manage that?"

"I'll try," Moza said. "But she doesn't like people prying. She told me that and she was quite definite."

"I'm very definite too. I'm definite about I don't like this lady and I want to know what she's up to. You find out where she comes from and Kinsey can take care of the rest. And I don't have to tell you, Moza, I don't want Lila Sams to know. You understand?"

Moza looked cornered. I could see her debate, trying to decide which was worse: infuriating Rosie or getting caught spying on Lila Sams. It was going to be a close contest, but I knew who I was betting on.

16

I went back to my office late in the day and typed up my notes. There wasn't much, but I don't like to get behind. With Bobby dead, I intended to write regular reports and submit itemized bills at intervals, even if it was just to myself. I had tucked his file back in the drawer and I was tidying up my desk when there was a tap at the door and Derek Wenner peered in.

He said, "Oh. Hello. I was hoping I'd catch you here."

"Hi, Derek. Come on in," I said.

He stood for a moment, undecided, his gaze tracing the perimeters of my small office space. "Somehow I didn't picture this," he said. "Nice. I mean, it's small, but efficient. Uh, how'd you do with Bobby's box? Any luck?"

"I haven't had a chance to look closely. I've been doing other things. Have a seat."

He pulled a chair up and sat down, still looking around. He was wearing a golf shirt, white pants, and two-tone shoes. "So this is it, huh?"

This was his version of small talk, I assumed. I sat down and let him ramble briefly. He seemed anxious and I couldn't imagine what had brought him in. We made mouth noises at each other, demonstrating goodwill. I'd just seen him a few hours earlier and we didn't have that much to talk about.

"How's Glen doing?" I asked.

"Good," he nodded. "She's doing pretty well. God, I don't know how she's gotten through, but you know she's made of substantial stuff." He tended to speak in doubtful tones, as if he weren't absolutely certain he was telling the truth.

He cleared his throat and the timbre of his voice changed.

"Say, I'll tell you why I stopped in," he said. "Bobby's attorney gave me a call a little while ago just to talk about the terms of Bobby's will. Do you know Varden Talbot?"

"We've never met. He sent me copies of the reports on Bobby's accident, but that's the extent of it."

"Smart fellow," Derek said. He was stalling. I thought I better goose him along or this could take all day.

"What'd he have to say?"

Derek's expression was a wonderful combination of uneasiness and disbelief. "Well, that's the amazing thing," he said. "From what he indicated, I guess my daughter inherits the bulk of Bobby's money."

It took me a moment to compute the fact that the daughter he referred to was Kitty Wenner, cokehead, currently residing in the psycho ward at St. Terry's. "Kitty?" I said.

He shifted in his seat. "I was surprised too, of course. From what Varden tells me, Bobby made out a will when he came into his inheritance three years ago. At that point, he left everything to Kitty. Then sometime after the accident, he added a codicil, so that a little money would go to Rick's parents as well."

I was about to say "Rick's parents?" as if I were suffering from echolalia, but I clamped my mouth shut and let him continue.

"Glen won't be back until late, so she's not aware of it. I'd imagine she'll want to talk to Varden in the morning. He said he'd make a copy of the will and send it over to the house. He's going to go ahead and file it for probate."

"And this is the first anybody's heard of it?"

"As far as I know." He went on talking while I tried to figure out what it meant. Money, as a motive, always seems so direct. Find out who benefits financially and start from there. Kitty Wenner. Phil and Reva Bergen.

"Excuse me," I said, cutting in. "Just how much money are we talking about?"

Derek paused to run a hand up along his jaw, as though deciding if he was due for a shave. "Well, a hundred grand to Rick's parents and gee, I don't know. Kitty probably stands to gain a couple mill. Now, you're going to have inheritance tax . . ."

All of the little zeros began to dance in my head like sugar plums. "Hundred grand" and "couple mill," as in a hundred thousand dollars and two million of them. I just sat and blinked at him. Why had he come in here to tell me this stuff?

"What's the catch?" I asked.

"What?"

"I'm just wondering why you're telling me about it. Is there some problem?"

"I guess I'm worried about Glen's reaction. You know how she feels about Kitty."

I shrugged. "It was Bobby's money to do with as he saw fit. How could she object?"

"You don't think she'd contest it?"

"Derek, I can't speculate about what Glen might do. Talk to her."

"Well, I guess I will when she gets back."

"I'm assuming the money was put in some kind of trust fund since Kitty's just seventeen. Who was named executor? You?"

"No, no. The bank. I don't think Bobby had a very high opinion of me. To tell you the truth, I'm a little worried about how this might look. Bobby claims someone's trying to kill him and then it turns out Kitty inherits all this money when he dies."

"I'm sure the police will have a chat with her."

"But you don't think she had anything to do with Bobby's accident, do you?"

Ah, the subtext of his visit.

I said, "Frankly, I'd find it hard to believe, but Homicide might see it differently. They might also want to take a look at you while they're at it."

"Me?!" He managed to pack a lot of punctuation into one syllable.

"What if something happens to Kitty? Who gets the money then? She's not exactly in the best of health."

He looked at me uncomfortably, probably wishing he'd never come in. He must have harbored the vague notion that I could reassure him. Instead, I'd only broadened the basis for his anxieties. He wound up the conversation and got up moments later, telling me he'd be in touch. When he turned to go, I could see that the golf shirt was sticking to his back and I could smell the tension in his sweat.

"Oh, Derek," I called after him. "Does the name Blackman mean anything to you?"

"Not that I know. Why?"

"Just curious. I appreciate your coming in," I said. "If you find out anything else, please let me know."

"I will."

Once he was gone, I put in a quick call to a friend of mine at the telephone company and asked about S. Blackman. He said he'd check into it and call me back. I went down to the parking lot and hauled out the cardboard box I'd picked up from Bobby's garage. I went back up to the office and checked the contents, taking the items out one by one. It was all just as I remembered it: a couple of radiology manuals, some medical texts, paper clips, ballpoint pens, scratch pads. Nothing of significance that I could see. I hauled the box back out and shoved it into the backseat again, thinking I'd drop it back at Bobby's house next time I was there.

What to try next? I couldn't think of a thing.

I went home.

As I pulled into a parking place out front, I found myself scanning the walk for signs of Lila Sams. For a woman I'd only seen three or four times in my life, she was looming large, spoiling any sense of serenity I'd come to attach to the notion of "home." I locked my car and went around to the backyard, glancing at the rear of Henry's house to see if he was there. The back door was open and I caught the spicy scent of yeast and cinnamon through the screen. I peered in and spotted Henry sitting at the table with a coffee mug and the afternoon paper in front of him.

"Henry?"

He looked up. "Well, Kinsey. There you are." He came over and unlatched the screen, holding the door open for me. "Come in, come in. Would you like some coffee? I've got a pan of sweet rolls coming out in a minute."

I entered hesitantly, still half expecting Lila Sams to jump out like a tarantula. "I didn't want to interrupt anything," I said. "Is Lila here?"

"No, no. She had some business to take care of, but she should be back by six. I'm taking her out to dinner tonight. We have reservations at the Crystal Palace."

"Oh, wow, impressive," I said. Henry pulled a chair out for me and then poured me some coffee while I looked around. Lila had apparently taken her fine hand to the place. The curtains were new: avocado green cotton with a print of salt and pepper shakers, vegetable clusters, and wooden spoons, tied back with green bows. There were matching placemats and napkins, with accessories in a contrasting pumpkin shade. There was a new trivet on the counter with a homely saying in wrought-iron curlicue. I thought it said, "God Bless Our Biscuits," but that couldn't have been right.

"You've fixed the place up," I said.

His face brightened and he looked around. "You like it? It was Lila's idea. I tell you, the woman has made such a difference in my life."

"Well, that's good. I'm glad to hear that," I said.

"She's made me feel . . . I don't know, *vital* is the word I guess. Ready to start all over again."

I wondered if he was going to pass right over her accusations about my cheating him. He got up and opened the oven door, checking the sweet rolls, which he apparently decided were not quite done. He shoved them back and shut the oven, leaving the pumpkin-colored mitt on his right hand like a boxing glove.

I shifted uncomfortably on the stool where I was perched. "I thought maybe you and I should have a talk about Lila's accusations about the rent."

"Oh, don't worry about it," he said. "She was just in one of her moods."

"But Henry, I don't want you to feel like I'm cheating you. Don't you think we should get that ironed out?"

"No. Piffle. I don't feel you're cheating me."

"But she does."

"No no, not at all. You misunderstood."

"Misunderstood?" I said incredulously.

"Look, this is all my fault and I'm sorry I didn't get it straightened out at the time. Lila flew off the handle and she realizes that. In fact, I'm sure she means to apologize. She and I had a long talk about it afterward and I know she felt bad. It had nothing to do with you personally. She's a little high-strung, but she's just the dearest woman you'll ever meet. Once you get to know her, you'll see what a wonderful person she is."

"I hope so," I said. "What worried me is that she and Rosie had that tiff and then she took off after me. I wasn't sure what was going on."

Henry laughed. "Well, I wouldn't take that too seriously. You know Rosie. She gets into tiffs with everyone. Lila's fine. She's got a heart of gold and she's just as loyal as a little pup."

"I just don't want to see you going off the deep end," I said. It was one of those sayings that doesn't really mean anything but somehow it seemed to apply.

"No need to worry about that," he said mildly. "I've been around a long time, you know, and I haven't gone off the deep end yet."

He checked the sweet rolls again, and this time, he took them out and put the pan on the trivet to cool. He glanced over at me. "I haven't had a chance to tell you. She and I are going into a real-estate venture together."

"Oh really?"

"Which is how the subject of your rent came up in the first place. Rental income affects the overall value of the property and that was her main concern. She said she didn't mean to interfere in our relationship at all. She's hard-headed when it comes to business but she didn't want to look like she was butting in."

"What kind of real-estate venture?"

"Well, she owns some property she's going to put up as collateral, and with this place thrown in, we'll just about have the down payment on the property we want."

"Something here in town?"

"I better not say. She swore me to secrecy. I mean, it's not firm yet anyway, but I'll tell you about it when we get the deal put together. It should be happening in the next couple of days. I had to swear I'd keep mum."

"I don't understand," I said. "You're selling your house?"

"I can't even begin to understand the details. Too complicated for me," he said.

"I wasn't aware that she was involved in real estate."

"Oh, she's been doing this sort of thing for years. She was married to some big wheeler-dealer in New Mexico, and when he died, he left her very well off. She's got a bundle. Does real-estate investments almost as a hobby, she says."

"And she's from New Mexico? I thought someone told me it was Idaho."

"Oh, she's lived everywhere. She's a gypsy at heart. She's even talking me into it. You know, just take off into the sunset. Big RV and a map of the States. Go where the road takes us. I feel like she's added twenty years to my life."

I wanted to question him more closely, but I heard Lila's "yoo hoo" at the screen door and her face appeared, wreathed in saucy curls. She put a hand to her cheek when she saw me, turning all sheepish and coy.

"Oh, Kinsey. I bet I know just what you're doing

here," she said. She came into the kitchen and paused for a moment, hands clasped in front of her as though she might drop to her knees in prayer. "Now don't say a word until I get this out," she went on. She paused to peer over at Henry. "Oh Henry, you did tell her how sorry I was to fuss at her that way." She was using a special "little" voice.

Henry put an arm around her, giving her a squeeze. "I've already explained and I'm sure she understands," he said. "I don't want you to worry any more about that."

"But I do worry, Puddy, and I won't feel right about it 'til I tell her myself."

Puddy?

She came over to the stool where I was perched and took my right hand, pressing it between her own.

"I am so sorry. I tell you I am so apologetic for what I said to you and I beg your forgiveness." Her tone was contrite and I thought Puddy was going to get all choked up. She was making deep eye contact with me and a couple of her rings were digging into my fingers rather painfully. She had apparently turned the ring around so that the stones were palm inward, producing maximum effect as she tightened her grip.

I said, "Oh, that's all right. Don't think another thing about it. I'm sure I won't."

Just to show her what a brick I was, I got up and put my left arm around her just the way Henry had. I gave her the same little squeeze, easing my foot across the toe of her right shoe and leaning forward slightly. She pulled back from the waist, but I managed to keep my foot where it was so that we were standing hip to hip. We locked eyes for a moment. She gave me a gooey smile and then eased her grip. I shifted my weight from her foot, but not before two coins of color had appeared high up on her cheeks like a cockatiel.

Puddy seemed pleased that we'd come to this new understanding and I was too. I made my excuses and departed soon after that. Lila had stopped looking at me altogether by then and I noticed that she had sat down abruptly, easing off one shoe.

17

I let myself into my apartment and poured a glass of wine and then I made myself a sandwich with creamed cheese and thinly sliced cucumbers and onions on dark bread. I cut it in half and used a piece of paper toweling as a combination napkin and dinner plate, toting sandwich and wineglass into the bathroom. I opened my bathroom window a crack and ate standing in the tub, peering out at intervals to see if Henry and Lila were departing for their dinner date. At 6:45, they came around the corner of the building and Henry unlocked his car, opening the door for her on the passenger side. I eased into an upright position, ducking back out of sight until I heard him start the car and pull away.

I'd finished dinner by then and I had nothing to do in the way of dishes except to wad up my paper towel and throw it in the trash, feeling inordinately pleased with myself. I traded my sandals for tennis shoes, grabbed up my master keys, my key picks, penknife, and a flashlight, then headed down the block to Moza Lowenstein's house, where I rang the bell. She peered out of the side window at me in perplexity, then opened the door.

"I couldn't think who it was at this hour," she said. "I thought Lila must be coming back for something she forgot."

I don't ordinarily visit Moza and I could tell she was wondering what I was doing on her doorstep. She moved back and admitted me, smiling timidly. The television was tuned to a rerun of *M.A.S.H.*, helicopters whipping up a cloud of dust.

"I thought I'd do a little background check on Lila Sams," I said, while "Suicide Is Painless" played merrily.

"Oh, but she's just gone out," Moza said in haste. It was already occurring to her that I was up to no good and I guess she thought she could head me off.

"Is this her room back here?" I asked, moving into the corridor. I knew Moza's bedroom was the one at the end of the hall to the left. I figured Lila's must be the former "spare" room.

Moza lumbered after me. She's a big woman, suffering from some condition that makes her feet swell. Her expression was a cross between pain and bewilderment.

I tried the knob. Lila's door was locked.

"You can't go in there."

"Really?"

She was looking fearful by now and she didn't seem reassured by the sight of the master key I was easing into the keyhole. This was a simple house lock requiring only a skeleton key, several styles of which I had on a ring.

"You don't understand," she said again. "That's locked."

"No, it's not. See?" I opened the door and Moza put a hand on her heart.

"She'll come back," she said with a quaking voice.

"Moza, I'm not going to take anything," I said. "I will work with great care and she'll never know I was here. Why don't you sit out there in the living room and keep an eye open, just in case? O.K.?"

"She'll be so angry if she finds out I let you in," she said to me. Her eyes were as mournful now as a basset hound's.

"But she won't find out, so there's nothing to worry about. By the way, did you ever find out what little town in Idaho she's from?"

"Dickey is what she told me."

"Oh good. I appreciate that. She never mentioned living in New Mexico, did she?"

Moza shook her head and began to pat her chest as if she were burping herself. "Please hurry," she said. "I don't know what I'd do if she came back."

I wasn't sure myself.

I eased into the room and closed the door, flipping on the light. On the other side of the door, I heard Moza shuffling back toward the front of the house, murmuring to herself.

The room was furnished with an ancient wood-veneer bedroom suite that I doubt could be called "antique." The pieces looked like the ones I've seen out on thrift-shop sidewalks in downtown Los Angeles: creaky, misshapen, smelling oddly of wet ash. There was a chiffonier, matching bedtables, a dressing table with a round mirror set between banks of drawers. The bed frame was iron, painted a flaking white, and the spread was chenille in a dusty rose with fringe on the sides. The wallpaper was a tumble of floral bouquets, mauve and pale rose on a gray background. There were several sepia photographs of a man whom I imagined was Mr. Lowenstein; someone, at any rate, who favored hair slicked down with water and spectacles with round gold rims. He appeared to be in his twenties, smooth and pretty with a solemn mouth pulled over slightly protruding teeth. The studio had tinted his cheeks a pinkish tone, slightly at odds with the rest of the photo, but the effect was nice. I'd heard that Moza was widowed in 1945. I would have loved seeing a picture of her in those days. Almost reluctantly, I turned back to the task at hand.

Three narrow windows were locked on the inside, shades drawn. I moved over and peered out of one, catching a glimpse of backyard through screens rusted into the old wooden frames. I checked my watch. It was only seven. They'd be gone, at the very least, an hour, and I didn't think I needed to provide myself an emergency exit. On the other hand, there isn't any point in being dumb about these things. I went back to the door and opened it, leaving it ajar. Moza had turned off the TV set and I pictured her peeking through the front curtain, heart in her throat, which is about where mine was.

It was still light outside, but the room was gloomy even with the overhead light on. I started with the chiffonier. I did a preliminary survey, using my flashlight to check for any crude attempts at security. Sure enough, Lila had booby-trapped a couple of drawers by affixing a strand of hair slyly across the crack. I removed these beauties and placed them carefully on the hand-crocheted runner on top.

The first drawer contained a jumble of jewelry, several belts coiled together, embroidered handkerchiefs, a watch case, hairpins, a few stray buttons, and two pairs of white cotton gloves. I stared for a long time, without touching anything, wondering why any of it warranted a protective strand of hair. Actually, anybody snooping in Lila's things would probably start here and work down, so maybe it was just a ready reference on her part, a checkpoint each time she returned to her room. I tried the next drawer, which was filled with neat piles of nylon underpants in a quite large old-lady style. I ran an experimental finger down between the stacks, being careful not to disturb the order. I couldn't feel anything significant; no handgun, no unidentifiable boxes or bumps.

On an impulse, I opened the first drawer again and peered up at the underside. Nothing taped to the bottom. I pulled the whole drawer out and checked along the back. Hello! Score one for my team. There was an envelope encased in plastic, sealed flat against the back panel of the drawer and secured by masking tape on all four sides. I took out my penknife and slid the small blade under one corner of the tape, peeling it up so I could remove the envelope from the plastic housing. In it was an Idaho driver's license in the name of Delilah Sampson. The woman had a real biblical sense of humor here. I made a note of the address, date of birth, height, weight, hair and eye color, much of which seemed to apply to the woman I knew as Lila Sams. God, I had really hit pay dirt. I slipped the license back into the envelope, returned the envelope to its hiding place, and pressed the masking tape securely against the wood. I squinted critically at my handiwork. Looked untouched to me, unless she'd powdered everything with some kind of tricky dust that would dye my hands bright red the instant I washed them again. Wouldn't that be a bitch!

The back of the second drawer was also being used as a little safe-deposit box, containing a stack of credit cards and yet another driver's license. The name on this one was Delia Sims, with an address in Las Cruces, New Mexico, and a date of birth that matched the first. Again, I made a note of the details and carefully returned the document to its hiding place. I replaced the drawer, glancing quickly at my watch. Seven thirty-two. I was still O.K., but I had a lot of ground to cover yet. I continued my search, working with delicacy, leaving the contents of each drawer undisturbed. When I finished with the chiffonier, I retrieved the two hairs and moored them across the drawer cracks again.

The dressing table revealed nothing and the bed-tables were unremarkable. I went through the closet, checking coat pockets, suitcases, handbags, and shoe boxes, one of which still contained the receipt for the red wedgies she'd been wearing the first time we met. There was a credit-card slip stapled to the receipt and I tucked both in my pocket for later inspection. There was nothing under the bed, nothing stashed behind the chiffonier. I was checking back to see if I'd missed anything when I heard a peculiar warbling from the living room.

"Kinsey, they're back!" Moza wailed, her voice hoarse with dread. From out on the street, I caught the muffled thump of a car door slamming.

"Thanks," I said. Adrenaline flooded through me like water through a storm drain and I could have sworn my heart was boinging up against my tank top as in a cartoon. I did a hasty visual canvas. Everything looked O.K. I reached the door to the hallway, eased out, and pulled it shut behind me, snatching the ring of skeleton keys out of my jeans pocket. The flashlight. Shit! I'd left it on the dressing table.

Murmurs at the front door. Lila and Henry. Moza was making nice, asking about dinner. I yanked the door open and did a running tiptoe to the dressing table, snagged the flashlight, and bounded, like a silent gazelle, back to the door again. I tucked the flashlight up under my arm and prayed that I was inserting the proper key into the lock. A twist to the left and I heard the latch slide into the hole. I turned the key back quietly, extracting it with shaking hands, careful not to let the keys jingle together noisily. I glanced back over my shoulder, at the same time looking for an escape route.

The hallway extended about three feet to the right, where the archway to the living room cut through. At the extreme end of the hall was Moza's bedroom. To my left, there was an alcove for the telephone, a closet, the bathroom, and the kitchen, with an archway to the dining room visible beyond that. The dining room, in turn, opened into the living room again. If they were heading back this way, I had to guess they'd come straight through the archway to my right. I took two giant steps to the left and slipped into the bathroom. The minute I did it, I knew I'd made a bad choice. I should have tried the kitchen, with its outside exit. This was a dead end.

There was a separate shower to my immediate left with an opaque glass door, bathtub adjacent. To my right was a pedestal sink, and next to it, the toilet. The only window in the room was small and probably hadn't been opened in years. By now, I could hear voices growing louder as Lila moved into the hall. I stepped into the enclosed shower and pulled the door shut. I didn't dare latch it. I was certain the distinct sound of the metallic click would carry, alerting her to my presence. I set the flashlight down and held on to the door from the inside, bracing my fingers against the title. I sank down to a crouch, thinking that if someone came in, I'd be less conspicuous if I was hunkered down. The voices in the hall bumbled on and I heard Lila unlock her bedroom door.

The shower was still damp from recent use, scented

with Zest soap. A washrag hanging over the cold-water knob dripped intermittently on my shoulder. I listened intently, but I couldn't hear much. In situations like this, you have to get into the Zen of hiding. Otherwise your knees ache, your leg muscles go into spasms, and pretty soon you lose all sense of caution and just want to leap out, shrieking, regardless of the consequence. I leaned my face on my right arm, looking inward. I could still taste the onion from my sandwich. I was longing to clear my throat. Also I needed to pee. I hoped I wouldn't get caught, because I was going to feel like such an ass if Lila or Henry whipped open the shower door and found me crouching there. I didn't even bother to think up an explanation. There wasn't one.

I lifted my head. Voices in the hall. Lila had come out of her room, locking it after her. Maybe she'd gone in to make sure the hairs were in place. I wondered if I should have confiscated the duplicate licenses while I had the chance. No, better that I left them where they were.

Suddenly the bathroom door flew back and Lila's voice echoed against the bathroom walls like a bullhorn. My heart leapt into action so fast it was like being flung in an icy swimming pool. She was right on the other side of the shower door, her plump form vaguely defined through the milky glass. I closed my eyes like a kid, willing myself invisible.

"I'll be right there, dearie love," she sang from two feet away.

She crossed to the john and I heard the rustle of her

polyester dress and the snap of her girdle as she struggled with it.

Please God, I thought, don't let her decide to take an impromptu shower or a dump. My tension level was so high that I was bound to sneeze or cough or groan or cackle maniacally. I willed myself into a hypnotic state, feeling my armpits dampen with sweat.

The toilet flushed. Lila took forever putting herself back together again. Rustle, pop, snap. I heard her jiggle the handle when the toilet continued to run. She washed her hands, the faucet squeaking as she turned it off. How long could she drag this out? Finally, she moved toward the bathroom door and opened it, and then she was gone, footsteps receding toward the living room. Yakety-yak, chit chat, soft laughter, good-bye sounds, and the front door closed.

I stayed exactly where I was until I heard Moza in the hall.

"Kinsey? They're gone. Are you still here?"

I let out the breath I'd been holding and stood up, shoving my flashlight into my back pocket. This is not a dignified way to make a living, I thought. Hell, I wasn't even getting paid for this. I peered out of the shower door, making sure I hadn't been set up in some elaborate ruse. The house felt quiet except for Moza, who was opening the broom-closet door, still whispering, "Kinsey?"

"I'm in here," I said, voice booming.

I went out into the hall. Moza was so thrilled we hadn't been caught that she couldn't even get mad at me. She leaned against the wall, fanning herself. I figured I better get out of there before they came back for something else, taking ten more years off my projected life-span.

"You're terrific," I murmured. "I'm indebted for life. I'll buy you dinner at Rosie's."

I moved through the kitchen, peering out the back door before I exited. It was fully dark by then, but I made sure the street was deserted before I stepped out of the shadow of Moza's house. Then I walked the half-block toward home laughing to myself. Actually, it's fun to horse around with danger. It's fun to snoop in people's dresser drawers. I might have turned to burgling houses if law enforcement hadn't beckoned to me first. With Lila, I was finally beginning to take control of a situation I didn't like and the surge of power made me feel nearly giddy with relief. I wasn't sure what she was up to, but I intended to find out.

18

When I was safely back in my apartment again, I took out the credit-card receipt I'd lifted from Lila's shoe box. The date on it was May 25 and the store was located in Las Cruces. The credit-card imprint read "Delia Sims." In the box marked "phone number," someone had obligingly penned in a phone number. I hauled out my telephone book and looked up the area code for Las Cruces. Five-oh-five. I picked up the receiver and dialed the number, wondering as I heard it ring on the far end just what I intended to say.

"Hello?" Man's voice. Middle-aged. No accent.

"Oh hello," I said smoothly. "I wonder if I might speak to Delia Sims."

There was a moment of silence. "Hang on."

A palm was secured across the mouthpiece and I could hear muffled conversation in the background.

The receiver was apparently taken over by someone else, because a new voice inquired, "May I help you?"

This one was female and I couldn't classify the age.

"Delia?" I said.

"Who is this, please?" The tone was guarded, as though the call might be obscene.

"Oh, sorry," I said. "This is Lucy Stansbury. That's not you, is it, Delia? It doesn't sound like your voice."

"This is a friend of Delia's. She not here at the moment. Was there something I might help you with?"

"Well, I hope so," I said, mind racing. "Actually, I'm calling from California. I just met Delia recently and she left some of her things in the backseat of my car. I couldn't figure out any other way to reach her except to try this number, which was on a credit-card receipt for a purchase she made in Las Cruces. Is she still in California or is she home again?"

"Just a minute."

Again, a palm across the mouthpiece and the drone of conversation in the background. The woman came back on the line.

"Why don't you give me your name and number and I'll have her get back to you?"

"Oh sure, that's fine," I said. I gave her my name again, spelling it out laboriously and then I made up a telephone number with the area code for Los Angeles. "You want me to mail this stuff back to her or just hang on to it? I'd feel bad if I thought she didn't realize where she'd left it."

"What exactly did she leave?"

"Well, most of it's just clothes. A summer dress I know she's fond of, but I don't guess that matters much. I do have that ring of hers with the square-cut emerald and the little diamond baguettes," I said, describing the ring I'd seen Lila wearing that first after-noon in Henry's garden. "Do you expect her back soon?"

After the barest hesitation, the woman's chill reply came. "Who is this?"

I hung up. So much for trying to fool the folks in Las Cruces. I couldn't imagine what she was up to, but I sure didn't like the notion of this real-estate venture she'd proposed to Henry. He was so smitten, she could probably talk him into anything. She was moving quickly too, and I thought I better come up with some answers before she took him for all he was worth. I reached for a pile of blank index cards in my top desk drawer, and when the phone rang moments later, I jumped. Shit, could someone have put a trace on the call that fast? Surely not.

I lifted the receiver with caution, listening for the white noise of a long-distance connection. There was none.

"Hello?"

"Miss Millhone?" Male. The voice sounded famil-iar, though I couldn't for the moment figure out who it was. Music blasting in the background was forcing him to yell, and I found myself yelling too.

"This is she."

"This is Gus," he hollered, "Bobby's friend from the skate-rental place."

"Oh, it's you. Hello. I'm glad you called. I hope you have some information for me. I could sure use the help."

"Well, I've been thinking about Bobby and I guess I

owe him that much. I should have spoken up this afternoon."

"Don't worry about it. I appreciate your getting back to me. You want to get together or just talk on the phone?"

"Either way is fine. One thing I wanted to mention—and I don't know if this would be a help or not—but Bobby gave me this address book you might want to take a look at. Did he ever talk to you about that?"

"Of course he did. I've been turning the town upside down looking for that thing," I said. "Where are you?"

He gave me an address on Granizo and I said I'd be right there. I hung up the phone and grabbed my handbag and car keys.

Gus's neighborhood was poorly lighted and the yards were flat patches of dirt, graced with occasional palm trees. The cars parked along the curbs were primer-painted low riders with bald tires and ominous dents. My VW fit right in. About every third property boasted a brand-new chain link fence, erected to corral God knows what kind of beast. As I passed one house, I heard something that sounded ugly and snappish scramble forward to the length of its choke chain, whimpering hoarsely when it couldn't quite get to me. I picked up my pace.

Gus lived in a tiny frame cottage in a U-shaped courtyard ringed with cottages. I passed through an ornamental entranceway with the street number in wrought iron arched across it in a rainbow shape. There were eight units altogether, three on each side of a central walkway and two at the end. All were cream-colored and even in the darkness looked drab with soot. I identified Gus's place because the music thundering out was the same stuff I'd heard on the phone. Up close, it didn't sound as good. His front drape consisted of a bedsheet slung over a curtain rod and the knob on his screen was an empty wooden spool on a nail. I had to wait for a brief silence between cuts to pound on the door-frame. The music started up again with a vengeance, but he'd apparently caught my knock.

"Yo!" he called. He opened the door and held the screen for me. I stepped into the room, assaulted by heat, loud rock, and the strong smell of catbox.

"Can you turn that shit down?" I yelled.

He nodded, moving to the stereo, which he flicked off. "Sorry," he said sheepishly. "Have a seat."

His place was about half the size of mine and jammed with twice the furniture. King-sized bed, a big chest of drawers in pecan-wood plastic laminate, the stereo cabinet, sagging brick-and-board bookcases, two upholstered chairs with shredded sides, a space heater, and one of those units the size of a television console, housing sink, stove, and refrigerator. The bathroom was separated from the main room by a panel of material hanging on a length of twine. The room's two lamps were draped with red terry-cloth towels that muted their two-hundred-and-fifty-watt bulbs to a rosy glow. Both chairs were filled with cats, which he seemed to notice about the same time I did.

He gathered one batch of them up by the armload as if they were old clothes and I sat down in the space he had cleared. As soon as he tossed the cats on the bed, they made their way back to their original places. One of them kneaded my lap as if it were a hunk of bread dough and then curled up when he was satisfied with the job he'd done. Another one crowded in beside me and a third one settled on the arm of the chair. They seemed to eye each other, trying to figure out who had the best deal. They appeared to be full-grown and probably from the same litter, as they all sported thick tortoiseshell coats and heads the size of softballs. There were two adolescent cats curled up in the other chair, a buff and a black, tangled together like mismatched socks. A sixth cat emerged from under the bed and paused, pointing each hind foot in turn. Gus watched this feline activity with a shy smile, his face flushed with pride.

"Aren't they great?" he said. "I just never get tired of these little peckerheads. At night, they pile on the bed with me like a quilt. I got one sleeps on my pillow with his feet in my hair. I can kiss their little faces anytime I want." He snatched one up and cradled it like a baby, an indignity the cat endured with surprising passivity.

"How many do you have?"

"Six right now, but Luci Baines and Lynda Bird are both pregnant. I don't know what I'm gonna do about that."

"Maybe you could get them fixed," I said helpfully.

"Well, after this batch is born, I guess I should. I'm real good at finding homes for the kittens, though, and they're always so sweet."

I wanted to mention how good they smelled too, but I didn't have the heart for sarcasm when he was clearly so crazy about his brood. There he was, looking like a police artist's composite of a sex killer, making a fool of himself over this collection of domesticated furs.

"I guess I should have spoken up sooner about this stuff," he was saying. "I don't know what got into me." He crossed to the bookshelf and sorted through the mess on top, coming up with an address book about the size of a playing card, which he held out to me.

I took it, leafing through. "What's the significance? Did Bobby fill you in?"

"Well no. He told me to keep it and he said it was important, but he didn't explain. I just assumed it must be a list or a code, *some* kind of information he had, but I don't know what."

"When did he give you this?"

"I don't remember exactly. It was sometime before the accident. He stopped over one day and gave it to me and asked me if I'd just hold on to it for him, so I said sure. I'd forgotten all about it until you brought it up."

I checked the index tab for *B*. There wasn't a Blackman listed there, but I did find the name penciled inside the back cover, with a seven-digit number beside it. No area code indicated, so it was probably local, though I didn't think it matched the number for S. Blackman I'd found in the telephone book.

"What did he actually say at the time?" I asked. I knew I was repeating myself, but I kept hoping to solicit some indication of Bobby's intent.

"Nothing really. He wanted me to hang on to it is all. He didn't tell you either, huh?"

I shook my head. "He couldn't remember. He knew it was important, but he had no idea why. Have you ever heard the name Blackman? S. Blackman? Anybody Blackman?"

"Nope." The cat was squirming and he put it down.

"I understand Bobby had fallen in love with someone. I wonder if it might have been this S. Blackman."

"If it was, he didn't tell me. A couple of times he did meet some woman down at the beach. Right out in that parking lot by the skate shack."

"Before the accident or afterwards?"

"Before. He'd sit in his Porsche and wait and she'd pull in and then they'd talk."

"He never introduced you or mentioned who she was?"

"I know what she looked like but not her name. I saw 'em go in the coffee shop once and she was built odd, you know? Kind of like a Munchkin. I couldn't figure that out. Bobby was a good-lookin' guy and he always hung out with these real foxy chicks, but she was a dog."

"Blond wispy hair? Maybe forty-five?"

"I never saw her up close so I don't know about her

age, but the hair sounds right. She drives this Mercedes I see around now and then. Dark green with a beige interior. Looks like a 'fifty-five or 'fifty-six, but it's in great shape."

I glanced through the address book again. Sufi's address and telephone number were listed under the D's.

Had he been having an affair with *her*? It seemed so unlikely. Bobby had been twenty-three years old and, as Gus said, a good-looking kid. Carrie St. Cloud had mentioned a blackmailing scheme, but if Sufi was being blackmailed by someone, why would she turn to him for help? Surely it wasn't a matter of her blackmailing *him*. Whatever it was, it gave me a lead and I was grateful for that. I tucked the book in my handbag and looked up. Gus was watching me with amusement.

"God, you should see your face. I could really watch the old wheels turn," he said.

"Things are beginning to happen and I like that," I said. "Listen, this has been a big help. I don't know what it means yet, but believe me, I'll figure it out."

"I hope so. I'm just sorry I didn't speak up when you asked. If there's anything else I can do, just let me know."

"Thanks," I said. I shifted the cat off my lap and got up, shaking hands with him.

I went out to my car, brushing at my jeans, picking cat hair off my lip. It was now ten o'clock at night and I should have headed home, but I was feeling wired. The episode at Moza's and the sudden appearance of Bobby's address book were acting on me like a stimulant. I wanted to talk to Sufi. Maybe I'd stop by her place. If she was up, we could have a little chat. She'd tried once to steer me away from this investigation and I wondered now what that was about.

19

I pulled into the shadows across the street from Sufi's place on Haughland Road in the heart of Santa Teresa. For the most part, the houses I had passed were two-story frame-and-stone on large lots complete with junipers and oaks. Many lawns sported the ubiquitous California crop of alarm-company signs, warning of silent surveillance and armed patrols.

Sufi's yard was darkened by the interlacing tree branches overhead, the property stretching back in a tangle of shrubs and surrounded by a picket fence with wide pales. The house was done in a dark shingle siding, possibly a muted brown or green, though it was hard to tell which at this hour of the night. The side porch was narrow and deeply recessed with no exterior light visible. A dark green Mercedes was parked in the drive to the left.

It was a quiet neighborhood. The sidewalks were deserted and there was no traffic. I got out of my car and crossed to the front of the house. Up close, I could see that the place was massive, the kind being converted now to bed-and-breakfast establishments with odd names: The Gull and Satchel, The Blue Tern, The Quackery. They're all over town these days: renovated Victorian mansions impossibly quaint, where for ninety bucks a night, you can sleep in a bed with a fake brass frame and struggle, the next morning, with a freshly baked croissant that will drop pastry flakes in your lap like dandruff.

From the look of it, Sufi's was still a single-family dwelling, but it had a shabby air. Maybe, like many single women her age, she'd reached that point where the absence of a man translates out to dripping faucets and rain gutters in need of repair. A single woman my age would haul out a crescent wrench or shinny up the down spout, feeling that odd joyousness that comes with self-sufficiency. Sufi had let her property decline to a state of lingering disrepair and it made me wonder what she did with her salary. I thought surgical nurses made good money.

At the rear of the house, there was a glass-enclosed porch, the windows flickering with the blue/gray reflections of a television set. I fumbled my way up several crumbling concrete steps and tapped on the door. After a moment, the porch light came on and Sufi looked through the curtain.

"Hi, it's me," I said. "Can I talk to you?"

She leaned closer to the glass, peering around, apparently checking to see whether I was accompanied by roving bands of thugs.

She opened the door in her robe and slippers, clutching the lapels together at her throat, one arm circling her waist. "Oh my God, you scared me to death," she said. "What are you doing here at this hour? Is something wrong?"

"Not at all. Sorry to alarm you. I was in the neighborhood and I needed to talk to you. Can I come in?"

"I was on my way to bed."

"We can talk out here on the porch, then."

She gave me a grudging look, stepping back reluctantly so I could enter. She was half a head shorter than I and her blond hair was so thin, I could see stretches of scalp underneath. I hadn't pegged her as the type who'd lounge around in a slinky peach satin wrapper and matching mules with dandelion fuzz across the instep. This was hotsy-totsy stuff. I wanted to say, "Hubba-hubba" but I was afraid she'd take offense.

Once inside, I took a quick mental picture and stored it away for future assessment. The room was cluttered, disorganized, and probably unclean judging from the used dishes piled here and there, the dead flowers in a vase, and the wastebasket spilling trash out onto the floor. The water in the bottom of the vase was cloudy with bacteria and probably smelled like the last stages of some disease. There was a crumpled cellophane packet on the arm of the easy chair and I saw that she'd been sneaking Ding Dongs. A *Reader's Digest* condensed book was open facedown on the ottoman. The place smelled like pepperoni pizza, some of which I spied sitting in a box on top of the television set. The heat from the circuitry was keeping it warm, the scent of oregano and mozzarella cheese mingling with the odor of hot cardboard. God, I thought, when did I last eat?

"You live alone?" I asked.

She looked at me as if I were casing the joint. "What of it?"

"I've been assuming you were single. I just realized no one had ever really said as much."

"It's very late to be doing a survey," she said tartly. "What did you want?"

I find it so liberating when other people are rude. It makes me feel mild and lazy and mean. I smiled at her. "I found Bobby's address book."

"Why tell me?"

"I was curious about your relationship with him."

"I didn't have a relationship with him."

"That's not what I hear."

"Well, you heard wrong. Of course I *knew* him. He was Glen's only child and she and I are best friends and have been for years. Aside from that, Bobby and I didn't have that much to say to one another."

"Why'd you need to meet him down at the beach, then?"

"I never 'met' Bobby at the beach," she snapped.

"Somebody saw you with him on more than one occasion."

She hesitated. "Maybe I ran into him once or twice. What's wrong with that? I used to see him at the hospital, too."

"I wondered what you talked about, that's all."

"I'm sure we talked about lots of things," she said. I

could see her shifting gears, trying another tack. Some of the huffiness dropped away. She'd apparently decided to roll out the charm. "God, I don't know what's the matter with me. I'm sorry if I sounded rude. As long as you're here, you might as well sit down. I have wine chilled if you want some."

"I'd like that. Thanks."

She left the room, probably grateful for the chance to stall while she figured out how to cover her tracks. For my part, I was delighted with the opportunity to nose around. I crossed in haste to the easy chair, checking the table beside it. The top was littered with things I didn't want to touch. I eased the drawer open. The interior looked like a catchall for household fallout. Batteries, candles, an extension cord, receipts, rubber bands, packets of matches, two buttons, a sewing kit, pencils, junk mail, a dinner fork, a stapler gun—all of it surrounded by accumulated grit. I ran a hand down along the chair cushion and came up with a nickel, which I left there. I heard the chirp of a wine cork in the kitchen and the tinkle of wineglasses as she removed them from a cabinet. The glass rims began to clink together as she moved back toward the TV room. I abandoned my search and perched myself casually on the arm of the couch.

I was trying to think of something nice to say about her house, but I was secretly worried about my tetanus shots being out of date. This was the kind of place if you had to use the john, you'd want to put paper down on the seat. "Quite a house," I remarked.

Sufi made a face. "The cleaning lady comes tomorrow," she said. "Not that she does much. She worked for my parents for years and I don't have the heart to let her go."

"Do they live with you?"

She shook her head. "Dead. Cancer."

"Both of them?"

"That's the way it goes," she said with a shrug.

So much for family sentiment.

She poured a glass of wine and handed it to me. I could tell from the label, it was the same ultra-crummy stuff I drank before I got into the boxed brand with the picture of a phony-looking vineyard on the front. Clearly, neither of us had the budget or the palate for anything decent.

She settled into the easy chair, wineglass in hand. The change in her manner was conspicuous. She must have come up with a good one while she was gone.

She took a sip of wine, staring at me over the rim of her glass. "Have you talked to Derek lately?" she asked.

"He stopped by my office this afternoon."

"He moved out. When Glen got back from San Francisco this evening, she had the maid pack his bags and put them out in the driveway. Then she changed the locks."

"My, my," I said, "I wonder what brought that on."

"You'd be smart to talk to him before you worry about me."

"Why's that?"

"He had a motive for killing Bobby. I didn't, if that's what you're getting at."

"What motive are you referring to?"

"Glen discovered he'd taken out a big life-insurance policy on Bobby eighteen months ago."

"What?" My wineglass tipped and wine slopped out on my hand. I couldn't disguise the fact that I was startled, but I didn't like the smug look that crossed her face in response.

"Oh yes. The insurance company tracked her down to ask for a copy of the death certificate. I guess the agent read about Bobby in the paper and remembered the name. That's how Glen found out."

"I thought you couldn't take out a policy on someone without their signature."

"Technically, that's true, but it can be done."

I busied myself wiping up spilled wine with a tissue. In the midst of the mop-up procedure, I realized, like a cartoon light bulb going on overhead, that she felt an intense dislike for. Derek. "What's the story?" I asked.

"Derek got caught with his pants down," she said. "His claim is that he got the policy ages ago after Bobby'd totaled his car a couple of times. He thought Bobby would self-destruct. You know the type. One accident after another until the kid winds up dead. It becomes a socially acceptable form of suicide. Personally, I'm not sure Derek was that far off. Bobby drank like a fish and I'm sure he did drugs. He and Kitty were both a mess. Rich and spoiled and self-indulgent—"

"Be careful what you say here, Sufi. I liked Bobby Callahan. I think he had guts."

"I think we're all aware of that," she said. She was using that superior tone of voice that drove me mad, but I couldn't afford to react at this point. She crossed her legs, swinging one foot. The dandelion fuzz on that slipper undulated as the air passed over it. "You may not like it, but it *is* the truth. And that's not all of it. Word has it that Derek took out a policy on Kitty too."

"For how much?"

"Half a million bucks on each."

"Come on, Sufi. That doesn't make any sense. Derek wouldn't kill his own daughter."

"Kitty isn't dead, though, is she?"

"But why would he kill Bobby? He'd have to be nuts. The first thing the cops are going to do is turn around and look at him."

"Kinsey," she said patiently. "Nobody ever said Derek had brains. He's an idiot. A fool."

"He's not that big a fool," I said. "How could he hope to get away with it?"

"Nobody's got any proof that he did anything. There never was any evidence from the first accident and Jim Fraker seems to think this one came about because Bobby had a seizure first. How can they pin that on Derek?"

"But why would he do it? He's got money."

"*Glen's* got money. Derek doesn't have a dime. He'd go for anything that would get him out from under her. Don't you know that?"

All I could do was stare at her, running the information through my mental computer. She took another sip of wine and smiled at me, loving the effect she'd produced.

Finally, I said, "I just don't believe it."

"You can believe anything you like. All I'm saying is you better check that out before you do anything else."

"You don't like Derek, do you?"

"Of course not. I think he's the biggest ass who ever lived. I don't know what Glen saw in him in the first place. He's poor. He's dumb. He's pompous. And those are his *good* qualities," she said with energy. "Aside from all that, he's ruthless."

"He doesn't seem ruthless to me," I said.

"You haven't known him as long as I have. He's a man who'd do anything for money and I suspect he's got lots he's not anxious to discuss. Doesn't he strike you as a man with a past?"

"Like what?"

"I'm not sure. But I'd be willing to bet you his buffoonery is just a cover for something else."

"Are you saying Glen's been hoodwinked? She seems smarter than that."

"She's smart about everything but men. This is her third time around, you know, and Bobby's father was a mess. Husband number two I don't know about. She was living in Europe when she married him and it didn't last long."

"Let's get back to you for a minute. The day of Bobby's funeral, I got the impression you were trying to steer me away from the investigation. Now you're giving me leads. Why the switch?"

She had to stop and pay attention to the tie on her robe, though she was talking to me the whole time. "I guess I thought you'd be prolonging Glen's pain and heartache," she said, looking up at me then. "It's clear now that nothing I say is going to dissuade you in any event, so I might as well tell you what I know."

"Why'd you meet Bobby down at the beach? What was going on?"

"Oh, poo. Nothing," she said. "I ran into him a couple of times and he wanted to bitch about Derek. Bobby couldn't stand him either and he knew I made a good audience. That's all it amounted to."

"Why didn't you say that in the first place?"

"I'm not accountable to you. You show up at my door uninvited and quiz me about all this bullshit. It's none of your business so why should I answer to you? I don't think you know how you come off sometimes."

I felt myself flush at the well-placed insult. I drank the last of my wine. I was having trouble believing her story about meeting Bobby, but it was clear I wasn't going to get much more out of her. I decided to drop it for the moment, but it didn't sit well with me. If she'd only been listening to his complaints, why not just say so to begin with?

A glance at my watch showed that it was just after eleven and I decided to try to catch Glen at home. I excused myself abruptly and got out. I'm sure the haste of my departure wasn't lost on her.

There are times when things begin to break by sheer dint of dumb luck. I don't pretend to take credit for what happened next. By the time I got to my little VW, I realized how chilly it was. I hopped in and shut the door, locking it as is my habit, and then I turned and started rooting around in my junky backseat for a sweatshirt I'd tossed back there. I'd just laid my hands on it and I was in the process of hauling it out from under a pile of books when I heard a car start up. I glanced to my right. Sufi's Mercedes was being backed out of the driveway. I did a quick surface dive, disappearing from view. I wasn't sure if she knew my car or not, but she must have assumed I was gone because she pulled straight off. As soon as she did, I rolled into the driver's seat, fumbling for my keys. I started the car and did a quick U-turn, catching a glimpse of her taillights as she hung a right, heading toward State Street.

She couldn't have had time enough to change her clothes. At best, she might have thrown a coat over her satin lounging outfit. Who did she know well enough to visit unannounced in a Jean Harlow getup at this hour of the night? I couldn't wait to see.

20

In Santa Teresa, the rich are divided into two cliques: half live in Montebello, half in Horton Ravine. Montebello is the old money, Horton Ravine, the new. Both communities have acres of old trees, bridle paths, and country clubs requiring proper sponsorship and entrance fees of twenty-five grand. Both communities discourage fundamentalist churches, tacky yard ornaments, and door-to-door sales. Sufi was headed for Horton Ravine.

As she passed through the main gates on Los Piratas, she slowed to thirty miles an hour, reluctant perhaps to get picked up for speeding while dressed like a call girl on her way to a john. I slowed my car at a pace with hers, hanging back as far as I could. I was worried about having to pursue her along miles of winding road, but she surprised me by turning into one of the first driveways on the right. The house was set back about a hundred yards, a one-story California "bungalow": maybe five bedrooms, four thousand square feet, not remarkable to look at, but expensive nevertheless.

The property was probably five acres all told, surrounded by an ornamental split-rail fence, with rambling roses laid along its length. Exterior lights had come on when Sufi's Mercedes reached the house. She got out of the car in a blur of peach satin and mink, moving toward the front door, which opened and swallowed her up.

I had passed the house by then. I drove on as far as the first road on the right, where I did a turnaround, dousing my headlights as I drifted back. I parked my car on the berm on the left-hand side, hugging some shrubs. The area was shrouded in darkness, no streetlights at all. Across from me, the tag end of the golf course was visible and the narrow artificial lake that served as a water hazard. Moonlight glimmered on the surface of the lake, making it as glossy as a remnant of gray silk.

I removed the flashlight from the glove compartment and got out of my car, picking my way carefully through the tall grass growing by the road. It was thick and wet, soaking my tennis shoes and the legs of my jeans.

I reached the driveway. There wasn't any name on the mailbox, but I noted the numbers. I could always stop by my office and check my crisscross directory if I needed to. I had gone about halfway up the drive when I heard a dog barking at the house. I had no idea what kind it was, but it sounded big—one of those dogs that knows how to bark from its balls—deep, businesslike barks, suggestive of sharp teeth and a bad attitude. Furthermore, that sucker had picked up my scent and was anxious to make contact. There was no way I could creep any closer without alerting the occupants of the house. They were probably already wondering what was making Old Dog Tray wet himself with excitement. For all I knew, they'd release him from his three-eighths-inch chain and send him flying down the driveway after me, toenails scratching along the blacktop. I've been chased by dogs before and it's not that much fun.

I reversed my course and got back in the car. Common sense is no disgrace in the private-eye trade. I watched the house for an hour, but there was no sign of activity. I was getting tired and this felt like a waste of time. Finally, I started the engine and eased the car into gear, not flipping on my headlights until I was out through the gate again.

By the time I got home, I was exhausted. I made a few quick notes and packed it in for the night. It was nearly one o'clock when I finally turned out the light. I got up at six and did a three-mile run just to get my head on straight. Then I sped through my morning ablutions, grabbed an apple, and arrived at the office by seven. It was Tuesday and I was thankful I wasn't scheduled for physical therapy that day. Now that I thought about it, my arm was feeling pretty good, or maybe the fact that I was involved in an investigation distracted me from whatever pain or immobility remained.

There were no messages on my answering machine and no mail that needed dealing with from the day before. I hauled out my crisscross and checked the house numbers on Los Piratas. Well, well. I should have guessed. Fraker, James and Nola. I wondered which of them Sufi had gone to see and why the rush. It was possible, of course, that she'd consulted with both, but I couldn't quite picture that. Could Nola be the woman Bobby'd fallen in love with? I couldn't see how Dr. Fraker tied into this, but something was sure going on.

I took out Bobby's address book and tried the number for Blackman. I got a recorded message from that woman who sounds like the fairy godmother in a Walt Disney cartoon. "We're sorry, but the number you've dialed cannot be connected in the eight-oh-five area code. Please check the number and dial again. Thank you." I tried the codes for surrounding areas. No luck. I spent a long time looking through the other entries in the book. If all else failed, I'd have to sit here and contact each person in turn, but it seemed like a tiresome prospect and not necessarily productive. In the meantime, what?

It was too early in the morning to make house calls, but it occurred to me that a visit to Kitty might make sense. She was still at St. Terry's and, given hospital routine, she'd probably been rousted out of bed at dawn. I hadn't seen her for days anyway and she might be of help.

The chill of the day before was gone. The air was clear and the sun was already intense. I slid my VW into the last available space in the vistors' lot and went around to the front entrance. The information desk in the lobby was deserted but the hospital itself was in full swing. The coffee shop was jammed, the scent of cholesterol and caffeine wafting irresistibly through the open doorway. Lights were on in the gift shop. The cashier's office was busy, filled with young female clerks preparing final bills as if this were some grand hotel nearing check-out time. There was an aura of excitement—medical personnel gearing up for birth and death and complex surgeries, cracked bones and breakdowns and drug overdoses . . . a hundred life-threatening episodes any given day of the week. And through it all the insidious sexuality that made it the stuff of soaps.

I went up to the third floor, turning left when I got off the elevators near 3 South. The big double doors were locked, as usual. I pushed the buzzer. After a moment, a heavyset black woman in jeans and a royal blue T-shirt rattled some keys and opened the door a crack. She wore a nursy no-nonsense watch and those shoes with two-inch crepe soles designed to offset fallen arches and varicose veins. She had startling hazel eyes and a face that radiated competence. Her white plastic tag indicated that her name was Natalie Jacks, LVN. I showed Ms. Jacks the photostat of my license and asked if I could talk to Kitty Wenner, explaining that I was a friend of the family.

She looked my I.D. over carefully and finally stepped back to let me in.

She locked the door behind me and led the way down the corridor to a room near the end. I was sneaking peeks into rooms along the way. I don't know what I anticipated—women writhing and babbling to themselves, men imitating ex-Presidents and jungle beasts.

Or the lot of them in a drug-induced stupor that would swell their tongues and make their eyes roll back in their heads. Instead, as I passed each door, I saw faces raised in curiosity toward mine, as if I were a new admission who might shriek or do birdcalls while I tore off my clothes. I couldn't see any difference between them and me, which I thought was worrisome.

Kitty was up and dressed, her hair still wet from a shower. She was stretched out on her bed, pillows propped up behind her, a breakfast tray on the bed-table next to her. She wore a silk caftan that drooped on her frame as if she were a coat hanger. Her breasts were no bigger than buttons on a couch and her arms were bare bones fleshed out with skin as thin as tissue paper. Her eyes were enormous and haunted, the shape of her skull so pronounced that she looked as if she were seventy. Sally Struthers could have used her picture in an ad for foster parenting.

"You got a visitor," Natalie said.

Kitty's eyes flicked to me, and for a moment, I could see how scared she was. She was dying. She had to know that. The energy was seeping out of her pores like sweat.

Natalie inspected the breakfast tray. "You know they're going to put you on an I.V. if you don't do better than this. I thought you had a contract with Dr. Kleinert."

"I *ate* some," Kitty said.

"Well, I'm not supposed to pester you, but he'll be doing rounds soon. Try picking away at this while you talk to her, O.K.? We're on your team, baby. Honestly."

Natalie gave us both a brief smile and left, moving into the room next door, where we could hear her talking to someone else.

Kitty's face was suffused with pink and she was fighting back tears. She reached for a cigarette and lit it, coughing some against the back of her bony hand. She shook her head, conjuring up a smile that had some sweetness to it. "God, I can't believe I got myself into this," she said, and then wistfully, "You think Glen might come see me?"

"I don't know. I may go over there after I talk to you. I'll mention it to her if you like."

"She kicked Daddy out."

"So I heard."

"She'll probably kick me out next."

I couldn't look at her anymore. Her longing for Glen was so tangible it hurt me to see it. I studied the breakfast tray: a fresh fruit cup, a blueberry muffin, a carton of strawberry yogurt, granola, orange juice, tea. There was no indication that she'd eaten any of it.

"You want some of that?" she asked.

"No way. You'll tell Kleinert you ate it."

Kitty had the good grace to blush, laughing uneasily.

"I don't understand why you don't eat," I said.

She made a face. "Everything just looks so gross. There's this girl two doors down and she was suffering from anorexia, you know? So they brought her in here and she finally started to eat? Now she looks like she's pregnant. She's still thin. She's just got half a basketball for a stomach. It's disgusting."

"So what? She's alive, isn't she?"

"I don't want to look like that. Nothing tastes good anyway and it just makes me throw up."

There was no point in pursuing the subject so I let it go, shifting over to something else instead. "Have you talked to your father since Glen kicked him out?"

Kitty shrugged. "He's here every day in the afternoon. He's moved into the Edgewater Hotel until he finds a place."

"Did he tell you about Bobby's will?"

"Some. He says Bobby left me all this money. Is that true?" Her tone was one of dismay as much as anything.

"As far as I know, it is."

"But why would he do that?"

"Maybe he felt like he messed up your life and wanted to do right by you. Derek tells me he left some money to Rick's parents too. Or maybe he considered it a little incentive for you to get your shit together for a change."

"I never made any deals with him."

"I don't think he meant to make a 'deal.'"

"Well, I don't like to feel controlled."

"Kitty, I think you've demonstrated the fact that you can't be controlled. We're all getting that message loud and clear. Bobby loved you."

"Who asked him to? Sometimes I wasn't even nice to him. And I didn't exactly have his best interests at heart."

"Meaning what?"

"Nothing. Skip it. I wish he hadn't left me anything is all. It makes me feel crummy."

"I don't know what to tell you," I said.

"Well, I never asked him for a thing." Her tone was argumentative, but I couldn't understand what her position was.

"What's bothering you?"

"Nothing."

"What's all the fretting about, then?"

"I'm not fretting! God. Why should I fret? He did it so he'd feel good, right? It had nothing to do with me."

"It had *something* to do with you or he'd have left the money to someone else."

She started gnawing on her thumbnail, temporarily abandoning the cigarette, which sat on the lip of the ashtray and sent up a tiny trail of smoke like an Indian signal on a distant mountaintop. Her mood was getting dark. I wasn't sure why she was so upset at the notion of two million dollars being dumped in her lap, but I didn't want to alienate her. I wanted information. I shifted the subject again. "What about the insurance your father took out on Bobby's life? Did he mention that?"

"Yeah. That's weird. He does stuff like that, and later, he can't understand why people get upset. He doesn't see anything wrong with it at all. To him, it just makes sense. Bobby'd cracked up his car once or twice so Daddy just figured if he died, somebody might as well benefit. I guess that's why Glen threw him out, huh?"

"I think that's a safe bet. She'd never tolerate his profiting from Bobby's death. My God, it was the worst possible move he could have made as far as she's concerned. Besides which, it sets him up as a murder suspect."

"My father wouldn't kill anyone!"

"That's what he says about you."

"Well, it's true. I didn't have any reason to want Bobby dead. Neither of us did. I didn't even know about the money and I don't want it anyway."

"Money might not be the motive," I said. "It's an obvious place to start, but it doesn't necessarily go anywhere."

"But you don't think Daddy did it, do you?"

"I haven't made up my mind about that yet. I'm still trying to figure out what Bobby was up to and I need to fill in some gaps. Something was going on back then and I can't get a line on it. What was his relationship to Sufi? You have any idea?"

Kitty picked up her cigarette, averting her gaze. She took a moment to tap the ash from the end, and then she took a last, deep drag and put it out. Her nails were bitten down so far the pads of the fingers seemed like little round balls.

She was debating something with herself. I kept my mouth shut and gave her some room. "She was a contact," she said finally, her voice low. "Bobby was doing this investigation or something for somebody else."

"Who?"

"I don't know."

"It had to be the Frakers, right? I talked to Sufi last night, and the minute I left, she hightailed it over to their place. She was in there so long, I finally had to go home."

Kitty's eyes came up to mine. "I don't know for sure what it was."

"But how'd he get into it? What was it about?"

"All I know is he told me he was looking for something and he got the job out at the morgue so he could search at night."

"Medical records? Something stored out there?"

Her face closed down again and she shrugged.

"But Kitty, when you realized someone was trying to kill him, didn't you figure it was connected to that?"

She was chewing on her thumbnail in earnest by now. I saw her eyes flick and I turned around. Dr. Kleinert was standing in the doorway, staring at her. When he realized I'd seen him, he looked over at me. His smile seemed forced and it was not full of merriment.

"Well. I didn't know you were entertaining this morning," he said to her. Then briefly to me, "What brings you in so bright and early?"

"I just stopped by on my way to Glen's. I've been trying to persuade Kitty to eat," I said.

"No need for that," he said easily. "This young lady has an agreement with me." He gave a practiced glance at his watch, adjusting the face of it on his wrist before it disappeared up his cuff again. "I hope you'll excuse us. I have other patients to see and my time is limited."

"I'm on my way out," I said. I glanced at Kitty. "I may give you a call in a little while. I'll see if Glen can stop in to visit you."

"Great," she said. "Thanks."

I waved and moved out of the room, wondering how

long he'd been standing there and how much he'd heard. I was trying to remember what Carrie St. Cloud had said. She'd told me Bobby was involved in some kind of blackmail scheme, but not the usual kind with money changing hands. Something else. "Somebody had something on some friend of his and he was trying to help out," was the way she'd put it as nearly as I could remember. If it was extortion, why didn't he go to the police? And why was it up to him to do anything?

I got back in my car and headed out to Glen's place.

21

It was just after nine when I pulled into Glen's driveway. The courtyard was deserted. The fountain sent up a column of water fifteen feet high, cascading back on itself in a tumble of pale green and white. I could hear a power mower whining from one of the terraces in the rear and rainbirds were jetting a fine spray into the giant fern, dappled with sunlight, that bordered the gravel walks. The air seemed tropical, scented with jasmine.

I rang the bell and one of the maids admitted me. I asked for Glen and she murmured something in Spanish, raising her eyes to the second floor. I gathered that Glen was upstairs.

The door to Bobby's room was open and she was seated in one of his easy chairs, hands in her lap, her face impassive. When she caught sight of me, she smiled almost imperceptibly. She was looking drawn, dark lines etched under her eyes. Her makeup was subtle, but it only seemed to emphasize the pallor in her cheeks. She wore a knit dress in a shade of red too harsh for her. "Hello, Kinsey. Come sit down," she said.

I sat in the matching plaid chair. "How are you doing?"

"Not that well. I find myself spending much of the day up here. Just sitting. Waiting for Bobby."

Her eyes strayed to mine. "I don't mean that literally, of course. I'm far too rational a person to believe the dead return. I keep thinking there's something more, that it can't be over yet. Do you know what I mean?"

"No. Not quite."

She stared at the floor, apparently consulting her inner voices. "Part of it is a feeling of betrayal, I think. I was brave and I did everything I was supposed to. I was a trouper and now I want the payoff. But the only reward that interests me is having Bobby back. So I wait." Her gaze moved around the room as if she were taking a series of photographs. Her manner seemed very flat to me, despite the emotional content of her speech. It was curious, like talking to a robot. She said human things, but mechanically. "You see that?"

I followed her eyes. Bobby's footprints were still visible on the white carpeting.

"I won't let them vacuum in here," she said. "I know it's stupid. I don't want to turn into one of those dreadful women who erect a shrine for the dead, keeping everything just as it was. But I don't want him erased. I don't want him wiped out like that. I don't even want to go through his belongings."

"There's no need to do anything yet, is there?"

"No. I guess not. I don't know what I'll do with the room anyway. I have dozens and they're all empty. It's not like I need to convert it into a sewing room or a studio."

"Are you taking care of yourself otherwise?"

"Oh, yes. I know enough to do that. I feel like grief is an illness I can't recover from. What worries me is I notice there's a certain attraction to the process that's hard to give up. It's painful, but at least it allows me to feel close to him. Once in a while, I catch myself thinking of something else and then I feel guilty. It seems disloyal not to hurt, disloyal to forget even for a moment that he's gone."

"Don't get mean with yourself and suffer more than you have to," I said.

"I know. I'm trying to wean myself. Every day I mourn a little less. Like giving up cigarettes. In the meantime, I pretend to be a whole person, but I'm not. I wish I could think of something that would heal me. Ah, God, I shouldn't go on and on about it. It's like someone who's had a heart attack or major surgery. It's all I can talk about. So self-centered."

Again, she paused and then she seemed to remember polite behavior. She looked at me. "What have you been doing?"

"I went over to St. Terry's this morning to see Kitty."

"Oh?" Glen's expression was devoid of interest.

"Is there any chance you might stop by to see her?"

"Absolutely none. For one thing, I'm furious that

she's alive while Bobby's not. I hate it that he left her all that money. As far as I'm concerned, she's grasping, self-destructive, manipulative—" She broke off, closing her mouth. She was silent for a moment. "Sorry. I don't mean to be so vehement. I never liked her. Just because she's in trouble now doesn't change anything. She's done it to herself. She thought there'd always be someone who'd bail her out, but it won't be me. And Derek's not capable of it."

"I heard he left."

She stirred restlessly. "We had a terrible fight. I didn't think I'd ever get him out of here. I finally had to call one of the gardeners. I despise him. Truly. It makes me sick to think he was ever in my bed. I don't know which is worse . . . the fact that he took out that ghoulish policy on Bobby's life or the fact that he hadn't the faintest sense how despicable it was."

"Can he collect?"

"He seems to think so, but I intend to fight him every step of the way. I've put the insurance company on notice and I've contacted a firm of lawyers in L.A. I want him out of my life. I don't really care what it costs, though the less of mine he gets the better. Fortunately, we signed premarital agreements, though he swears he'll challenge me on that if I thwart his insurance claim."

"Jesus, you're really drawing up battle lines."

She rubbed her forehead wearily. "God, it was horrible. I called Varden to see if I can get a restraining order out on him. It's lucky there wasn't a gun in the house or one of us would be dead."

I was silent.

After a moment, she seemed to collect herself. "I don't mean to sound so crazy. Everything I say comes out so manic somehow. Anyway. Enough of that. I'm sure you didn't come here to listen to me rave. Would you like some coffee?"

"No thanks. I just wanted to touch base with you and bring you up to date. Most of this has to do with Bobby, so if you don't want to talk about it now, I can stop back another time."

"No, no. That's fine. Maybe it will give me something new to think about. I do want you to find out who killed him. It may be the only form of relief I can look forward to. What have you come up with so far?"

"Not a lot. I'm putting it together piece by piece and I'm not really sure of my facts. For one thing, I may have people lying to me, but since I don't really know the truth, I can't be sure," I said.

"I understand."

I hesitated, oddly reluctant to pass on my conjecture. It felt intrusive to speculate about his past, in poor taste somehow to discuss the intimate details of his life with the woman who was trying so hard to cope with his death. "I think Bobby was having an affair."

"That's not surprising. I think I mentioned that he was dating someone."

"Not her. Nola."

She stared at me as though waiting for the punch line. Finally, she said, "You can't be serious."

"From what I've heard, Bobby was having an affair with someone and he fell in love. That's why he broke up with Carrie St. Cloud in the first place. I have reason to believe it was Nola Fraker, though I haven't confirmed it yet."

"I don't like that. I hope that's not true."

"I don't know what to tell you. It seems to fit the facts."

"I thought you said he was in love with Kitty."

"Maybe not 'in love.' I think he loved her a lot. That doesn't mean he acted on it. She claims there was nothing going on between them and I tend to believe her. If they'd had a sexual relationship, I'm sure you'd have been the first to know—for the shock value if nothing else. You know how she is. She's obviously immature and confused and he was certainly aware of your attitude toward her. Anyway, whatever he felt for her wouldn't have precluded an involvement with someone else."

"But Nola's happily married. She and Jim have been here dozens of times. There was never even a hint of anything between her and Bobby."

"I hear what you're saying, Glen, but that's the way the game is played. You're having a clandestine affair. You and your lover end up at the same social event and walk around chatting politely, ignoring each other . . . but not too pointedly because that would be conspicuous. Sly little hand touches by the punch bowl, secret glances across the room. It's a big hot joke and later you giggle about it in bed like a couple of kids because you put one over on the grown-ups."

"But why Nola? The whole idea is ludicrous."

"Not at all. She's a beautiful woman. Maybe they ran into each other and suddenly the spark was there. Or maybe they'd been eyeing each other for years. Actually, it must have started last summer because I don't think his relationship to her could have overlapped his to Carrie by much. He didn't strike me as the type who'd have two affairs running at the same time."

Glenn's expression changed and she glanced at me with apparent discomfort.

"What?"

"I just remembered. Derek and I were in Europe for two months last summer. When we got back, I noticed we were suddenly seeing more of the Frakers, but I shrugged it off. You know how it is. Sometimes you see a lot of another couple and then they drop out of your life for a while. I just can't believe she'd do that to me or to Jim. It makes me feel like a jealous spouse. Like I've been duped."

"But Glen, come on. Maybe it was the best thing that ever happened to him. Maybe it helped him grow up some. Who knows? Bobby was a good kid. What difference could it possibly make at this point anyway?" I said. It felt mean but I didn't want her getting into this bullshit of denying who he was and what he did.

Her cheeks had taken on a tint of pink and she turned a cold eye toward me. "I get the message. I still don't understand why you're telling me this."

"Because it's not up to me to shield you from the truth."

"It's not up to you to carry tales either."

"Yes. All right. You're right about that. I'm not into gossip for the sake of it. There's a chance that it's tied up with Bobby's death."

"How?"

"I'll get to that, but I have to have your assurances first that this won't go any further."

"What's the connection?"

"Glen, you're not listening. I'll tell you as much as I can, but I can't tell you everything and I don't want you flying off the handle. If you turn around and repeat this to anyone, you could be putting both of us in jeopardy."

Her eyes came into focus and I felt she was finally taking in what I was saying. "I'm sorry. Of course. I won't say a word to anyone."

I told her briefly about Bobby's last message on my answering machine, and about the blackmail scheme, which I still didn't understand. I deleted mention of Sufi's part in all of this because I was still worried Glen would take matters into her own hands and do something dumb. She seemed volatile right now, unstable, like a vial of nitroglycerin. One minor bump and she might blow.

"I do need your help," I said when I finished.

"Doing what?"

"I want to talk to Nola. So far I still don't have confirmation on this and if I call or stop by out of a clear blue sky, it's going to scare the shit out of her. I'd like you to call her and see if you can set something up."

"For when?"

"This morning if possible."

"What would you want me to say to her?"

"Tell her the truth. Tell her I'm looking into Bobby's death, that we think he may have been involved with some woman last summer, and since you were gone, you thought maybe she might have seen him around with someone. Ask her if she'd mind talking to me."

"Won't she suspect? Surely, she'll figure out that you're onto her."

"Well, for starters, I could be wrong. Maybe it's not her. That's what I'm trying to determine. If she's innocent, she won't care one way or the other. And if she's not, let her cook up a cover so she'll feel secure. I don't care. The point is, she won't have the balls to shut the door in my face, which is what she'd probably do if I went over there unannounced."

She considered briefly. "All right."

She got up and crossed to the telephone on the night stand, punching in Nola's number from memory. She handled the request as deftly as anything I'd ever heard, and I could see how good she must be at fundraising. Nola couldn't have been nicer or more cooperative and in fifteen minutes I was on my way back to Horton Ravine.

By day, I could see that the Frakers' house was pale yellow with a shake roof. I went up the driveway and pulled onto the parking pad to the left of the house, where a dark maroon BMW and a silver Mercedes were parked. As I was not feeling suicidal, I leaned out of my car window, looking for the dog. Rover or Fido, whatever his name was, turned out to be a great dane with rubbery black-rimmed lips, complete with strings of slobber hanging down. From that distance, I swear it looked like his collar was studded with spikes. His food dish was a wide aluminum bowl with bite marks around the rim.

I got out of the car cautiously. He ran up to the fence and started barking bad breath in my direction. He stood up on his hind legs, his front paws tucked over the gate. His dick looked like a hot dog in a long, furry bun and he wagged it at me like a guy who's just stepped out of a phone booth to open his raincoat.

I was just on the verge of insulting him when I realized that Nola had come out on the porch behind me.

"Don't mind him," she said. She was wearing another jump suit, this one black, with spike heels that made her half a head taller than me.

"Nice pup," I remarked. People always love it when you say their dogs are nice. Just shows you how out of touch they are.

"Thanks. Come on in. I have something to do first, but you can wait in the den."

22

The interior of the Fraker house was cool and spare; gleaming dark wood floors, white walls, bare windows, fresh flowers. The furniture was upholstered in white linen and the den into which Nola ushered me was lined with books. She excused herself and I heard her high heels tap-tap-tapping away down the hall.

It's never a good idea to leave me in a room by myself. I'm an incurable snoop and I search automatically. Having been raised from the age of five by an unmarried aunt, I spent a lot of time as a child in the homes of her friends, most of whom had no children of their own. I was told to keep quiet and amuse myself, which I managed in the first five minutes with the latest in an endless series of coloring books we brought with us when visiting. The problem was that I was terrible at keeping in the lines and the pictures always seemed dumb to me—little children frolicking with dogs and visiting farms. I didn't like to color chickens or hogs, so I learned to search. In this manner, I discovered people's hidden lives—the prescriptions in the medicine cabinets, tubes of jelly in bed-table drawers, cash reserves in the back of coat closets, startling sex manuals and marital artifacts between the mattress and box springs. Of course, I could never quiz my aunt afterward about the extraordinary-looking objects I came across because I wasn't supposed to know about them in the first place. Fascinated, I would wander into the kitchen, where the adults in those days seemed to congregate, drinking highballs and talking about achingly dull things like politics and sports, and I would stare at women named Bernice and Mildred whose husbands were named Stanley and Edgar, and I would wonder who did what with the long doodad with the battery stuck in one end. It was not a flashlight. That much I knew. Early on, I discerned the sometimes remarkable distinction between public appearances and private tastes. These were the people my aunt forbade me to swear in front of no matter how we talked at home. Some of the phrases she used, I thought might have application here, but I could never confirm this. The whole process of education for me was learning the proper words to attach to things I already knew.

The Frakers' den exhibited a shocking lack of hiding places. No drawers, no cabinets, no end tables with cupboards underneath. The two chairs were chrome with leather straps. The coffee table was glass with narrow chrome legs, sporting a decanter of brandy and two snifters on a tray. There wasn't even a carpet to peek under. Jesus, what kind of people were they? I was reduced to touring the bookshelves, trying to divine their hobbies and avocations from the volumes on hand.

People do tend to hang on to hardbacked books, and I could see that Nola had gone through interior design, gourmet cooking, gardening, needlework, and personal beauty hints. What caught my attention, however, were the two shelves lined with books on architecture. What was that about? Surely, neither she nor Dr. Fraker was commissioned to design buildings in their spare time. I took out an oversized volume called *Architectural Graphic Standards* and checked the flyleaf. The engraved bookplate showed a lithograph of a seated cat staring at a fish in a bowl. Under the Ex Libris, the name Dwight Costigan was scratched in a masculine hand. A reminder bell tinkled at the back of my brain. I thought he was the architect who designed Glen's house. A borrowed book? I checked three more in rapid succession. All of them were "from the library of" Dwight Costigan. That was odd. Why here?

I heard Nola tapping back in my direction and I slipped the book into place, then eased over to the window and acted as though I'd occupied my time by looking out. She came into the den with a smile that went on and off again like a loose connection. "Sorry you had to wait. Have a seat."

I hadn't really given a lot of thought to how I was going to handle this. Every time I rehearse these little playlets in advance, I'm brilliant and the other characters say exactly what I want to hear. In reality, nobody gets it right, including me, so why worry about it before the fact?

I sat down in one of the chrome-and-leather chairs, hoping I wouldn't get lodged in the straps. She sat down on the edge of a white linen love seat, resting one hand gracefully on the surface of the glass coffee table in an attitude that suggested serenity, except that she was leaving little pads of perspiration at her finger-tips. I took in the sight of her at a quick glance. Slim, long-legged, with those perfect apple-sized breasts. Her hair was a paid-for shade of red, framing her face in a tumble of soft waves. Blue eyes, flawless skin. She had that clear ageless look that comes with first-rate cosmetic surgery, and the black jumpsuit she wore emphasized her lush body without being vulgar or crass. Her manner was solemn and sincere, and struck me as false.

"What can I help you with?" she asked.

I had a split second in which to make a judgment. Could Bobby Callahan *truly* have gotten involved with a woman as phony as this? Oh hell, who was I trying to kid? Of course!

I gave her a fifteen-watt smile, resting my chin on my fist. "Well, I have a little problem, Nola. May I call you Nola?"

"Certainly. Glen mentioned you were investigating Bobby's death."

"That's true. Actually Bobby just hired me a week ago and I feel like I ought to give him his money's worth."

"Oh. I thought maybe there was something wrong and that was why you were looking into it."

"There might be. I don't know yet."

"But shouldn't the police be doing that?"

"I'm sure they are. I'm conducting a . . . you know, an auxiliary investigation, just in case they're on the wrong track."

"Well, I hope somebody figures it out. Poor kid. We all feel so bad for Glen. Are you having any luck?"

"As a matter of fact, I am. Somebody told me half the story and all I have to do is figure out the rest."

"It sounds like you're doing pretty well, then." She hesitated delicately. "What kind of story?"

I suspect she didn't really want to ask, but the nature of the conversation dictated that she must. She was pretending to cooperate so, of course, she had to feign interest in a subject she'd probably prefer to ignore.

I let a moment pass while I stared down at the table-top. I thought it lent a note of credibility to the lie I was about to tell. I looked back at her, making significant eye contact. "Bobby told me he was in love with you."

"With me?"

"That's what he said."

The eyes blinked. The smile went off and on. "Well, I'm astonished. I mean, it's very flattering and I always thought he was a sweet kid, but really!"

"I didn't find it that astonishing."

Her laugh conveyed a wonderful combination of innocence and disbelief. "Oh, for heaven's sake. I'm married. And I'm twelve years older than he is."

Shit, she was quick—shaving years off her age without pausing to count on her fingers or anything. I'm not that fast at subtraction so it's probably fortunate that I don't lie about how old I am.

I smiled slightly. She was pissing me off and I found myself using a mild, deadly tone. "Age doesn't matter. Bobby's dead now. He's older than God. He's as old as anybody's ever going to get."

She stared at me, cuing in to the fact that I was mad. "You don't have to get nasty about it. I can't help it if Bobby Callahan decided he was in love with me. So the kid had a crush on me. So what?"

"So the kid had an *affair* with you, Nola. That's what. You got your tit in a wringer and the kid was helping you out. The *kid* was murdered because of you, ass eyes. Now, shall we quit bullshitting each other and get down to business on this or shall I call Lieutenant Dolan down at Homicide and let him have a chat with you?"

"I don't know what you're talking about," she snapped. She got up, but I was already on my feet and I clamped a hand around that dainty wrist so fast she gasped. She gave a little jerk and I released her, but I could feel myself expand with anger like a hot-air balloon.

"I'm telling you, Nola. You've got a choice. You tell me what was going on or I'm going to start leaning on you. In fact, I may do that anyway. I'll whip on down to the courthouse and I'll start going through public records and newspaper accounts and police files until I get a little background information on you and then I'm going to figure out what you're hiding and *then* I'm going to find a way to stick it to you so bad you'll wish you'd blabbed the whole story out right here."

That's when I got the jolt. In the back of my brain, I heard a sound like a parachute catching air. Thwunk . . . it opened up. It was one of those extraordinary moments when automatic recall clicks in and a piece of information pops up like a flash card. It must have been the adrenaline pumping through my head because I suddenly retrieved some data from my memory bank and it appeared on my mental screen just as clear as could be . . . not the whole of it, but enough. "Wait a minute. I know who you are. You were married to Dwight Costigan. I knew I'd seen you somewhere. Your picture was in all the papers."

Her face drained of color. "That has nothing to do with this," she said.

I laughed, primarily because sudden recollection does that to me. A mental leap has a little chemical component to it that gives a quick rush.

"Oh come on," I said. "It does connect. I don't know how yet, but it's all the same tale, isn't it?"

She sank back down on the love seat, one hand reaching for the glass tabletop to steady herself. She breathed deeply, trying to relax. "You would do well to let this pass," she said, not looking at me.

"Are you nuts?" I said. "Are you out of your tiny mind? Bobby Callahan hired me because he thought somebody was trying to kill him and he was right. He's dead now and he's got no way to rectify the situation, but *I* do and if you think I'll back off this sucker, you don't know me."

She was shaking her head. All the beauty was gone and what remained seemed drab. She looked, then, like we all look in fluorescent lighting—tired, sallow, shopworn. Her voice was low. "I'll tell you what I can. And then I beg you to drop the investigation. I mean that. For your own good. I did have an affair with Bobby." She paused, searching for the path she wanted to take. "He was a wonderful person. He really was. I was crazy about him. He was so uncomplicated and he had no history. He was just young and healthy, vigorous. God. He was twenty-three. Even the sight of his *skin*. He was like a—" Her eyes came up to mine and she broke off with embarrassment, a smile forming and faltering, this time from some emotion I couldn't read . . . pain or tenderness, perhaps.

I eased into the chair carefully, hoping I wouldn't spoil the mood.

"When you're that age," she said, "you still think things can be made right. You still think you can have anything you want. You think life's simple, that you only have to do one or two little things and it will all turn around. I told him it wasn't like that for me, but he had a streak of gallantry in him. Sweet fool."

She was silent for a long time.

" 'Sweet fool,' what?" I said quietly.

"Well, he died for it, of course. I can't tell you the guilt I've felt. . . ." She trailed off and she looked away.

"Tell me the front end. How does Dwight fit in? He was shot, right?"

"Dwight was much older than I. Forty-five when we were married. I was twenty-two. It was a good marriage . . . up to a point at any rate. He adored me. I admired him. He did incredible things for this town."

"He designed Glen's house, didn't he?"

"Not really. His father was the original architect when the house was built back in the twenties. Dwight did the restoration," she said. "I think I need a drink. Do you want one?"

"Sure, that's fine," I said.

She reached for the brandy decanter, removing the heavy glass stopper. She laid the neck of the decanter against the edge of one of the snifters, but her hands were shaking so badly I thought she'd crack the glass. I reached over and took the bottle from her, pouring her a stiff shot. I poured myself one too, though at ten in the morning, it was the last thing I wanted. She gave hers a perfunctory swirl and we both drank. I swallowed and my mouth came open automatically as if I'd just risen to the surface of a swimming pool. This was clearly fine stuff, but I didn't think I'd need my teeth cleaned for a *year*. I watched her calm herself, taking a deep breath or two.

I was trying desperately to recall the accounts I'd read of the incident in which Costigan was killed. It must have been five or six years ago. As nearly as I could remember, someone had broken into their Montebello house one night and had shot Dwight to death after a struggle in the bedroom. I'd been off in Houston for a client so I hadn't followed the events very closely, but as far as I knew, it was still sitting on the books as an unsolved homicide.

"What happened?" I asked.

"Don't ask and don't interfere. I pleaded with Bobby to let it go, but he wouldn't listen and it cost him his life. The past is the past. It's over and done with and I'm the only one paying for it now. Forget it. I don't care, and if you're smart, you won't either."

"You know I can't do that. Tell me what went on."

"What for? It won't change anything."

"Nola, I'm going to find out whether you tell me or not. If you lay it out for me maybe it won't have to go any further than this. Maybe I'll understand and agree to drop the whole thing. I'm not unreasonable, but you've gotta play fair."

I could see the indecision written in her face. She said, "Oh God," and put her head down for a moment. She looked at me with anxiety. "We're talking about a lunatic. Someone so crazy. You'd have to swear . . . you'd have to promise to back off."

"I can't make a promise like that and you know it. Tell me the story and then we'll figure out what has to be done."

"I've never told anyone except Bobby and look what happened to him."

"What about Sufi? She knows, doesn't she?"

She blinked at me, momentarily startled at the mention of Sufi's name. She looked away from me. "No, not at all. I'm sure she doesn't know what's going on. Why would she?" The answer seemed too hesitant to be convincing, but I let it pass for the time being. Could Sufi be blackmailing her?

"Well, *somebody* else knows," I said. "From what I gather, you're being blackmailed and that's what Bobby was trying to stop. What's the deal? What does this person have on you? What kind of leverage?"

I let the silence stretch, watching as she struggled with her need to unload.

Finally, she started talking, her voice so low I was forced to lean forward so I could hear her. "We'd been married nearly fifteen years. Dwight was on medication for high blood pressure and it made him impotent. We'd never had a highly charged sex life anyway. I got restless and found . . . someone else."

"A lover."

She nodded, eyes closed as if the recollection hurt her. "Dwight walked in on us one night in bed. He was crazed. He got a gun from the study and came back and there was a struggle."

I caught the sound of footsteps coming down the hall. I glanced toward the door and she did too, her voice becoming urgent.

"Don't breathe a word of this. Please."

"Trust me, I won't. What's the rest?"

She hesitated. "I shot Dwight. It was an accident, but somebody has the gun with my fingerprints on it."

"And that's what Bobby was searching for?"

She nodded almost imperceptibly.

"But who has it? Your ex-lover?"

Nola raised a finger to her lips. There was a tap at the door and Dr. Fraker stuck his head in, apparently surprised to see me sitting there. "Oh, hi, Kinsey. Is that your car in the drive? I was just about to take off, and I couldn't figure out who was here."

"I stopped by to talk to Nola about Glen," I said. "I

don't think she's doing too well and I was wondering if we shouldn't work out some arrangement to take turns spending time with her now that Derek's gone."

He shook his head regretfully. "Dr. Kleinert told me she'd kicked him out. Damn shame. Not that I have any use for him myself, but she's got her share of trouble right now. I hate to see her saddled with something else."

"Me, too," I said. "Do you need me to move my car?"

"No, that's fine," he said, looking over at Nola. "I've got some work to do at the hospital, but I shouldn't be back too late. Do we have dinner plans?"

She smiled pleasantly, though she had to clear her throat before she could speak. "I thought we'd eat here if that's all right with you."

"Sure, it's fine. Well. I'll let you two hatch your little schemes. Nice to see you, Kinsey."

"Actually we're finished," Nola said, getting up.

"Oh, well good," he said, "I'll walk you out."

I knew she was just using his appearance as a way to terminate the conversation, but I couldn't think of any delaying tactics, especially with the two of them standing there looking at me.

We exchanged brief good-byes and then Dr. Fraker held the door for me and I left the den. As I glanced back, I could see that Nola's expression was tinged with anxiety, and I suspected she was wishing she'd kept her secret to herself. She had a lot at stake: freedom, money, status, respectability. She was vulnerable to anyone who knew what I now knew. I wondered how desperate she was to hang on to what she had and what kind of payment had been extracted from her as a result.

23

I went into the office. There was a pile of mail on the floor under the door slot. I gathered that up and tossed it on my desk, opening the French doors to let in some fresh air. The message light on my answering machine was blinking. I sat down and pressed the play-back button.

The message was from my friend at the telephone company with a report on the disconnect for S. Blackman, whose full name was Sebastian S., male, age sixty-six, with a forwarding address in Tempe, Arizona. Well, that didn't sound very promising. If all else failed, I could double back and check that out to see if there was any tie to Bobby. Somehow I doubted it. I made a note in his file. There was a certain security in having it all committed to paper. At least that way, if anything happened to me, someone could come along afterward and pick up the thread—a grim notion, but not unrealistic given Bobby's fate.

I spent the next hour and a half going through my mail, catching up on my bookkeeping. A couple of checks had come in and I entered those in accounts receivable, making out a deposit slip. One statement had been shipped back to me unopened, marked "Addressee Unknown. Return to Sender" with a big purple finger pointing right at me. God, a deadbeat. I hated getting stung for services rendered. I'd done some good work for that guy, too. I'd known he was a slow pay, but I didn't think he'd actually stiff me for my fee. I set it aside. I'd have to track him down when I had some time.

It was almost noon by then and I glanced at the phone. I knew there was a call I should make and I picked up the receiver, punching in the number before I lost my nerve.

"Santa Teresa Police Department. Deputy Collins."

"I'd like to speak to Sergeant Robb in Missing Persons."

"Just a moment. I'll connect you."

My heart was thudding in a way that made my armpits damp.

I'd run into Jonah while I was investigating the disappearance of a woman named Elaine Boldt. He was a nice guy with a bland face, maybe twenty pounds overweight, amusing, direct, a bit of a rebel, pirating copies of some homicide reports for me against all the rules. He'd been married for years to his junior-high-school sweetheart, who'd abandoned him a year ago, departing with his two daughters, and leaving him with a freezer full of crappy dinners that she'd done up herself. He hadn't been flashy but I don't look for that anyway and I'd liked him a lot. We'd never been lovers, but he'd exhibited a bit of healthy male interest and I'd taken a dim view of it when he went back to his wife. Face it, I was miffed, and I'd kept my distance from him ever since.

"Robb here."

"Jesus," I said, "I haven't even talked to you yet and I'm already pissed."

I could hear him hesitate. "Kinsey, is that you?"

I laughed. "Yes, it's me and I just figured out how frosted I am."

He knew exactly what I was talking about. "God. I know, babe. What a load of pig swill that was. I've thought about you so often."

I was saying "uh-hun, uh-hun" in what I hoped was my most skeptical tone. "How's Camilla?"

He sighed and I could almost see him run a hand through his hair. "About the same. She treats me like dirt. I don't know why I let her back in my life."

"Must be nice to have the girls home though, isn't it?"

"Well, yeah, that's true," he said. "And we're seeing a counselor. Not them. Me and her."

"Maybe that will help."

"Maybe it won't." He caught himself and changed his tone. "Ah. Well. I shouldn't complain. I guess I did it to myself. I'm just sorry it ended up affecting you."

"Don't worry about it. I'm a big girl. Besides, I've got a way for you to redeem yourself. I thought maybe I could buy you lunch today and pick your brain."

"Sure. I'd love it, only lunch is on me. It'll help assuage my guilt. How you like that 'assuage' stuff? That's the word of the day on my vocabulary calendar. Yesterday was 'ineluctable.' I never did figure out how to sneak that one in. Where do you want to go? You name the place."

"Oh, let's keep it simple. I don't want to spend a lot of time on social niceties."

"How about the courthouse? I'll pick up some sandwiches and we can eat on the lawn."

"God, right out in public. Won't the department talk?"

"I hope so. Maybe Camilla will get wind of it and leave me again."

"See you at twelve-thirty."

"Is there something you want me to research in the meantime?"

"Oh right. Good point." I gave him a quick synopsis of the Costigan shooting, leaving Nola Fraker out of it. I'd decide later how much of the story I could trust him with. For now, I fed him the public version and asked if he could take a peek at the files.

"I have a vague recollection of that one. Let me see what I can dig up."

"And one more thing if you would," I said. "Could you run a check through NCIC on a woman named Lila Sams?" I gave him her two a.k.a.'s, Delia Sims and Delilah Sampson, the birthdate I'd taken off the driver's license, and the additional information I had in my notes.

"Right. Got it. I'll do what I can. See you shortly," he said and hung up.

It had occurred to me that if Lila was running some kind of scam on Henry, she might well have a prior record. There was no way I'd have access to the National Crime Information Center except through an authorized law-enforcement agency. Jonah could have the name run through the computer and get feedback in minutes and at least then I'd know if my instincts were accurate.

I tidied up my office, grabbed the bank deposit, and locked up, going next door for a few minutes to chat with Vera Lipton, one of the claims adjusters for California Fidelity Insurance. I stopped off at the bank on the way over to the courthouse, depositing most of the money to savings, with enough to my checking account to cover current expenses.

The day, which had started out on preheat, was cranked up to broil by now. The sidewalks shimmered and the palms looked bleached out by the sun. Where occasional potholes in the street had been filled, the asphalt was as soft and grainy as cookie dough.

The Santa Teresa Courthouse looks like a Moorish castle: hand-carved wooden doors, towers, and wrought-iron balconies. Inside, there's so much mosaic tile on the walls, it looks like someone's covered them with patchwork quilts. One courtroom sports a cycloramic mural that depicts the settling of Santa Teresa by the early Spanish missionaries. It's sort of the Walt Disney version of what really went on as the artist has omitted the introduction of syphilis and the corruption of the

Indians. I prefer it myself, if the truth be known. It would be hard to concentrate on justice if you had to stare up at some poor bunch of Indians in the last stages of paresis.

I cut through the great archway toward the sunken gardens in the rear. There were about two dozen people scattered across the lawn, some eating lunch, some napping or taking in the sun. Idly, I catalogued the merits of a good-looking man coming toward me in a pale blue short-sleeved shirt. I was doing one of those visual surveys that starts at the bottom and moves up. Uh-hun, nice hips, dressing left . . . uh-hun, flat belly, great arms, I thought. He'd almost reached me when I checked out the face and realized it was Jonah.

I hadn't seen him since June. Apparently the diet and his weight-lifting regimen had worked like a charm. His face, which in the past I'd labeled "harmless," was now nicely honed. His dark hair was longer and he'd picked up a tan so that his blue eyes now blazed in a face the color of maple sugar.

"Oh, God," I said, stopping dead in my tracks. "You look great."

He flashed me a smile, loving it. "You think so? Thanks. I must have lost twenty pounds since I saw you last."

"How'd you do it? Hard work?"

"Yeah, I did a little work."

He stood and stared at me and I stared back. He was exuding pheromones like a musky aftershave and I could feel my body chemistry start to shift. Mentally, I shook myself. I didn't need this. The only thing worse than a man just out of a marriage is a man who's still *in* one.

"I heard you got shot," he said.

"A mere .22, which hardly counts. I got beat up too, and that's what hurt. I don't know how guys put up with that shit," I said. I rubbed at the bridge of my nose ruefully. "Broke my schnoz."

He reached out impulsively and ran a finger down my nose. "Looks O.K. to me."

"Thanks," I said. "It still blows pretty good."

We endured one of those awkward pauses that had always punctuated our relationship.

I shifted my bag from one shoulder to the other, just for something to do. "What'd you bring?" I said, indicating the paper sack he held.

He glanced down. "Oh, yeah. I forgot. Uh, subs and Pepsis and Famous Amos cookies."

"We could even eat," I said.

He didn't move. He shook his head. "Kinsey, I don't remember going through this before," he said. "Why don't we fuckin' skip lunch and go over there behind that bush?"

I laughed, because I'd just had this quick flash of something hot and nasty that I don't care to repeat. I tucked my hand through his arm. "You're cute."

"I don't want to hear about cute."

We went down the wide stone steps and headed toward the far side of the courthouse lawn, where shaggy evergreens shade the grass. We sat down, distracted by the business of eating lunch. Pepsis were opened and lettuce fell out of sandwiches and we exchanged paper napkins and murmured about how good it all was. By the time we finished eating, we'd recovered some professional composure and conducted most of our remaining conversation like adults instead of sex-starved kids.

He shoved his empty Pepsi can in the sack. "I'll tell you the scuttlebutt on that Costigan shooting. The guy I talked to used to work Homicide and he says he always thought it was the wife. It was one of those situations where the whole story stank, you know? She claimed some guy broke in, husband gets a gun, big struggle, boom! The gun goes off and hubby's dead. Intruder runs away and she calls the cops, distraught victim of a random burglary attempt. Well, it didn't look right, but she stuck to her guns. Hired some hotshot lawyer right off the bat and wouldn't say a word until he got there. You know how it goes. 'Sorry my client can't answer this.' 'Sorry I won't let her respond to that.' Nobody believed a word she said, but she never broke down and in the end there wasn't any proof. No evidence, no informant, no weapon, no witness. End of tale. I hope you're not working for her because if you are, you're screwed."

I shook my head. "I'm looking into Bobby Callahan's death," I said. "I think he was murdered and I think it connects back to Dwight Costigan." I sketched the whole story out for him, avoiding his gaze. We were stretched out in the grass by then and I kept having these images of sexual misbehavior that I didn't think would serve. I plowed right ahead, talking more than I should have just to create a diversion.

"God, you come up with something on the Costigan killing and Lieutenant Dolan's gonna crochet you a watch," he said.

"What about Lila Sams?"

He held a finger up. "I was saving the best for last," he said. "I ran a field check on her and came up with a hit. This lady has a string of wants and warrants as long as your arm. Priors going back to 1968."

"What for?"

"Fraud, obtaining property by false pretenses, larceny by trick and device. She's been passing bad paper, too. She's got six outstanding warrants on her even as we speak. Well, wait. Take a look for yourself. I brought the print-out."

He held out the computer print-out and I took it. Why didn't I feel more elated at the notion of nailing her? Because it would break Henry's heart and I didn't want to take responsibility for that. I ran an eye down the sheet. "Can I keep this?"

"Sure, but don't jump up and down like that. Calm yourself," he said. "I take it you know where she is."

I looked over at him with a weak smile "Probably sitting in my backyard drinking iced tea," I said. "My landlord is head over heels in love with her and I suspect she's on the verge of taking him for everything he's worth."

"Talk to Whiteside in Fraud and he'll have her picked up."

"I think I better talk to Rosie first."

"That old bag who runs the dive down the street from you? What's she got to do with it?"

"Oh, neither one of us can stand Lila. Rosie wanted me to do the background check for the aggravation if nothing else. We needed to know where she was coming from."

"So now you know. What's the problem?"

"I don't know. It just feels crummy somehow, but I'll figure it out. I don't want to rush into anything I'll regret."

There was a momentary silence and then Jonah gave my shirt a tug. "You been up to the shooting range lately?"

"Not since we were there together," I said.

"You want to go up there sometime?"

"Jonah, we can't do that."

"Why not?"

"Because it might feel like a date and confuse us both."

"Come on. I thought we were friends."

"We are. We just can't hang out together."

"Why not?"

"Because you're too good-looking and I'm too smart," I said tartly.

"We're back to Camilla again, right?"

"Right. I'm not going to interfere with that. You've been with her a long time."

"I tell you something. I'm still kicking myself. I could have gone to the other junior high school, you know? Seventh grade. How did I know I was making a decision that would haunt me in middle-age?"

I laughed. "Life is full of that stuff. You had to choose between metal or woodshop, right? You could have turned out to be an auto mechanic. Instead you're a cop. You know what my choices were? Child psychology or home ec. I didn't give a shit about either one."

"I wish I hadn't seen you again."

I could feel my smile fade. "Well, I'm sorry for that. It was my fault." I could tell we'd been looking at each other too long, so I got up, brushing grass off my jeans. "I have to go."

He got up too and we said some good-bye things. We parted company shortly thereafter. I walked backward for a few steps, watching him head back to the station. Then I continued on toward my office, turning my attention back to the matter of Henry Pitts. I realized then that there wasn't any point in talking to Rosie about it. Of course I'd have to tell the cops where Lila was. She'd been a con for nearly twenty years and she wasn't going to reform and make Henry a happy man in the twilight of their days. She was going to cheat him silly, thus breaking his heart anyway. What difference did it make how she got caught or who turned her in? Better to do it now before she took every cent he had.

I'd been walking rapidly, head down, but when I got to the corner of Floresta and Anaconda, I did an abrupt left and headed for the police station.

24

I was at the police station for an hour and forty-five minutes. Fortunately, the Missing Persons Department and Fraud were nowhere near each other so I didn't have to worry about running into Jonah again. First, Whiteside was at lunch and then he had a quick meeting to attend. Then when I explained the situation to him, he had to place a call to a county in northern New Mexico where three of the warrants had been issued. While he was waiting for a response to that inquiry, he contacted the county sheriff in some little town up near San Francisco, trying to get confirmation on a no-bail warrant that originated in Marin. The charge on the fifth warrant in Boise, Idaho, turned out to be a misdemeanor and the fraud detective said he couldn't afford to come get her in any event. The sixth warrant, in Twin Falls, had been recalled for reasons unspecified. So far, Lila Sams was home free.

At 3:20, Marin County finally returned Whiteside's call, confirming the no-bail warrant and indicating that they'd have someone pick her up once they knew she was actually in custody. Their cooperation was largely due to the fact that one of their deputies was vacationing in Santa Teresa anyway and had agreed to accompany her back to Marin. Whiteside said as soon as a telexed copy of the warrant came through, he'd send the beat officer over to make the arrest. He didn't really have to have the warrant in hand, but I think he'd sensed by now that she was slippery. I gave him Moza's address, my address, and a thorough description of Lila Sams.

It was 3:40 by the time I got home. Henry was sitting on a chaise in the backyard, surrounded by books. He looked up from his legal pad as I came around the corner.

"Oh, it's you," he said. "I thought it might be Lila. She said she'd stop in and say good-bye before she took off."

That caught me by surprise. "She's leaving?"

"Well, she's not really 'leaving.' She's going to Las Cruces for a few days, but she hopes to be back by the end of the week. I guess a little problem came up on some property she owns and she has to get things squared away. It's a darn nuisance, but what can you do?"

"She's not gone already, though, is she?"

He checked his watch. "I can't imagine she would be. Her plane takes off about five. She said she had to go to the title company and then she'd toss a few things in a suitcase. Did you want to talk to her?"

I shook my head, unable to say yet what needed to be said. I could see that he was mapping out a new crossword puzzle, jotting down preliminary notes. At the top of the page, he'd written two titles, "Elementary, Dear Watson!" and "Home Sweet Holmes."

He smiled shyly when he saw me take note. "This one's for the Sherlockeans in the crowd," he said. He set the legal pad aside, as though self-conscious at having someone watch him work. "Well, now, how are things with you?"

He seemed so innocent, nothing more on his mind than his passion for words. How could she deceive a man like that?

"Something's come up I think you ought to know about," I said. I unfolded the computer print-out and handed it to him.

He looked down at it. "What's this?"

Lila's name apparently caught his eye then, because his gaze settled on the page. His face lost animation as he assimilated the facts. When he finished reading, he gestured aimlessly. He was silent for a moment and then he glanced up at me. "Well. Makes me look like a fool, doesn't it?"

"Come on, Henry. Don't talk like that. I don't think so at all. You took a risk and she brought you some happiness. Hey, so later it turns out she's a crook. That's not your fault."

He stared at the paper like a kid just learning to sound out words. "What made you check into it?"

I thought there might be a tactful explanation, but nothing occurred to me. "I didn't like her much, to tell you the truth. I guess I felt protective, especially when you talked about doing business with her. I just didn't think she was on the level and it turns out she's not. You haven't given her any money, have you?"

He folded the print-out. "I closed out one of my accounts this morning."

"How much?"

"Twenty thousand in cash," he said. "Lila said she'd deposit it to an escrow account at the title company. The bank manager urged me to reconsider, but I thought he was simply being conservative. I see now, he was not." His manner had become very formal and it nearly broke my heart.

"I'm going down to Moza's to see if I can intercept her before she takes off You want to come?"

He shook his head, his eyes bright. I turned on my heel and moved off at a quick clip.

I trotted the half-block to Moza's. A taxicab was cruising at half speed, the driver scanning house numbers. The two of us reached Moza's at just about the same time. He pulled over to the curb. I crossed to the passenger side, peering into the open window. He had a face like a beachball made of flesh.

"You the one wanted a cab?"

"Uh, sure. Lila Sams?"

He checked his trip sheet. "Right. You got any bags you need help with?"

"Actually, I don't need the cab. A neighbor said she'd run me out to the airport. I called back, but I guess the dispatcher didn't head you off in time. Sorry."

He gave me a look, then heaved an exasperated sigh, making a big display of crossing the address off his sheet. He shifted gears with annoyance, pulling away from the curb with a shake of his head. God, he could go on stage with an act like that.

I crossed Moza's yard at an angle and took the porch steps two at a time. She was holding the screen door open, looking out anxiously at the departing taxi. "What did you say to him? That was Lila's cab. She has to get to the airport."

"Really? He told me he had the wrong address. He was looking for Zollinger, one street over, I think."

"I better try another company. She ordered a cab thirty minutes ago. She's going to miss her plane."

"Maybe I can help," I said. "Is she in here?"

"You're not going to cause any trouble, Kinsey. I won't have that."

"I'm not causing trouble," I said. I moved through the living room and into the hall. The door to Lila's room was open.

The place had been stripped of personal possessions. One of the drawers where she'd concealed a phony I.D. was sitting on top of the chest of drawers, its back panel bare. She'd left the masking tape in a wad like a hunk of chewing gum. One suitcase was packed and sat near the door. Another was open on the bed, half filled, and beside it was a white plastic purse.

Lila had her back to me, bending over to remove a stack of folded clothes from one of the dressing-table drawers. The polyester pantsuit she wore was not very flattering. From the rear, her ass looked like two hanging foam-rubber hams. She caught sight of me as she turned. "Oh! You scared me. I thought it was Moza. What can I do for you?"

"I heard you were leaving. I thought maybe I could help."

Uncertainty flickered in her eyes. Her abrupt departure was probably at the urging of her cohorts in Las Cruces, alerted by my phone call of the night before. She might have suspected it was me, but she couldn't be sure. For my part, I was just hoping to stall until the cops showed up. I had no intention of confronting her. For all I knew, she might whip out a little two-shot Derringer or fly at me with some kind of old-lady karate-type move that would take me right out.

She checked her watch. It was now almost 4:00. It took twenty minutes to get to the airport and she'd have to be there by 4:30 or risk losing her seat. That gave her ten minutes. "Oh dear. Well, I don't know why my taxi isn't here. I might need a ride to the airport, if you could do that," she said.

"No problem," I said. "My car's right down the street. Henry said you'd be stopping by his place anyway to say good-bye."

"Of course I am, if I have time. He's such a sweetie." She finished laying in the armload of clothes and I could see her look around the room to see if she'd missed anything.

"Did you leave anything in the bathroom? Shampoo? Hand laundry?"

"Oh, I believe I did. I'll be right back." She moved past me, heading for the bathroom.

I waited until she rounded the corner and then reached over and opened her purse. Inside was a fat manila envelope with Henry's name penciled on the front. I took off the rubber band and checked the contents. Cash. I closed her purse again and tucked the envelope into the waistband of my jeans at the small of my back. I figured Henry was never going to press charges and I hated to see his savings confiscated and itemized as police property. No telling when he'd get it back. I was just adjusting my T-shirt over the bulge when she returned, toting shampoo, shower cap, hand lotion. She tucked them in around the sides of her folded clothes and closed up the suitcase, snapping the locks shut.

"Here, I'll get it," I said. I hauled that suitcase off the bed and picked up the other one, moving out into the hall like a pack mule. Moza was standing there, wringing out an imaginary dish towel in her anxiety.

"I can take one of those," she said.

"I got it."

I headed for the door, with Moza and Lila bringing up the rear. I certainly hoped the cops would show. Lila and Moza were saying those last-minute things to one another, Lila faking it out the whole time. She was taking off. She was gone. She had no intention of coming back.

As we reached the front, Moza moved ahead so she could hold the screen door open for me. A black-and-white patrol car had just pulled up in front. I was afraid if Lila spotted them too soon, she'd bolt for the rear.

"Did you get that pair of shoes under the bed?" I asked over my shoulder. I paused in the doorway, blocking her view.

"I don't know. I just looked and I didn't see any."

"You probably got them, then," I said.

"No, no. I better check." She hurried toward the bedroom while I set the two suitcases on the porch.

Moza, meanwhile, was staring at the street with puzzlement. Two uniformed officers were coming up the walk, one male, one female, both bareheaded, in short-sleeved shirts. In Santa Teresa, there's been a move afoot to divest the police of their authoritarian images, but these two managed to seem ominous anyway. Moza probably thought she'd violated some civil code—grass too long, TV too loud.

I left her to have a little conversation with them while I herded Lila up this way, so she wouldn't spot the cops and try slipping out the back. "Lila, your ride's here," I called.

"Well thank heaven for that," she said, as she came through the living room. "I didn't find anything under the bed, but I'd left my ticket right up on the chest, so it's lucky I went back."

As she reached the front door, I eased behind her. She glanced up, catching sight of the officers.

The guy, according to his name tag, was G. Pettigrew. He was black, maybe in his thirties, with big arms and a barrel chest. His partner, M. Gutierrez, looked almost as hefty as he.

Pettigrew's eyes settled on Lila. "Are you Lila Sams?"

"Yes." She loaded that one syllable with puzzlement, blinking at him. Her body seemed to change so that she looked older and more squat.

"Could you step out onto the porch, please?"

"Of course, but I can't think what this is about." Lila made a move toward her purse, but Gutierrez intercepted, checking the contents quickly for weapons.

Pettigrew told Lila she was under arrest, reciting her rights to her from a card he held. I could tell he'd done it all a hundred times and didn't really need the cue, but he read it anyway so there wouldn't be any question later.

"Could you turn around and face the wall, please?"

Lila did as she was told and Gutierrez did a patdown, then snapped on a pair of handcuffs. Lila was starting to wail pitifully. "But what have I done? I haven't done anything. This is all a terrible mistake." Her desperation seemed to set Moza off.

"What's going on, officer?" Moza said. "This woman is my tenant. She hasn't done anything wrong."

"Ma'am, we'd appreciate it if you'd step back, please. Mrs. Sams is entitled to contact an attorney when we get downtown." Pettigrew touched at Lila's elbow, but she pulled away, her voice rising to a shrill pitch.

"Help! Oh no! Let go of me. Help!"

The two officers took control of her, one on either side, moving her off the porch at a businesslike pace, but Lila's shrieks were beginning to bring curious neighbors out onto their porches. She went limp, sagging heavily between them, craning her face toward Moza with a piteous cry. They hustled her into the squad car, picking her feet up to deposit her in the rear. Lila somehow conveyed the impression that this was a Gestapo arrest, that she was being hauled off by the

Nazis and might never be heard from again. Shaking his head, Officer Pettigrew gathered up her belongings, which were now strewn along the walk. He tucked her suitcases in the trunk.

The man next door apparently felt called upon to intercede and I saw him in conversation with Pettigrew while Gutierrez called in to the station and Lila thrashed about, flinging herself at the mesh that separated her from Gutierrez in the front seat. Finally Pettigrew got in the car on the driver's side, slamming the door shut, and they pulled away.

Moza was dead white and she turned a stricken face to me. "This was your doing! What in heaven's name were you thinking of? The poor woman."

But I'd caught sight of Henry half a block away. Even at that distance, his face seemed blank with disbelief, his body tense. "I'll talk to you later, Moza," I said and headed toward him.

25

By the time I reached my place, Henry was nowhere in sight. I pulled the envelope out of my waistband and knocked on his back door. He opened it. I held the envelope up and he took it, glancing at the contents. He gave me a searching look, but I didn't explain how I'd come by it and he didn't ask.

"Thank you."

"We'll talk later," I said, and he closed the door again, but not before I caught a glimpse of his kitchen counter. He had gotten out the sugar canister and a new blue-and-white sack of flour, turning to the activity he knew best while he worked through his pain. I felt awful for him but I had to let him sort it out for himself. God, it was all so unpleasant. In the meantime, I had to get back to work.

I let myself into my apartment and got out the telephone book, looking for Kelly Borden. If Bobby'd been searching for the gun out at the old county building, I wanted to have a crack at it too and I thought maybe Kelly could tell me where to start. No sign of him in the telephone book. I tried to find the number for the former medical facility, but there wasn't a listing for it and the information operator was being obtuse, pretending she had no idea what I was talking about. If he worked a seven-to-three shift, he'd be gone anyway. Shit. I looked up the number of Santa Teresa Hospital and put a call in to Dr. Fraker. His secretary, Marcy, told me he was "away from his desk" (meaning in the men's room), but would be back shortly. I told her I needed to talk to Kelly Borden and asked for his address and telephone number.

"Gee, I don't know," she said. "Dr. Fraker probably wouldn't mind my giving you the information, but I'm not really supposed to do it without his O.K."

"Look, I've got some errands to run anyway so why don't I stop by. It'll take me ten minutes," I said. "Just make sure he doesn't leave work before I get there."

I drove over to St. Terry's. Parking turned out to be a trick and I had to leave my car three blocks away, which was okay with me because I had to stop at a drugstore. I went in through the back entrance, following varicolored lines on the floor, as though on my way to Oz. Finally, I reached a set of elevators and took one down to the basement.

By the time I reached Pathology, Dr. Fraker was off again, but Marcy had told him I was coming and he'd instructed her to forward me, like a piece of mail. I trailed after her through the lab and finally came across him in surgical greens, standing at a stainless-steel counter with a sink, disposal, and hanging scales.

He was apparently about to launch into some procedure and I was sorry I had to interrupt.

"I really didn't mean to disturb you," I said. "All I need is Kelly Borden's address and telephone number."

"Pull up a chair," he said, indicating a wooden stool at one end of the counter. And then to Marcy, "Why don't you look up the information for Kinsey and I'll keep her amused in the meantime."

As soon as she departed, I pulled the stool over and perched.

For the first time, I cued in to what Fraker was actually doing. He was wearing surgical gloves, scalpel in hand. There was a white plastic carton on the counter, a one-pint size, like the kind used for chicken livers in the meat section of the supermarket. As I watched, he dumped out a glistening blob of organs, which he began to sort through with a pair of long tweezers. Against my will, I felt my gaze fix on this small pile of human flesh. Our entire conversation was conducted while he trimmed off snippets from each of several organs.

I could feel my lips purse in distaste. "What are those?"

His expression was mild, impersonal, and amused. He used the tweezers to point, touching each of several hunks in turn. I half expected the little morsels to draw away from his probing, like live slugs, but none of them moved. "Well, let's see. That's a heart. Liver. Lung. Spleen. Gall bladder. This fella died suddenly during surgery and nobody can figure out what his problem was."

"And you can? Just from doing that?"

"Well, not always, but I think we'll come up with something in this case," he said.

I didn't think I'd ever look at stew meat in quite the same way. I couldn't take my eyes away from his dicing process and I couldn't get it through my head that these had once been functioning parts of a human being. If he was aware of my fascination, he didn't give any indication of it and I tried to be as nonchalant about the whole deal as he was.

He glanced over at me. "How does Kelly Borden figure into this?"

"I'm not sure," I said. "Sometimes I have to look at things that end up having no connection whatever to a case. Maybe it's the same as what you do—inspecting all the pieces of the puzzle until you come up with a theory."

"I suspect this is a lot more scientific than what you do," he remarked.

"Oh, no doubt about it," I said. "But I'll tell you one advantage I have."

He paused, looking over at me again, but with the first genuine interest I'd seen.

"I know the man whose death I'm dealing with and I have a personal stake in the outcome. I think he was murdered and it pisses me off. Disease is neutral. Homicide's not."

"I think your feeling for Bobby is coloring your judgment. His death was accidental."

"Maybe. Or maybe I can persuade Homicide that he died as a result of a murder attempt nine months ago."

"If you can prove that," he said. "So far I gather you don't have much to go on, which is where your work differs from mine. I can probably come up with something conclusive here and I won't have to leave the room."

"I do envy you that," I said. "I mean, I don't doubt Bobby was killed, but I don't have any idea who did it and I may never have any evidence."

"Then I have it all over you," he said. "For the most part, I deal in certainty. Once in a while, I'm stumped, but not often."

"You're lucky."

Marcy returned with Kelly's address and telephone number on a slip of paper, which she handed to me.

"I prefer to think I'm talented," he was saying wryly. "I better not keep you in any case. Let me know how it comes out."

"I'll do that. Thanks for this," I said, holding up the slip of paper.

It was now five o'clock. I found a pay phone in an offshoot of one of the hospital corridors and tried Kelly's number.

He picked up on the third ring. I identified myself, reminding him of Dr. Fraker's introduction.

"I know who you are."

"Listen," I said, "could I stop by and talk to you? There's something I need to check out."

He seemed to hesitate at first. "Sure, O.K. You know where I am?"

Kelly's apartment was on the west side of town, not far from St. Terry's. I trotted back to my car and drove over to an address on Castle. I parked in front of a frame duplex and walked down a long driveway to a small wooden outbuilding at the rear of the property. His place, like mine, had probably been a garage at one time.

As I rounded some shrubs, I spotted him sitting on his front step, smoking a joint. He wore jeans and a leather vest over a plaid shirt, feet bare. His hair was pulled back in the same neat braid, beard and mustache looking grayer somehow than I remembered. He seemed very mellow, except for his eyes, which were aquamarine and impossible to read. He held the joint out to me, but I declined with a shake of my head.

"Didn't I see you at Bobby's funeral?" I asked.

"Might have. I saw you." His eyes settled on me with a disconcerting gaze. Where had I seen that color before? In a swimming pool where a dead man was floating like a lily pad. That had been four years ago, one of the first investigations I ever did.

"Chair over there if you have time to sit." He managed to get this sentence out while holding his breath, dope smoke locked in his lungs.

I glanced around and spotted an old wooden lawn chair, which I dragged over to the step. Then I took the address book out of my handbag and passed it to him, open to the back cover. "Any idea who this is? It's not a local number."

He glanced at the penciled entry and then gave me a quick look. "You tried calling?"

"Sure. I also tried the only Blackman listed in the book. It's a disconnect. Why? Do you know who it is?"

"I know the number, but it's not a telephone listing. Bobby moved the hyphen over."

"What's it for? I don't understand."

"These first two digits indicate Santa Teresa County. Last five are the morgue code. This is the I.D. number on a body we got in storage. I told you we had two that had been out there for years. This is Franklin."

"But why list it under Blackman?"

Kelly smiled at me, taking a long pull off his joint before he spoke. "Franklin's black. He's a black man. Maybe it was Bobby's joke."

"Are you sure?"

"Reasonably sure. You can check it yourself if you don't believe me."

"I think he was searching for a handgun out there. Would you have any idea where he might have started?"

"Nope. Place is big. They must have eighty, ninety rooms out there that haven't been used in years. Could be anywhere. Bobby would have worked his shift by himself. He had the run of the building as long as no one found out he was away from his work."

"Well. I guess I'll just have to wing it. I appreciate your help."

"No problem."

I went back to my office. Kelly Borden had told me that a kid named Alfie Leadbetter would be working the three-to-eleven shift at the morgue. The guy was a friend of his and he said he'd call ahead and let him know I was coming out.

I hauled out my typewriter again and made some notes. What was this? What did the corpse of a black man have to do with the murder of Dwight Costigan and the blackmailing of his former wife?

The phone rang and I picked it up like an automaton, my mind on the problem at hand. "Yes?"

"Kinsey?"

"Speaking."

"I wasn't sure that was you. This is Jonah. You always answer that way?"

I focused. "God, sorry. What can I do for you?"

"I heard about something I thought might interest you. You know that Callahan accident?"

"Sure. What about it?"

"I just ran into the guy who works Traffic and he says the lab boys went over the car this afternoon. The brake lines were cut just as clean as you please. They transferred the whole case to Homicide."

I could feel myself doing the same kind of mental double take I'd done just minutes before when I finally heard what the name Blackman meant. "What?"

"Your friend Bobby Callahan was murdered," Jonah said patiently. "The brake lines on his car had been cut, which means all the brake fluid ran out, which means he crashed into that tree because he rounded the curve with no way to slow down."

"I thought the autopsy showed he had a stroke."

"Maybe he did when he realized what was happening. That's not inconsistent as far as I can tell."

"Oh, you're right." For a moment I just breathed in Jonah's ear. "How long would that take?"

"What, cutting the brake lines or the fluid running out?"

"Both, now that you mention it."

"Oh, probably five minutes to cut the lines. That's no big deal if you know where to look. The other depends. He probably could have driven the car for a little while, pumped the brakes once or twice. Next thing he knew, he'd have tried 'em and boom, gone."

"So it happened that night? Whoever cut the lines?"

"Had to. The kid couldn't have driven far."

I was dead silent, thinking of the message Bobby'd left on my machine. He'd seen Kleinert the night he died. I remember Kleinert mentioning it too.

"You there?"

"I don't know what it means, Jonah," I said. "This case is starting to break and I just can't figure out what's going on."

"You want me to come over and we'll talk it out?"

"Not, not yet. I need to be by myself. Let me call you later when I have more to go on."

"Sure. You've got my home number, haven't you?"

"Better give it to me again," I said and jotted it down.

"Now, listen," he said to me. "Swear to me you won't do anything stupid."

"How can I do anything stupid? I don't even know what's going on," I said. "Besides, 'stupid' is after the fact. I always feel smart when I think things up."

"God damn it, you know what I'm talking about."

I laughed. "You're right. I know. And believe me, I'll call you if anything comes up. Honestly, my sole object in life is to protect my own ass."

"Well," he said grudgingly. "That's good to hear, but I doubt it."

We said our good-byes and he hung up. I left my hand on the receiver.

I tried Glen's number. I felt she should have the information and I couldn't be sure the cops would bring her up to date, especially since, at this point, they probably didn't have any more answers than I did.

She picked up the phone and I told her what was going on, including the business about Blackman in Bobby's address book. Of necessity, I told her as much as I knew about the blackmailing business. Hell, why not? This was no time to keep secrets. She already knew that Nola and Bobby were lovers. She might as well understand what he had undertaken in Nola's behalf. I even took the liberty of mentioning Sufi's involvement, though I still wasn't sure about that. I suspected that she was a go-between, ferrying messages between Nola and Bobby, counseling Bobby, perhaps, when his passion clashed with his youthful impatience.

She was quiet for a moment in the same way I had been. "What happens now?"

"I'll talk to Homicide tomorrow and tell them everything I know. They can handle it after that."

"Be careful in the meantime," she said.

"No sweat."

26

There was still an hour and a half of daylight left when I reached the old county medical complex. From the number of parking spaces available, it was clear that most of the offices were closed, personnel gone for the day. Kelly had told me there was a second parking lot around the side that was used by the janitorial staff at night. I didn't see any reason to park that far away. I pulled into a slot as close to the entrance as I could get, noting with interest that there was a bicycle chained to a rack just off to my left. It was a banged-up old Schwinn with fat tires and a fake license plate wired onto the rear, reading "Alfie." Kelly had told me the building was generally locked up by seven, but that I could buzz in and Alfie would buzz back to admit me.

I grabbed my flashlight and my key picks, pausing to pull a sweatshirt over my tank top. I remembered the building as chilly, even more so, I imagined, if I was there after sunset. I locked my car and headed for the entrance.

I paused at the double doors in front and pressed a bell to my right. After a moment, the door buzzed back, releasing the lock, and I went in. The lobby was already accumulating shadows and reminded me vaguely of an abandoned train station in a futuristic movie. It had that same air of vintage elegance: inlaid marble floors, high ceilings, beautiful woodwork of buffed oak. The few remaining fixtures must have been there since the twenties, when the place was built.

I crossed the lobby, glancing idly at the wall directory as I passed. Almost subliminally, a name caught my eye. I paused and looked again. Leo Kleinert had an office out here, which I hadn't realized before. Had Bobby driven this far for weekly psychiatric sessions? Seemed a bit out of the way. I went downstairs, footsteps scratching on the tile steps. As before, I could feel the temperature dropping, like a descent into the waters of a lake. Down here, it was gloomier, but the glass door to the morgue was lighted, a bright rectangle in the gathering darkness of the hall. I checked my watch. It wasn't even 7:15.

I tapped on the glass for form's sake and then tried the knob. It was unlocked. I opened the door and peered in.

"Hello?"

There was no one in evidence, but that had happened to me before when Dr. Fraker and I had visited. Maybe Alfie was in the refrigerated storage room where the bodies were kept.

"Heellloo!"

No response. He'd buzzed me in, so he had to be around here someplace.

I closed the door behind me. The fluorescent lighting was harsh, giving the illusion of winter sunlight. There was a door to my left. I crossed and knocked before I opened it to find an empty office with a dark brown Naugahyde couch. Maybe the guy on the graveyard shift snagged some shut-eye in here when nothing else was going on. There was a desk and a swivel chair. The outside of the window was covered with ornamental wrought-iron burglar bars, the daylight blocked out by a mass of unruly shrubs. I closed the door and moved over to the refrigerated room where the bodies were kept, peering in.

No Alfie in sight. Inside, the light was constant, occupants laid out on blue fiberglass berths, engaged in their eternal, motionless naps, some wrapped in sheets, some in plastic, necks and ankles wound with what looked like masking tape. Somehow, it reminded me of quiet time at summer camp.

I returned to the main room and sat for a while, staring at the autopsy table. My customary procedure would have been to snoop into every cabinet, drawer, and storage bin, but it felt disrespectful here. Or maybe I was afraid I'd stumble onto something grotesque: trays of dentures, a Mason jar chock-full of floating eyeballs. I don't know what I thought I'd see. I shifted restlessly. I felt as if I were wasting time. I went to the door and looked out into the hall, tilting my head to listen. Nothing.

"Alfie?" I called. I listened again, then shrugged and closed the door. It occurred to me that as long as I was there, I could at least verify that the number Bobby'd written down was, in fact, the same as the number on Franklin's toe tag. That wouldn't do any harm. I took the address book out of my handbag and turned to the penciled entry on the back cover. I went into the cold-storage room again, moving from body to body, checking I.D. tags. This was like some kind of bargain-basement sale only nothing was marked down.

When I got to the third body, the numbers matched. Kelly was right. Bobby'd shifted the hyphen over so the seven-digit code looked like a telephone number. I stared at the body, or what I could see of it. The plastic that Franklin was wrapped in was transparent but yellowing, as though stained with nicotine. Through the swaddling, I could see that he was a middle-aged black man of medium height, slim, with a face of stone. Why was this corpse significant? I was feeling anxious. I figured Alfie would be back shortly and I really didn't want to be caught nosing around in here. I went back to my chair.

Coming out of the cold-storage room was like leaving an air-conditioned theater. It made the autopsy room feel balmy by comparison. I was getting itchy to explore. I couldn't help myself. I was irritated that no one was there to help me and feeling edgy from the quiet. This was not a fun place. Ordinarily, I don't hang out in morgues and it was making me tense.

Just to soothe my nerves, I peered into a drawer, testing the contents against the grisly images I'd conjured up. This one contained scratch pads, order blanks, and miscellaneous paper supplies. Reassured, I tried the next drawer: small vials of several drugs, the names of which I did not recognize. I was warming up here and I checked on down the line. Everything appeared to be related to the business of dissecting the dead; not surprising, given the locale; but not very enlightening.

I straightened up and looked around the room. Where were the files? Didn't anybody keep records around this place? Somebody had mentioned that there were medical charts stored out here, but where? This floor? Somewhere on one of the floors above? I didn't relish the idea of creeping through the empty building by myself. I'd been picturing Alfie Leadbetter at my side, telling me what was accessible and where I might start. I'd even pictured slipping him a twenty-dollar bill if that's what it took to enlist his aid.

I glanced at my watch. I'd now been here forty-five minutes and I wanted some results. I grabbed my handbag and went out in the hall, looking in both directions. It was getting darker down here, although I could see through a window at the end of the hall that it was still light outside. I found a wall switch and flipped on the lights and then I wandered along the corridor, reading the small white signs mounted above each office door. The radiology offices were right next to the morgue. Beyond that, Nuclear Medicine, and nursing offices. I wondered if Sufi Daniels had occasion to come out here.

Something was beginning to stir at the back of my

brain. I was thinking about the cardboard box full of Bobby's belongings. What was in it? Medical texts and office supplies and two radiology manuals. What was he actually doing with those? He hadn't even been a medical student and I couldn't think why he'd need the manuals for equipment he might not be using for years, if ever. He'd indicated no particular interest in radiology.

I went upstairs. It wouldn't hurt to look at that stuff again. When I reached the front entrance, I slipped off my sweatshirt and wedged it in the opening. I could push the door open with no problem, but I didn't want the lock snapping shut behind me as I went out. I crossed to my car and unlocked it, wrestling the carton out the backseat. I removed the two radiology books and leafed through them quickly. These were technical manuals for specific equipment, information about the various gauges and dials and switches, with a lot of esoteric talk about exposures, rads, and roentgens. At the top of one page was a penciled number, like a doodle, surrounded by curlicues. Franklin's again. The sight of the now familiar seven-digit code seemed eerie, like the sound of Bobby's voice on my answering machine five days after he died.

I tucked the two manuals under my arm and locked my car again, leaving the box on the front seat. Slowly, I returned to the building. I let myself in, pausing to pull on my sweatshirt. As long as I was on the first floor, I did a superficial survey. I kept thinking it was medical records I was looking for, the handgun tucked down in a banker's box packed with old charts. This had been a working hospital at one time and there had to be a records department somewhere. Where else would old charts be kept? If my memory of St. Terry's served me, the Medical Records Department was fairly centrally located so that doctors and other authorized personnel would have easy access.

Not many offices on this floor appeared to be occupied. I tried door handles randomly. Most were locked. I rounded the corner at the end of the hall and there it was, "Medical Records" painted above a set of double doors in a faded scrawl. I could see now that many of the old departments were similarly marked: florid lettering on a painted scroll, as though by declaration of the conquistadors.

I tried the knob, expecting to have to experiment with my key picks. Instead, the door swung open with a low-pitched creak that might have been contrived by a special effects man. Waning daylight filtered in. The room yawned before me, barren, stripped of everything. No file cabinets, no furniture, no fixtures. A crumpled cigarette pack, some loose boards, and a couple of bent nails were scattered across the floor. This department had literally been dismantled at some point and God only knew where the old records were now. It was possible they were somewhere in one of the abandoned hospital rooms above, but I really didn't want to go up there by myself. I'd promised Jonah I wouldn't be stupid and I was trying to be a good scout on that score. Besides, something else was nagging at me.

I returned to the stairs, descending. What was that little voice in the back of my head murmuring? It was like a radio playing in the next room. I could pick up only a faint phrase now and then.

When I reached the basement, I crossed to the radiology office and tried the knob. Locked. I got out my key picks and played around for a while. This was one of those "burglar-proof" locks that *can* be picked, but it really is a pain in the ass. Still, I wanted to see what was in there and I worked patiently. I was using a set of rocker picks, with random depth cuts spaced along the top, the back side of each pick ground to an oval. The whole idea is that with enough different cut combinations, together with an applied rocking motion, somewhere along the way all the pins will, by chance, be raised to the shear line at the same time, popping the lock.

Like hiding, the only way to approach the whole process is to give oneself up to it. I stood there for maybe twenty minutes, easing the pick forward, rocking it, applying slight pressure when I felt movement of any sort. Lo and behold, the sucker gave way and I let out a little exclamation of delight. "Oh, wow. Hey, that's great." It's this sort of shit that makes my job fun. Also illegal, but who was going to tell?

I eased into the office. I flipped the overhead light on. It looked like ordinary office space. Typewriters and telephones and file cabinets, plants on the desks, pictures on the walls. There was a small reception area where I imagined patients seated, waiting to be called for their X rays. I wandered through some of the rooms in the rear, picturing the procedures for chest X rays and mammograms, upper G.I. series. I stood in front of the machines and opened one of the manuals I'd brought in from the car.

I checked the diagrams against the various dials and gauges on the X-ray equipment itself. It was a match, more or less. Maybe some variation according to year, make, or model of the actual machinery installed. Some of it looked like the stuff of science fiction. Massive nose cone on a swinging arm. I stood there, manual open in my arms, pages pressed to my chest while I stared at the table and the lead apron that looked like a baby bib for a giant. I thought about the X rays I'd had taken of my left arm two months ago, just after I'd been shot.

It wasn't as if the idea came to me all at once. It formed around me, like fairy dust, gradually taking shape. Bobby had been out here all by himself, just like this. Night after night, searching for the handgun that had Nola's fingerprints on it. He knew who had hidden it, so he must have formed some kind of theory about the hiding place. I had to guess that he'd found the gun and that's why he was killed. Maybe he'd actually retrieved it, but I didn't think so. I'd been operating on the assumption that it was still hidden out here and that still seemed like a good bet. He'd made some little notes to himself, doodling the I.D. number of a corpse in his little red book and again in the pages of a radiology manual he'd acquired.

The phrases running through my head began to connect. Maybe you should X-ray the corpse, said I to myself. Maybe that's what Bobby did and maybe that's why he made the penciled notation in the radiology book. Maybe the gun is *inside* the corpse. I thought about it briefly, but I couldn't see why I shouldn't give it a try. The worst that could happen (aside from my getting caught) was that I'd be wasting time and making a colossal fool of myself. This would not be a first.

I left my handbag and the manuals on one of the X-ray tables and went next door to the morgue. In the refrigerated storage room, I spotted a gurney against the right wall. I was on automatic pilot by now, simply doing what I knew had to be done. There was still no sign of Alfie Leadbetter and no one was going to help me. I might be wrong, so maybe it was just as well that no one knew what I was up to. The building was deserted. It was early yet. Even if I fumbled the X-ray procedure, it couldn't hurt the dead man.

I rolled the gurney over to the fiberglass bunk where the body lay. I pretended I was a morgue attendant. I pretended I was an X-ray technician or a nurse, some thoroughly professional person with a job to do.

"Sorry to disturb you, Frank," I said, "but you have to go next door for some tests. You're not looking so good."

Tentatively, I reached out and eased a hand under Franklin's neck and knees and pulled, slipping him from his resting place onto the gurney. He was surprisingly light, and cold to the touch, about the consistency of a package of raw chicken breasts just out of the fridge. God, I thought, why do I plague myself with these domestic images? I'd never be motivated to learn to cook at this rate.

It took incredible maneuvering to get the gurney

through the morgue and out into the corridor, then into the reception area of the radiology offices and into one of the X-ray rooms in the rear. I lined the gurney up parallel to the X-ray table and shoved the body into place. I raised and lowered the nose cone a couple of times experimentally, sliding it along its overhead track until it was right over Franklin's abdomen. At some point, I was going to have to figure out how far away from the body it should be. Meanwhile, since I intended to take some pictures, I thought I better find some film of some kind.

I looked through the four cabinets in the room and found nothing. I circled the room. There was a shallow cupboard mounted on the wall, like a fuse box with double doors. A strip of masking tape was pasted on one side, with the word *exposed* printed on it in ballpoint pen. A second strip of tape said *unexposed*. I opened that door. There were film cassettes of varying sizes lined up like serving trays. I took one out.

I went over to the table and studied the layout of the machinery. I didn't see any way to slide the cassette into the apparatus above the table, but there was a sliding tray in the table itself, just under the padded edge. I pulled it out and inserted the cassette. I hoped I had guessed right about which side should be up. Looked right to me. Maybe I could fashion a whole new career out of this.

I figured Franklin didn't need protecting, so I picked up the full-length lead apron and put it on myself, feeling somehow like the goalie in a hockey match. Actually, I'd never seen an X-ray technician running around in one of these things, but it made me feel secure. I pointed the nose cone at Franklin's belly, about three feet up, and then went behind the screen in one corner of the room.

I checked the manual again, leafing through until I found diagrams that seemed relevant. There were numerous gauges with little arrow-shaped pointers at rest, ready to whip into the green zone, the yellow, or the red at the flick of a switch. There was a lever on the right marked "power supply," which I flipped to the "on" position. Nothing went on. A puzzlement. I flipped it off and then checked the wall to my left. There were two breaker boxes with big switches that I shifted from "off" to "on." There was a murmur of power being generated. I flipped the power supply lever to "on" again. The machine came on. I smiled. That was great.

I studied the panel in front of me. There was a timer that would apparently have to be set on a scale from 1/120 of a second to six seconds. A gauge for kilovolts. One marked "milliamperes." God, three rows of lighted green squares to choose from. I started with a midrange setting on everything, figuring I could use one gauge as a control and adjust the other two in some sort of rotating system. In between, I would check my results on the finished film and see what kind of picture I was getting.

I peered around the screen. "O.K., Frank, take a deep breath and hold."

Well, at least he got the "holding" part right.

I pressed the switch on the handgrip. I heard a brief

bzzt. Cautiously, I came out from behind the screen as though X rays might still be flying around the room. I crossed to the table and removed the cassette. Now what? There had to be some kind of developing process, but it didn't appear to be in here. I left the machine on and carried the cassette with me, checking into rooms nearby.

Two doors away, I found what looked right to me. On the wall was a flow chart, giving the step-by-step procedure for developing plates. I could get a job out here after this.

Again, it was necessary to switch the power on. After that, I worked in the dull red glow of the safelights, squinting my way through the process slowly. I filled the wall-mounted tank with water as specified. I flipped the cassette over and unlatched the back, removing the film, which I eased into the tray. It disappeared into the machine with a sound.

Shoot, where'd it go? I couldn't see anything in the room that looked like it would produce a piece of processed film. I felt like a puppy learning what happens when a ball rolls under the couch. I left the room and went next door. The hind end of the automatic developer was there, looking like a big Xerox machine with a slot. I waited. A minute and a half later, a finished piece of film slid out. I looked at it. Pitch black. Shit. What had I done wrong? How could it be overexposed when I'd been so careful? I stared at the developer. The lid was open a crack. I peered at it. Experimentally, I gave it a push. It snapped shut. Maybe that would do it.

I went back into the other room and got a second cassette out and went through the entire process again. Two rounds later, I found what I was looking for. The overall quality of the picture was poor, but the image was distinct. In the center of Franklin's belly was the solid white silhouette of a handgun. It looked like a large-frame automatic, arranged at an angle, maybe to accommodate his skeletal structure or internal organs. There was something unnerving about the sight. I rolled up the X ray and put a rubber band around it. Time to get out of here.

Hastily, I shut down the machinery and shifted Franklin onto the cart for the ride back to the morgue, turning off lights and locking up the office in my wake.

I navigated the gurney back through the hall and into the morgue. I was easing Franklin onto his berth again when something caught my eye. I glanced over at the next tier of bunks. A man's hand was resting just about at eye level and it didn't look right. The bodies I'd seen had been deadly pale, the flesh like a doll's skin, rubbery and unreal. This hand seemed too pink. I could see now that the body itself was only loosely covered with plastic sheeting. Had it been there before? I moved closer, reaching out hesitantly. I think I made that little humming sound you make when you're close to a shriek, but haven't yet committed yourself.

Tentatively, I lifted the plastic away from the face. Male, white, in his twenties. There was no pulse evident but that was probably because there was a ligature wound around his neck so tightly that it had all but disappeared, sinking into the flesh until his tongue bugged out. The body was cool, but not cold. I stopped breathing. I thought my heart would stop as well. I was reasonably sure I'd just made the acquaintance of Alfie Leadbetter, newly deceased. At that instant I wasn't as worried about who had killed him as who had buzzed the door open to let me in. I didn't think it was Alf. I suddenly suspected that I'd been cruising around that deserted building in the company of a killer who was undoubtedly still there, waiting to see what I was up to, waiting to do to me what had been done to the hapless morgue attendant who'd gotten in the way.

I backed out of the room as fast as I could, my heart banging away, sending sick spurts of fear through my electrified frame. The morgue was reassuringly bright, but so deadly still.

Mentally, I traced an escape route, wondering what choices I had. The windows down here were covered with burglar bars too narrow to slip through. The exterior doors were heavy glass, embedded with wire that I might or might not be able to penetrate. I certainly wasn't going to smash through them without calling attention to myself. I'd have to try for the stairs, pushing out of the same double doors I'd come through in the first place, though the idea of even going out into the *hall* at this point was nearly more than I could bear.

Somewhere above me, a door slammed and I jumped. I heard someone coming down the stairs, whistling aimlessly. A security guard? Someone coming back after work? I absolutely could not move. It was too late for action, too late for escape, and there was no place to hide. Transfixed, I stared at the door as footsteps approached. Someone paused in the corridor, singing the first few snatches of "Someone to Watch over Me." The knob turned and Dr. Fraker came in, glancing up, startled, at the sight of me.

"Oh! Hello. I didn't expect to see you here," he said. "I thought you were off talking to Kelly."

I let out a breath and found my voice. "I did that. A little while ago."

"Jesus, what's wrong? You're as white as a ghost."

I shook my head. "I was just on my way out when I heard the door slam. You scared the shit out of me." My voice cracked in the middle of the sentence as if I'd just reached puberty.

"Sorry. I didn't mean to spook you like that." He had on his surgical greens. I watched him cross the counter and open a drawer, taking out instruments. From the next drawer down, he took out a vial and a syringe.

"Listen, we've got a problem," I said.

"Oh really. What's that?" Dr. Fraker turned to smile at me and Nola's line popped into my head. "We're talking about a lunatic. Someone so crazy," she had whispered. Dr. Fraker's eyes were fixed on mine as he filled the syringe. The penny dropped. She hadn't wanted to stay *in* the marriage. She had wanted *out*. Bobby Callahan in his naïveté had thought he could help.

It was there in his face and the lazy way he moved. This man meant to kill me. Judging from the tools he'd assembled, he had all of the equipment he needed—nice table with a drain, hacksaws, scalpels, a working disposal just under the sink. He knew anatomy too, all the tendons and ligaments. I pictured a turkey wing, how you have to bend it backward to ease the blade into that joint.

I usually cry when I'm scared and I could feel tears well up. Not sorrow, but horror. Given all the lies I'd told in my life, right then I couldn't think of one. My mind was empty of thought. There I stood with the X ray in my hand, the truth, I'm sure, written all over my face. My only hope was to act before he did and move twice as fast.

I dove for the door, fumbling with the knob. I yanked it open and ran for the stairs, taking two at a time, then three, looking back with a moan of raw fear. He was coming out of the door, syringe held loosely in one hand. What scared me was that he was moving slowly, as if he had all the time in the world. He'd taken up the song lyric where he left off, a sort of tuneless rendition that didn't do the Gershwins justice.

"Like a little lamb who's lost in the wood . . . I know I could always be good . . . to one who'll watch over me . . ."

I reached the top of the stairs. What did he know that I didn't know? Why did he feel that this leisurely pace would suit when I was flying toward the entrance? I lowered a shoulder and slammed up against the double doors, but neither gave way. I rammed them again.

The entranceway, locked like this, formed a small cul-de-sac. If I gave him time to reach the corridor, I'd have no way out. I reached the hall just as he got to the top of the stairs.

Chit, chit. I could hear his footsteps scratch on the tile while he sang on.

"Although he may not be the man some girls think of as handsome, to my heart he'll carry the key . . ."

Still taking his time. I wanted to scream, but what was the point? The building was empty. It was locked up tight. Dark except for the pale light filtering in from the parking lot. I needed a weapon. Dr. Fraker had his little syringe filled with whatever he meant to pop me with. He was a big guy too, and once he made contact, I was in trouble.

I flew down the hall to the old medical-records room and slammed the door back on its hinge. I snatched up a two-by-four, still running, and headed back out into the corridor, racing for the far end. There had to be stairs. There had to be windows to smash, *some* way out.

Behind me, from a man who couldn't even carry a tune, I heard . . . *"Won't you tell him please to put on some speed, follow my lead, oh how I need, someone to watch over me . . ."*

I reached the stairwell and headed up, beginning to analyze the situation as I ran. At this rate, he could chase me all over the building. I'd soon be exhausted and he wouldn't even be breaking a sweat. Not a good idea, this form of pursuit. I reached the landing and snatched for the door. Locked. There was just one more floor. Was I being trapped or herded? In either case, I had the feeling he was in charge, that he'd set this all up in advance.

He was just coming into the stairwell below me as I took to the stairs again, heading toward the third floor, the two-by-four clutched in my hot little hand. I didn't like this. The door at the third floor flew back at a touch and I stepped into the darkened hall. I took off to my right, forcing myself to slow my pace. I was out of breath from climbing the stairs, bathed in sweat. I considered searching out a place to hide, but my choices were limited. There were rooms opening off on either side of me, but I was afraid I was going to get cornered in one. All he had to do was check each one in turn and pretty soon he'd figure out where I was. Also I hate hiding. It turns me into a six-year-old and I'm sick of that. I wanted to be on my feet, in motion, taking action instead of crouching down with my hands held over my face hoping God had rendered me transparent.

I made another right-hand turn. Behind me, I heard the door to the third-floor landing slam shut. I spotted an elevator halfway down the corridor on the right-hand side. I sprinted, and when I reached it, pounded on the "down" button with my palm.

Dr. Fraker had just taken up a new tune, this time whistling the first few bars of "I Don't Stand a Ghost of a Chance with You." Was this man sick or what?

I banged on the button again, listening fervently as

the elevator cable whirred softly on the other side of the door. I looked to my right. There he came, his surgical greens showing up as a pale glow in the shadows. I heard the mechanism stop. He seemed to be moving faster, but he was still twenty yards away from me. The elevator doors slid open. Oh fuck!

I stepped forward just as I flashed on the fact that there was nothing there except a yawning shaft and a gust of cold air wafting up from below. I caught myself half a second from tumbling into that pitch-black hole. A low cry escaped me as I caught at the doorframe, swinging out over the pit for an instant before I managed to right myself. I stumbled backward to safety but I'd lost my purchase. I was down and the two-by-four flew out of my hand, skittering off. I flipped over on my hands and knees scrambling toward it.

He had caught up to me by then and he grabbed me by the hair, hauling me upright just as my hand closed around the board. I swung it up, whacking at him. I made contact but the angle was awkward and there was no force behind the blow. I felt the sting of the needle in my left thigh. Both of us barked out a sound at the same time. Mine was a shrill yelp of pain and surprise, his the low grunt as the impact from the two-by-four registered. I had the advantage of a split second and I took it, lashing out with a side kick that caught him in the shin. No good, too low. The wisdom of self-defense would have it that there's no point in simply inflecting pain on your attacker. It'll just piss him off. Unless I could disable him, I didn't have a chance.

He grabbed at me from behind. I snapped my left

elbow back, but again I was slightly off the mark. I pushed at him, kicking repeatedly at his shin until he backed off, breathing hard. I cracked him one across the shoulder with the two-by-four and ran, pounding down the hall. I stumbled briefly, but regained my footing. I felt as if I'd stepped in a hole, and it occurred to me belatedly that whatever he'd injected me with was taking effect. My left leg was feeling wobbly, my kneecap loose, both feet going numb. The same fear that had sent adrenaline coursing through my body was speeding some drug on its way. Like snakebite. They say you shouldn't run.

I glanced back. He was clutching his shoulder, just beginning to move in my direction, coming slowly again. He didn't seem worried that I'd get away, so I had to guess that he had jammed the door to the stairwell as he came through. Either that or he knew that the shit he'd popped me with would soon knock me out. I was losing contact with my extremities and I could scarcely sense my own grip on the board. A chill was seeping from my skin toward my core as if I were being put through a quick-freeze process for shipping to God knows where. I was working as hard as I could, but the darkness had become gelatinous and I felt slow. Time was grinding down too as my body labored against the drug. My mind was working, but I felt myself distracted by the odd sensations I experienced.

Oh, the bothersome details that finally fall into place like a little right-brain joke. It did come to me, in a flash, like a bubble through my veins, that Fraker was the one supplying Kitty with drugs, probably in exchange for information about Bobby's search for the gun. The stash in her bed-table drawer was a plant. He'd been there that night. Maybe he thought it was time to take her out, lest she in her guilt admit to her own duplicity where Bobby was concerned.

The distance to the corner of the hallway had been extended. I'd been running forever. The simple commands I was managing to send to my body were taking too long and I was losing the feedback system that records a response. Was I, in fact, running? Was I going anywhere? Sound was being stretched out, the echo of my own footsteps coming belatedly. I felt as if I were bounding down a corridor with a floor like a trampoline. Flash number two. Fraker had rigged the autopsy report. No seizure. He'd cut the brake lines. Too bad I hadn't figured it out before now. God, what a dummy I was.

I reached the corner slowing, and I could feel my body folding down on itself. As I rounded the corner, I had to pause. I propped myself against the wall, working to breathe. I had to clear my head. Stay upright. I had to lift my arms if I could. Time had begun to stretch out like taffy, long strands, sticky, hard to manage.

He was singing again, treating me to some oldies but goodies in his own private hit parade. He'd moved on now to "Accentuate the positive . . . eliminate the negative" . . . vowels dragged out like a phonograph record slowing when the power shuts off.

Even the voice in my own brain got hollow and remote.

Crouch, Kinsey, it said.

I thought I might be crouching but I couldn't tell anymore where my legs were or my hips or much of my spine. My arms were feeling heavy and I wondered if my elbows were bent.

Batter up, the voice said and I believed, but couldn't have sworn to the fact, that I was drawing the two-by-four back, elbow crooked as my aunt had taught me long long ago.

Day was passing into night, life into death.

Fraker's voice droned out the song. *"Acceeennntuate the pooosssitive, eeeellliiiiminaaate the neeegatiiiive . . ."*

When he came around the corner, I stepped into the swing, the two-by-four aimed straight at his face. I could see the board begin its march through space, like a series of time-lapse photographs, light against dark, closing down the distance. I felt the board connect with a sweet popping sound.

It was out of the ball park and I went down with the roar of the crowd in my ears.

Epilogue

They told me later, though I remember little of it, that I managed to make my way down to the morgue, where I dialed 911, mumbling a message that brought the cops. What comes back to me most clearly is the hangover I endured after the cocktail of barbiturates I was injected with. I woke in a hospital bed, as sick as a dog. But even with a pounding head, retching into a kidney-shaped plastic basin, I was glad to be among the living.

Glen spoiled me silly and everyone came to see me, including Jonah, Rosie, Gus, and Henry, bearing hot cross buns. Lila, he said, had written to him from a jail up north, but he didn't bother to reply. Glen never relented in her determination to reject both Derek and Kitty, but I introduced Kitty Wenner to Gus. Last I heard, they were dating and Kitty was cleaning up her act. Both had gained weight.

Dr. Fraker is currently out on bail, awaiting trial on charges of attempted murder and two counts of first-degree murder. Nola pleaded guilty to voluntary manslaughter, but served no time. When I got back to the office, I typed up my report, submitting a bill for thirty-three hours, plus mileage; a total I rounded off to an even $1000. The balance of Bobby's advance I returned to Varden Talbot's office to be factored into his estate. The rest of the report is a personal letter. Much of my last message to Bobby is devoted to the simple fact that I miss him. I hope, wherever he may be, that he sails among the angels, untethered and at peace.

—Respectfully submitted,
Kinsey Millhone

D is for Deadbeat

For my sister, Ann,
and the memories of Maple Hill

The author wishes to acknowledge the invaluable assistance of the following people: Steven Humphrey, Florence Clark, Joyce Mackewich, Steve Stafford, Bob Ericson, Ann Hunnicutt, Charles and Mary Pope of the Rescue Mission, Michael Thompson of the Santa Barbara Probation Department, Michelle Bores and Bob Brandenburg of the Santa Barbara Harbor Master's Office, Mary Louise Days of the Santa Barbara Building Department, and Gerald Dow, Crime Analyst, Santa Barbara Police Department.

1

Later, I found out his name was John Daggett, but that's not how he introduced himself the day he walked into my office. Even at the time, I sensed that something was off, but I couldn't figure out what it was. The job he hired me to do seemed simple enough, but then the bum tried to stiff me for my fee. When you're self-employed, you can't afford to let these things slide. Word gets out and first thing you know, everybody thinks you can be had. I went after him for the money and the next thing I knew, I was caught up in events I still haven't quite recovered from.

My name is Kinsey Millhone. I'm a private investigator, licensed by the state of California, operating a small office in Santa Teresa, which is where I've lived all my thirty-two years. I'm female, self-supporting, single now, having been married and divorced twice. I confess I'm sometimes testy, but for the most part I credit myself with an easygoing disposition, tempered (perhaps) by an exaggerated desire for independence. I'm also plagued with the sort of doggedness that makes private investigation a viable proposition for someone with a high school education, certification from the police academy, and a constitutional inability to work for anyone else. I pay my bills on time, obey most laws, and I feel that other people should do likewise . . . out of courtesy, if nothing else. I'm a purist when it comes to justice, but I'll lie at the drop of a hat. Inconsistency has never troubled me.

It was late October, the day before Halloween, and the weather was mimicking autumn in the Midwest— clear and sunny and cool. Driving into town, I could have sworn I smelled woodsmoke in the air and I half expected the leaves to be turning yellow and rust. All I actually saw were the same old palm trees, the same relentless green everywhere. The fires of summer had been contained and the rains hadn't started yet. It was a typical California *un*season, but it *felt* like fall and I was responding with inordinate good cheer, thinking maybe I'd drive up the pass in the afternoon to the pistol range, which is what I do for laughs.

I'd come into the office that Saturday morning to take care of some bookkeeping chores—paying personal bills, getting out my statements for the month. I had my calculator out, a Redi-Receipt form in the typewriter, and four completed statements lined up, addressed and stamped, on the desk to my left. I was so intent on the task at hand that I didn't realize anyone was standing in the doorway until the man cleared his throat. I reacted with one of those little jumps you do when you open the evening paper and a spider runs out. He apparently found this amusing, but I was having to pat myself on the chest to get my heart rate down again.

"I'm Alvin Limardo," he said. "Sorry if I startled you."

"That's all right," I said, "I just had no idea you were standing there. Are you looking for me?"

"If you're Kinsey Millhone, I am."

I got up and shook hands with him across the desk and then suggested that he take a seat. My first fleeting impression had been that he was a derelict, but on second glance, I couldn't find anything in particular to support the idea.

He was in his fifties, too gaunt for good health. His face was long and narrow, his chin pronounced. His hair was an ash gray, clipped short, and he smelled of citrus cologne. His eyes were hazel, his gaze remote. The suit he wore was an odd shade of green. His hands seemed huge, fingers long and bony, the knuckles enlarged. The two inches of narrow wrist extending, cuffless, from his coat sleeves suggested shabbiness though his clothing didn't really look worn. He held a slip of paper which he'd folded twice, and he fiddled with that self-consciously.

"What can I do for you?" I asked.

"I'd like for you to deliver this." He smoothed out the piece of paper then and placed it on my desk. It was a cashier's check drawn on a Los Angeles bank, dated October 29, and made out to someone named Tony Gahan for twenty-five thousand dollars.

I tried not to appear as surprised as I felt. He didn't look like a man with money to spare. Maybe he'd borrowed the sum from Gahan and was paying it back. "You want to tell me what this is about?"

"He did me a favor. I want to say thanks. That's all it is."

"It must have been quite a favor," I said. "Do you mind if I ask what he did?"

"He showed me a kindness when I was down on my luck."

"What do you need me for?"

He smiled briefly. "An attorney would charge me a hundred and twenty dollars an hour to handle it. I'm assuming you'd charge considerably less."

"So would a messenger service," I said. "It's cheaper still if you do it yourself." I wasn't being a smart-mouth about it. I really didn't understand why he needed a private detective.

He cleared his throat. "I tried that, but I'm not entirely certain of Mr. Gahan's current address. At one time, he lived on Stanley Place, but he's not there now. I went by this morning and the house is empty. It looks like it hasn't been lived in for a while. I want someone to track him down and make sure he gets the money. If you can estimate what that might run me, I'll pay you in advance."

"That depends on how elusive Mr. Gahan turns out to be. The credit bureau might have a current address, or the DMV. A lot of inquiries can be done by phone, but they still take time. At thirty bucks an hour, the fee does mount up."

He took out a checkbook and began to write out a check. "Two hundred dollars?"

"Let's make it four. I can always refund the balance if the charges turn out to be less," I said. "In the meantime, I've got a license to protect so this better be on the up and up. I'd be happier if you'd tell me what's going on."

This was where he hooked me, because what he said was just offbeat enough to be convincing. Liar that I am, it still didn't occur to me that there could be so much falsehood mixed in with the truth.

"I got into trouble with the law awhile back and served some time. Tony Gahan was helpful to me just before I was arrested. He had no idea of my circumstances so he wasn't an accessory to anything, nor would you be. I feel indebted."

"Why not take care of it yourself?"

He hesitated, almost shyly I thought. "It's sort of like that Charles Dickens book, *Great Expectations*. He might not like having a convicted felon for a benefactor. People have strange ideas about ex-cons."

"What if he won't accept an anonymous donation?"

"You can return the check in that case and keep the fee."

I shifted restlessly in my chair. What's wrong with this picture, I asked myself. "Where'd you get the money if you've been in jail?"

"Santa Anita. I'm still on parole and I shouldn't be playing the ponies at all, but I find it hard to resist. That's why I'd like to pass the money on to you. I'm a gambling man. I can't have that kind of cash around or I'll piss it away, if you'll pardon my French." He closed his mouth then and looked at me, waiting to see what else I might ask. Clearly, he didn't want to volunteer more than was necessary to satisfy my qualms, but he seemed amazingly patient. I realized later, of course, that his tolerance was probably the function of his feeding me so much bullshit. He must have been entertained by the game he was playing. Lying is fun. I can do it all day myself.

"What was the felony?" I asked.

He dropped his gaze, addressing his reply to his oversized hands, which were folded in his lap. "I don't think that pertains. This money is clean and I came by it honestly. There's nothing illegal about the transaction if that's what's worrying you."

Of *course* it worried me, but I wondered if I was being too fastidious. There was nothing wrong with his request on the face of it. I chased the proposition around in my head with caution, wondering what Tony Gahan had done for Limardo that would net him this kind of payoff. None of my business, I supposed, as long as no laws had been broken in the process. Intuition was telling me to turn this guy down, but it happens that the rent on my apartment was due the next day. I had the money in my checking account, but it seemed providential to have a retainer drop in my lap unexpectedly. In any event, I didn't see a reason to refuse. "All right," I said.

He nodded once, pleased. "Good."

I sat and watched while he finished signing his name to the check. He tore it out and pushed it toward me, tucking the checkbook into the inner pocket of his suit coat. "My address and telephone number are on that in case you need to get in touch."

I pulled a standard contract form out of my desk drawer and took a few minutes to fill it in. I got his signature and then I made a note of Tony Gahan's last known address, a house in Colgate, the township just north of Santa Teresa. I was already feeling some low-level dread, wishing I hadn't agreed to do anything. Still, I'd committed myself, the contract was signed, and I figured I'd make the best of it. How much trouble could it be, thought I.

He stood up and I did too, moving with him as he walked toward the door. With both of us on our feet, I could see how much taller he was than I . . . maybe six-four to my five-foot-six. He paused with his hand on the knob, gazing down at me with the same remote stare.

"One other thing you might need to know about Tony Gahan," he said.

"What's that?"

"He's fifteen years old."

I stood there and watched Alvin Limardo move off down the hall. I should have called him back, folks. I should have known right then that it wasn't going to turn out well. Instead I closed the office door and returned to my desk. On impulse, I opened the French doors and went out on the balcony. I scanned the street below, but there was no sign of him. I shook my head, dissatisfied.

I locked the cashier's check in my file cabinet. When the bank opened on Monday, I'd put it in my safe deposit box until I located Tony Gahan and then turn it over to him. Fifteen?

At noon, I closed up the office and went down the back stairs to the parking lot, where I retrieved my VW, a decaying sedan with more rust than paint. This is not the sort of vehicle you'd choose for a car chase, but then most of what a P.I. does for a living isn't that exciting anyway. I'm sometimes reduced to serving process papers, which gets hairy now and then, but much of the time I do preemployment background checks, skip-tracing, or case-and-trial preparation for a couple of attorneys here in town. My office is provided by California Fidelity Insurance, a former employer of mine. The company headquarters is right next door and I still do sporadic investigations for them in exchange for a modest two rooms (one inner, one outer) with a separate entrance and a balcony overlooking State Street.

I went by the post office and dropped the mail in the box and then I stopped by the bank and deposited Alvin Limardo's four hundred dollars in my checking account.

Four business days later, on a Thursday, I got a letter from the bank, informing me that the check had bounced. According to their records, Alvin Limardo had closed out his account. In proof of this, I was presented with the check itself stamped across the face with the sort of officious looking purple ink that makes it clear the bank is displeased.

So was I.

My account had been debited the four hundred dollars and I was charged an additional three bucks, apparently to remind me, in the future, not to deal with deadbeats. I picked up the phone and called Alvin Limardo's number in Los Angeles. A disconnect. I'd been canny enough to ignore the search for Tony Gahan until the check cleared, so it wasn't as if I'd done any work to date. But how was I going to get the check replaced? And what was I going to do with the twenty-five grand in the meantime? By then, the cashier's check was tucked away in my safe deposit box, but it was useless to me and I didn't want to proceed with delivery until I knew I'd be paid. In theory, I could have dropped Alvin Limardo a note, but it might have come bouncing back at me with all the jauntiness of his rubber check, and then where would I be? Crap. I was going to have to drive down to L.A. One thing I've learned about collections—the faster you move, the better your chances are.

I looked up his street address in my *Thomas Guide to Los Angeles Streets*. Even on the map, it didn't look like a nice neighborhood. I checked my watch. It was then 10:15. It was going to take me ninety minutes to reach L.A., probably another hour to locate Limardo, chew him out, get the check replaced, and grab a bite of lunch. Then I'd have to drive ninety minutes back, which would put me in the office again at 3:30 or 4:00. Well, that wasn't too bad. It was tedious, but necessary, so I decided I might as well quit bellyaching and get on with it.

By 10:30, I'd gassed up my car and I was on the road.

2

I left the Ventura Freeway at Sherman Oaks, taking the San Diego Freeway south as far as Venice Boulevard. I exited, turning right at the bottom of the off-ramp. According to my calculations, the address I wanted was somewhere close. I doubled back toward Sawtelle, the street that hugs the freeway on a parallel route.

Once I saw the building, I realized that I'd spotted the rear of it from the freeway as I passed. It was painted the color of Pepto-Bismol and sported a sagging banner of Day-Glo orange that said NOW RENTING. The building was separated from the roadway by a concrete rain wash and protected from speeding vehicles by a ten-foot cinderblock wall sprayed with messages for passing motorists. Spiky weeds had sprung up along the base of the wall and trash had accumulated like hanging ornaments in the few hearty bushes that managed to survive the gas fumes. I had noted the building because it seemed so typical of L.A.: bald, cheaply constructed, badly defaced. There was something meanspirited about its backside, and the entrance turned out to be worse.

The street was largely made up of California "bungalows," small two-bedroom houses of wood and stucco with ragged yards and no trees. Most of them had been painted in pastel hues, odd shades of turquoise and mauve, suggestive of discount paints that hadn't quite covered the color underneath. I found a parking space across the street and locked my car, then crossed to the apartment complex.

The building was beginning to disintegrate. The stucco looked mealy and dry, the aluminum window frames pitted and buckling. The wrought-iron gate near the front had been pulled straight out of the supporting wall, leaving holes large enough to stick a fist into. Two apartments at street level were boarded up. The management had thoughtfully provided a number of garbage bins near the stairs, without (apparently) paying for adequate trash removal services. A big yellow dog was scratching through this pile of refuse with enthusiasm, though all he seemed to net for his efforts was a quarter moon of pizza. He trotted off, the rim of crust clenched in his jaws like a bone.

I moved into the shelter of the stairs. Most of the mailboxes had been ripped out and mail was scattered in the foyer like so much trash. According to the address on the face of the check, Limardo lived in apartment 26, which I surmised was somewhere above. There were apparently forty units, only a few marked with the occupants' names. That seemed curious to me. In Santa Teresa, the post office won't even deliver junk mail unless a box is provided, clearly marked, and in good repair. I pictured the postman, emptying out his mail pouch like a wastepaper basket, escaping on foot then before the inhabitants of the building swarmed over him like bugs.

The apartments were arranged in tiers around a courtyard "garden" of loose gravel, pink paving stones, and nut grass. I picked my way up the cracked concrete steps.

At the second-floor landing, a black man was seated in a rickety metal folding chair, whittling with a knife on a bar of Ivory soap. There was a magazine open on his lap to catch the shavings. He was heavyset and shapeless, maybe fifty years old, his short-cropped frizzy hair showing gray around his ears. His eyes were a muddy brown, the lid of one pulled askew by a vibrant track of stitches that cut down along his cheek.

He took me in at a glance, turning his attention then to the sculpture taking form in his hands. "You must be looking for Alvin Limardo," he said.

"That's right," I said, startled. "How'd you guess?"

He flashed a smile at me, showing perfect teeth, as snowy as the soap he carved. He tilted his face up at me, the injured eye creating the illusion of a wink.

"Baby, you ain't live here. I know ever'body live here. And from the look on your face, you ain't thinkin' to rent. If you knew where you were going, you'd be headed straight there. Instead, you be lookin' all around like somethin' might jump out on you, including me," he said and then paused to survey me. "I'd say you do social work, parole, something like that. Maybe welfare."

"Not bad," I said. "But why Limardo? What made you think I was looking for him?"

He smiled then, his gums showing pink. "We *all* Alvin Limardo 'round here. It's a joke we play. Just a name we take when we jivin' folk. I been Alvin Limardo myself lass week at the food stamp line. He get welfare checks, disability, AFDC. Somebody show up lass week wid a warrant on him. I tole 'em, 'Alvin Limardo's done leff. He gone. Ain't nobody here by that name about now.' The Alvin Limardo you want . . . he be white or black?"

"White," I said and then described the man who'd come into my office on Saturday. The black man started nodding about halfway through, his knife blade still smoothing the surface of the soap. It looked like he'd carved a sow lying on her side with a litter of piglets scrambling over her to nurse. The whole of it couldn't have been more than four inches long.

"That's John Daggett. Whooee. He bad. He the one you want, but he gone for sure."

"Do you have any idea where he went?"

"Santa Teresa, I heard."

"Well, I know he was up there last Saturday. That's where I ran into him," I said. "Has he been back since then?"

The man's mouth drooped with skepticism. "I seen him on Monday and then he gone off again. Only other peoples must want him too. He ack like a man who's runnin' and don't want to be caught. What you want wid him?"

"He wrote me a bum check."

He shot me a look of astonishment. "You take a check from a man like that? Lord God, girl! What's the matter wid you?"

I had to laugh. "I know. It's my own damn fault. I thought maybe I could catch him before he skipped out permanently."

He shook his head, unable to sympathize. "Don't take nothin' from the likes of him. That's your first mistake. Comin' 'round this place may be the next."

"Is there anybody here who might know how to get in touch with him?"

He pointed the blade of his knife toward an apartment two doors down. "Axe Lovella. She might know. Then again, she might not."

"She's a friend of his?"

"Not hardly. She's his wife."

I felt somewhat more hopeful as I knocked at apartment 26. I was afraid he'd moved out altogether. The door was a hollowcore with a hole kicked into the bottom about shin high. The sliding glass window was open six inches, a fold of drapery sticking out. A crack ran diagonally across the pane, held together by a wide band of electrician's tape. I could smell something cooking inside, kale or collard greens, with a whisper of vinegar and bacon grease.

The door opened and a woman peered out at me. Her upper lip was puffy, like the kind of scrape children get falling off bicycles when they first learn to ride. Her left eye had been blackened not long ago and it was streaked now with midnight blue, the surrounding tissue a rainbow of green and yellow and gray. Her hair was the color of hay, parted in the middle and snagged up over each ear with a bobby pin. I couldn't even guess how old she might be. Younger than I expected, given John Daggett's age, which had to be fifty plus.

"Lovella Daggett?"

"That's right." She seemed reluctant to admit that much.

"I'm Kinsey Millhone. I'm looking for John."

She licked uneasily at her upper lip as if she was still unfamiliar with its new shape and size. Some of the scraped area had formed a scab, which resembled nothing so much as half a moustache. "He's not here. I don't know where he's at. What'd you want him for?"

"He hired me to do some work, but he paid me with a bum check. I was hoping we could get it straightened out."

She studied me while she processed the information. "Hired you to do what?"

"Deliver something."

She didn't believe a bit of that. "You a cop?"

"No."

"What are you, then?"

I showed her the photostat of my license by way of reply. She turned and walked away from the door, leaving it open behind her. I gathered this was her method of inviting me in.

I stepped into the living room and closed the door behind me. The carpeting was that green cotton shag so admired by apartment owners everywhere. The only furniture in the room was a card table and two plain wooden chairs. A six-foot rectangle of lighter carpeting along one wall suggested that there'd once been a couch on the spot, and a pattern of indentations in the rug indicated the former presence of two heavy chairs and a coffee table, arranged in what decorators refer to as "a conversational grouping." Instead of conversation these days, Daggett apparently got right down to busting her chops, breaking anything else that came to hand. The one lamp I saw had been snapped off at the socket and the wires were hanging out like torn ligaments.

"Where'd the furniture go?"

"He hocked it all last week. Turns out he used the payments for his bar bill. The car went before that. It was a piece of junk, anyway, but I'd paid for it. You ought to see what I've got for a bed these days. Some peed-on old mattress he found out on the street."

There were two bar stools at the counter and I perched on one, watching as Lovella ambled into the small space that served as a kitchen. An aluminum saucepan sat on a gas flame on the stove, the water in it boiling furiously. On one of the other back burners, there was a battered aluminum kettle filled with simmering greens.

Lovella wore blue jeans and a plain white tee shirt wrong-side out, the Fruit of the Loom label visible at the back of her neck. The bottom of the shirt had been pulled tight and knotted to form a halter, leaving her midriff bare. "You want coffee? I was just fixing some."

"Yes, please," I said.

She rinsed a cup under the hot water faucet and gave it a quick swipe with a paper towel. She set it on the counter and spooned instant coffee into it and then used the same paper towel as a potholder when she reached for the saucepan. The water sputtered against the edge of the pan as she poured. She added water to a second cup, gave a quick stir to the contents, and pushed it toward me with the spoon still resting up against the rim.

"Daggett's a jerk. They should lock him up for life," she remarked, almost idly, I thought.

"Did he do that to you?" I asked, my gaze flicking across her bruised face.

She fixed a pair of dead gray eyes on me without

bothering to reply. Up close, I could see that she wasn't much more than twenty-five. She leaned forward, resting her elbows on the counter, her coffee cup cradled in her hands. She wasn't wearing a bra and her breasts were big, as soft and droopy as balloons filled with water, her nipples pressing against the tee-shirt fabric like puckered knots. I wondered if she was a hooker. I'd known a few with the same careless sexuality—all surface, no feeling underneath.

"How long have you been married?"

"You care if I have a cigarette?"

"It's your place. You can do anything you want," I said.

That netted me a wan smile, the first I'd seen. She reached for a pack of Pall Mall 100s, flipped on the gas burner, and lit her cigarette from it, tilting her head so her hair wouldn't catch fire. She took a deep drag and exhaled it, blowing a cloud of smoke at me. "Six weeks," she said, answering my question belatedly. "We were pen pals after he got sent to San Luis. Wrote for a year and then I married him the minute he got out. Dumb? Jesus. Can you believe I did that?"

I shrugged noncommittally. She didn't really care if I believed it or not. "How'd you connect in the first place?"

"A buddy of his. Guy named Billy Polo I used to date. They'd sit and talk about women and my name came up. I guess Billy made me sound like real hot stuff, so Daggett got in touch."

I took a sip of my coffee. It had that flat, nearly sour taste of instant, with tiny clumps of coffee powder floating at the edge. "Do you have any milk for this?"

"Oh, sure. Sorry," she said. She moved over to the refrigerator where she took out a small can of Carnation.

It wasn't quite what I had in mind, but I added some to my coffee, intrigued as evaporated milk rose to the surface in a series of white dots. I wondered if a fortune teller could read the pattern, like tea leaves. I thought I spied some indigestion in my future, but I wasn't sure.

"Daggett's a charmer when he wants," she said. "Give him a couple of drinks, though, and he's mean as a snake."

That was a story I'd heard before. "Why don't you leave?" said I, as I always do.

"Because he'd come after me is why," she said snappishly. "You don't know him. He'd kill me without giving it a second thought. Same thing if I called the cops. Talk back to that man and he'll punch your teeth down your throat. He hates women is what's the matter with him. Of course, when he sobers up, he can charm your socks off. Anyway, I'm hoping he's gone for good. He got a phone call Monday morning and he was out of here like a shot. I haven't heard from him since. Of course, the phone was disconnected yesterday so I don't know how he'd reach me even if he wanted to."

"Why don't you talk to his parole officer?"

"I guess I could," she said reluctantly. "He reports to the guy every time he turns around. For two days he had a job, but he quit that. Of course, he's not supposed to drink. I guess he tried to play by the rules at first, but it was too much."

"Why not get out while you have the chance?"

"And go where? I don't have a nickel to my name."

"There are shelters for battered women. Call the rape crisis center. They'll know."

She gestured dismissively. "Jesus, I love people like you. You ever had a guy punch you out?"

"Not one I was married to," I said. "I wouldn't put up with that shit."

"That's what I used to say, sister, but I'll tell you what. You don't get away as easy as all that. Not with a bastard like Daggett. He swears he'd follow me to the ends of the earth and he would."

"What was he in prison for?"

"He never said and I never asked. Which was also dumb. It didn't make any difference to me at first. He was fine for a couple weeks. Just like a kid, you know? And sweet? Lord, he trotted around after me like a puppy dog. We couldn't get enough of each other and it all seemed just like the letters we wrote. Then he got into the Jack Daniel's one night and the shit hit the fan."

"Did he ever mention the name Tony Gahan?"

"Nuh-uh. Who's he?"

"I'm not sure. Some kid he asked me to find."

"What'd he pay you with? Can I see the check?"

I took it out of my handbag and laid it on the counter. I thought it best not to mention the cashier's check. I didn't think she'd take kindly to his giving money away. "I understand Limardo is a fabricated name."

She studied the check. "Yeah, but Daggett did keep some money in this account. I think he cleaned it out just before he left." She took a drag of her cigarette as she handed back the check. I managed to turn my head before she blew smoke in my face again.

"That phone call he got Monday, what was it about? Do you know?"

"Beats me. I was off at the Laundromat. I got home and he was still on the phone, his face as gray as that dish rag. He hung up quick and then started shovin' stuff in a duffel. He turned the place upside down lookin' for his bank book. I was afraid he'd come after me, thinkin' I took it, but I guess he was too freaked out to worry about me."

"He told you that?"

"No, but he was cold sober and his hands were shaking *bad*."

"You have any idea where he might have gone?"

A look flashed through her eyes, some emotion she concealed by dropping her gaze. "He only had one friend and that was Billy Polo up in Santa Teresa. If he needed help, that's where he'd go. I think he used to have family up there too, but I don't know what happened to them. He never talked much about that."

"So Polo's out of prison?"

"I heard he got out just recently."

"Well, maybe I'll track him down since that's the only lead I have. In the meantime, would you find a phone and call me if you hear from either one?" I took out a business card and jotted my home address and phone on the back. "Call collect."

She looked at both sides of the card. "What do you think is goin' on?"

"I don't know and I don't much care. As soon as I run him down, I'll clean up this business and *bail out*."

3

As long as I was in the area, I went by the bank. The woman in charge of customer service couldn't have been less helpful. She was dark haired, in her early twenties, and new at the job I gathered because she greeted my every request with the haunted look of someone who isn't quite sure of the rules and therefore says no to everything. She would not verify "Alvin Limardo's" account number or the fact that the account had been closed. She would not tell me if there was, perhaps, another account in John Daggett's name. I knew there had to be a registered copy of the cashier's check itself, but she refused to verify the information he'd given at the time. I kept thinking there was some other tack I might take, especially with that much money at stake. Surely, the bank must care what happened to twenty-five thousand dollars. I stood at the counter and stared at the woman, and she stared back. Maybe she hadn't understood.

I took out the photostat of my license and pointed. "Look," I said, "You see this? I'm a private investigator. I've got a real problem here. I was hired to deliver a cashier's check, but now I can't find the man who gave it to me and I don't know the whereabouts of the person who's supposed to receive it and I'm just trying to get a lead so I can do what I was hired to do."

"I understand that," she said.

"But you won't give me any information, right?"

"It's against bank regulations."

"Isn't it against bank regulations for Alvin Limardo to write me a bad check?"

"Yes."

"Then what am I supposed to do with it?" I said. I really knew the answer . . . eat it, dum-dum . . . but I was feeling stubborn and perverse.

"Take him to small claims court," she said.

"But I can't find him. He can't be hauled into court if nobody knows where he is."

She stared at me blankly, offering no comment.

"What about the twenty-five thousand?" I said. "What am I supposed to do with that?"

"I have no idea."

I stared down at the desk. When I was in kindergarten, I was a biter and I still struggle with the urge. It just feels good, you know? "I want to speak to your supervisor."

"Mr. Stallings? He's gone for the day."

"Well, is there anybody else here who might give me some help on this?"

She shook her head. "I'm in charge of customer service."

"But you're not doing a thing. How can you call it customer service when you don't do shit?"

Her mouth turned prim. "Please don't use language like that around me. It's very offensive."

"What do I have to do to get help around here?"

"Do you have an account with us?"

"If I did, would you help?"

"Not with this. We're not supposed to divulge information about bank customers."

This was silly. I walked away from her desk. I wanted to make a withering remark, but I couldn't think of one. I knew I was just mad at myself for taking the job to begin with, but I was hoping to lay a little ire off on her . . . a pointless enterprise. I got back in my car and headed toward the freeway. When I reached Santa Teresa, it was 4:35. I bypassed the office altogether and went home. My disposition improved the minute I walked in. My apartment was once a single-car garage and consists now of one room, fifteen feet on a side, with a narrow extension on the right that serves as a kitchenette, separated from the living area by a counter. The space is arranged with cunning: a stackable washer-dryer tucked in beside the kitchenette, bookshelves, drawers, and storage compartments built into the wall. It's tidy and self-contained and all of it suits me absolutely. I have a six-foot convertible sofa that I usually sleep on as is, a desk, a chair, an endtable, and plump pillows that serve as additional seating if anyone comes over to sit. My bathroom is one of those preformed fiberglass units with everything molded into it, including a towel bar, a soap holder, and a cutout for a window that looks out at the street. Sometimes I stand in the bathtub, elbows resting on the sill, and stare at passing cars, just thinking how lucky I am. I love being single. It's almost like being rich.

I dropped my handbag on the desk and hung my jacket on a peg. I sat on the couch and pulled off my boots, then padded over to the refrigerator and took out a bottle of white zinfandel and a corkscrew. At intervals, I try to behave like a person with class, which is to say I drink wine from a bottle instead of a cardboard box. I pulled the cork and poured myself a glass. I crossed to the desk, taking the telephone book from the top drawer, trailing telephone cord, directory, and wine glass over to the sofa. I set the wine glass on the endtable and thumbed through the book to see if Billy Polo was listed. Of course, he wasn't. I looked up the name Gahan. No dice. I drank some wine and tried to think what to do next.

On an impulse, I checked for the name Daggett. Lovella had mentioned that he once lived up here. Maybe he still had relatives in town.

There were four Daggetts listed. I started dialing

them in order, saying the same thing each time. "Oh, hi. I'm trying to reach a John Daggett, who used to live in this area. Can you tell me if this is the correct number?"

On the first two calls, I drew a blank, but with the third, the man who answered responded to my query with one of those odd silences that indicate that information is being processed.

"What did you want with him?" he asked. He sounded like he was in his sixties, his phrasing tentative, alert to my response, but undecided how much he was willing to reveal.

He was certainly skipping right down to the tricky part. From everything I'd heard about Daggett, he was a bum, so I didn't dare claim to be a friend of his. If I admitted he owed me money, I was going to have the phone slammed down in my ear. Ordinarily, in a situation like this, I'd insinuate that I had money for *him*, but somehow I didn't think that would fly. People are getting wise to that shit.

I laid out the first lie that occurred to me. "Well, to tell you the truth," I said, "I've only met John once, but I'm trying to get in touch with a mutual acquaintance and I think John has his address and telephone number."

"Who were you looking to get in touch with?"

That caught me off-guard, as I hadn't made that part up yet. "Who? Um . . . Alvin Limardo. Has John ever mentioned Alvin?"

"No, I don't believe so. But, now, you may have the wrong party. The John Daggett that used to live here is currently in prison and he's been there, oh I'd say nearly two years." His manner suggested a man whose retirement has invested even a wrong number with some interesting possibilities. Still, it was clear I'd hit pay dirt.

"That's the one I'm talking about," I said. "He was up in San Luis Obispo."

"He still is."

"Oh, no. He's out. He was released six weeks ago."

"John? *No*, ma'am. He's still in prison and I hope he stays there. I don't mean to speak ill of the man, but you'll find he's what I call a problematic person."

"Problematic?"

"Well, yes. That's how I'd have to put it. John is the type of person that creates problems and usually of a quite serious nature."

"Oh, really," I said. "I didn't realize that." I loved it that this man was willing to chat. As long as I could keep him going, I might figure out how to get a bead on Daggett. I took a flyer. "Are you his brother?"

"I'm his brother-in-law, Eugene Nickerson."

"You must be married to his sister then," I said.

He laughed. "No, he's married to *my* sister. She was a Nickerson before she became a Daggett."

"You're Lovella's brother?" I was trying to picture siblings with a forty-year age span.

"No, Essie's."

I held the receiver away from my ear and stared at it. What was he talking about? "Wait a minute. I'm confused. Maybe we're *not* talking about the same man." I gave a quick verbal sketch of the John Daggett I'd met. I didn't see how there could be two, but there was something going on here.

"That's him all right. How did you say you knew him?"

"I met him last Saturday, right here in Santa Teresa."

The silence on the other end of the line was profound.

I finally broke into it. "Is there some way I might stop by so we can talk about this?"

"I think you'd best," he said. "What would your name be?"

"Kinsey Millhone."

He told me how to get to the place.

The house was white frame with a small wooden porch, tucked into the shadow of Capillo Hill on the west side of town. The street was abbreviated, only three houses on each side before the blacktop petered out into the gravel patch that formed a parking pad beside the Daggett residence. Beyond the house, the hill angled upward into sparse trees and underbrush. No sunlight whatever penetrated the yard. A sagging chicken wire fence cut along the lot lines. Bushes had been planted at intervals, but had failed to thrive, so that now there were only globes of dried twigs. The house had a hangdog look, like a stray being penned up until the dogcatcher comes.

I climbed the steep wooden steps and knocked. Eugene Nickerson opened the door. He was much as I had pictured him: in his sixties, of medium height, with wiry gray hair and eyebrows drawn together in a knot. His eyes were small and pale, his lashes nearly white. Narrow shoulders, thick waist, suspenders, flannel shirt. He carried a Bible in his left hand, his index finger closed between the covers, keeping his place.

Uh-oh, I thought.

"I'll have to ask your name again," he said as he admitted me. "My memory's not what it was."

I shook his hand. "Kinsey Millhone," I said. "Nice to meet you, Mr. Nickerson. I hope I didn't interrupt anything."

"Not at all. We're preparing for our Bible class. We usually get together on Wednesday nights, but our pastor has been down with the flu this week, so the meeting was postponed. This is my sister, Essie Daggett. John's wife," he said, indicating the woman seated on the couch. "You can call me Eugene if you like," he added. I smiled briefly in assent and then concentrated on her.

"Hello. How are you? I appreciate your letting me

stop by like this." I moved over and offered my hand. She allowed a few fingers to rest in mine briefly. It was like shaking hands with a Playtex rubber glove.

She was broad-faced and colorless, with graying hair in an unbecoming cut and glasses with thick lenses and heavy plastic frames. She had a wen on the right side of her nose about the size of a kernel of popcorn. Her lower jaw jutted forward aggressively, with protrusive cuspids on either side. She smelled virulently of lilies of the valley.

Eugene indicated that I should have a seat, my choice being the couch where Essie sat, or a Windsor chair with one of the wooden spokes popped out. I opted for the chair, sitting forward slightly so as not to pop anything else. Eugene seated himself in a wicker rocker that creaked under his weight. He took up the narrow purple ribbon hanging out of the Bible and marked his place, then set the book on the table in front of him. Essie had said nothing, her gaze fixed on her lap.

"May I get you a glass of water?" he asked. "We don't hold with caffeinated beverages, but I'd be happy to pour you some 7-Up, if you like."

"I'm fine, thanks," I said. I was seriously alarmed. Being with devout Christians is like being with the very rich. One senses that there are rules at work, some strange etiquette that one might inadvertently breech. I tried to hold bland and harmless thoughts, hoping I wouldn't blurt out any four-letter words. How *could* John Daggett be related to these two?

Eugene cleared his throat. "I was explaining to Essie this confusion we're having over John Daggett's whereabouts. Our understanding is that John is still incarcerated, but now you seem to have a different point of view."

"I'm as baffled as you are," I said. I was thinking fast, wondering how much information I might elicit without giving anything away. As bugged as I was with Daggett, I still didn't feel I should be indiscreet. Not only was there the issue of his being out on parole— there was Lovella. I didn't want to be the one to spill the beans about this new bride of his to a woman he was apparently still married to. "Do you happen to have a picture of him?" I asked. "I suppose it's possible the man I talked to was simply claiming to be your brother-in-law."

"I don't know," Eugene said, dubiously. "It surely sounded like him from what you described."

Essie reached over and picked up a color studio photograph in an ornate silver frame. "This was taken on our thirty-fifth wedding anniversary," she said. Her voice had a nasal cast and a grudging undertone. She passed the photograph to her brother as though he'd never seen it before and might like to have a peek.

"Shortly before John left for San Luis," Eugene

amended, passing the photo to me. His tone suggested John was off on a business trip.

I studied the picture. It was Daggett all right, looking as self-conscious as someone in one of those booths where you dress up as a Confederate soldier or a Victorian gent. His collar looked too tight, his hair too slicked down with pomade. His face looked tight too, as if any minute he might cut and run. Essie was seated beside him, as placid as a blancmange. She was wearing what looked like a crepe de chine dress in lilac, with shoulder pads and glass buttons, a big orchid corsage pinned to her left shoulder.

"Lovely," I murmured, feeling guilty and false. It was a terrible picture. She looked like a bulldog and John looked like he was suppressing a fart.

I handed the picture to Essie again. "What sort of crime did he commit?"

Essie inhaled audibly.

"We prefer not to speak of that," Eugene interjected smoothly. "Perhaps you should tell us of your own acquaintance with him."

"Well, of course, I don't know him well. I think I mentioned that on the phone. We have a mutual friend and he's the one I was hoping to get in touch with. John mentioned that he had family in this area and I just took a chance. I'm assuming you haven't spoken to him recently."

Essie shifted on the couch. "We stuck by him as

long as we could. The pastor said in his opinion we'd done enough. We don't know what John might be wrestling with in the dark of his soul, but there's a limit to what others can *take*." The edge was there in her voice and I wondered what it was made of: rage, humiliation perhaps, the martyrdom of the meek at the hands of the wretched.

I said, "I gather John's been a bit of a trial."

Essie pressed her lips together, clutching her hands in her lap. "Well, it's just like the Bible says. '*Love* your enemies, *bless* them that curse you, do *good* to them that hate you, and pray for them which despitefully use you and persecute you'!" Her tone was accusatory. She began to rock with agitation.

Whoa, I thought, this lady's heat gauge has shot right up into the red.

Eugene creaked in his chair, snagging my attention with a gentle clearing of his throat. "You said you saw him on Saturday. May I ask what the occasion was?"

I realized then that I should have devoted a lot more time to the fib I'd told because I couldn't think how to respond, I was so unnerved by Essie Daggett's outburst that my mind went blank.

She leaned forward then. "Have you been saved?"

"Excuse me, what?" I said, squinting.

"Have you taken Jesus into your heart? Have you set aside *sin*? Have you *repented*? Have you been washed in the Blood of the *Lamb*?"

A spark of spit landed on my face, but I didn't dare react. "Not lately," I said. What is it about me that attracts women like this?

"Now Essie, I'm sure she didn't come by to ponder the state of her soul," Eugene said. He glanced at his watch. "My goodness, I believe it's time for your medication."

I took the opportunity to rise. "I don't want to take up any more of your time," I said, conversationally. "I really appreciate your help on this and if I need any more information, I'll give you a call." I fumbled in my handbag for a business card and left it on the table.

Essie had kicked into high gear by now. "'And they shall stone thee with stones, and *thrust* thee through with their swords. And they shall burn thine houses with fire, and execute judgments upon thee in the sight of many women; and I will cause thee to *cease* from playing harlot, and thou also shalt give no hire anymore . . .'"

"Well, okay now, thanks a lot," I called, easing toward the door. Eugene was patting Essie's hands, too distracted to worry about my departure.

I closed the door and trotted back to my car at a quick clip. It was getting dark and I didn't like the neighborhood.

4

Friday morning I got up at 6:00 and headed over to the beach for my run. For much of the summer, I'd been unable to jog because of an injury, but I'd been back at it for two months and I was feeling good. I've never rhapsodized about exercise and I'd avoid it if I could, but I notice the older I get, the more my body seems to soften, like butter left out at room temp. I don't like to watch my ass drop and my thighs spread outward like jodhpurs made of flesh. In the interest of tight-fitting jeans, my standard garb, I jog three miles a day on the bicycle path that winds along the beach front.

The dawn was laid out on the eastern skyline like watercolors on a matte board: cobalt blue, violet, and rose bleeding together in horizontal stripes. Clouds were visible out on the ocean, plump and dark, pushing the scent of distant seas toward the tumbling surf. It was cold and I ran as much to keep warm as I did to keep in shape.

I got back to my apartment at 6:25, showered, pulled on a pair of jeans, a sweater, and my boots, and then ate a bowl of cereal. I read the paper from front to back, noting with interest the weather map, which showed the radiating spiral of a storm sweeping toward us from Alaska. An 80 percent chance of showers was forecast for the afternoon, with scattered showers through the weekend, clearing by Monday night. In Santa Teresa, rain is not a common event, and it takes on a festive air when it comes. My impulse, always, is to shut myself inside and curl up with a good book. I'd just picked up a new Len Deighton novel and I was looking forward to reading it.

At 9:00, reluctantly, I dug out a windbreaker and picked up my handbag, locked the apartment, and headed over to the office. The sun was shining with a brief show of warmth while the bank of charcoal clouds crept in from the islands twenty-six miles out. I parked in the lot and went up the back stairs, passing the glass double doors of California Fidelity, where business was already under way.

I unlocked my office and dropped my bag on the chair. I really didn't have much to do. Maybe I'd put in a little bit of work and then head home again.

My answering machine showed no messages. I sorted through the mail from the day before and then typed up the notes from my visit with Lovella Daggett, Eugene Nickerson, and his sister, Essie. Since no one seemed to know where John Daggett was, I decided I'd try to get a line on Billy Polo instead. I was going to need data for an effective paper search. I put a call through to the Santa Teresa Police Department and asked to be connected to Sergeant Robb.

I'd met Jonah back in June when I was working on a missing persons case. His erratic marital status made a relationship between us inadvisable from my point of view, but I still eyed him with interest. He was what they called Black Irish: dark-haired, blue-eyed, with (perhaps) a streak of masochism. I didn't know him well enough to determine how much of his suffering was of his own devising and I wasn't sure I wanted to find out. Sometimes I think an unconsummated affair is the wisest course, in any event. No hassles, no demands, no disappointments, and both partners keep all their neuroses under wraps. Whatever the surface appearances, most human beings come equipped with convoluted emotional machinery. With intimacy, the wreckage starts to show, damage rendered in the course of passions colliding like freight trains on the same track. I'd had enough of that over the years. I wasn't in any better shape than he was, so why complicate life?

Two rings and the call was picked up.

"Missing Persons, Sergeant Robb."

"Hello, Jonah. It's Kinsey."

"Hey, babe," he said, "What can I do for you that's legal in this state?"

I smiled. "How about a field check on a couple of ex-cons?"

"Sure, no sweat," he said.

I gave him both names and what little information I had. He took it down and said he'd get back to me. He'd fill out a form and have the inquiry run through the National Crime Information Computer, a federal offense since I'm really not entitled to access. Generally, a private investigator has no more rights than the average citizen and relies on ingenuity, patience, and resourcefulness for facts that law enforcement agencies have available as a matter of course. It's a frustrating, but not impossible, state of affairs. I simply cultivate relationships with people plugged into the system at various points. I have contacts at the telephone company, the credit bureau, Southern California Gas, Southern Cal Edison, and the DMV. Occasionally I can make a raid on certain government offices, but only if I have something worthwhile to trade. As for information of a more personal sort, I can usually depend on people's tendencies to rat on one another at the drop of a hat.

I made up a check sheet for Billy Polo and went to work.

Knowing Jonah, he'd call Probation and pick up Polo's current address. In the meantime, I wanted to tag some bases of my own. A personal search always pays unexpected dividends. I didn't want to bypass the possibility of surprise, as that's half the fun. I knew Polo wasn't listed in the current phone book, but I tried information, thinking he might have had a phone put in. There was no new listing for him.

I put a call through to my pal at the utility company, inquiring about a possible service connection. Their records showed nothing. Apparently he hadn't applied for water, gas, or electricity in the area in his own name, but he could be renting a room somewhere, paying a flat rate, with utilities thrown in.

I put calls through to five or six fleabag hotels on lower State Street. Polo wasn't registered and nobody seemed to spark to the name. While I was at it, I tried John Daggett's name and got nowhere.

I knew I wouldn't get so much as a by-your-leave from the local Social Security office and I doubted I'd find Billy Polo's name among the voter registration files.

Which left what?

I checked my watch. Only thirty minutes had passed since I talked to Jonah. I wasn't sure how long it would take him to call back and I didn't want to waste time sitting around until I heard from him. I grabbed my windbreaker, locked the office, and went down the front stairs to State Street, walking two blocks over and two blocks up to the public library.

I found an empty table in the reference department and hauled out Santa Teresa telephone directories for the past five years, checking back year by year. Four books back, I found Polo. Great. I made a note of the

Merced Street address, wondering if his prison sentence accounted for the absence of a listing since then.

I went over to the section on Santa Teresa history and pulled out the city directory for that year. In addition to an alphabetical listing by name, the city directory lists *addresses* alphabetically so that if you have an address and want to know the resident, you can thumb to the street and number and pick up the name of the occupant and a telephone number. In the back half, telephone numbers are listed sequentially. If all you have is a telephone number, the city directory will provide you with a name and address. By cross referencing the address, you can come up with the name again, an occupation, and the names of neighbors all up and down the same street. In ten minutes, I had a list of seven people who had lived in range of Billy Polo on Merced. By checking for those seven in the current directory, I determined that two were still living there. I jotted down both current telephone numbers, returned the books to their proper places, and headed back toward my office.

The sunlight, intermittent for the last hour, was now largely blocked by incoming clouds which had crowded out blue sky, leaving only an occasional patch, like a hole in a blanket. The air was beginning to cool rapidly, a damp breeze worrying at women's hems. I looked toward the ocean and spotted that silent veil of gray that betokens rain already falling some miles out. I quickened my pace.

Once in my office again, I entered the new information in the file I'd opened. I was just on the verge of closing up for the day when I heard a tap at the door. I hesitated, then crossed to the door and peered out.

There was a woman standing in the corridor, late thirties, expressionless and pale.

"Can I help you?" I said.

"I'm Barbara Daggett."

Quickly, I prayed this wasn't wife number three. I tried the optimistic approach. "John Daggett's daughter?"

"Yes."

She was one of those icy blondes, with skin as finely textured as a percale bedsheet, tall, substantially built, with short coarse hair fanning straight back from her face. She had high cheekbones, a delicate brow, and her father's piercing gaze. Her right eye was green, her left eye blue. I'd seen a white cat like that once and it had had the same disconcerting effect. She was wearing a gray wool business suit and a prim, high-necked white blouse with a froth of lace at the throat. Her heels were a burgundy leather and matched her shoulder bag. She looked like an attorney or a stockbroker, someone accustomed to power.

"Come on in," I said, "I was trying to figure out how to get in touch with him. I take it your mother told you I stopped by."

I was making small talk. She wasn't having any of it. She sat down, turning those riveting eyes on me as I moved around to my side of the desk and took a seat. I thought of offering her coffee, but I really didn't want her to stay that long. Even the air around her seemed chilly and I didn't like the way she looked at me. I rocked back in my swivel chair. "What can I do for you?"

"I want to know why you're looking for my father."

I shrugged, underplaying it, sticking to the story I'd started with. "I'm not really. I'm looking for a friend of his."

"Why weren't we told Daddy was out of prison? My mother's in a state of collapse. We had to call the doctor and have her sedated."

"I'm sorry to hear that," I said.

Barbara Daggett crossed her legs and smoothed her skirt, her movements agitated. "Sorry? You don't know what this has done to her. She was just beginning to feel safe. Now we find out he's in town somewhere and she's very upset. I don't understand what's going on."

"Miss Daggett, I'm not a parole officer," I said. "I don't know when he got out or why nobody notified you. Your mother's problems didn't start yesterday."

A bit of color came to her cheeks. "That's true. Her problems started the day she married him. He's ruined her life. He's ruined life for all of us."

"Are you referring to his drinking?"

She brushed right over that. "I want to know where he's staying. I have to talk to him."

"At the moment, I have no idea where he is. If I find

him, I'll tell him you're interested. That's the best I can do."

"My uncle tells me you saw him on Saturday."

"Only briefly."

"What was he doing in town?"

"We didn't discuss that," I said.

"But what did you talk about? What possible business could he have had with a private detective?"

I had no intention of giving her information, so I tried her technique and ignored the question.

I pulled a legal pad over and picked up a pen. "Is there a number where you can be reached?"

She opened her handbag and took out a business card which she passed across the desk to me. Her office address was three blocks away on State and her title indicated that she was chairman and chief executive officer of a company called FMS.

As if in response to a question, she said, "I develop financial management software systems for manufacturing firms. That's my office number. I'm not listed in the book. If you need to reach me at home, this is the number."

"Sounds interesting," I remarked. "What's your background?"

"I have a math and chemistry degree from Stanford and a double masters in computer sciences and engineering from USC."

I felt my brows lift appreciatively. I couldn't see any evidence that Daggett had ruined *her* life, but I kept the observation to myself. There was clearly more to Barbara Daggett than her professional status indicated. Maybe she was one of those women who succeeds in business and fails in relationships with men. As I'd been accused of that myself, I decided not to make a judgment. Where is it written that being part of a couple is a measure of anything?

She glanced at her watch and stood up. "I have an appointment. Please let me know if you hear from him."

"May I ask what you want with him?"

"I've been urging Mother to file for divorce, but so far she's refused. Maybe I can persuade him instead."

"I'm surprised she didn't divorce him years ago."

Her smile was cold. "She says she married him 'for better or for worse.' To date, there hasn't been any 'better.' Maybe she's hoping for a taste of that before she gives up."

"What about his imprisonment? What was that for?"

Something flickered in her face and I thought at first she wouldn't answer me. "Vehicular manslaughter," she said, finally. "He was drunk and there was an accident. Five people were killed, two of them kids."

I couldn't think of a response and she didn't seem to expect one. She stood up, closed the conversation with a perfunctory handshake, and then she was gone. I could hear her high heels tapping away down the corridor.

5

By the time I closed up the office and got down to my car, the clouds overhead looked like dark gray vacuum cleaner fluff and the rain had begun to splatter the sidewalk with polka dots. I stuck Daggett's file on the passenger seat and backed out of my space, turning right from the parking lot onto Cannon, and right again onto Chapel. Three blocks up, I made a stop, ducking into the supermarket to pick up milk, Diet Pepsi, bread, eggs, and toilet paper. I was into my siege mentality, looking forward to pulling up the drawbridge and waiting out the rain. With luck, I wouldn't have to go out for days.

The phone was ringing as I let myself in. I put the grocery bag on the counter and snatched up the receiver.

"God, I was just about to give up," Jonah said. "I tried the office, but all I got was your answering machine."

"I closed up for the day. I can work at home if I'm in the mood, which I'm not. Have you seen the rain?"

"Rain? Oh yeah, so there is. I haven't even looked out the window since I got in. God, that's great," he said. "Listen, I have some of the information you're looking for and the rest will have to wait. Woody's got a priority request and I had to back off. I'm working tomorrow so I can pick it up then."

"You're working Saturday?"

"I'm filling in for Sobel. My good deed for the week," he said. "Got a pencil? Polo's the one I got a line on."

He rattled out Billy Polo's age, date of birth, height, weight, hair and eye color, his a.k.a., and a hasty rundown of his record, all of which I noted automatically. He'd picked up the name of Billy's parole officer, but the guy was out of the office and wouldn't be available until Monday afternoon.

"Thanks. In the meantime, I'm nosing around on my own," I said. "I bet I'll get a line on him before you do." He laughed and hung up.

I put groceries away and then sat down at my desk, hauling out the little portable Smith-Corona I keep in the knee hole. I consigned the data Jonah'd given me to index cards and then sat and stared at it. Billy Polo, born William Polokowski, was thirty years old, five-foot-eight, a hundred and sixty pounds, brown hair, brown eyes, no scars, tattoos, or "observable physical oddities." His rap sheet sounded like a pop quiz on the

California Penal Code, with arrests that ranged from misdemeanors to felonies. Assault, forgery, receiving stolen property, grand theft, narcotics violations. Once he was even convicted of "injuring a public jail," a misdemeanor in this state. Had this occurred in the course of an escape attempt, the charge would have been bumped up to a felony. As it was, he'd probably been caught scratching naughty words on the jail house walls. A real champ, this one.

Apparently, Billy Polo was pretty shiftless when it came to breaking the law and had never even settled on an area of expertise. He'd been arrested sixteen times, with nine convictions, two acquittals, five dismissals. Twice, he'd been put on probation, but nothing seemed to have affected the nature of his behavior, which appeared nearly pathological in its thrust. The man was determined to screw up. Since the age of eighteen, he'd spent an accumulated nine years in jail. No telling what his juvenile record looked like. I assumed his acquaintance with John Daggett dated from his latest offense, an armed robbery conviction, for which he'd served two years and ten months at the California Men's Colony at San Luis Obispo, a medium security facility about ninety miles north of Santa Teresa.

I pulled out the telephone book again and checked for a listing under the name Polokowski. Nothing. God, why can't anything be simple in this business? Oh well. I wasn't going to worry about it for the moment.

By now, I could hear the rain tapping on the glass-enclosed breezeway that connects my place to Henry Pitt's house. He's my landlord and has been for nearly two years. In dry weather, he places an old Shaker cradle out there, filled with rising bread. When the sun is out, the space is like a solar oven, warm and sheltered, dough puffing up above the rim of the cradle like a feather pillow. He can proof twenty loaves at a time, then bake them in the big industrial-sized oven he had installed when he retired from commercial baking. Now he trades fresh bread and pastries for services in the neighborhood and stretches his Social Security payments by clipping coupons avidly. He picks up additional income constructing crossword puzzles which he sells to a couple of those pint-sized "magazines" you can purchase in a supermarket checkout line. Henry Pitts is eighty-one years old and everyone knows I'm half in love with him.

I considered popping over to see him, but even the fifty-foot walk seemed like too much to deal with in the wet. I put some tea water on and picked up my book, stretching out on the sofa with a quilt pulled over me. And that's how I spent the rest of the day.

During the night, the rain escalated and I woke up twice to hear it lashing at the windows. It sounded like somebody spraying the side of the place with a hose. At intervals, thunder rumbled in the distance and my windows flickered with blue light, tree branches illuminated briefly before the room went black again. It was clear I'd have to cancel my 6:00 A.M. run, an obligatory day off, so I burrowed into the depths of my quilt like a little animal, delighted at the idea of sleeping late.

I woke at 8:00, showered, dressed, and fixed myself a soft-boiled egg on toast with lots of Lawry's Seasoned Salt. I'm not going to give up salt. I don't care what they say.

Jonah called as I was washing my plate. He said, "Hey, guess what? Your friend Daggett showed."

I tucked the receiver into the crook of my neck, turning off the water and drying my hands. "What happened? Did he get picked up?"

"More or less. A scruffy drifter spotted him face down in the surf this morning, tangled up in a fishing net. A skiff washed ashore about two hundred yards away. We're pretty sure it connects."

"He died last night?"

"Looks like it. The coroner estimates he went into the water sometime between midnight and five A.M. We don't have a determination yet on the cause and manner of death. We'll know more after the autopsy's done, of course."

"How'd you find out it was him?"

"Fingerprints. He was over at the morgue listed as a John Doe until we ran the computer check. You want to take a look?"

"I'll be right there. What about next of kin? Have they been notified?"

"Yeah, the beat officer went over as soon as we made the I.D. You know the family?"

"Not well, but we've met. I wouldn't want to be quoted on this, but I think you'll find out he's a bigamist. There's a woman down in L.A. who also claims she's married to him."

"Cute. You better come talk to us when you leave St. Terry's," he said and hung up.

The Santa Teresa Police Department doesn't really have a morgue of its own. There's a coroner-sheriff, an elected officer in this county, but the actual forensic work is contracted out among various pathologists in the tri-county area. The morgue space itself is divided between Santa Teresa Hospital (commonly referred to as St. Terry's) and the former County General Hospital facility on the frontage road off 101. Daggett was apparently at St. Terry's, which was where I headed as soon as I'd rounded up my slicker, an umbrella, and my handbag.

The visitors' lot at the hospital was half empty. It was Saturday and doctors would probably be making rounds later in the day. The sky was thick with clouds and, high up, I could see the wind whipping through like a fan, blowing white mist across the gray. The pavement was littered with small branches, leaves plastered flat against the ground. Puddles had formed everywhere, pockmarked by the steady rainfall. I parked as close to the rear entrance as I could and then locked my car and made a dash for it.

"Kinsey!"

I turned as I reached the shelter of the building. Barbara Daggett hurried toward me from the far side of the lot, her umbrella tilted against the slant of the rain. She was wearing a raincoat and spike-heeled boots, her white-blonde hair forming a halo around her face. I held the door open for her and we ducked into the foyer.

"You heard about my father?"

"That's why I'm here. Do you know how it happened?"

"Not really. Uncle Eugene called me at eight-fifteen. I guess they tried to notify Mother and he interceded. The doctor has her so doped up it doesn't make any sense to tell her yet. He's worried about how she'll take it, as unstable as she is."

"Is your uncle coming down?"

She shook her head. "I said I'd do it. There's no doubt it's Daddy, but somebody has to sign for the body so the mortuary can come pick it up. Of course, they'll autopsy first. How did you find out?"

"Through a cop I know. I'd told him I was trying to get a line on your father, so he called me when they got a match on the fingerprints. Did you manage to locate him yesterday?"

"No, but it's clear someone did." She closed her umbrella and gave it a shake, then glanced at me. "Frankly, I'm assuming somebody killed him."

"Let's not be too quick off the mark," I said, though privately, I agreed.

The two of us moved through the inner door and into the corridor. The air was warmer here and smelled of latex paint.

"I want you to look into it for me, in any event," she said.

"Hey, listen. That's what the police are for. I don't have the scope for that. Why don't you wait and see what they have to say first?"

She studied me briefly and then moved on. "They don't give a damn what happened to him. Why would they care? He was a drunken bum."

"Oh come on. Cops don't have to *care*," I said. "If it's homicide, they have a job to do and they'll do it well."

When we reached the autopsy room, I knocked and a young black morgue attendant came out, dressed in surgical greens. His name tag indicated that his name was Hall Ingraham. He was lean, his skin the color of pecan wood with a high-gloss finish. His hair was cropped close and gave him the look of a piece of sculpture, his elongated face nearly stylized in its perfection.

"This is Barbara Daggett," I said.

He looked in her direction without meeting her eyes. "You can wait right down here," he said. He moved two doors down and we followed, pausing politely while he unlocked a viewing room and ushered us in.

"It'll be just a minute," he said.

He disappeared and we took a seat. The room was small, maybe nine by nine, with four blue molded-plastic chairs hooked together at the base, a low wooden table covered with old magazines, and a television screen affixed, at an angle, up in one corner of the room. I saw her gaze flick to it.

"Closed circuit," I said. "They'll show him up there."

She picked up a magazine and began to flip through it distractedly. "You never really told me why he hired you," she said. An ad for pantyhose had apparently caught her eye and she studied it as if my reply were of no particular concern.

I couldn't think of a reason not to tell her at this point, but I noticed that I censored myself to some extent, a habit of long standing. I like to hold something back. Once information is out, it can't be recalled so it's better to exercise caution before you flap your mouth. "He wanted me to find a kid named Tony Gahan," I said.

That remarkable two-toned gaze came up to meet mine and I found myself trying to decide which eye color I preferred. The green was more unusual, but the blue was clear and stark. The two together presented a contradiction, like the signal at a street corner, flashing Walk and Don't Walk simultaneously.

"You know him?" I asked.

"His parents and a younger sister were the ones killed in the accident, along with two other people in the car with them. What did Daddy want with him?"

"He said Tony Gahan helped him once when he was on the run from the cops. He wanted to thank him."

Her look was incredulous. "But that's bullshit!"

"So I gather," I said.

She might have pressed for more information, but the television screen flashed with snow at that moment and then flipped over to a closeup of John Daggett. He was lying on a gurney, a sheet neatly pulled up to his neck. He had the blank, plastic look that death sometimes brings, as if the human face were no more than an empty page on which the lines of emotion and experience are transcribed and then erased. He looked closer to twenty years old than fifty-five, with a stubble of beard and hair carelessly arranged. His face was unmarked.

Barbara stared at him, her lips parting, her face diffused with pink. Tears rose in her eyes and hung there, captured in the well of her lower lids. I looked away from her, unwilling to intrude any more than I had to. The morgue attendant's voice reached us through the intercom.

"Let me know when you're done."

Barbara turned away abruptly.

"Thank you. That's fine," I called. The television screen went dark.

Moments later, there was a tap at the door and he reappeared with a sealed manila envelope and a clipboard in hand.

"We'll need to know what arrangements you want made," he said. He was using that tone of studied neutrality I've heard before from those who deal with the bereaved. Its effect is impersonal and soothing, liberating one to transact business without intrusive emotionalism. He needn't have bothered. Barbara Daggett was a businesswoman, bred to that awesome poise that so unsettles men accustomed to female subservience. Her manner now was smooth and detached, her tone as impassive as his.

"I've talked to Wynington-Blake," she said, indicating one of the funeral homes in town. "If you'll notify them once the autopsy's done, they'll take care of everything. Is that form for me?"

He nodded and held the clipboard out to her with a pen attached. "A release for his personal effects," he said.

She dashed off a signature as if she were signing an autograph for a pesky fan. "When will you have the autopsy results?"

He handed her the envelope, which apparently contained Daggett's odds and ends. "Probably by late afternoon."

"Who's doing the post?" I asked.

"Dr. Yee. He's scheduled it for two-thirty."

Barbara Daggett glanced at me. "She's a private investigator. I want all information released to her. Will I need to sign a separate authorization for that?"

"I don't know. There's probably some procedure, but it's a new one on me. I can check into it and contact you later, if you like."

She slipped her business card under the clamp as she handed the clipboard back to him. "Do that."

His eyes met hers for the first time and I could see him register the oddity of the mismatched irises. She brushed past him, moving out of the room. He stared after her. The door closed.

I held my hand out. "I'm Kinsey Millhone, Mr. Ingraham."

He smiled for the first time. "Oh yeah. I heard about you from Kelly Borden. Nice to meet you."

Kelly Borden was a morgue attendant I'd met during a homicide investigation I'd worked on in August.

"Nice to meet you too," I said. "What's the story on this one?"

"I can't tell you much. They brought him in about seven, just as I was coming to work."

"Do you have any idea how long he'd been dead?"

"I don't know for sure, but it couldn't have been long. The body wasn't bloated and there wasn't any putrefaction. From what I've seen of drowning victims, I'd guess he went in the water late last night. Don't quote me on that. The watch he had on was stopped at two thirty-seven, but it could have been broken. It's a crummy watch and looks all beat up. It's in with his effects. Hell, what do I know? I'm just a flunkie, lowest of the low. Dr. Yee hates it if we talk to people like this."

"Believe me, I'm not going to say anything. I'm just asking for my own purposes. What about his clothing? How was he dressed?"

"Jacket, pants, shirt."

"Shoes and socks?"

"Well, shoes. He didn't have socks on and he didn't have a wallet or anything like that."

"Any signs of injury?"

"None that I've seen."

I couldn't think of anything else I wanted to ask for the moment so I thanked him and said I'd be in touch.

Then I went out to look for Barbara Daggett. If I was going to work for her, we needed to get business squared away.

6

I found her standing in the foyer, looking out at the parking lot. The rain was falling monotonously, occasional gusts of wind tossing the treetops. Cozy-looking lights were on in all the buildings that rimmed the parking lot, which only emphasized the dampness and the chill outside. A nurse, her white uniform flashing from the flaps of a dark blue raincoat, approached the doorway, leaping over puddles like a kid playing hopscotch. Her white hose were speckled with flesh-colored blotches where the rain had soaked through and the tops of her white shoes were spattered with mud. She reached the entrance and I held the door for her.

She flashed me a smile. "Whoo! Thanks. It's like an obstacle course out there." She shook the water from her raincoat and padded down the hallway, crepe soles leaving a pattern of damp footprints in her wake.

Barbara Daggett seemed rooted to the spot. "I have

to go to Mother's," she said. "Somebody has to tell her." She turned and looked at me. "How much do you charge for your services?"

"Thirty an hour, plus expenses, which is standard for the area. If you're serious, I can drop a contract off at your office this afternoon."

"What about a retainer?"

I made a quick assessment. I usually ask for an advance, especially in a situation like this, when I know I'll be talking to the cops. There's no concept of privilege between a P.I. and a client, but at least the front money makes it clear where my loyalties lie.

"Four hundred should cover it," I said. I wondered if the figure came to mind because of Daggett's bounced check. Oddly enough, I felt protective of him. He'd conned me—there was no doubt of that—but I *had* agreed to work for him, and in my mind, I still had a duty to discharge. Of course, I might not have felt as charitable if he were still alive, but the dead are defenseless, and somebody in this world has to look out for them.

"I'll have my secretary cut you a check first thing Monday morning," she said. She turned back, looking out the double doors into the gloom. She leaned her head against the glass.

"Are you okay?"

"You don't know how many times I've wished him dead," she said. "Have you ever dealt with an alcoholic?"

I shook my head.

"They're so maddening. I used to look at him and I was convinced he could quit drinking if he wanted to. I don't know how many times I talked to him, begging him to stop. I thought he didn't understand. I thought he just wasn't aware of what we were going through, my mother and me. I can remember the look he'd get in his eyes when he was drunk. Little pink piggy eyes. His whole body radiated this odor. Bourbon. God, I hate that stuff. He smelled like somebody'd dropped a bottle of Early Times down a heater vent . . . waves of smell. He reeked of it."

She looked over at me, her eyes dry and pitiless. "I'm thirty-four and I've hated him with every cell in my body for as long as I can remember. And now I'm stuck with it. He won, didn't he? He never changed, never straightened up, never gave us an inch. He was such a shitheel. It makes me want to smash this glass door out. I don't even know why I care how he died. I should be relieved, but I'm pissed. The irony is that he's probably still going to dominate my life."

"How so?"

"Look what he's done to me already. I think of him every time I have a drink. I think of him if I decide *not* to have a drink. If I even *meet* a man who drinks or if I see a bum on the street or smell bourbon, his face is the first thing that comes to mind. Oh God, and if I'm around someone who's had too much, I can't stand it. I disconnect. My life is filled with reminders of him. His apologies and his phony, wheedling charm, his boo-hooing when the booze got to him. The times he fell, the times he got put in jail, the times he spent every dime we had. When I was twelve, Mother got religion and I don't know which was worse. At least Daddy woke up most days in okay shape. She had Jesus for breakfast, lunch, and dinner. It was grotesque. And then there were the joys of being an only child."

She broke off abruptly and seemed to shake herself. "Oh hell. What difference does it make? I know I sound sorry for myself, but it's been such a bitch and there's no end in sight."

"Actually, you look like you've done pretty well," I said.

She turned her gaze back to the parking lot and I could see her faint, bitter smile reflected in the glass. "You know what they say about living well as the best revenge. I did well because it was the one defense I had. Escape has been the motivating force in my life. Getting away from him, getting away from her, putting that household behind me. The funny thing is, I haven't moved an inch, and the harder I run, the faster I keep slipping back to them. There are spiders that work like that. They bury themselves and create a little pocket of loose dirt. Then when their prey comes along, the soil gives way and the victim slides right down into the trap. There are laws for everything except the harm families do."

She turned, shoving her hands down in her raincoat

pockets. She pushed the door open with her backside and a draft of cold air rushed in. "What about you? Are you leaving or will you stick around?"

"I guess I'll hit the office as long as I'm out," I said.

She pressed a button on the handle of her umbrella and it lifted into the open position with a muffled *thunk*. She held it for me and we walked toward my car together. The raindrops tapping on the umbrella fabric made a muted sound, like popcorn in a covered saucepan.

I unlocked my car and got in, while she moved off toward hers, calling back over her shoulder. "Try me at the office as soon as you hear anything. I should be there by two."

My office building was deserted. California Fidelity is closed on weekends so their offices were dark. I let myself in, picking up the batch of morning mail that had been shoved through the slot. There were no messages on my answering machine. I pulled a contract out of my top drawer and spent a few minutes filling in the blanks. I checked Barbara Daggett's business card to verify the address, then I locked up again and went down the front stairs.

I walked the three blocks and dropped the contract off at her office, then headed over to the police station on Floresta. The combination of the weekend and the bad weather lent the station much the same deserted air as my office building. Crime doesn't adhere to a forty-hour week, but there are days when even the criminals don't seem to feel like doing much. The linoleum showed a gridwork of wet footprints, like a pattern of dance steps too complex to learn. The air smelled of cigarette smoke and damp uniforms. I could see where someone had fashioned a folded newspaper into a rain hat and then abandoned it on the wooden bench just inside the door.

One of the clerks in the identification and records section buzzed Jonah and he came out to the locked foyer door and admitted me.

He wasn't looking good. During the summer, he'd shed an excess twenty pounds and he'd told me he was still working out at the gym, so it wasn't that. His dark hair seemed poorly trimmed and the lines around his eyes were pronounced. He also had that weary aura that unhappiness seems to breed.

"What happened to you?" I asked as we walked back to his office. He'd been reconciled with his wife since June, after a year's separation, and from what I'd gathered, it was not going well.

"She wants an open relationship," he remarked.

"Oh come *on*," I said, with disbelief.

That netted me a tired smile. "That's what the lady says." He held the door open for me and we passed into an L-shaped room, furnished with big wooden desks.

Missing Persons is included in Crimes Against Persons, which in turn is considered part of the Investigations Division, along with Crimes Against Property,

Narcotics, and Special Investigations. The room was deserted at the moment, but people came and went at intervals. From the interview room off the inside corridor, I could hear the rise and fall of a shrill female voice and I guessed that an interrogation was under way. Jonah closed the hall door, automatically protective of department business.

He filled two Styrofoam cups with coffee and brought them over, handing me packets of Cremora and Equal. Just what I needed, a cup of hot chemicals. We went through the motions of doctoring the coffee, which smelled like it'd been on the burner too long.

I took a few minutes to lay out the Daggett situation. At this point, we didn't have the results of the autopsy, so the idea of murder was purely theoretical. Still, I told Jonah what had gone on to date, detailing the principal characters. I was talking to him as a friend instead of a cop and he listened as an interested, but unofficial, party.

"So how long was he up here before he died?" Jonah asked.

"Since Monday presumably," I said. "It's possible he went somewhere else first, but Lovella seemed to think he'd head straight for Billy Polo if he needed help."

"Did that information on Polo do you any good?"

"Not yet, but it will. I'm just waiting to see what we've got on our hands before I proceed. Even if the death was accidental, I suspect Barbara Daggett will want me to look into it. I mean, for starters, what was he doing on a boat in a rainstorm? And where has he been all this time?"

"Where have *you* been?" Jonah asked.

I focused on him and realized he'd shifted the subject. "Who, me? I've been around."

He picked up a pencil and began to tap out a beat, like a man auditioning for a tiny blues band. He was giving me a look I'd seen before, full of heat and speculation. "Are you dating anyone?"

I shook my head, smiling slightly. "The only good men I know are married." I was being flirtatious and he seemed to like that.

His blue eyes locked into mine and the color rose in his face. "What do you do for sex?"

"Jog on the beach. How about you?"

He smiled, breaking off eye contact. "In other words, it's none of my business."

I laughed. "I'm not avoiding the question. I'm telling the truth."

"Really? That's funny. I always pictured you out raising hell."

"I did some of that years ago, but I can't stand it these days. Sex is a bonding process. I'm careful who I connect up with. Besides, you don't know what the marketplace is like. A one-night stand is more like a wrestling match with a couple of quick take-downs. Talk about demoralizing. I'd rather be alone."

"I know what you mean. I was out there hustling some the year she was gone, but I never got the hang of it. I'd go in a bar and some babe would sidle up to me, but I never made the right moves. Couple of times, women told me I was rude when I just thought I was making small talk."

"It's worse if you're successful at it," I said. "Be grateful you never learned the gamesmanship. I know a couple of guys on the circuit and they're hard as nails, you know? Unhappy. Hostile toward women. They get laid, but that's about all they get."

Behind him, Lieutenant Becker came in and took a seat at a desk across the room. Jonah's pencil tapping started again and then stopped. He tossed it aside and rocked back in his chair.

"I wish life were simple," he said.

I kept my tone of voice mild. "Life *is* simple. You're the one making things complex. You were doing great without Camilla, as far as I could see. She crooks her finger, though, and you go running back. And now you can't figure out what went wrong. Quit acting like a victim when you did it to yourself."

This time he laughed. "God, Kinsey. Why don't you just say what's on your mind."

"Well, I don't understand voluntary suffering. If you're unhappy, change something. If you can't make it work, then bail out. What's the big deal?"

"Is that what you did?"

"Not quite. I dumped the first and the second one dumped me. With both, I did my share of suffering, but when I look back on it, I can't understand why I endured so long. It was dumb. It was a big waste of time and cost me a lot."

"I've never even heard you mention those guys."

"Yeah, well I'll tell you about them sometime."

"You want to have a drink when I get off work?"

I looked at him briefly and then shook my head. "We'd end up in bed, Jonah."

"That's the point, isn't it?" He smiled and did a Groucho Marx wiggle with his eyebrows.

I laughed and turned the subject back to Daggett as I got up. "Call me when Dr. Yee has results on the post."

"I'll call for more than that."

"Get your life squared away first."

When I left, he was still staring after me, and it was all I could do to get out of there. I had this troubling urge to gallop over and leap onto his lap, laughing while I covered his face with licks, but I didn't think the department would ever be the same. As I glanced back, I could see Becker giving us a speculative look while he pretended to check his "in" box.

7

Daggett's death was ruled accidental. Jonah called me at home at 4:00 to give me the news. I'd spent the afternoon again wrapped up in a quilt, hoping to finish the book. I'd just put on a fresh pot of coffee and I was scurrying back under the covers as the phone rang. When he told me, I was puzzled, but I wasn't convinced. I kept waiting for the punchline, but there wasn't one.

"I don't get it," I said. "Does Yee know the background on this?"

"Babe, Daggett's blood alcohol was point three-five. You're talking acute ethanol intoxication, almost coma stage."

"And that was the cause of death?"

"Well no, he drowned, but Yee says there's no evidence of foul play. None. Daggett went out in a boat, got tangled up in a fishing net, and fell overboard, too drunk to save himself."

"Bullshit!"

"Kinsey, some people die accidentally. It's a fact."

"I don't believe it. Not this one."

"The crime scene investigation unit didn't find a thing. Not even a *hint*. What can I say? You know these guys. They're as good as they come. If you think it's murder, come up with some evidence. In the meantime, we're calling it an accident. As far as we're concerned, the case is closed."

"What was he doing dead drunk in a boat?" I asked. "The man was broke and it was raining cats and dogs. Who'd he rent the boat from?"

I could hear Jonah sigh. "He didn't. Apparently, he took a little ten-foot skiff from its mooring off the dock at Marina One. The harbor master identified the boat and you can see where the line was cut."

"Where'd they find it?"

"On the beach near the pier. There weren't any usable prints."

"I don't like it."

"Look, I know what you're saying and you've got a point. I tend to agree, if that makes you feel any better, but who's asking us? Look at it as a gift. If the death is ruled a homicide, you can't get near it. This way, you've got carte blanche . . . within limits, of course."

"Does Dolan know I'm interested?" Lieutenant Dolan was an assistant division commander and an old antagonist of mine. He hated private investigators getting involved in police business.

"The case is Feldman's. He won't give a shit. You want me to talk to him?"

"Yeah, do that," I said. "And clear it with Dolan, while you're at it. I'm tired of getting my hand smacked."

"Okay. I'll get back to you first thing Monday then," Jonah said. "In the meantime, let me know if anything turns up."

"Right. Thanks."

I put a call through to Barbara Daggett, repeating the information I'd just received. When I finished, she was silent.

"What do you think?" she asked, finally.

"Let's put it this way. *I'm* not satisfied, but it's your money. If you like, I can nose around for a couple of days and if nothing turns up, we'll dump the whole business and you'll just have to live with it."

"What are the odds?"

"I have no idea. All I know to do is pick up a thread and see where it leads. We may come up with six dead ends, but at least you'll know we gave it a shot."

"Let's do it."

"Great. I'll be in touch."

I pushed the quilt aside and got up. I hoped Billy Polo was still around. I didn't know where else to start.

I unplugged the coffeepot, poured the balance of the coffee into a thermos, and then made myself a peanut butter and dill pickle sandwich, which I put in a brown paper bag like a school kid. I had just about that same feeling in my gut too . . . the dull dread I'd experienced when I was eight, trudging off to Woodrow Wilson Elementary. I didn't want to go out in the rain. I didn't want to connect up with Billy Polo, who was probably a creep. He sounded like one of the sixth-grade boys I'd been so fearful of . . . lawless, out of control, and mean.

I searched through my closet until I found my slicker and an umbrella. I left my warm apartment behind and drove over to Billy Polo's old address on Merced. It was 4:15 and getting prematurely dark. The neighborhood had probably been charming once, but it was gradually being overtaken by apartment buildings and was now no more than a hapless mix of the down-at-the-heel and the bland. The little gingerbread structures were wedged between three-story stucco boxes with tenant parking underneath and everywhere there was evidence of the same tasteless disregard for history.

I parked under a pepper tree, using the overhanging branches as brief shelter while I put up my umbrella. I checked the names and house numbers of the two former neighbors, hoping one of them could give me a lead on Polo's current whereabouts.

The first door I knocked on was answered by an elderly woman in a wheelchair, her legs wrapped in Ace bandages and stuffed into lace-up shoes with slices cut out of the sides to accommodate her bunions. I stood on her leaky front porch, talking to her through the screen door, which she kept latched. She had a vague recollection of Billy, but had no idea what had happened to him or where he'd gone. She did direct me to a little rental unit at the rear of the property next door. This was not one of the addresses I'd picked up from the city directory. She said Billy's family had lived in the front house, while the rear was still occupied by an old gent named Talbot, who had been there for the last thirty years. I thanked her and picked my way down the rain-slicked stairs and back along the driveway.

The front unit must have been one of the early houses in the area—a story and a half of white frame, with a peaked roof, two dormers, and a front porch that was screened in now and furnished with junk. I could see the coils on the backside of an old refrigerator and beside it, what looked like a pillar of milk cartons, filled with paperback books. Hydrangeas and bougainvillea grew together in a tangle along the side of the house and the runoff from the rain gutter threw a gush of water out on the drive, forcing me to cut wide to the right.

The rear unit looked like it was originally a tool shed, with a lean-to attached to the left side and a tiny carport on the right. There was no car visible and most of the sheltered space was taken up by a cord of firewood, stacked against the wall. There was room left for a bicycle maybe, but not much else.

The structure was white frame, propped up on cinderblocks, with a window on either side of a central door, and a tiny chimney poking up through the roof. It looked like the drawing we all did in grade school, even to the smoke curling up from the chimney pipe.

I knocked and the door was opened by a wizened old man with no teeth. His mouth was a wide line barely separating the tip of his nose from the upward thrust of his chin. When he caught sight of me and realized that I was no one he knew, he left the doorway briefly and returned with his dentures, smiling slightly as he shifted them into place. His false teeth made a crunching sound like a horse chewing on a bit. He looked to be in his seventies, frail, his pale skin speckled with red and blue. His white hair was brushed into a pompadour in front, shaggy over his ears and touching his collar in the back. He wore a shirt that looked soft from years of washing and a cardigan sweater that probably belonged to a woman at some point. The buttons were rhinestone and the buttonholes were on the wrong side. He smoothed his hair back with a trembling hand and waited to see what I could possibly want.

"Are you Mr. Talbot?"

"Depends on who's asking," he said.

"I'm Kinsey Millhone. The woman next door suggested that I talk to you. I'm looking for Billy Polo. His family lived in that front house about five years ago."

"I know Billy quite well. Why are you looking for him?"

"I need some information about a friend of his," I said and then gave him a brief explanation. I couldn't see any reason to prevaricate so I simply stated my purpose and left it at that.

He blinked at me. "Billy Polo's a very bad fella. I wonder if you're aware of that." His voice was powdery and I noticed that he had a tremor, his head oscillating as he spoke. I guessed that he suffered from some form of parkinsonism.

"Yeah, I am. I heard he was up at the California Men's Colony until recently. I think that's where he met the man I'm referring to. Do you have any idea how I might reach him?"

"Well, you know, his mother is the one who owned that place," he said, nodding toward the front house. "She sold it about two years ago when she remarried."

"Is she still here in town?"

"Yes, and I believe she's living on Tranvia. Her married name is Christopher. Just a minute and I'll give you the address." He shuffled away and a few moments later was back with a small address book in hand. "She's a lovely woman. Sends me a card every year at Christmastime. Yes, here it is. Bertha Christopher. Goes by the nickname of Betty. If you chance to see her, I wish you'd give her my best."

"I'll do that, Mr. Talbot. Thanks so much."

Tranvia turned out to be a wide, treeless street off Milagro on the east side of town, a neighborhood of one-story frame houses on small lots, with chicken wire fences, unruly head-high poinsettia bushes pelted by the rain, and soggy children's toys abandoned in driveways paved with parallel strips of concrete. The level of maintenance here seemed erratic, but the address I now had for Bertha Christopher showed one of the better-kept houses on the block, mustard-colored with dark brown trim. I parked my VW on the opposite side of the street, about fifty yards away, so I could sit and watch the place inconspicuously. Most of the parked cars were crummy so mine fit right in.

It was now after 5:00 and the light was fading fast, the chill in the air more pronounced. The rain had eased somewhat so I left my umbrella where it was. I grabbed my yellow slicker and slipped into it, pulling up the hood. I locked the car and crossed the street, splashing through puddles that darkened the leather of my boots. The rain drummed against the fabric of the slicker with a pocking sound that made me feel like I was in a pup tent.

The Christopher property was surrounded by a low rock wall, constructed with sandstone boulders the size of cantaloupes, held together with concrete. A row of hanging planters screened the front windows from the street and a set of glass windchimes, suspended in one corner of the porch, tinkled with the wind. There were two lightweight aluminum lawn chairs arranged on either side of a metal table. Everything was soggy and smelled of wet grass.

There was no doorbell, but I tapped on the pane of

glass in the front door, cupping a hand so I could peer in. The interior was in shadow, no lights showing from the rear of the house. I moved to the porch rail and checked the adjacent houses, both of which were dark. My guess was that many of these people were off at work. After a few minutes, I went back to my car.

I started the engine and ran the heater for a while, fogging up the windows until I could barely see. I rubbed a clear spot in the middle of the windshield and then sat and stared. Streetlights came on. At 5:45, I ate my sandwich just for something to do. At 6:15, I drank some coffee and flipped on my car radio, listening to a talk-show host interview a psychic. Fifteen minutes later, right after the 6:30 news, a car approached and slowed, turning into the Christophers' driveway.

A woman got out, dimly illuminated by the street light. She paused as if to raise her umbrella and then apparently decided to make a dash for it. I watched her scuttle up the driveway and around toward the back of the house. Moments later, the lights went on in se-quence . . . first the rear left room, probably a kitchen, then the living room, and finally the front porch light. I gave her a few minutes to get her coat hung up and then I returned to her front door.

I knocked again. I could see her peer into the hall-way from the rear of the house and then approach the front door. She stared at me blankly, then leaned her head close to the glass for a better look.

She appeared to be in her fifties, with a sallow complexion and a deeply creased face. Her hair was too uniform a shade to be a natural brown. She wore it parted on the side with big puffy bangs across her lined forehead. Her eyes were the size and color of old pennies and her makeup looked like it needed renewing at this hour of the day. She wore a uniform I'd seen before, brown pants and a brown-and-yellow-checked tunic. I couldn't place the outfit offhand.

"Yes?" she called through the glass.

I raised my voice against the sound of the rain. "I'm looking for Billy. Is he back yet?"

"He don't live here, hon, but he said he'd be by at eight o'clock. Who are you?"

I picked a name at random. "Charlene. Are you his mother?"

"Charlene who?"

"A friend of his said I should look him up if I was ever in Santa Teresa. Is he at work?"

She gave me an odd look, as if the notion of Billy working had never crossed her mind. "He's out checking the used car lots for an automobile."

She had one of those faces that seemed tantalizingly familiar and it dawned on me, belatedly, that she was a checker at the supermarket where I shop now and then. We'd even chatted idly about the fact that I was a P.I. I eased back out of the porch light, hoping she hadn't recognized me at the same time I recognized her. I held the corner of the slicker up as though to shield my face from the wind.

She seemed to pick up on the fact that something odd was going on. "What'd you want him for?"

I ignored that, pretending I couldn't hear. "Why don't I come back when he gets home?" I hollered. "Just tell him Charlene stopped by and I'll catch up with him when I can."

"Well, all right," she said reluctantly. I gave her a casual wave as I turned. I went down the porch steps and into the dark, aware that she was peering after me suspiciously. I must have disappeared from her field of vision then because she turned the porch light off.

I got back in my car with one of those quick, involuntary shudders that racks you from head to toe. When I caught up with Billy, I might well admit who I was and what I wanted with him, but for the moment, I didn't want to tip my hand. I checked my watch and settled in, prepared to wait. Already, it was feeling like a long night.

8

Four hours passed. The rain stopped. It became apparent that Billy was not only late, but possibly not coming at all. Maybe he'd bought a car and hightailed it out of town, or maybe at some point he'd phoned his mother and decided to skip the visit when he heard about "Charlene." I finished all the coffee in the thermos, my brain fairly crackling from caffeine. If I smoked cigarettes, I could have gone through a pack. Instead, I listened to eight more installments of the news, the farm report, and an hour of Hispanic music. I pondered the possibility of learning the Spanish language by simply listening to these gut-wrenching tunes. I thought about Jonah and the husbands I'd known. Surely, if my heart broke again, it would sound just like this, though for all I knew, the lyrics were about cut worms and inguinal hernias, matters only made soulful through soaring harmonies. Altogether, I came perilously close to boring myself insensible with my own mental processes, so it was with real relief that I saw the car approach and pull into the curb in front of the house across the street. It looked like a 1967 Chevrolet, white, with a temporary registration sticker on the windshield. I couldn't tell much about the guy who got out, but I watched with interest as he took the porch steps in two bounds and rang the bell.

Betty Christopher came to the door to let him in. The two of them disappeared. A moment later, shadows wavered against the kitchen light. I figured they'd sit down for a couple of beers and a heart-to-heart talk. The next thing I knew, however, the front door opened again and he came out. I slipped down on the car seat until my eyes were level with the bottom of the window. The cloud cover was still heavy, obscuring the moon, and the cars along the curb created deeper shadows still. He stared out at the street, taking in the line of parked cars one by one. I felt my heart start to thump as I watched him come down the steps and head in my direction.

He paused in the middle of the street. He moved over to a van parked two cars away from mine. He flicked on a flashlight and opened the door on the driver's side, apparently to check the registration. I lost sight of him. Moments went by. I watched the shadows, wondering if he'd crept around the other side and was coming up on my right. I heard a muffled sound as he closed the door to the van. The beam from his flashlight swept over the car in front of me and flashed across my windshield, the light too dif-fused by the time it reached me to illuminate much. He flicked it off. He waited, scanning the street on both sides. Apparently, he decided there was nothing to worry about. He crossed back to the house. As he reached the porch, she came out, clutching a robe around her. They talked for a few minutes and then he got in his car and took off. The minute she went in-side, I started the VW and did a big U-turn, follow-ing. I hoped this wasn't all some elaborate ruse to flush me into the open.

He had already made a left turn and then a right by the time I caught sight of him two blocks ahead of me. We were driving along the back streets with no traffic lights at all and only an occasional stop sign to slow our progress. I had to close the gap or risk losing him. A "one-man" tail is nearly pointless unless you know who you're following and where he's going to begin with. At this hour, there were very few cars on the road, and if he drove far, he'd realize the presence of my VW was no accident.

I thought he was headed toward the freeway, but be-fore he reached the northbound on-ramp, he slowed and made a right-hand turn. By then, I was only half a block back so I whipped over to the curb and parked, killing the engine. I locked the car and took off on foot, heading diagonally across the corner lot at a dead run. I caught sight of his taillights half a block ahead. The car was making a left-hand turn into a shabby trailer park.

Puente is a narrow street that parallels Highway 101 on the east side of town, with the trailer park itself squeezed into the space between the two roadways, screened off from the highway by a ten-foot board fence and masses of oleander. I was covering ground at a quick clip. The houses I passed were dark, driveways crowded with old cars, most of them sporting dents. The street lighting here was poor, but ahead of me I caught traces of light from the trailer park, which was strung with small multicolored bulbs.

By the time I got to the entrance, there was no sign of the Chevrolet, but the place was small and I didn't think the car would be hard to spot. The road twisting through the trailer park was two lanes wide. The blacktop still glistened from the rain and water was dripping from the eucalyptus trees that towered at intervals. There were signs posted everywhere: SLOW. SPEED BUMPS. TENANT PARKING ONLY. DO NOT BLOCK DRIVEWAY.

Most of the trailers were "single-wides," fifteen to twenty feet long, the kind that once upon a time you could actually hitch to your car and travel in. Nomad, Airstream, and Concord seemed to predominate. Each had a numbered cardboard sign in the window, indicating the number of the lot on which it sat. Some were moored in narrow patches of grass, temporary camper spaces for RVs passing through, but many were permanent and, by the look of them, had been there for years. The lots were stingy squares of poured concrete, surrounded by sections of white picket fence two feet high, or separated from one another by sagging lengths of bamboo matting. The yards, when they existed, harbored an assortment of plastic deer and flamingos.

It was almost eleven and many of the trailers were dark. Occasionally, I could see the blue-gray flicker of a TV set. I found the Chevrolet, hood warm, the engine still ticking, parked beside a dark green battered trailer with a torn awning and half the aluminum skirting ripped away. From inside, I could hear the dull thump of rock and roll music being played too loudly in too small a space.

The trailer windows were ovals of hot yellow light, positioned about a foot higher than eye level. I edged around to the right-hand side, easing in as close as I could, checking the area to see if any of the neighbors had spotted me. The trailer next door had a FOR RENT sign taped to the siding, and the one across the lane had the curtains pulled. I turned back to the window and got up on tiptoe, peering in. The window was opened slightly and the air seeping out was hot and smelled of fried onions. The curtains consisted of old cotton dish towels, with a brass rod threaded through one end, hanging crookedly enough to provide a clear view of Billy Polo and the woman he was talking to. They were both seated at a flop-down table in the galley, drinking beer, mouths working, words inaudible in the thumping din of music. The interior of the trailer was a depressing collage of cheap paneled walls, dirty dishes, junk, torn upholstery, newspapers, and canned goods stacked on countertops. A bumper sticker pasted above the front door said, I'VE BEEN TO ALL 48 STATES!

There was a small black-and-white television set perched on a cardboard box, tuned to what looked like the tag end of a prime-time private-eye show. The action was speeding up. A car careened out of control, flipping end over end before it went off a cliff, exploding in midair. The picture cut to two men in an office, one talking on the phone. Neither Billy nor his companion seemed to be watching and the music must have made it impossible for them to hear the dialogue anyway.

I could feel a cramp forming in my right calf. I cast about for something to stand on to ease the strain. The yard next door was a jungle of overgrown shrubs, the parking space choked with discards. There was a set of detached wooden steps tucked up under the trailer door. I blundered through the bushes, my jeans and boots getting drenched in the process. I was counting on the thunder of music to cover the sound of my labors as I hefted the box steps, tramped back through the shrubs, and set the steps under the window.

Cautiously, I mounted, peering in again. Billy Polo had a surprisingly boyish face for a man who'd lived his thirty years as a thug. His hair was dark, a curly mass standing out around his face. His nose was small, his mouth generous, and he had a dimple in his chin that looked like a puncture wound. He wasn't a big man, but he had a wiry musculature that suggested strength. There was something manic about him, a hint of tension in his gestures. His eyes were restless and he tended to stare off to one side when he spoke, as if direct eye contact made him anxious.

The woman was in her early twenties, with a wide mouth, strong chin, and a pug nose that looked as if it was made of putty. She wore no makeup and her fair hair was dense, a series of tight ripples that she wore shoulder length, brittle and illcut. Her skin was very pale, mottled with freckles. She was wearing a man's oversized silk bathrobe and apparently nursing a cold. She kept a wad of Kleenex in her pocket which she honked into from time to time. She was so close to me I could see the chapping where the frequent blowing had reddened her nose and upper lip. I wondered if she was an old girlfriend of Billy's. There was no overt sexuality in the way they related to one another, but there was a curious intimacy. An old love affair gone flat perhaps.

The continuous rock and roll music was driving me

nuts. I was never going to hear what they were saying with that stuff booming out all over the place. I got down off the steps and went around the other side of the trailer to the front door. The window to the right was wide open, though the curtains were pinned shut.

I waited until there was a brief pause between cuts. I took a deep breath and pounded on the door. "Hey! Could you cut the goddamn noise," I yelled. "We're tryin' to get some sleep over here!"

From inside the trailer, the woman hollered, "Sorry!" The music ceased abruptly and I went back around to the other side to see how much of their conversation I could pick up.

The quiet was divine. The volume on the television set must have been turned all the way down, because the string of commercials that now appeared was antic with silence and I could actually catch snatches of what they were saying, though they mumbled unmercifully.

". . . course, she's going to say that. What did you expect?" she said.

"I don't like the pressure. I don't like havin' her on my back . . ." He said something else I couldn't make out.

"What difference does it make? Nobody forced her. Shit, she's free, white, and twenty-one . . . the point is . . . getting into . . . just so she doesn't think . . . the whole thing, right?"

Her voice had dropped and when Billy answered, he had one hand across his mouth so I couldn't understand him at all. He was only half attentive anyway, talking to her with his gaze straying to the television picture. It must have been 11:00 because the local news came on. There was the usual lead-in, a long shot of the news desk with two male newscasters, one black, one white, like a matched set, sitting there in suits. Both looked properly solemn. The camera cut to a head shot of the black man. A photograph of John Daggett appeared briefly behind him. There was a quick shot of the beach. It took me a moment to realize that it must have been the spot where Daggett's body had been found. In the background, I could see the mouth of the harbor and the dredge.

Billy jerked upright, grabbing the woman's arm. She swiveled around to see what he was pointing to. The announcer talked on, smoothly moving the top sheet of paper aside. The camera cut to the co-anchor and the picture shifted to a still shot of a local waste disposal site.

Billy and the woman traded a long, anxious look. Billy started cracking his knuckles. "Christ!"

The woman snatched up the paper and tossed it at him. "I told you it was him the minute I read some bum washed up on the beach. Goddamn it, Billy! Everything with you comes down to the same old bullshit. You think you're so smart. You got all the angles covered. Oh sure. Turns out you don't even know what you're talking about!"

"They don't even know we knew him. How would they know that?"

She gave him a scornful look, exasperated that he'd try to defend himself. "Give the cops some credit! They probably identified him by his fingerprints, right? So they know he was up in San Luis. It's not going to take a genius to figure out you were up there with him. Next thing we know somebody's coming around knocking at the door. 'When'd you last see this guy?' Shit like that."

He got up abruptly. He crossed to a kitchen cabinet and opened it. "You got any Black Jack?"

"No, I don't have any Black Jack. You drank it all last night."

"Get some clothes on. Let's go over to the Hub."

"Billy, I've got a cold! I'm not going out at this hour. You go. Why do you need a drink anyway?"

He reached for his jacket, hunching into it. "You have any cash? All I got on me is a buck."

"Get a job. Pay your own way. I'm tired of givin' you money."

"I said you'd get it back. What are you worried about? Come on, come on," he said, snapping his fingers impatiently.

She took her time about it, but she did root through her purse, coming up with a crumpled five-dollar bill, which he took without comment.

"Are you crashing here?" she asked.

"I don't know yet. Probably. Don't lock up."

"Well, just keep it down, okay? I feel like hell and I don't want to be woke up."

He put his hands on her arms. "Hey," he said. "Cool it. You worry too much."

"You know what your problem is? You think all you have to do is say shit like that and it's all okay. The world doesn't work that way. It never did."

"Yeah, well there's always a first time. Your problem is you're a pessimist. . . ."

At that point, I figured I'd better cut out and head back to my car. I eased down off my perch, debating briefly about whether I should move the steps or leave them there. Better to move them. I hefted them, swiftly pushing through the undergrowth to a cleared space where the junk was stacked up. I set the box down and then took off through the darkened trailer park and out to the street.

I jogged to my car, started it, and did another U-turn, anticipating that Billy would head back the same way he came. Sure enough, in my rearview mirror I saw the Chevrolet make a left turn onto the main thoroughfare, coming up behind me. He followed me for a block and a half, tailgating, a real A-type. With an impatient toot of the horn, he passed me, squealed into another left-hand turn, and zoomed off toward Milagro. I knew where he was headed so I took my time. There's a bar called the

Hub about three blocks up. I walked into the place maybe ten minutes after he did. He'd already bought his Jack Daniel's, which he was nursing while he played pool.

9

The Hub is a bar with all the ambience of a converted warehouse. The space is too vast for camaraderie, the air too chill for relaxation. The ceiling is high, painted black, and covered with a gridwork of pipes and electrical conduits. The tables in the main room are sparse, the walls lined with old black-and-white photographs of the bar and its various clientele over the years. Through a wide archway is a smaller room with four pool tables. The juke box is massive, outlined in bands of yellow, green, and cherry red, with bubbles blipping through the seams. The place was curiously empty for a Saturday night. A Willie Nelson single was playing, but it wasn't one I knew.

I was the only woman in the bar and I could sense the male attention shift to me with a bristling caution. I paused, feeling sniffed at, as if I were a dog in an alien neighborhood. Cigarette smoke hung in the air, and the men with their pool cues were caught in the hazy light, bent above the tables in silhouette. I identified Billy Polo by the great puff of hair around his head. Upright, he was taller than I'd pictured him, with wide, hard shoulders and slim hips. He was playing pool with a Mexican kid, maybe twenty-two, with a gaunt face, tattooed arms, and a strip of pinched-looking chest which was visible in the gap of the Hawaiian shirt he wore unbuttoned to the waist. He sported maybe six chest hairs in a shallow depression in the middle of his sternum.

I crossed to the table and stood there, waiting for Billy to finish his game. He glanced at me with disinterest and lined up the cue ball with the six ball, which he smacked smartly into a side pocket. He moved around the table without pause, lining up the two ball which he fired like a shot into the corner pocket. He chalked his cue, eyeing the three ball. He tested an angle and rejected it, leaning into the table then with a shot that sent the three ball rocketing into the side pocket, while the five ball glanced off the side, rolled into range of the corner pocket, hung there, and finally dropped in. A trace of a smile crossed Billy's face, but he didn't look up.

Meanwhile, the Mexican kid stood there and grinned at me, leaning on his cue stick. He mouthed, "I love you." One of his front teeth was rimmed in gold, like a picture frame, and there was a smudge of blue chalk near his chin. Behind him, Billy cleaned up the table and put his cue stick back in the rack on the wall. As he passed, he plucked a twenty from the kid's shirt pocket and tucked it into his own. Then, with his face averted, he said, "You the chick came looking for me at my mom's house earlier?"

"That's right. I'm a friend of John Daggett's."

He cocked his head, squinting, his right hand cupped behind his ear. "Who?"

I smiled lazily. We were apparently playing charades. I raised my voice, enunciating. "Daggett. John."

"Oh, yeah, him. How's he doing these days?" He started snapping his fingers lightly to the music, which had switched from Willie Nelson to a George Benson tune.

"He's dead."

I have to credit him. He did a nice imitation of casual surprise, not overdoing it. "You're shittin' me. Daggett's dead? Too bad. What happened to the dude, heart attack?"

"Drowned. It just happened last night, down at the marina." I wagged a thumb over my shoulder in the direction of the beach so he'd know which marina I meant.

"Here in town? Hey, that's tough. I didn't know that. He was in L.A. last I heard."

"I'm surprised you didn't see it on the news."

"Yeah, well I never pay attention to that shit, you know? Bums me out. I got better things to do with my time."

His eyes were all over the place and his body was half turned away. I had to guess that he was busy trying to figure out who I was and what I was up to. He flicked a look at me. "I'm sorry. I didn't catch your name."

"Kinsey Millhone."

He studied me fleetingly. "I thought my mom said the name was Charlene."

I shook my head. "I don't know where she got that."

"And you do what?"

"Basic research. I free-lance. What's that got to do with it?"

"You don't look like a friend of Daggett's. He was kind of a lowlife. You got too much class for a scumbag like him."

"I didn't say we were close. I met him recently through a friend of a friend."

"Why tell me about it? I don't give a damn."

"I'm sorry to hear that. Daggett said if anything happened to him, I should talk to you."

"Me? Naww," he said with disbelief. "That's fuckin' weird. You must have got me mixed up with somebody else. I mean, I knew Daggett, but I didn't *know* him, you dig?"

"That's funny. He told me you were the best of friends."

He smiled and shook his head. "Old Daggett gave you a bum steer, baby doll. I don't know nothin' about it. I don't even remember when I saw him last. Long time."

"What was the occasion?"

He glanced at the Mexican kid who was eavesdropping shamelessly. "Catch you later, man," he said to him. Then under his breath, with contempt, he said, "Paco." Apparently, this was a generic insult that applied to all Hispanics.

He touched my elbow, steering me into the other room. "These beaners are all the same," he confided. "Think they know how to play pool, but they can't do shit. I don't like talking personal in front of spics. Can I buy you a beer?"

"Sure."

He indicated an empty table and held a chair out for me. I hung my slicker over the back and sat down. He caught the bartender's eye and held up two fingers. The bartender pulled out two bottles of beer which he opened and set on the bar.

Billy said, "You want anything else? Potato chips? They make real nice french fries. Kinda greasy, but good."

I shook my head, watching him with interest. At close range, he had a curious charisma . . . a crude sexuality that he probably wasn't even aware of. I meet men like that occasionally and I'm always startled by the phenomenon.

He ambled over and picked up the beers, dropping a

couple of crumpled bills on the bar. He said something to the bartender and then waited while the guy placed a glass upside down on each bottle, shooting a smirk in my direction.

He came back to the table and sat down. "Jesus, ask for a glass in this place and they act like you're puttin' on airs. Bunch of bohunks. I only hang out here because I got a sister works here three nights a week."

Ah, I thought, the woman in the trailer.

He poured one of the beers and pushed it over to me, taking his time then as he poured his own. His eyes were deepset, and he had dimples that formed a crease on either side of his mouth. "Look," he said, "I can see you got your mind made up I know something I don't. The truth is, I didn't like Daggett much and I don't think he liked me. Where you got this yarn about me bein' some pal of his, I don't know, but it wasn't from him."

"You called him Monday morning, didn't you?"

"Nuh-uh. Not me. Why would I call him?"

I went on as though he hadn't said anything. "I don't know what you told him, but he was scared."

"Sorry I can't help you out. Must have been somebody else. What was he doin' up here anyway?"

"I don't know. His body washed up in the surf this morning. I thought maybe you could fill me in on the rest. Do you have any idea where he was last night?"

"Nope. Not a clue." He'd gotten interested in a

speck of dust in the foam on his beer and he had to pick that out.

"When did you see him last? I don't think you said."

His tone became facetious. "Geez, I don't have my Day-Timer with me. Otherwise, I could pin it down. We might've had lunch at some little out of the way place, just him and me."

"San Luis perhaps?"

There was a slight pause and his smile dimmed a couple of watts. "I was at San Luis with him," he said, cautiously. "Me and thirty-seven hundred other guys. So what?"

"I thought maybe you'd kept in touch."

"I can tell you didn't know Daggett too good. Being with him is like walking around with dog-do on your shoe, you know? It's not something you'd seek out."

"Who else did he know here in town?"

"Can't help you there. It's not my week to keep track."

"What about your sister? Did he know her?"

"Coral? No way. She don't hang out with bums like that. I'd break her neck. I don't get why you're goin' on and on about this. I told you I don't know nothin'. I didn't see him, didn't hear from him. Why can't you just take my word for it?"

"Because I don't think you're telling the truth."

"Says who? I mean, you came lookin' for me, re-member? I don't have to talk to you. I'm doin' you a favor. I don't know who you are. I don't even know what the fuck you're up to."

I shook my head, smiling slightly. "God, Billy. Such foul talk. I didn't think you dealt with women that way. I'm shocked."

"Now you're makin' fun of me, right?" He scrutinized my face. "You some kind of cop?"

I ran my thumbnail down the bottle, snagging an accordion strip of label, which I picked off. "Actually I am."

He snorted. Now he'd heard everything. "Come on. Like what," he said.

"I'm a private investigator."

"Bullshit."

"It's a fact."

He tipped back in his chair, amused that I'd try to lay such a line on him. "Jesus, you're too much. Who do you think you're talkin' to? I might have been born at night, but it wasn't *last* night. I know the private eyes around town and you ain't one, so try somethin' else."

I laughed. "All right, I'm not. Maybe I'm just a nosy chick looking into the death of a man I once met."

"Now, that I'd buy, but it still don't explain why you're crankin' on my case."

"You introduced him to Lovella, didn't you?"

That stopped him momentarily. "You know Lovella?"

"Sure. I met her down in L.A. She has an apartment on Sawtelle."

"When was this?"

"Day before yesterday."

"No foolin'. And she told you to look me up?"

"How else would I know where you were?"

He stared at me, going through some sort of mental debate.

I thought a little coaxing might loosen his tongue. "Are you aware that Daggett's been beating the shit out of her?"

That made him restless and his eyes dropped away from mine. "Yeah, well Lovella's a big girl. She has to learn how to take care of herself."

"Why don't you help her out?"

He smiled bitterly. "I know people who'd laugh at the notion of me helping anyone," he said. "Besides, she's tough. You don't want to underestimate that one, I'm tellin' you."

"You've known her a long time, haven't you?"

His knee had started to jump. "Seven years, eight. I met her when she was seventeen. We lived together for a while, but it didn't work out. We used to knock heads too much. She's a bullheaded bitch, but I loved her a lot. Then I got busted on a burglary rap and me and her, hell, I don't know what it was. We wrote to each other for a while, but you can't go back to something once it's dead, you know? Anyway, now we're friends, I guess. At least I dig her. I don't know how she feels about me."

"Have you seen her recently?"

The knee stopped. "No, I haven't seen her recently," he said. "What about you? Why'd you go down there?"

"I was looking for Daggett. The phone was disconnected."

"What exactly did she say?"

I shrugged. "Nothing much. I wasn't there long and she wasn't feeling that good. She was nursing a big black eye."

"Jesus," he said. He rocked back in his chair. "Tell me something. How come women do that? Let guys punch 'em out?"

"I have no idea."

He drained his beer glass and set it down. "I bet you don't take crap from anyone, am I right?"

"We all take crap from someone," I said.

Billy got up. "Sorry to cut this off, but I gotta split." He turned, tucking his shirt down into his pants more securely. His body language said he'd already taken off and hoped his clothing would catch up with him by the time he hit the street.

I got up, reaching for my slicker. "You're not leaving town, are you?"

"What business is it of yours?"

"It doesn't seem like a good idea with Daggett's death hanging fire. Suppose the cops want to talk to you."

"About what?"

"Where you were last night, for starters."

His tone rose. "Where *I* was? What are you talkin' about?"

"They might want to know about the connection between Daggett and you."

"What connection? That's a crock. I don't know where you come up with that."

"It's not me you have to worry about. It's the cops who count."

"What cops?"

I shook my head. "You know who your friendly local cops are," I said. "If somebody puts a bug in the wrong ear, you'll be sitting in the hot seat."

He was all outrage. "Why would you do that to me?"

"Because you're not leveling with me, William."

"I *am* leveling with you! I've told you everything I know."

"I don't think so. I think you knew about Daggett's death. I think you saw him this week."

He put his hands on his hips and looked off across the room, shaking his head. "Man, this is all I need. This is no lie. I've been straight. I'm minding my own business, doing like I been told. I didn't even know the dude was up here."

"You can stick to your story if you like," I said, "but I'll give you a word of advice. I've got the license number of that car you bought. You bolt and I'm calling Lieutenant Dolan down at Homicide."

He seemed as much puzzled as dismayed. "What is this? A shakedown? Is that what this is about?"

"What's to shake? You don't have a cent. I want information, that's all."

"I don't *have* any information. How many times I gotta tell you that?"

"Look," I said patiently. "Why don't I let you think about the situation and then we can talk again."

"Why don't you go fuck yourself!"

I put my slicker on, tucking the strap of my handbag over my shoulder. "Thanks for the beer. I'll buy yours next time."

He made an exaggerated gesture of dismissal, too pissed off to reply. He headed toward the door and I watched him go. I glanced at my watch. It was well after midnight and I was exhausted. My head was starting to ache and I knew everything about me smelled like stale cigarette smoke. I wanted to go home, strip down, shower, and then crawl into the folds of my quilt. Instead, I took a deep breath and went after him.

10

I gave him a good head start, then followed him back to the trailer. The temperature felt like it had dropped into the fifties. The eucalyptus trees were still tossing occasional showers at me when the wind cut through, but for the most part, the night was clear. Above me, I could see pale puffs of rain clouds receding, wide patches of starry sky breaking through. I parked half a block away and padded into the park on foot as I had before. Billy's car was parked beside the trailer. I was getting bored, but I had to be certain he wasn't heading off to consult with some confederate I didn't know about.

The same lights were on in the galley, but a dim light now glowed at the rear of the trailer, where I imagined the bedroom to be. I picked my way through the bushes to that end. Curtains were pulled across the windows, but the venting system was piping a murmured conversation right out through a mesh-covered opening. I hunkered down by the torn skirting, leaning my head against the aluminum. I could smell cigarette smoke, which I guessed was Coral's.

". . . want to know why she showed up now," she was saying. "That's what we have to worry about. For all we know, they're in it together."

"Yeah, but doin' what? That's what I can't figure out."

"When'd she say she'd get in touch?"

"She didn't. Said I should think about the situation. Jesus. How'd she get a bead on the Chevy so fast? That's what bugs me. I had that car two hours."

"Maybe she followed you, dimwit."

The silence was profound. "Goddamn it," he said.

I heard footsteps thump toward the front of the trailer. By the time the door banged open I was easing my way around the end. I peered out into the carport. The nose of the Chevy was about six feet away, the space on either side of it crowded with junk.

The door to the trailer had been flung open. Light poured out, washing as far as the point where the asphalt began. With a quick look over my shoulder, I waded into the refuse, picking my way around to the far side of the car, where I crouched, listening intently. Sometimes I feel like I spend half my life this way. I heard Billy fumble his way around the bedroom end of the trailer just as I had.

"Jesus!" he hissed.

Coral peered out the side window, whispering hoarsely. "What's wrong?"

"Shut up! Nothing. I banged my goddamn shin on the trailer hitch. Why don't you clean up this crap?"

My sentiments exactly.

Coral laughed and the curtain dropped back into place.

Billy appeared again at the far end of the carport, rubbing his left shin. He did a quick visual survey, apparently convinced by then there wasn't anybody lurking about the premises. He shook his head and thumped up the steps, banging the door shut behind him. The carport went dark. I let out my breath.

I could hear them murmuring together, but by then I didn't really care what else they discussed. As soon as I was convinced it was safe, I crept out of the driveway and headed for my car.

Sunday morning was overcast. The very air looked gray, and dampness seemed to rise up out of the earth like a mist. I went through my usual morning routine, getting a three-mile run in before the skies opened up again. At 9:00, I put a call through to Barbara Daggett at home. I brought her up to date, filling her in on my night's activities.

"What now?" she asked.

"I'm going to let Billy Polo stew for a day or two and then get back to him."

"What makes you think he won't skip?"

"Well, he *is* on parole and I'm hoping he won't want to mess that up. Besides, it feels like a waste of money to pay me to sit there all day."

"I thought you said he was the only lead you had."

"Maybe not," I said cautiously. "I've been thinking about Tony Gahan and the other people killed in the accident."

"Tony Gahan?" she said with surprise. "How could he be involved in this?"

"I don't know. Your father hired me originally to track him down. Maybe he found the kid himself and that's where he was early in the week."

"But Kinsey, why would Daddy want to track him down? That boy must hate his guts. His whole family was wiped out."

"That's my point."

"Oh."

"Do you have any idea how to locate him? Your father had an address on Stanley Place, but the house was apparently empty. I can't find a Gahan listed in the telephone book."

"He lives with his aunt now, I think, somewhere in Colgate. Let me see if I've got an address."

Colgate is the bedroom community, attached to Santa Teresa like a double star. The two are just about the same size, but Santa Teresa has all the character and Colgate has the affordable housing, along with hardware stores, paint companies, bowling alleys, and drive-in theaters. Colgate is the Frostee-Freeze capital of the world.

There was a pause and I could hear pages rattle. She came back on the line. "My mistake. They live near the Museum. Her last name is Westfall. Ramona."

"I wonder why your father didn't know about her."

"I don't know. She was there for the trial. I do remember that, because someone pointed her out to me. I wrote her a note afterward, saying that of course we'd do anything we could to help, but I never heard back."

"You know anything else about her? Is she married, for instance?"

"I think so, yes. Her husband manufactures industrial supplies or something like that. Actually, now that I think about it, she *was* working at that kitchenware place on Capilla because I spotted her when I was in there shopping a couple of months ago. Maybe you could catch her this afternoon if she still works there."

"On Sunday?"

"Sure, they're open from twelve to five."

"I'll try her first and see how far I get," I said. "What about your mother? How's she holding up?"

"Surprisingly well. Turns out she handles death like a champ. If it's covered in the Bible, she trots out all the appropriate attitudes and goes through the sequence automatically. I thought she'd flip out, but it seems to have put her back on her feet. She's got church women sitting with her, and the pastor's there. The kitchen table's stacked with tuna casseroles and chocolate cakes. I don't know how long it will last, but for now, she's in her element."

"When's the funeral?"

"Tuesday afternoon. The body's been transported to the mortuary. I think they said he'd be ready for viewing early this afternoon. Are you coming by?"

"Yes, I think I will. I can tell you then if I've talked to this Westfall woman or the kid."

Jorden's is a gourmet cook's fantasy, with every imaginable food preparation device. Rack after rack of cookware, utensils, cookbooks, linens, spices, coffees, and condiments; chafing dishes, wicker baskets, exotic vinegars and oils, knives, baking pans, glassware. I stood in the entrance for a moment, amazed by the number and variety of food-related implements. Pasta machines, cappuccino makers, food warmers, coffee grinders, ice cream freezers, food processors. The air smelled of chocolate and made me wish I had a mother. I spotted three saleswomen, all wearing wrap-around aprons made of mattress ticking, with the store's name embroidered in maroon across the bib.

I asked for Ramona Westfall and was directed toward the rear aisle. She was apparently doing a shelf count. I found her perched on a small wooden stool, clipboard in hand, checking off items on a list that in-

cluded most of the nonelectrical gadgets. She was sorting through a bin of what looked like small stainless
steel sliding boards with a blade across the center that
would slice your tiny ass off.

"What are those?" I asked.

She glanced up at me with a pleasant smile. She appeared to be in her late forties, with short, pale sandy
hair streaked with gray, hazel eyes peering at me over a
pair of half-glasses which she wore low on her nose.
She used little if any makeup, and even seated, I could
tell she was small and slim. Under the apron, she wore
a white, long-sleeved blouse with a Peter Pan collar, a
gray tweed skirt, hose, and penny loafers.

"That's a mandoline. It's made in West Germany."

"I thought a mandolin was a musical instrument."

"The spelling's different. This is for slicing raw veg-
etables. You can waffle-cut or julienne."

"Really?" I said. I had sudden visions of homemade
French fries and cole slaw, neither of which I've ever
prepared. "How much is that?"

"A hundred and ten dollars. With the slicing guard,
it's one thirty-eight. Would you like a demonstration?"

I shook my head, unwilling to spend that much
money on behalf of a potato. She got to her feet,
smoothing the front of her apron. She was half a head
shorter than I and smelled like a perfume sample I'd
gotten in the mail the week before. Lavender and
crushed jasmine. I was impressed with the price of the

stuff, if not the scent. I stuck it in a drawer and I'm assailed with the fragrance now every time I pull out fresh underwear.

"You're Ramona Westfall, aren't you?"

Her smile was modified to a look of expectancy. "That's right. Have we met?"

I shook my head. "I'm Kinsey Millhone. I'm a private investigator here in town."

"Is there something I can help you with?"

"I'm looking for Tony Gahan. I understand you're his aunt."

"Tony? Good heavens, what for?"

"I was asked to locate him on a personal matter. I didn't know how else to get in touch with him."

"What personal matter? I don't understand."

"I was asked to deliver something to him. A check from a man who's recently deceased."

She looked at me blankly for a moment and then I saw recognition leap into her eyes. "You're referring to John Daggett, aren't you? Someone told me it was on the news last night. I assumed he was still in prison."

"He's been out for six weeks."

Her face flooded with color. "Well, isn't that typical," she snapped. "Five people dead and he's back on the streets."

"Not quite," I said. "Could we go someplace and talk?"

"About what? About my sister? She was thirty-eight,

a beautiful person. She was decapitated when he ran a stoplight and plowed into them. Her husband was killed. Tony's sister was crushed. She was six, just a baby. . . ." She bit off her sentence abruptly, suddenly aware that her voice had risen. Nearby, several people paused, looking over at us.

"Who were the others? Did you know them?" I asked.

"You're the detective. You figure it out."

In the next aisle, a dark-haired woman in a striped apron caught her eye. She didn't open her mouth, but her expression said, "Is everything all right?"

"I'm taking a break," Ramona said to her. "I'll be in the back room if Tricia's looking for me."

The dark-haired woman glanced at me briefly and then dropped her gaze. Ramona was moving toward a doorway on the far side of the room. I followed. The other customers had lost interest, but I had a feeling that I'd be facing an unpleasant scene.

By the time I entered the back room, Ramona was fumbling in her handbag with shaking hands. She opened a zippered compartment and took out a vial of pills. She extracted a tablet and broke it in half, downing it with a slug of cold coffee from a white mug with her name on the side. On second thought, she took the second half of the tablet as well.

I said, "Look, I'm sorry to have to bring this up . . ."

"Don't apologize," she spat. "It doesn't do any

good." She searched through the bag and came up with a hard pack of Winston's. She pulled out a cigarette and tamped it repeatedly on her thumbnail, then lit it with a Bic disposable lighter she'd tucked in her apron pocket. She hugged her waist with her left arm, propping the right elbow on it so she could hold the cigarette near her face. Her eyes seemed to have darkened and she fixed me with a blank, rude stare. "What is it you want?"

I could feel my face warm. Somehow the money was suddenly beside the point and seemed like too paltry a sum in any event. "I have a cashier's check for Tony. John Daggett asked me to deliver it."

Her smile was supercilious. "Oh, a *check*. Well, how much is it for? Is it per *head* or some sort of lump sum payment by the carload?"

"Mrs. Westfall," I said patiently.

"You can call me Ramona, dear, since the subject matter's so intimate. We're talking about the people I loved best in this world." She took a deep drag of her cigarette and blew smoke toward the ceiling.

I clamped down on my temper, controlling my response. "I understand that the subject is painful," I said. "I know there's no way to compensate for what happened, but John Daggett was making a gesture, and regardless of your opinion of him, it's possible that Tony might have a use for the money."

"We provide for him very nicely, thanks. We don't

need anything from John Daggett *or* his daughter or from *you*."

I plowed on, heading into the face of her wrath like a swimmer through churning surf. "Let me just say something first. Daggett came to me last week with a cashier's check made out to Tony."

She started to speak, but I held up one hand. "Please," I said.

She subsided, allowing me to continue.

"I put the check in a safe deposit box until I could figure out how to deliver it, as agreed. You can toss it in the trash for all I care, but I'd like to do what I said I'd do, which is to see that Tony Gahan gets it. In theory, it's Tony's to do with as he sees fit, so I'd appreciate it if you'd talk to him before you do anything else."

She thought about that one, her eyes locked on mine. "How much?"

"Twenty-five thousand. That's a good chunk of education for Tony, or a trip abroad. . . ."

"I get the point," she cut in. "Now maybe you'll allow me to have my say. That boy has been with us for almost three years now. He's fifteen years old and I don't think he's slept a full eight hours since the accident. He has migraines, he bites his nails. His grades are poor, school attendance is *shit*. We're talking about a kid with an I.Q. right off the charts. He's a wreck and John Daggett did that to him. There's no way . . . no *way* anyone can ever make up to Tony for what that man did."

"I understand that."

"No, you don't." Her eyes filled suddenly with tears. She was silent, hands shaking again so badly now that she could scarcely get the Winston to her lips. She managed to take another drag, fighting for control. The silence lengthened. She seemed to shudder and I could almost see the tranquilizer kick in. She turned away abruptly, dropped the cigarette, and stepped on it. "Give me a number where I can reach you. I'll talk to my husband and see what he says."

I handed her my card, taking a moment to jot down my home address and telephone number on the back, in case she needed to reach me there.

11

After I left Ramona Westfall, I stopped by my apartment and changed into pantyhose, low heels, and my all-purpose dress. This garment, which I've owned for five years, is made of some magic fabric that doesn't wilt, wrinkle, or show dirt. It can be squashed down to the size of a rain hat and shoved in the bottom of my handbag without harm. It can also be rinsed out in any bathroom sink and hung to dry overnight. It's black, lightweight, has long sleeves, zips up the back, and should probably be "accessorized," a women's clothing concept I've never understood. I wear the dress "as is" and it always looks okay to me. Once in a while I see this look of recognition in someone's eye, but maybe it's just a moment of surprise at seeing me in something other than jeans and boots.

The Wynington-Blake Mortuary—Burials, Cremation, and Shipping, Serving All Faiths—is located on the east side of town on a shady side street with ample

parking. It was originally built as a residence and re-
tains the feeling of a substantial single-family dwelling.
Now, of course, the entire first floor has been converted into the equivalent of six spacious living rooms,
each furnished with metal folding chairs and labeled
with some serene-sounding word.

The gentleman who greeted me, a Mr. Sharonson,
wore a subdued navy blue suit, a neutral expression,
and used a public library voice. John Daggett was laid
out in "Meditation," which was just down the corridor
and to my left. The family, he murmured, was in the
Sunrise Chapel if I cared to wait. I signed in. Mr.
Sharonson removed himself discreetly and I was left to
do as I pleased. The room was rimmed with chairs, the
casket at the apex. There were two sprays of white
gladioli that looked somehow like pristine fakes provided by the mortuary, instead of wreaths sent by
those who mourned Daggett's passing. Organ music
was being piped in, a nearly subliminal auditory cue
meant to trigger thoughts about the brevity of life.

I tiptoed across the room to have a peek at him. The
color and texture of Daggett's skin looked about like a
Betsy-Wetsy doll I'd had as a kid. His features had a
flattened appearance, which I suspected was a side effect of the autopsy process. Peel somebody's face back
and it's hard to line it all up again. Daggett's nose
looked crooked, like a pillowcase put on with the seam
slightly skewed.

I was aware of a rustling behind me and Barbara

Daggett appeared on my right. We stood together for a moment without a word. I don't know why people stand and study the dead that way. It makes about as much sense as paying homage to the cardboard box your favorite shoes once came in. Finally, she murmured something and turned away, moving toward the entrance where Eugene Nickerson and Essie Daggett were just coming in through the archway.

Essie was wearing a dark navy dress of rayon jersey, her massive arms dimpled with pale flesh. Her hair looked freshly "done," puffed and thick, sprayed into a turban of undulating gray. Eugene, in a dark suit, steered her by the elbow, working her arm as if it were the rudder on a ship. She took one look at the casket and her wide knees buckled. Barbara and Eugene caught her before she actually hit the floor. They guided her to an upholstered chair and lowered her into the seat. She fumbled for a handkerchief, which she pressed to her mouth as if she meant to chloroform herself.

"Sweet Jesus Lord," she mewed, her eyes turned up piteously. "Lamb of God . . ." Eugene began to pat at her hand and Barbara sat down beside her, putting one arm around her protectively.

"You want me to bring her some water?" I asked.

Barbara nodded and I moved toward the doorway. Mr. Sharonson had sensed the disturbance and had appeared, his face forming a question. I passed the request along and he nodded. He left the room and I returned to Mrs. Daggett's side. She was having a pretty good time by now, rolling her head back and forth, reciting scriptures in a high-pitched voice. Barbara and Eugene were working to restrain her and I gathered that Essie had expressed a strong desire to fling herself into the coffin with her beloved. I might have given her a boost myself.

Mr. Sharonson returned with a paper envelope full of water, which Barbara took, holding it to Essie's lips. She jerked her head back, unwilling to accept even this small measure of solace. "By night on my bed, I sought him whom my soul loveth," she warbled. "I sought him, but I found him not. I will rise now, and go about the city in the streets, and in the broad ways I will seek him whom my soul loveth. The watchmen that go about the city found me . . . Lord in Heaven . . . O God. . . ."

With surprise, I realized she was quoting fragments from the Song of Solomon, which I recognized from my old Methodist Sunday School days. Little kids were never allowed to read that part of the Bible as it was considered too smutty, but I was real interested in the idea of a man with legs like pillars of marble set upon sockets of fine gold. There was some talk of swords and thighs that caught my attention too. I believe I lasted three Sundays before my aunt was asked to take me down the street to the Presbyterians.

Essie was rapidly losing control, whipping herself into such an agitated state that Eugene and Mr.

Sharonson had to assist her to her feet and help her out of the room. I could hear her cries becoming feebler as she was moved down the hall. Barbara rubbed her face wearily. "Oh God. Count on Mother," she said. "How has your day been?"

I sat down beside her. "This doesn't seem like the best time to talk," I said.

"Oh, don't worry about it. She'll calm down. This is the first she's seen of him. There's some kind of lounge upstairs. She can rest for a while and she'll be fine. What about Ramona Westfall? Did you talk to her?"

I filled her in on my brief interview, bringing the subject around to my real question at this point, which had to do with the two other victims in the accident. Barbara closed her eyes, the matter clearly causing her pain.

"One was a little friend of Hilary Gahan's. Her name was Megan Smith. I'm sure her parents are still in the area. I'll check the address and telephone number when I get home. Her father's name is Wayne. I forget the name of the street, but it's probably listed."

I took my notebook out and jotted the name down. "And the fifth?"

"Some kid who'd bummed a ride with them. They picked him up at the on-ramp to the freeway to give him a lift into town."

"What was his name?"

"Doug Polokowski."

I stared at her. "You're kidding."

"Why? Do you know him?"

"Polokowski is Billy Polo's real last name. It's on his rap sheet."

"You think they're related?"

"They'd almost have to be. There's only one Polokowski family in town. It's got to be a cousin or a brother, *something*."

"But I thought Billy Polo was supposed to be Daddy's best friend. That doesn't make sense."

Mr. Sharonson returned to the room and caught her eye. "Your mother is asking for you, Miss Daggett."

"You go ahead," I said. "I've got plenty to work on at this point. I'll call you later at home."

Barbara followed Mr. Sharonson while I headed out to the foyer and hustled up a telephone book. Wayne and Marilyn Smith were listed on Tupelo Drive out in Colgate, right around the corner from Stanley Place, if my memory served me correctly. I considered calling first, but I was curious what the reaction would be to the fact of Daggett's death, if the news hadn't already reached them. I stopped to get gas in the VW and then headed out to the freeway.

The Smiths' house was the single odd one in a twelve-block radius of identical tract homes and I guessed that theirs was the original farmhouse at the heart of what had once been a citrus grove. I could still spot orange trees in irregular rows, broken up now by winding roads, fenced lots, and an elementary school. The Smiths' mailbox was a small replica of the house and the street number was gouged out of a thick plank of pine, stained dark and hung above the porch steps. The house itself was a two-story white frame with tall, narrow windows and a slate roof. A sprawling vegetable garden stretched out behind the house, with the garage beyond that. A tire swing hung by a rope from a sycamore that grew in the yard. Orange trees extended on all sides, looking twisted and barren, their producing years long past. It was probably cheaper to leave them there than to tear them out. An assortment of boys' bicycles in a rack on the porch suggested the presence of male offspring or an in-progress meeting of a cycling club.

The bell consisted of a metal twist in the middle of the door. I cranked it once and it trilled harshly. As with the Christopher house, the upper portion of the door was glass, allowing me a glimpse of the interior—high ceilings, waxed pine floors, a scattering of rag rugs, and Early American antiques that looked authentic to my untrained eye. The walls were covered with patchwork quilts, the colors washed out to pale shades of mauve and blue. Numerous children's jackets hung from a row of pegs to the left, rainboots lined up underneath.

A woman in jeans and an oversized white shirt trotted down the stairs, trailing one hand along the banister. She gave me a quick smile and opened the front door.

"Oh hi. Are you Larry's mom?" She read instantly

from my expression that I hadn't the faintest idea what she was talking about. She gave a quick laugh. "I guess not. The boys got back from the movie half an hour ago and we've been waiting for Larry's mother to pick him up. Sorry."

"That's all right. I'm Kinsey Millhone," I said. "I'm a private investigator here in town." I handed her my card.

"Can I help you with something?" She was in her mid-thirties, her blonde hair pulled straight back from her face in a clumsy knot. She was dark-eyed, with the tanned good looks of someone who works outdoors. I imagined her to be the kind of mother who forbade her children to eat refined sugar and supervised the television shows they watched. Whether such vigilance pays off or not, I'm never sure. I tend to place kids in a class with dogs, preferring the quiet, the smart, and the well trained.

"John Daggett was killed here in town Friday night," I said.

Something flickered across her face, but maybe it was just the realization that a painful subject was coming up again. "I hadn't heard about that. What happened?"

"He fell out of a boat and drowned."

She thought about that briefly. "Well, that's not too bad. Drowning's supposed to be fairly easy, isn't it?" Her tone of voice was light, her expression pleasant. It took me a minute to realize the savagery of the sentiment. I wondered what kind of torture she'd wished on him.

"Most of us don't get to choose our death," I said.

"My daughter certainly didn't," she said tartly. "Was it an accident or did someone give him a nice push?"

"That's what I'm trying to find out," I said. "I heard he came up from L.A. on Monday, but nobody seems to know where he spent the week."

"Not here, I can assure you. If Wayne so much as set eyes on him, he'd have. . . ." The words tapered off to a faint smile and her tone became almost bantering. "I was going to say, he'd have killed him, but I didn't mean that literally. Or maybe I did. I guess I shouldn't speak for Wayne."

"What about you? When did you see him last?"

"I have no idea. Two years ago at least."

"At the trial?"

She shook her head. "I wasn't there. Wayne sat in for a day, but he couldn't take it after that. He talked to Barbara Daggett once, I think, but I'm sure there's been nothing since. I'm assuming somehow that the man was murdered. Is that what you're getting at?"

"It's possible. The police don't seem to think so, but I'm hoping they'll revise their opinion if I can come up with some evidence. I get the impression a lot of people wanted Daggett dead."

"Well, I sure did. I'm thrilled to hear the news. Somebody should have killed him at birth," she said. "Would you like to come in? I don't know what I can tell you, but we might as well be comfortable." She glanced at my business card again, double-checking the name and then tucking it in her shirt pocket.

She held the door and I passed over the threshold, pausing to see where she meant for us to go. She led me into the living room.

"You and your husband were home Friday night?"

"Why? Are we suspects?"

"There isn't even a formal investigation yet," I said.

"I was here. Wayne was working late. He's a C.P.A."

She indicated a chair and I sat down. She took a seat on the couch, her manner relaxed. She was wearing a thin gold bracelet on her right wrist and she began to turn that, straightening a kink in the chain. "Did you ever meet John Daggett yourself?" she asked.

"Once. He came to my office a week ago Saturday."

"Ah. Out on parole, no doubt. He must have served his ten minutes."

I made no comment, so she went on.

"What was he doing in Santa Teresa? Returning to the scene of the slaughter?"

"He was trying to locate Tony Gahan."

This seemed to amuse her. "To what end? It's probably none of my business, but I'm curious."

I was discomfited by her attitude, which seemed an odd mix of the wrathful and the jocular. "I'm not really sure what his intentions were," I said carefully. "The story he told me wasn't true anyway, so it's probably not worth repeating. I gathered he wanted to make restitution."

Her smile faded, dark eyes boring into mine with a look that chilled me. "There's no such thing as 'restitution' for what that man did. Megan died horribly. Five-and-a-half years old. Has anyone given you the details?"

"I have the newspaper clippings in the car. I talked to Ramona Westfall too, and she filled me in," I said, lying through my teeth. I didn't want to hear about Megan's death. I didn't think I could bear it, whatever it was. "Have you kept in touch with the other families?"

For a moment, I didn't think I could distract her. She was going to sit there and tell me some blood-curdling tale that I was never going to forget. Cruel images seemed to play across her face. She faltered and her expression underwent that transformation that precedes tears—her nose reddening, mouth changing shape, lines drawing down on either side. Then her self-control descended and she looked at me with clouded eyes. "I'm sorry. What?"

"I was wondering if you'd talked to the others recently. Mrs. Westfall or the Polokowskis."

"I've hardly even talked to Wayne. Megan's death has just about done us in."

"What about your other children? How are they handling it?"

"Better than we are, certainly. People always say,

'Well, you still have the boys.' But it doesn't work that way. It's not like you can substitute one child for another." Belatedly, she took out a Kleenex and blew her nose.

"I'm sorry I had to bring it all up again," I said. "I've never had children, but I can't imagine anything more painful than losing one."

Her smile returned, fleeting and bitter. "I'll tell you what's worse. Knowing there's a man out there doing a few months in jail for 'vehicular manslaughter' when he murdered five people. Do you know how many times he got picked up for drunk driving before that accident? Fifteen. He paid a few fines. He got his hand smacked. Once he did thirty days, but most of the time. . . ." She broke off, then changed her tone. "Oh hell. What difference does it make? Nothing changes anyway and it never ends. I'll tell Wayne you stopped by. Maybe he knows where Daggett was."

12

I sat in the car and shuddered. I couldn't think when an interview had made me feel so tense. Daggett *had* to have been murdered. I just didn't see how it could come down any other way. What I couldn't figure out was how to get my thinking straight. Usually the morality of homicide seems clear to me. Whatever the shortcomings of the victim, murder is wrong and the penalties levied against the perpetrator had better be substantial to balance out the gravity of the crime. In this case, that seemed like a simplistic point of view. It was *Daggett* who had caused the world to tilt on its axis. Because of him, five people had died, so that his death, whatever the instrument, was swinging the planet upright again, restoring a moral order of sorts. At the moment, I still didn't know whether his desire to make restitution was sincere or part of some elaborate con. All I knew was that I'd been caught up in the loop and I had a part to play, though I had no idea yet what it was.

I started the car and headed back to my place. The sky was clouding over again. It was after 5:00 and a premature twilight already seemed to be spilling down the mountainside. I pulled up in front of my apartment and switched off the ignition. I glanced over at my windows, which were dark. I was feeling edgy and I wasn't ready to go home yet. On impulse, I started the car again and headed for the beach, drawn by the scent of salt in the air. Maybe a walk would ease my restlessness.

I pulled into one of the municipal lots and parked, slipping out of my shoes and pantyhose, which I tossed in the back seat along with my handbag. I zipped up my windbreaker and locked the car, tucking my keys in my jacket pocket as I crossed the bike path to the beach. The ocean was silver, but the breaking waves were a muddy brown and the sand along the surf line was peppered with rocks. This was the winter beach, dark boulders having surfaced with the shifting coastal sands. Gulls hovered overhead, eyeing the thundering waves for signs of edible sea life.

I walked along the wet sand with a buffeting wind at my back. A windsurfer clung to the crossbar on a bright green sail, arching himself against the force of the wind, his board streaking toward the beach. Two big fishing boats were chugging into the marina.

Everywhere there was the sense of urgency and threat—the torn white of storm surf, the darkening gray of the sky. Across the harbor, the ocean drove at the shore without pity, pounding at the breakwater with a grudging monotony. A rocketing spray shot straight up on impact, fanning along the seawall. I could almost hear the splats as successive waves hit the concrete walkway on the landward side.

I passed the entrance to the wharf. Ahead the beach widened, curving left toward the marina where the bare masts of sailboats tilted in the wind like metronomes. The sand was softer here, deeper too, so that walking became a labor. I turned and walked backward for a few steps, trying to get my bearings. Somewhere along this part of the beach was the spot where Daggett's body had been found. A brief glimpse of the site had appeared on the newscast and I was hoping now to get a fix on the place. I thought it was probably this side of the boat launch. Ahead and to my right was the kiddie park with its playground equipment and a fenced-in area with a wading pool.

The newscast had shown a portion of the dredge in the background, intersected by the breakwater and a line of rocks. I trudged on until I had the three lined up in the same configuration. The dry sand was trampled and there were signs that vehicles had crossed the beach. Where waves slapped against the shore, all traces of activity had been erased. The crime scene investigators had, no doubt, done at least a cursory search. I scanned the area without any expectation of finding "evidence." If you murder a man by tossing him, dead drunk, out of a rowboat, there aren't any telltale clues to dispose of afterward. The boat itself had been left to drift and, from what Jonah said, must have washed ashore closer to the pier.

I drank in the heady perfume of the sea, watching the restless surge of the waves, turning myself slowly until the ocean was at my back and I was staring at the line of motels across the boulevard. Daggett had apparently died sometime between midnight and 5:00 A.M. I wondered if it would be productive to canvas the neighborhood for witnesses. It was possible, of course, that Daggett had actually cut the line on the skiff himself, rowing out of the harbor alone. With a 0.35 blood alcohol level, it seemed unlikely. By the time blood alcohol concentrations reach 0.40 percent, a drunk is essentially in a state of deep anesthesia, incapable of anything so athletic as working an oar. He might have maneuvered his way out of the harbor first and *then* sat in the bobbing boat, drinking himself insensible, but I couldn't picture that. I kept visualizing somebody with him . . . waiting, watching . . . finally hefting his feet and toppling him backward. "A lesson in the back flip, Daggett. Oh shit, you blew it. Too bad, sucker. You die."

Getting him in the boat in the first place might have

been a trick, as drunk as he was, but the rest of it must have been a snap.

I glanced to my right. An old bum with a shopping cart was picking through a trash container. I crossed the sand, heading toward him. As I approached, I could see that his skin was nearly gray with accumulated filth, tanned by the wind, with an overlay of rosiness from recent sunburn or Mogen David wine . . . Mad Dog 20–20, as it's better known among the scruffy drifters. He looked in his seventies and was bulked up by layers of clothing. He wore a watch cap, his gray hair hanging out of it like mop strings. He smelled as musky as an old buffalo. The odor radiated from his body in nearly visible wavy lines, like a cartoon rendition of a skunk.

"Hello," I said.

He went about his business, ignoring me. He pulled out a pair of spike heels, inspecting them briefly before he tucked them into one of his plastic trash bags. A two-day-old newspaper didn't interest him. Beer cans? Yes, he seemed to like those. A Kentucky Fried Chicken barrel was a reject. A skirt? He held it up with a critical eye and then shoved it into the trash bag with the shoes. Someone had discarded a plastic beach ball with a hole punched in it. The old man set that aside.

"Did you hear about the guy they found in the surf yesterday?" I asked. No response. I felt like an apparition, calling to him from the netherworld. I raised my voice. "I heard somebody down here spotted him and called the cops. Do you happen to know who?"

I guess he didn't care to discuss it. He resolutely avoided eye contact. I didn't have my handbag with me so I didn't have a business card or even a dollar bill as a letter of reference. I had no choice but to let it drop. I moved away. By then, he had worked his way down in the bin, his head almost out of sight. So much for my interviewing techniques.

By the time I got back to the parking lot, the light had faded, so I registered the fact that something was wrong long before I realized what it was. The door on the passenger side of my car was ajar. I stopped in my tracks.

"Oh no," I said.

I approached with caution, as if the vehicle might be booby-trapped. It looked like someone had run a coathanger in through the wind-wing in an attempt to jimmy the lock. Failing that, the shitheel had simply smashed the window out on the passenger side and had opened the door. The glove compartment hung open, the contents spilling out across the front seat. My handbag was missing. *That* generated a flash of irritation, swiftly followed by dread. I jerked the seat forward and hauled out my briefcase. The strap that secured the opening had been cut and my gun was gone.

"Oh nooo," I wailed. I gave vent to a string of expletives. In high school, I had hung out with some bad-ass boys who taught me to cuss to perfection. I tried some combinations I hadn't thought of in years. I was mad at myself for leaving the stuff in plain sight on the seat and mad at the jerk who ripped me off. Mine was one of the last cars left in the lot and had probably stood out like a beacon. I slammed the car door shut and headed off across the street, still barefoot, gesturing and muttering to myself like a mental case. I didn't even have the spare change to call the cops.

There was a hamburger stand close by and I conned the fry cook into making the call for me. Then I went back and waited until the black-and-white arrived. The beat officers, Pettigrew and Gutierrez (Gerald and Maria, respectively), I'd encountered some months before when they made an arrest in my neighborhood.

She took the report now, while he made sympathetic noises. Somehow the two of them managed to console me insofar as that was possible, calling for a crime scene investigator who obligingly came out and dusted for prints. We all knew it was pointless, but it made me feel better. Pettigrew said he'd check the computer for the serial number on my gun, which was registered, thank God. Maybe it would turn up later in a pawn shop and I'd get it back.

I love my little semiautomatic, which I've had for years . . . a gift from the aunt who raised me after my parents' death. That gun was my legacy, representing the odd bond between us. She'd taught me to shoot when I was eight. She had never married, never had children of her own. With me, she'd exercised her many odd notions about the formation of female character. Firing a handgun, she felt, would teach me to appreciate both safety and accuracy. It would also help me develop good hand-eye coordination, which she thought was useful. She'd taught me to knit and crochet so that I'd learn patience and an eye for detail. She'd refused to teach me to cook as she felt it was boring and would only make me fat. Cussing was okay around the house, though we were expected to monitor our language in the company of those who might take offense. Exercise was important. Fashion was not. Reading was essential. Two out of three illnesses would cure themselves, said she, so doctors could generally be ignored except in case of accident. On the other hand, there was no excuse for having bad teeth, though she viewed dentists as the persons who came up with ludicrous schemes for the human mouth. Drilling out all of your old fillings and replacing them with gold, was one. She had dozens of these precepts and most are still with me.

Rule Number One, first and foremost, above and beyond all else, was financial independence. A woman should never, never, never be financially dependent on anyone, especially a man, because the minute you were dependent, you could be abused. Financially dependent persons (the young, the old, the indigent) were inevitably treated badly and had no recourse. A woman should *always* have recourse. My aunt believed that every woman should develop marketable skills, and the more money she was paid for them the better. Any feminine pursuit that did not have as its ultimate goal increased self-sufficiency could be disregarded. "How to Get Your Man" didn't even appear on the list.

When I was in high school, she'd called Home Ec "Home Ick" and applauded when I got a D. She thought it would make a lot more sense if the boys took Home Ec and the girls took Auto Mechanics and Wood Shop. Make no mistake about it, she liked (some) men a lot, but she wasn't interested in tending to one like a charwoman or a nurse. She was nobody's mother, said she, not even mine, and she didn't intend to behave like one. All of which constitutes a long-winded account of why I wanted my gun back, but there it is. I didn't have to explain any of this to G. Pettigrew or M. Gutierrez. They both knew I'd been a cop for two years and they both understood the value of a gun.

By the time everyone left the parking lot, it was fully dark and starting to rain again. Oh perfect.

I drove home and started making out a list of items I'd have to replace, including my driver's license, gasoline charge card, checkbook, and God knows what else. While I was at it, I looked up three "800" numbers, phoning in the loss of my credit cards from the Xerox copy I keep in my file drawer at home. I'd only been carrying about twenty bucks in cash, but I resented the loss. It was all too irritating to contemplate for long. I showered, pulled on jeans, boots, and a sweater, and headed up to Rosie's for a bite to eat.

Rosie's is the tavern in my neighborhood, run by herself, a Hungarian woman in her sixties, short and top-heavy, with dyed red hair that recently had looked like a cross between terra cotta floor tile and canned pumpkin pie filling. Rosie is an autocrat—outspoken, overbearing, suspicious of strangers. She cooks like a dream when it suits her, but she usually wants to dictate what you should eat at any given meal. She's protective, sometimes generous, often irritating. Like your best friend's cranky grandmother, she's someone you endure for the sake of peace. I hang out at her establishment because it's unpretentious and it's only half a block away from my place. Rosie apparently feels that my patronage entitles her to boss me around . . . which is generally true.

That night when I walked in, she took one look at my face and poured me a glass of white wine from her personal supply. I moved to my favorite booth at the rear. The backs are high, cut from construction grade plywood and stained dark, with side pieces shaped like the curve of a wingback chair. Within moments, Rosie materialized at the table and set the glass of wine in front of me.

"Somebody just busted out the window of my car and stole everything I hold dear, including my gun," I said.

"I've got some *sóska leves* for you," she announced.

"And after that, you gonna have a salad made with celery root, some chicken paprikas, some of Henry's good rolls, cabbage strudel, and deep-fried cherries if you're good and clean up your plate. It's on the house, on account of your troubles, only think about this one thing while you eat. If you had a good man in your life, this would never happen to you and that's all I'm gonna say."

I laughed for the first time in days.

13

The next morning, Monday, I began the laborious process of replacing the contents of my handbag. I hit the DMV first, since the offices opened at 8:00 A.M. I set in motion the paperwork for a new driver's license, paying three dollars for a duplicate. The minute the bank opened, I closed out my checking account and opened a new one. I stopped by the apartment then and put a call through to Sacramento to the Bureau of Collection and Investigative Services, Department of Consumer Affairs, requesting application for a certified replacement for my private investigator's registration card. I armed myself with a batch of business cards from my ready supply and hunted up an old handbag to use until I could buy a new one. I drove over to the drugstore and made purchases to replace at least a few of the odds and ends I carry with me as a matter of course, birth control pills being one. At some point, I'd have to have my car window replaced too. Irksome, all of it.

I didn't reach the office until almost noon and the message light on my answering machine was blinking insistently. I tossed the morning mail aside and punched the playback button as I passed the desk, listening to the caller as I opened the French doors to let in some fresh air.

"Miss Millhone, this is Ferrin Westfall at 555-6790. My wife and I have discussed your request to speak with our nephew, Tony, and if you'll get in touch, we'll see what we can work out. Please understand, we don't want the boy upset. We trust you'll conduct whatever business you have with him discreetly." There was a click, breaking the connection. His tone had been cold, perfectly suited to his formal, well-organized speaking voice. No "uh"s, no hesitations, no hiccups in the presentation. I lifted my brows appreciatively. Tony Gahan was in capable hands. Poor kid.

I made myself a pot of coffee and waited until I'd downed half a cup before I returned the call. The phone rang twice.

"Good morning. PFC," the woman said.

PFC turned out to be Perforated Formanek Corporation, a supplier of industrial abrasives, grinders, clamps, epoxy, cutters, end mills, and precision tools. I know this because I asked and she recited the entire inventory in a sing-song tone, thinking perhaps that I was in the market for one of the above. I asked to speak to Ferrin Westfall and was thanked for my request.

There was a click. "Westfall," said he.

I identified myself. There was a silence, meant (perhaps) to intimidate. I resisted the urge to rush in with a lot of unnecessary chatter, allowing the pause to go on for as long as it suited him.

Finally, he said, "We'll see that Tony's available this evening between seven and eight if that's acceptable." He gave me the address.

"Fine," I said. "Thank you." Ass, I added mentally. Then I hung up.

I tipped back in my swivel chair and propped my feet up. So far, it was a crummy day. I wanted my handbag back. I wanted my gun. I wanted to get on with life and quit wasting time with all this clerical nonsense. I glanced out at the balcony. At least it wasn't raining at the moment. I pulled the mail over and started going through it. Most of it was junk.

I was feeling restless again, thinking about John Daggett and his boat trip across the harbor. Yesterday, at the beach, the notion of canvassing the neighborhood for witnesses had seemed pointless. Now I wasn't so sure. Somebody might have seen him. Public drunkenness is usually conspicuous, especially at an hour when not many people are about. Weekend guests at the beach motels had probably checked out by now, but it might still be worth a shot. I grabbed my jacket and my car keys, locked the office, and headed down the back stairs.

My VW was looking worse every time I turned around. It's fourteen years old, an oxidized beige model with dents. Now the window was smashed out on the passenger side. Not a class act by any stretch of the imagination, but it was paid for. Every time I think about a new car, it makes my stomach do a flip-flop. I don't want to be saddled with car payments, a jump in insurance premiums, and hefty registration fees. My current registration costs me twenty-five dollars a year, which suits me just fine. I turned the ignition key and the engine fired right up. I patted the dashboard and backed out of the space, taking State Street south toward the beach.

I parked on Cabana, just across from the entrance to the wharf. There are eight motels strung out along the boulevard, none with rooms for under sixty dollars a night. This was the "off" season and there were still no vacancies. I started with the first, the Sea Voyager, where I identified myself to the manager, found out who'd been working the night desk the previous Friday, jotted down the name, and left my card with a handwritten note on the back. As with many other aspects of the job I do, this door-to-door inquiry requires dogged patience and a fondness for repetition that doesn't really come naturally. The effort has to be made, however, on the off chance that someone, somewhere can fill in a detail that might help. Having worked my way to the last motel, I returned to my car and headed on down the boulevard toward the marina, half a mile away.

I parked this time near the Naval Reserve Building, in the lot adjacent to the harbor. There didn't seem to be much foot traffic in the area. The sky was overcast, the air heavy with the staunch smells of fresh fish and diesel fuel. I ambled along the walk that skirts the waterfront, with its eighty-four acres of slips for eleven hundred boats. A wooden pier, two lanes wide, juts out into the water topped with a crane and pulleys for hoisting boats. I could see the fuel dock and the city guest dock, where two men were securing the lines on a big power boat that they'd apparently just brought in.

On my right, there was a row of waterfront businesses—a fish market with a seafood restaurant above, a shop selling marine and fishing supplies, a commercial diving center, two yacht brokers. The building fronts are all weathered gray wood, with bright royal blue awnings that echo the blue canvas sail covers on boats all through the harbor. For a moment, I paused before a plate glass window, scanning the snapshots of boats for sale—catamarans, luxury cabin cruisers, sailboats designed to sleep six. There's a small population of "live-aboards" in the harbor—people who actually use their boats as a primary residence. The idea is mildly appealing to me, though I wonder about the reality of chemical toilets in the dead of night and showering in marina restrooms. I crossed the walk and leaned on the iron railing, looking out across the airy forest of bare boat masts.

The water itself was dark hunter green. Big rocks were submerged in the gloomy depths, looking like sunken ruins. Few fish were visible. I spotted two little crabs scuttling along the boulders at the water's edge, but for the most part, the shallows seemed cold and sterile, empty of sea life. A beer bottle rested on a shelf of sand and mud. Two harbor patrol boats were moored not far away.

I spotted a line of skiffs tied up at one of the docks below and my interest perked up. Four of the marinas are kept locked and can only be entered with a card key issued by the Harbor Master's Office, but this one was accessible to the public. I moved down the ramp for a closer look. There were maybe twenty-five small skiffs, wood and fiberglass, most of them eight to ten feet long. I had no way of knowing if one of these was the boat Daggett had taken, but this much seemed clear: if you cut the line on one of these boats, you'd have to row it out around the end of the dock and through the harbor. There was no current here and a boat left to drift would simply bump aimlessly against the pilings without going anyplace.

I went up the ramp again and turned left along the walkway until I reached Marina One. At the bottom of the ramp, I could see the chain-link fence and locked gate. I loitered on the walk, keeping an eye on passersby. Finally, a middle-aged man approached, his card key in one hand, a bag of groceries in the other. He was trim and muscular, tanned to the color of rawhide. He wore Bermuda shorts, Topsiders, and a loose cotton sweater, a mat of graying chest hairs visible in the V.

"Excuse me," I said. "Do you live down there?"

He paused, looking at me with curiosity. "Yes." His face was as lined as a crumpled brown grocery bag pressed into service again.

"Do you mind if I follow you out onto Marina One? I'm trying to get a line on the man who washed up on the beach Saturday."

"Sure, come on. I heard about that. The skiff he stole belongs to a friend of mine. By the way, I'm Aaron. You are?"

"Kinsey Millhone," I said, trotting down the ramp after him. "How long have you lived down here?"

"Six months. My wife and I split up and she kept the house. Nice change, boat life. Lot of nice people. You a cop?"

"Private investigator," I said. "What sort of work do you do?"

"Real estate," he said. "How'd you get into it?" He inserted his card and pushed the gate open. He held it while I passed through. I paused on the other side so he could lead the way.

"I was hired by the dead man's daughter," I said.

"I meant how'd you get into investigative work."

"Oh. I used to be a cop, but I didn't like it much. The law enforcement part of it was fine, but not the bureaucracy. Now I'm self-employed. I'm happier that way."

We passed a cloud of sea gulls converging rapidly on an object bobbing in the water. The screeches from the birds were attracting gulls from a quarter of a mile away, streaking through the air like missiles.

"Avocado," Aaron said idly. "The gulls love them. This is me." He had paused near a thirty-seven-foot twin-diesel trawler, a Chris-Craft, with a flying bridge.

"God, it's a beautiful boat."

"You like it? I can sleep eight," he said, pleased. He hopped down into the cockpit and turned, holding a hand out to me. "Pop your boots off and you can come on board and take a look around. Want a drink?"

"I better not, thanks. I've got a lot of ground to cover yet. Is there any way you can introduce me to the guy whose skiff was stolen?"

Aaron shrugged. "Can't help you there. He's out on a fishing boat all day, but I can give him your name and telephone number if you like. I think the police impounded the skiff, so if you want to see that, you better talk to them."

I didn't expect anything to come of it, but I thought I'd leave the door open just in case. I took out a business card, jotting down my home number on the back before I passed it on to him. "Have him give me a call if he knows anything," I said.

"I'll tell you who you might want to talk to. Go down here six slips and see if that guy's in. *The Seascape* is the name of the boat. His is Phillip Rosen. He knows all the gossip down here. Maybe he can help."

"Thanks."

The Seascape was a twenty-four-foot Flicka, a gaff-rigged sloop with a twenty-foot mast, teak deck, and a fiberglass hull that mimicked wood.

I tapped on the cabin roof, calling a hello toward the open doorway. Phillip Rosen appeared, ducking his head as he came up from down below. His emerging was like a visual joke: he was one of the tallest men I'd seen except on a basketball court. He was probably six-foot-ten and built on a grand scale—big hands and feet, big head with a full head of red hair, a big face with red beard and moustache, bare-chested and bare-foot. Except for the ragged blue jean cut-offs, he looked like a Viking reincarnated cruelly into a vessel unworthy of him. I introduced myself, mentioning that Aaron had suggested that I talk to him. I told him briefly what I wanted.

"Well, I didn't see them, but a friend of mine did. She was coming down here to meet me and passed 'em in the parking lot. Man and a woman. She said the old guy was drunk as a skunk, staggering all over the place. The little gal with him had a hell of a time trying to keep him upright."

"Do you have any idea what she looked like?"

"Nope. Dinah never said. I can give you her number though, if you want to ask her about it yourself."

"I'd like that," I said. "What time was this?"

"I'd say two-fifteen. Dinah's a waitress over at the Wharf and she gets off at two. I know she didn't close up that night and it only takes five minutes to get here. Shoot, if she walked on water, she could skip across the harbor in the time it takes her to get to the parking lot."

"Is she at work now by any chance?"

"Monday afternoon? Could be. I never heard what her schedule was this week, but you can always try. She'd be up in the cocktail lounge. A redhead. You can't miss her if she's there."

Which turned out to be true. I drove the half mile from the marina to the wharf, leaving my car with the valet who handles restaurant parking. Then I went up the outside staircase to the wooden deck above. Dinah was crossing from the bar to a table in the corner, balancing a tray of margaritas. Her hair was more orange than red, too carroty a shade to be anything but natural. She was probably six feet tall in heels, wearing dark mesh hose, and a navy blue "sailor" suit with a skirt that skimmed her crotch. She had a little sailor cap pinned to her head and an air about her that suggested she'd known starboard from port since the day she reached puberty.

I waited until she'd served the drinks and was on her way back to the bar. "Dinah?"

She looked at me quizzically. Up close, I could see the overlay of pale red freckles on her face and a long, narrow nose. She wore false eyelashes, like a series of commas encircling her pale hazel eyes, lending her a look of startlement. I gave her a brief rundown, patiently repeating myself. "I know who the old guy is," I said. "What I'm trying to get a fix on is the woman he was with."

Dinah shrugged. "Well, I can't tell you much. I just saw them as I went past. I mean, the marina's got *some* lights, but not that great. Plus, it was raining like a son of a bitch."

"How old would you say she was?"

"On the young side. Twenties, maybe. Blonde. Not real big, at least compared to him."

"Long hair? Short? Buxom? Flat-chested?"

"The build, I don't know. She was wearing a raincoat. Some kind of coat, anyway. Hair was maybe shoulder length, not a lot of curl. Kind of bushy."

"Pretty?"

She thought briefly. "God, all I remember thinking was there was something off, you know? For starters, he was such a mess. I could smell him ten feet away. Bourbon fumes. Phew! Actually, I kind of thought she might be a hooker on the verge of rolling him. I nearly said something to her, but then I decided it was none of my business. He was having a great old time, but you know how it is. Drunk as he was, she really could have ripped him off."

"Yeah, well, she did. *Dead* is about as ripped off as you can get."

14

By the time I pulled out of the restaurant parking lot, it was 2:00 and the air felt dank. Or maybe it was only the shadowy image of Daggett's companion that chilled me. I'd been half convinced there was someone with him that night and now I had confirmation—not proof of murder, surely, but some sense of the events leading up to his death, a tantalizing glimpse of his consort, that "other" whose ghostly passage I tracked.

From Dinah's description, Lovella Daggett was the first name that popped into my head. Her trashy blonde looks had made me think she was hooking when I met her in L.A. On the other hand, most of the women I'd run across to date were on the young side and fair-haired—Barbara Daggett, Billy Polo's sister Coral, Ramona Westfall, even Marilyn Smith, the mother of the other dead child. I'd have to start pinning people down as to their whereabouts the night of the murder, a tricky matter as I had no way to coerce a reply. Cops have some leverage. A P.I. has none.

In the meantime, I went by the bank and removed the cashier's check from my safe deposit box. I ducked into a coffee shop and grabbed a quick lunch, then spent the afternoon in the office catching up on paperwork. At 5:00, I locked up and went home, puttering around until 6:30 when I left for Ferrin and Ramona Westfall's house to meet Tony Gahan.

The Westfalls lived in an area called the Close, a deadend street lined with live oaks over near the Natural History Museum. I drove through stone gates into the dim hush of privacy. There are only eight homes on the cul-de-sac, all Victorian, completely restored, immaculately kept. The neighborhood looks, even now, like a small, rural community inexplicably lifted out of the past. The properties are surrounded by low walls of fieldstone, the lots overgrown with bamboo, pampas grass, and fern. It was fully dark by then and the Close was wreathed in mist. The vegetation was dense, intensely scented, and lush from the recent rain. There was only one street light, its pale globe obscured by the branches of a tree.

I found the number I was looking for and parked on the street, picking my way up the path to the front. The house was a putty-colored, one-story wood frame with a wide porch, white shutters and trim. The porch furniture was white wicker with cushions covered in a white-and-putty print. Two Victorian wicker plant stands held massive Boston ferns. All too perfect for my taste.

I rang the bell, refusing to peer in through the etched glass oval in the door. I suspected the interior was going to look like something out of *House and Garden* magazine, an elegant blend of the old, the new, and the offbeat. Of course, my perception was probably colored by Ferrin Westfall's curt treatment of me and Ramona's outright hostility. I'm not above holding grudges.

Ramona Westfall came to the door and admitted me. I kept my tone pleasant, but I didn't fall all over myself admiring the place, which, at a glance, did appear to be flawlessly done. She showed me into the front parlor and removed herself, closing the oak-paneled sliding doors behind her. I waited, staring resolutely at the floor. I could hear murmuring in the hall. After a moment, the doors slid open and a man entered, introducing himself as Ferrin Westfall . . . as if I hadn't guessed. We shook hands.

He was tall and slim, with a cold, handsome face and silver hair. His eyes were a dark green, as empty of warmth as the harbor. There were hints of something submerged in the depths, but no signs of life. He wore charcoal gray pants and a soft gray cashmere sweater that fairly begged to be stroked. He indicated that I should have a seat, which I did.

He surveyed me for a moment, taking in the boots, the faded jeans, the wool sweater beginning to pill at the elbows. I was determined not to let his disapproval get through to me, but it required an effort on my part. I stared at him impassively and warded off his withering assessment by picturing him on the toilet with his knickers down around his ankles.

Finally, he said, "Tony will be out in a moment. Ramona's told me about the check. I wonder if I might examine it."

I removed the check from my jeans pocket and smoothed it out, passing it to him for his inspection. I wondered if he thought it was forged, stolen, or in some way counterfeit. He scrutinized it, fore and aft, and returned it, apparently satisfied that it was legitimate.

"Why did Mr. Daggett come to you with this?" he asked.

"I'm not really sure," I said. "He told me he'd tried to find Tony at an old address. When he had no luck, he asked me to track him down and deliver it."

"Do you know how he acquired the money?"

Again, I found myself feeling protective. It was really none of this man's business. He probably wanted to assure himself that Daggett hadn't come by the money through some tacky enterprise—drugs, prostitutes, selling dogs and kitty cats to labs for medical experiments.

"He won it at the track," I said. Personally, I hadn't quite believed this part of Daggett's tale, but I didn't mind if Ferrin Westfall got sucked in. He didn't seem any more convinced than I. He shifted the subject.

"Would you prefer to be alone with Tony?"

I was surprised at the offer. "Yes, I would. I'd really like to go off somewhere with him and have a Coke."

"I suppose that would be all right, as long as you don't keep him too long. This is a school night."

"Sure. That's very nice of you."

There was a tap at the door. Mr. Westfall rose and crossed the room. "This will be Tony," he said.

The doors slid back and Tony Gahan came in. He looked like an immature fifteen. He was maybe five-foot-six, a hundred and twenty-five pounds. His uncle introduced me. I proferred my hand and we fumbled through a handshake. Tony's eyes were dark, his hair a medium brown, attractively cut, which struck me as odd. Most of the high school kids I've seen lately looked like they're being treated for the same scalp disease. I suspected Tony's hairstyle was a concession to Ferrin Westfall's notions of good taste and I wondered how that sat with him.

His manner was anxious. He seemed like a kid trying desperately to please. He shot a cautious look at his uncle, searching for visual cues as to what was expected of him and how he was meant to behave. It was painful to watch.

"Miss Millhone would like to take you out for a Coke, so she can talk to you," Mr. Westfall said.

"How come?" he croaked. Tony looked like he was going to drop dead on the spot and I remembered in a flash how much I'd hated eating and drinking in the presence of strange adults when I was his age. Meals represent a series of traps when you haven't yet mastered the appropriate social skills. I hated adding to his distress, but I was convinced I'd never have a decent conversation with him in this house.

"She'll explain all that," Mr. Westfall said. "Obviously, you're not required to go. If you'd prefer to stay here, simply say so."

Tony seemed unable to get a reading from his uncle's statement, which was neutral on the surface, but contained some tricky side notes. It was the word "simply" that tripped him, I thought, and the "obviously" didn't help.

Tony glanced at me with a half shrug. "It's okay, I guess. Like, right now?"

Mr. Westfall nodded. "It won't be for long. You'll need a jacket, of course."

Tony moved out into the hall and I followed, waiting until he found his jacket in the hall closet.

At fifteen, I thought he could probably figure out if he needed a jacket or not, but neither of them consulted me on the subject. I opened the front door and held it while he went out. Mr. Westfall watched us for a moment and then closed the door behind us. God, it was just like a date. I nearly swore I'd have him home by 10:00. Absurd.

We made our way down the path in the dark. "You go to Santa Teresa High School?"

"Right."

"What year?"

"Sophomore."

We got in the car. Tony tried to roll down the smashed window on his side without much success. A shard of glass tinkled down into the door frame. He finally gave up.

"What happened to this?"

"I was careless," I said, and let it go at that.

I did a U-turn in the lane and I headed for the Clockworks on State Street, a teen hangout generally regarded as seedy, unclean, and corrupt, which it is . . . a training ground for junior thugs. Kids come here (stoned, no doubt) to drink Cokes, smoke clove cigarettes, and behave like bad-asses. I'd been introduced to the place by a seventeen-year-old pink-haired dope dealer named Mike, who made more money than I did. I hadn't seen him since June, but I tend to look for him around town.

We parked in a small lot out back and went in through the rear entrance. The place is long and narrow, painted charcoal gray, the high ceiling rimmed with pink and purple neon. A series of mobiles, looking like big black clock gears, revolve in the smoky air. The noise level, on weekends, is deafening, the music so loud it makes the floor vibrate. On week nights, it's quiet and oddly intimate. We found a table and I went over to the counter to pick up a couple of Cokes. There was a tap on my shoulder and I turned to find Mike standing there. I felt a rush of warmth. "I was just thinking about you!" I said. "How are you?"

A pink tint crept across his cheeks and he gave me a slow seductive smile. "I'm okay. What are you doin' these days?"

"Nothing much," I said. "Great hair." Formerly, he'd sported a Mohawk, a great cockscomb of pink down the center of his head, with the sides shaved close. Now it was arranged in a series of purple spurts, each clump held together with a rubber band, the feathery tips bleached white. Aside from the hair, he was a good-looking kid, clear skin, green eyes, good teeth.

I said, "Actually, I'm about to have a talk with that guy over there . . . a schoolmate of yours."

"Yeah?" He turned and gave Tony a cursory inspection.

"You know him?"

"I've seen him. He doesn't hang out with the kind of people I do." His gaze returned to Tony and I thought he was going to say more, but he let it pass.

"What are you up to?" I asked. "Still dealing?"

"Who me? Hey, no. I told you I'd quit," he said, sounding faintly righteous. The look in his eyes, of course, suggested just the opposite. If he was doing something illegal, I didn't want to know about it anyway, so I bypassed the subject.

"What about school? You graduate this year?"

"June. I got college applications out and everything."

"Really?" I couldn't tell if he was putting me on or not.

He caught the look. "I get good grades," he protested. "I'm not just your average high school dunce, you know. The bucks I got, I could go anyplace I want. That's what private enterprise is about."

I had to laugh. "For sure," I said. The "bar maid" set two Cokes on the counter and I paid her. "I have to get back to my date."

"Nice seeing you," he said. "You ought to come in sometime and talk to me."

"Maybe I'll do that," I said. I smiled at him, mentally shaking my head. Flirtatious little shit. I moved over to the table where Tony was sitting. I handed him a Coke and sat down.

"You know that guy?" Tony asked cautiously.

"Who, Mike? Yes, I know him."

Tony's eyes strayed to Mike and back again, resting on my face with something close to respect. Maybe I wasn't such a geek after all.

"Did your uncle tell you what this is about?" I asked.

"Some. He said the accident and that old drunk."

"You feel okay discussing it?"

He shrugged by way of reply, avoiding eye contact.

"I take it you weren't in the car," I said.

He smoothed the front of his hair to the side. "Uh-uh. Me and my mom got into this argument. They were going to my granny's for this Easter egg hunt and I didn't want to go."

"Your grandmother's still in town someplace?"

He shifted in his chair. "In a rest home. She had a stroke."

"She's your mother's mother?" I didn't care particularly about any of this. I was just hoping the kid would relax and open up.

"Yeah."

"What's it like living with your aunt and uncle?"

"Fine. No big deal. He comes down on my case all the time, but she's nice."

"She said you were having some problems at school."

"So?"

"Just curious. She says you're very smart and your grades are in the toilet. I wondered what that was about."

"It's about school sucks," he said. "It's about I don't like people butting into my fuckin' business."

"Really," I said. I took a sip of Coke. His hostility was like a sewer backing up and I thought I'd give the efflux a chance to subside. I didn't care if he cussed. I could outcuss him any day of the week.

When I didn't react, he filled the silence. "I'm trying

to get my grades pulled up," he said somewhat grudgingly. "I had to take all this bullshit math and chemistry. That's why I didn't do good."

"What's your preference? English? Art?"

He hesitated. "You some kind of shrink?"

"No. I'm a private investigator. I assumed you knew that."

He stared at me. "I don't get it. What's this got to do with the accident?"

I took out the check and laid it on the table. "The man responsible wanted me to look you up and give you this."

He picked the check up and glanced at it.

"It's a cashier's check for twenty-five thousand dollars," I said.

"What for?"

"I'm not really sure. I think John Daggett was hoping to make restitution for what he did."

Tony's confusion was clear and so was the anger that accompanied it. "I don't want this," he said. "Why give it to me? Megan Smith died too, you know, and so did that other guy, Doug. Are they gettin' money too, or just me?"

"Just you, as far as I know."

"Take it back then. I don't want it. I hate that old bastard." He tossed the check on the table and gave it a push.

"Look. Now just wait and let me say something first. It's your choice. Honestly. It's up to you. Your aunt was offended by the offer and I understand that. No one can force you to accept the money if you don't want it. But just hear me out, okay?"

Tony was staring off across the room, his face set.

I lowered my voice. "Tony, it's true John Daggett was a drunk, and maybe he was a totally worthless human being, but he did something he felt bad about and I think he was trying to make up for it. Give him credit for that much and don't say no without giving it consideration first."

"I don't *want* money for what he did."

"I'm not done yet. Just let me finish this."

His mouth trembled. He made a dash at his eyes with the sleeve of his jacket, but he didn't get up and walk away.

"People make mistakes," I said. "People do things they never meant to do. He didn't kill anyone deliberately . . ."

"He's a fuckin' drunk! He was out on the fuckin' street at fuckin' nine in the morning. Dad and Mom and Hilary . . ." His voice broke and he fought for control. "I don't want anything from him. I hate his guts and I don't want his crummy check."

"Why don't you cash it and give it all away?"

"No! You take it. Give it back to him. Tell him I said he could get fucked."

"I can't. He's dead. He was killed Friday night."

"Good. I'm glad. I hope somebody cut his heart out. He deserved it."

"Maybe so. But it's still possible that he felt something for you and wanted to give you back some of what he took away."

"Like what? It's done. They're all dead."

"But you're not, Tony. You have to find a way to get on with life . . ."

"Hey! I'm doing that, okay? But I don't have to listen to this bullshit! You said what you had to say and now I want to go home."

He got up, radiating rage, his whole body stiff. He moved swiftly toward the rear entrance, knocking chairs aside. I snatched up the check and followed.

When I reached the parking lot, he was kick-boxing the remaining glass out of the smashed window of my car. I started to protest and then I stopped myself.

Oh why not, I thought. I had to replace the damn thing anyway. I stood and watched him without a word. When he was done, he leaned against the car and wept.

15

By the time I got Tony home again, he was calm, shut down, as if nothing out of the ordinary had occurred. I pulled up in front of the house. He got out, slammed the door, and headed up the path without a word. I was reasonably certain he wouldn't mention his outburst to his aunt and uncle, which was fortunate as I'd sworn I could talk to him without his getting upset. I was, of course, still in possession of Daggett's check, wondering if I'd be toting it around for life, trying in vain to get someone to take it off my hands.

When I got back to my place, I spent twenty minutes unloading my VW. While I tend to maintain an admirable level of tidiness in the apartment, my organizational skills have never extended to my car. The back seat is usually crowded with files, law books, my briefcase, piles of miscellaneous clothing—shoes, pantyhose, jackets, hats, some of which I use as "disguises" in the various aspects of my trade.

I packed everything in a cardboard box and then proceeded around to the backyard where the entrance to my apartment is located. I opened the padlock on the storage bin attached to the service porch and stowed the box, snapping the padlock into place again.

As I reached my door, a dark shape loomed out of the shadows. "Kinsey?"

I jumped, realizing belatedly that it was Billy Polo. I couldn't distinguish his features in the dark, but his voice was distinctly his own.

"Oh Jesus, what are you doing here?" I said.

"Hey, I'm sorry. I didn't mean to scare you. I wanted to talk to you."

I was still trying to recover from the jolt he'd given me, my temper rising belatedly. "How'd you know where to find me?"

"I looked you up in the telephone book."

"My home address isn't in the book."

"Yeah, I know. I tried your office first. You weren't in, so I asked next door at that insurance place."

"California Fidelity gave you my home address?" I said. "Who'd you talk to?" I didn't believe for a minute that CFI would release that kind of information to him.

"I didn't get her name. I told her I was a client and it was urgent."

"Bullshit."

"No, it's the truth. She only gave it to me because I leaned on her."

I could tell he wasn't going to budge on the point, so I let it pass. "All right, what is it?" I said. I knew I sounded cranky, but I didn't like his coming to my place and I didn't believe his tale about how he found out where it was.

"We're just gonna stand around out here?"

"That's right, Billy. Now get on with it."

"Well, you don't have to get so huffy."

"Huffy! What the hell are you talking about? You loom up out of the dark and scare me half to death! I don't know you from Jack the Ripper so why should I invite you in?"

"Okay, okay."

"Just say what you have to say. I'm beat."

He did some fidgeting around . . . for effect, I thought. Finally, he said, "I talked to my sister, Coral, and she told me I should be straight with you."

"Oh goody, what a treat. Straight about what?"

"Daggett," he mumbled. "He did get in touch."

"When was this?"

"Last Monday when he got to town."

"He called you?"

"Yeah, that's right."

"How'd he know where you were?"

"He tried my mom's house and talked to her. I wasn't home at the time, so she got his number and I called him back."

"Where'd he call from?"

"I don't know for sure. Some dive. There was all this noise in the background. He was drunk and I figured he must have parked himself in the first bar he found."

"What time of day was this?"

"Maybe eight at night. Around in there."

"Go on."

"He said he was scared and needed help. Somebody called him down in Los Angeles and told him he was dead meat on account of a scam he pulled up in prison just before he got out."

"What scam?"

"I don't know all the details. What I heard was his cellmate got snuffed and Daggett helped himself to a big wad of cash the guy had hidden in his bunk."

"How much?"

"Nearly thirty grand. It was some kind of drug deal went sour, which is why the guy got killed in the first place. Daggett walked off with the whole stash and somebody wanted it back. They were comin' after him. At least that's what they told him."

"Who?"

"I don't want to mention names. I got a fair idea and I could find out for sure if I wanted to, but I don't like puttin' my neck in a noose unless I have to. The point is I shined him on. I wasn't going to help that old coot. No way. He got himself in a hole, let him get himself out. I didn't want to be involved. Not with those guys after him. I'm too fond of my health."

"So what happened? You talked on the phone and that was it?"

"Well, no. I met him for a drink. Coral said I should level with you about that."

"Really," I said. "What for?"

"In case something came up later. She didn't want it to look like I was holding out."

"So you think they caught up with him?"

"He's dead, ain't he?"

"Proving what?"

"Don't ask me. I mean, all I know is what Daggett said. He was on the run and he thought I'd help."

"How?"

"A place to hide."

"When did you meet with him?"

"Not till Thursday. I was tied up."

"Pressing social engagements, no doubt."

"Hey, I was looking for work. I'm on parole and I got requirements to meet."

"You didn't see him Friday?"

"Uh-uh. I just saw him once and that was Thursday night."

"What'd he do in the meantime?"

"I don't know. He never said."

"Where'd you meet him?"

"At the bar where Coral works."

"Ah, now I see. She got worried I'd ask around and somebody'd say they saw you with him."

"Well, yeah. Coral don't like me to mess with the law, especially with me on parole anyway."

"How come it took the bad guys so long to catch up with him? He's been out of prison for six weeks."

"Maybe they didn't figure it was him at first. Daggett wasn't the brightest guy, you know. He never did nothin' right in his life. They prob'bly figured he was too dumb to stick his hand in a mattress and walk off with the cash."

"Did Daggett have the money with him when you talked to him?"

"Are you kidding? He tried to borrow ten bucks from me," Billy said, aggrieved.

"What was the deal?" I asked. "If he gave the money back, they'd let him off the hook?"

"Probably not. I doubt that."

"So do I," I said. "How do you think Lovella figures into this?"

"She doesn't. It's got nothing to do with her."

"I wouldn't be too sure about that. Somebody saw Daggett down at the marina last Friday night, dead drunk, in the company of a trashy-looking blonde."

Even in the dark, I could tell Billy Polo was staring at me.

"A blonde?"

"That's right. She was on the young side from what I was told. He was staggering, and she had to work to keep him on his feet."

"I don't know nothin' about that."

"Neither do I, but it sure sounded like Lovella to me."

"Ask her about it then."

"I intend to," I said. "So what happens next?"

"About what?"

"The thirty thousand, for starters. With Daggett dead, does the money go back to the guys who were after him?"

"If they found it, I guess it does," he said, uncomfortably.

"What if they didn't find it?"

Billy hesitated. "Well, I guess if it's stashed somewhere, it'd belong to his widow, wouldn't it? Part of his estate?"

I was beginning to get the drift here, but I wondered if he did. "You mean Essie?"

"Who?"

"Daggett's widow, Essie."

"He's divorced from her," Billy said.

"I don't think so. At least not as far as the law is concerned."

"He's married to Lovella," he said.

"Not legally."

"You're shittin' me."

"Come to the funeral tomorrow and see for yourself."

"This Essie has the money?"

"No, but I know where it is. Twenty-five thousand of it, at any rate."

"Where?" he said, with disbelief.

"In my pocket, sweetheart, in the form of a cashier's check made out to Tony Gahan. You remember, Tony, don't you?"

Dead silence.

I lowered my voice. "You want to tell me who Doug Polokowski is?"

Billy Polo turned and walked away.

I stood there for a moment and then followed reluctantly, still pondering the fact that he had my home address. Last time I'd talked to him, he didn't even buy the fact that I was a private investigator. Now suddenly he was seeking me out, having confidential chats about Daggett on my front step. It didn't add up.

I heard his car door slam as I reached the street. I hung back in the shadows, watching as he swung the Chevrolet out of a parking place four doors down. He gunned it, speeding off toward the beach. I debated about whether to pursue him, but I couldn't bear the thought of lurking about outside Coral's trailer again. Enough of that stuff. I turned back and let myself into my apartment. I kept thinking about the fact that my car was broken into, my handbag stolen, along with all of my personal identification. Had Billy Polo done that? Is that how he came up with my home address? I couldn't figure out how he'd tracked me to the beach in the first place, but it would explain how he knew where to find me now.

I was sure he was maneuvering, but I couldn't figure

out what he'd hoped to get. Why the yarn about Daggett and the bad guys in jail? It did fit with some of the facts, but it didn't have that nice, untidy ring of truth.

I hauled out a stack of index cards and wrote it all down anyway. Maybe it would make sense later, when other information came to light. It was 10:00 by the time I finished. I pulled the white wine out of the refrigerator, wiggled the cork loose, and poured myself a glass. I stripped my clothes off, turned the lights out, and toted the wine into the bathroom where I set it on the window sill in the bathtub and stared out at the darkened street. There's a streetlight out there, buried in the branches of a jacaranda tree, largely denuded now by the rain. The window was half opened and a damp slat of night wind wafted in, chilly and secretive. I could hear rain begin to rattle on my composition roof. I was restless. When I was a young girl, maybe twelve or so, I wandered the streets on nights like this, barefoot, in a raincoat, feeling anxious and strange. I don't think my aunt knew about my nocturnal excursions, but maybe she did. She had a reckless streak of her own and she may have honored mine. I was thinking a lot about her, of late, perhaps because of Tony. His family had been wiped out in a car accident, just as mine had, and he was being raised now by an aunt. Sometimes, I had to admit to myself . . . especially on nights like this . . . that the death of my parents may not have been as tragic as it seemed. My aunt, for all her failings, was a perfect guardian for me . . . brazen, remote, eccentric, independent. Had my parents lived, my life would have taken an altogether different route. There was no doubt of that in my mind. I like my history just as it is, but there was something else going on as well.

Looking back on the evening, I realized how much I'd identified with Tony's kicking my car window out. The rage and defiance were hypnotic and touched off deep feelings of my own. Daggett's funeral was coming up the next afternoon and that touched off something else . . . old sorrows, good friends gone down into the earth. Sometimes I picture death as a wide stone staircase, filled with a silent procession of those being led away. I see death too often to worry about it much, but I miss the departed and I wonder if I'll be docile when my turn comes.

I finished my wine and went to bed, sliding naked into the warm folds of my quilt.

16

The dawn was accompanied by drizzle, dark gray sky gradually shading to a cold white light. Ordinarily, I don't run in the rain, but I hadn't slept well and I needed to clear away the dregs of nagging anxiety. I wasn't even sure what I was worried about. Sometimes I awaken uncomfortably aware of a low-level dread humming in my gut. Running is the only relief I can find short of drink and drugs, which at 6:00 A.M. don't appeal.

I pulled on a sweat suit and hit the bike path, jogging a mile and a half to the recreation center. The palm trees along the boulevard had shed dried fronds in the wind and they lay on the grass like soggy feathers. The ocean was silver, the surf rustling mildly like a taffeta skirt with a ruffle of white. The beach was a drab brown, populated by sea gulls snatching at sand fleas. Pigeons lifted in a cloud, looking on. I have to admit I'm not an outdoor person at heart. I'm always aware that under the spritely twitter of birds, bones are being crunched and ribbons of flesh are being stripped away, all of it the work of bright-eyed creatures without feeling or conscience. I don't look to nature for comfort or serenity.

Traffic was light. There were no other joggers. I passed the public restrooms, housed in a cinderblock building painted flesh pink, where two bums huddled with a shopping cart. One I recognized from two nights before and he watched me now, indifferently. His friend was curled up under a cardboard comforter, looking like a pile of old rags. I reached the turnaround and ran the mile and a half back. By the time I got home, my Etonics were soaked, my sweat pants were darkened by the drizzle, and the mist had beaded in my hair like a net of seed pearls. I took a long hot shower, optimism returning now that I was safely home again.

After breakfast, I tidied up and then checked my automobile insurance policy and determined that the replacement of my car window was covered, after a fifty-dollar deductible. At 8:30, I started soliciting estimates from auto glass shops, trying to persuade someone to work me in before noon that day. I zipped myself into my all-purpose dress again, resurrected a decent-looking black leather shoulder bag that I use for "formal" wear and filled it with essentials, including the accursed cashier's check.

I dropped the car off at an auto glass shop not far from my office and hoofed it the rest of the way to work. Even with low-heeled pumps, my feet hurt and my pantyhose made me feel like I was walking around with a hot, moist hand in my crotch.

I let myself into the office and initiated my usual morning routines. The phone rang as I was plugging in the coffeepot.

"Miss Millhone, this is Ramona Westfall."

"Oh hello," I said. "How are you?" Secretly, my stomach did a little twist and I wondered if Tony Gahan had told her about his freak-out at the Clockworks the night before.

"I'm fine," she said. "I'm calling because there's something I'd like to discuss with you and I hoped you might have some time free this morning."

"Well, my schedule's clear, but I don't have a car. Can you come down here?"

"Yes, of course. I'd prefer that anyway. Is ten convenient? It's short notice, I know."

I glanced at my watch. Twenty minutes. "That's fine," I said. She made some good-bye noises and clicked off. I depressed the line and then put a call through to Barbara Daggett at her mother's house to verify the time of the funeral. She was unavailable to come to the phone, but Eugene Nickerson told me the services were at 2:00 and I said I'd be there.

I took a few minutes to open my mail from the day

before, posting a couple of checks to accounts receivable, then made a quick call to my insurance agent, giving her the sketchy details about my car window. I'd no more than put the phone down when it rang again.

"Kinsey, this is Barbara Daggett. Something's come up. When I arrived here this morning, there was some woman sitting on the porch steps who says she's Daddy's wife."

"Oh God. Lovella."

"You know about her?"

"I met her last week when I was down in L.A., trying to get a line on your father's whereabouts."

"And you knew about this claim of hers?"

"I never heard the details, but I gathered they were living in some kind of common-law relationship."

"Kinsey, she has a marriage certificate. I saw it myself. Why didn't you tell me what was going on? I was speechless. She stood out on the front porch, screaming bloody murder until I finally had to call the police. I can't believe you didn't at least *mention* it."

"When was I supposed to do that? At the morgue? Over at the funeral home with your mother in a state of collapse?"

"You could have called me, Kinsey. Any time. You could have come to my office to discuss it."

"Barbara, I could have done half a dozen things, but I didn't. Frankly, I was feeling protective of your father and I was hoping you wouldn't have to find out about this 'alleged' marriage. That certificate could be a fake.

The whole thing could be trumped up, and if not, you've still got problems enough without adding bigamy to his list of personal failings."

"That isn't yours to decide. Now Mother wants to know what the ruckus was about and I have no idea what to say."

"Well, I can see why you're upset, but I'm not sure I'd do it any differently."

"I can't believe you'd take that attitude! I don't appreciate being kept in the dark," she said. "I hired you to investigate and I expect you to pass on whatever comes to light."

"Your father hired me long before you did," I said.

That silenced her for a moment and then she took off again. "To do what? You never did specify."

"Of course I didn't. He talked to me confidentially. It was all bullshit, but it's still not mine to flap around. I couldn't stay in business if I blabbed all the information that came my way."

"I'm his daughter. I have a right to know. Especially if my father's a *bigamist*. What else am I paying you for?"

"You might be paying me to exercise a little judgment of my own," I said. "Come on, Barbara. Be reasonable. Suppose I'd told you. What purpose would that have served? If your parents are still legally married, Lovella has no claim whatever and, for all I know, she's perfectly aware of that. Why add to your grief when she might well have slunk away without a word?"

"How did she know he died in the first place?"

"Not from me, I can tell you that. I'm not an idiot. The last thing in the world I wanted was her up here camping out on your doorstep. Maybe she read it in the paper. Maybe she heard it on the news."

She murmured something, temporarily mollified.

"What happened when the cops got there?" I asked.

There was another pause while she debated whether to move on or continue berating me. I sensed that she enjoyed chewing people out and it was hard for her to give up the opportunity. From my point of view, she wasn't paying me enough to take much guff. A little bit, perhaps. I probably should have told her.

"The two officers took her aside and had a talk with her. She left a few minutes ago."

"Well, if she shows up again, I'll take care of it," I said.

"Again? Why would she do that?"

I remembered then that aside from the matter of her father's apparent bigamy, I hadn't told her about the infamous twenty-five thousand dollars, which Billy Polo assumed was part of Daggett's "estate." Maybe Lovella had come up here to collect. "I think we better have a chat soon," I said.

"Why? Is there something *else*?"

I looked up. Ramona Westfall was standing in my doorway. "There's always something else," I said. "That's what makes life so much fun. I've got someone here. I'll talk to you this afternoon."

I hung up and rose to my feet, shaking hands with Mrs. Westfall across the desk. I invited her to take a seat and then poured coffee for us both, using social ritual as a way of setting her at ease, or so I hoped.

She was looking drawn, the fine skin under her mild eyes smudged with fatigue. She wore a tan poplin shirtwaist with shoulder epaulets and carried a mesh-and-canvas handbag that looked like it could be packed for a quick safari somewhere. Her pale hair had the sheen of a Breck shampoo ad in a magazine. I tried to picture her in a raincoat, lurching around the marina with Daggett's arm draped over her shoulder. Could she have flipped him, ass over teakettle, right out of that skiff? Hey, sure. Why not?

She stared at me uneasily, reaching out automatically to straighten some items on my desk. She lined up three pencils with the points facing me, like little ground-to-air missiles, and then she cleared her throat.

"Well. We were wondering. Tony never said anything so we thought perhaps we should ask you about it. Did you tell Tony about the money when you talked to him last night?"

"Sure," I said. "Not that it did any good. I got nowhere. He was adamant. He wouldn't even discuss it."

She colored slightly. "We're thinking to take it," she said. "Ferrin and I talked about it last night while Tony was out with you and we're beginning to believe we should put the money in a trustee account for him . . .

at least until he's eighteen and really has a sense of what he might do with it."

"What brought about the change?"

"Oh everything, I guess. We've been in family counseling and the therapist keeps hoping we can work through some of the anger and the grief. He feels Tony's migraines are stress-related in part, a sort of index of his unwillingness . . . or maybe inability is a better word . . . to process his loss. I've been wondering how much I've contributed to that. I haven't dealt with Abby's death that well and it can't have helped him." She paused and then shook her head slightly as though embarrassed. "I know it's a reversal. I suppose we've been unnecessarily rude to you and I'm sorry."

"You don't have to apologize," I said. "Personally, I'd be delighted to have you take the check. At least then I could feel I'd discharged my responsibilities. If you change your mind later, you can always donate the money to a worthy cause. There are lots of those around."

"What about his family? Daggett's. They may feel they're entitled to the money, don't you think? I mean, I wouldn't want to take it if there are going to be any legal ramifications."

"You'd have to talk to an attorney about that," I said. "The check is made out to Tony, and Daggett hired me to deliver it to him. I don't think there's any question about his intention. There may be other legal issues I don't know about, but you're certainly welcome to talk to someone first." Secretly, I wanted her to take the damn thing and be done with it.

She stared at the floor for a moment. "Tony said . . . last night he mentioned that he might want to go to the funeral. Do you think he should? I mean, does that seem like a good idea to you?"

"I don't know, Mrs. Westfall. That's way out of my line. Why don't you ask his therapist?"

"I tried, but he's out of town until tomorrow. I don't want Tony any more upset than he is."

"He's going to feel what he feels. You can't control that. Maybe it's something he has to go through."

"That's what Ferrin says, but I'm not sure."

"What's the story on the migraines? How long has that been going on?"

"Since the accident. He had one last night as a matter of fact. It's not your fault," she added hastily. "His head started bothering him about an hour after he got home. He threw up every twenty minutes or so from midnight until almost four A.M. We finally had to take him over to the emergency room at St. Terry's. They gave him a shot and that put him out, but he woke up a little while ago and he's talking now about going to the funeral. Did he mention it to you?"

"Not at all. I told him Daggett was dead, but he didn't react much at the time, except to say he was glad. Is he well enough to go?"

"He will be, I think. The migraines are odd. One minute you think he's never going to pull out of it and the next minute he's on his feet and starving to death. It happened last Friday night."

"Friday?" I said. The night of Daggett's death.

"That episode wasn't quite as bad. When he came home from school, he knew he was on the verge of a headache. We tried to get some medication down him to head it off, but no luck. Anyway, he pulled out of it after a while and I ended up fixing him two meatloaf sandwiches in the kitchen at two A.M. He was fine. Of course, he had another headache on Tuesday, and then the one last night. Two the week before that. Ferrin thinks maybe his going to the funeral will have some symbolic significance. You know, finish it off for him and set him free."

"That's always possible."

"Would Barbara Daggett object?"

"I don't see why she would," I said. "I suspect she feels as guilty as her father did, and she's offered to help."

"I guess I'll see how he's doing when I get home, then," she said. She glanced at her watch. "I better go."

"Let me give you the check." I pulled my handbag out of the bottom drawer and took out the check, which I passed across the desk to her. As her husband had done the night before, she smoothed out the folds, looking at it closely as if it might be some preposterous fake. She folded it up again and slipped it in her bag as she got to her feet. She hadn't touched her mug of coffee. I hadn't drunk mine either.

I told her the time and place of the services and walked her to the door. After she left, I sat down at my desk again, reviewing everything she'd said. At some point, I wanted to take Tony Gahan aside and see if he could verify her presence at the house the night Daggett died. It was hard to picture her as a killer, but I'd been fooled before.

17

John Daggett's funeral service took place in the sanctuary of some obscure outpost of the Christian church. The building itself was a one-story yellow stucco, devoid of ornament, located just off the freeway—the sort of chapel you glimpse through the bushes when you're going someplace else. I arrived late. I'd retrieved my VW from the auto glass shop at 1:45 after countless delays, and I confess I'd spent a few contented moments cranking my new car window up and down. The drizzle was beginning to turn serious and I was heartened by the notion that it wouldn't blow straight in on me.

When I reached the gravel parking lot beside the church, there were already fifty cars jammed into space for thirty-five. Some vehicles had nosed out into the vacant lot next door and some hugged the fence along the frontage road. I was forced to pass the place, snag a spot at the end of a long line of cars, and walk back. I could already hear electronic organ music thumping out in a style better suited to a skating rink than a house of God. I noticed from the sign out front that the minister was called a pastor instead of "Reverend" and I wondered if that was significant. Pastor Howard Bowen. The church name was composed of a long string of words and reminded me uneasily of the outfit that distributes pamphlets door-to-door. I hoped they weren't keen on converts.

Mr. Sharonson, from Wynington-Blake, was standing by himself on the low front steps and he gave me a pained look as he passed me a mimeographed copy of the program with a hand-drawn lily on the front. His manner suggested that the services were spiritually second-rate, this being the K mart of churches.

I went in. An usher peeled a metal folding chair from a stack near the door and flipped it open for me. The congregation had risen to its feet to sing so I stood in the back row, wedged in among other late arrivals. The woman on my left offered to share her hymnal and I took my half, my gaze sliding over the page in haste. They were on verse four of a ditty that went on and on about blood and sin. I made some mouth noises which I hoped were being lost in the general din. Aside from the fact I don't believe in this stuff, I don't sing too good and I was worried I might be denounced on both counts.

Way up at the front, I thought I spotted Barbara Daggett's blonde head, but I didn't see anyone else I knew. We sat down with a rustle of clothing and the scrape of metal chair legs. While Pastor Bowen, in a matte black suit, talked about what wretches we were, I stared at the brown vinyl tile floor and studied the staunch row of stained glass windows which depicted forms of spiritual torment that made me squirm. Already, I could feel a burgeoning urge to repent.

I could see Daggett's casket up by the altar, looking somehow like one of those boxes magicians use when they cut folk in half. I checked my program. We'd whipped through the opening prayer and the invocation, and now that we'd dispensed with the first hymn, we were apparently settling in for an energetic discourse on the temptations of the flesh, which put me in mind of the numerous and varied occasions on which I'd succumbed. That was entertaining.

Pastor Bowen was in his sixties, balding, a small man with a tight round face, who looked like he would suffer from denture breath. He'd chosen as his subject matter a passage from Deuteronomy: "The Lord shall smite thee in the knees, and in the legs, with a sore botch that cannot be healed, from the sole of thy foot unto the top of thy head," and I heard more on that subject than I thought possible without falling asleep. I was curious what he could find to say about John Daggett, whose transgressions were many and whose repentances were few, but he managed to tie Daggett's passing into "He shall lend to thee, and thou shalt not lend to him; he shall be the head, and thou shalt be the tail," and sailed right into an all-encompassing prayer.

When we stood for the final hymn, I felt someone's eyes on me and I looked over to spot Marilyn Smith two rows down, in the company of a man I assumed to be her husband, Wayne. She was wearing red. I wondered if she would leap up and do a tap dance on the coffin lid. The congregation by now was really getting into the spirit of things and hosannas were being called out on all sides, accompanied by amens, huzzahs, and much rending and tearing of clothes. I wanted to excuse myself, but I didn't dare. This was beginning to feel like soul-aerobics.

The woman next to me began to sway, her eyes closed, while she hooted out an occasional "Yes, Lord." I'm not given to this sort of orthodox public outburst and I commenced to edge my way to the door. I could see now that the minister, doing what looked like deltoid releases, was leading his merry band of church elders in the equivalent of a canonical conga line with Essie Daggett bringing up the rear.

At the exit, I came face to face with Billy Polo and his sister, Coral. He took me by the arm and pulled me aside as the service drew to a close behind me and people began to crowd through the door. Essie Daggett was wailing, nearly borne aloft like a football coach after a big win. Barbara Daggett and Eugene Nickerson had arranged themselves on either side, giving her what protection they could. For some reason, the other mourners were reaching out to touch and pat and grasp at Essie, as if her grief lent her healing powers.

The pallbearers came last, pulling the coffin along on a rolling cart instead of toting it. None of the six of them appeared to be under sixty-five and Wynington-Blake may have worried that they'd collapse, or topple their cargo right out into the aisle. As it was, the cart seemed to have one errant wheel which caused it to meander, squeaking energetically. The coffin, as though with a will of its own, headed for the chairs first on one side and then the other. I could see the pallbearers struggle to maintain mournful expressions while correcting its course, dragging it up the aisle like a stubborn dog.

I caught sight of Tony Gahan briefly, but he was gone again before I could speak to him. The hearse pulled up in front and the coffin was angled down the low steps and into the rear. Behind it, the limousine pulled up and Essie was helped into the back seat. She was wearing a black suit, with a broad-brimmed black straw hat, swathed in veiling. She looked more like a beekeeper than anything else. Stung by the Holy Spirit, I thought. Barbara Daggett wore a charcoal gray suit and black pumps, her two-toned eyes looking almost electric in the pale oval of her face. The rain was falling steadily and Mr. Sharonson was distributing big black umbrellas as people ducked off the porch and hurried to the parking lot.

Cars were being started simultaneously in a rumble of exhaust fumes, gravel popping as we pulled out onto the frontage road and began the slow procession to the cemetery, maybe two miles away. Again, we parked in a long line, car doors slamming as we crossed the soggy grass. This was apparently a fairly new cemetery, with few trees—a wide flat field planted to an odd crop. The headstones were square cut and low, without any of the worn beauty of stone angels or granite lambs. The grounds were well kept, but consisted primarily of asphalt roadways winding among sections of burial plots that had apparently been sold "pre-need." I wondered if cemeteries, like golf courses, had to be designed by experts for maximum aesthetic effect. This one felt like a cut-rate country club, low membership fees for the upstart dead. The rich and respectable were buried someplace else and John Daggett couldn't possibly qualify for inclusion among them.

Wynington-Blake had set up a canopy over the grave itself and, nearby, a second larger one with folding chairs arranged under it. No one seemed to know who was supposed to go where and there was a bit of milling around. Essie and Barbara Daggett were led into the big tent and placed in the front row, with Eugene Nickerson on one side and a fat woman on the other in a set of four folding chairs connected at the base. The back legs were already beginning to sink into the rain-softened soil, tilting the four of them backward at a slight angle. I had a brief image of them trapped like that, staring at the tent top, legs dangling, unable to right themselves again. Why is it that grief always seems edged with absurdity?

I eased over to one side, under shelter, but remained standing. Most of the mourners appeared to be elderly and (perhaps) needed folding chairs more than I. It looked like the entire church membership had turned out in Essie Daggett's behalf.

Pastor Bowen had declined a raincoat and he stood now in the open air, rain collecting on his balding head, waiting patiently for everyone to get settled. At this range, I saw evidence of a hearing aid tucked into the tiny ear cave on his right. Idly, he fiddled with the device, keeping his expression benign so as not to call attention to himself. I wondered if the battery was shorting out from the damp. I could see him tap on the aid with his index finger, flinching then as though it had suddenly barked to life again.

On the far side of the tent, I saw Marilyn and Wayne Smith, and behind them Tony Gahan, accompanied by his aunt Ramona. He looked like the perfect prep school gentleman in gray wool slacks, white shirt, navy blazer, rep tie. As though sensing that he was being watched, his eyes strayed to mine, his expression as empty as a robot's. If he was expunging raw hate or an old sorrow, there was no sign of it. Billy Polo and his sister stood outside the tent in the rain, sharing an umbrella. Coral looked miserable. She was apparently still caught up in the throes of a cold, clutching a fistful of Kleenex. She belonged in bed with a flannel rag on her chest reeking of Vick's Vaporub. Billy seemed restless, scanning the crowd with care. I followed his gaze, wondering if he was looking for someone in particular.

"Dear friends," the minister said in a powdery voice. "We are gathered here on the sad occasion of John Daggett's death, to witness his return to the earth from which he was formed, to acknowledge his passing, to celebrate his entry into the presence of our Lord Jesus. John Daggett has left us. He is free now of the cares and worries of this life, free of sin, free of his burdens, free of blame. . . ."

From somewhere near the back, a woman hollered out "Yes, Lord!" and a second woman yelled out "Buulll-shiit!" in just about the same tone. The minister, not hearing that well, apparently took both as spiritual punctuation marks, Biblical whoopees to incite him to greater eloquence. He raised his voice, closing his eyes as he began quoting admonitions against sin, filth, defiled flesh, lasciviousness, and corruption.

"John Daggett was the biggest asshole who ever lived so get it straight!" came the jeering voice again. Heads whipped around. Lovella had gotten to her feet near the back. The people turned to stare, their faces blank with amazement.

She was drunk. She had the little bitty pink eyes that suggest some high-grade marijuana toked up in addition to the booze. Her left eye was still slightly puffy, but the bruising had lightened up to a mild yellow on that side and she looked more like she was suffering from an allergy than a rap up the side of the head from the dead man. Her hair was the same blonde bush I remembered, her mouth a slash of dark red. She'd been weeping copiously and her mascara was speckled under her lower lids like soot. Her skin was splotchy, her nose hot pink and running. For the occasion she'd chosen a black sequined cocktail dress, low cut. Her breasts looked almost transparent and bulged out like condoms inflated as a joke. I couldn't tell if she was weeping out of rage or grief and I didn't think this crowd was prepared to deal with either one.

I was already headed toward the rear. Out of the corner of my eye, I saw Billy Polo make a beeline toward her on the far side of the tent. The minister had figured out by now that she was not on his team and he shot a baffled look at Mr. Sharonson, who motioned the ushers to take charge. We all reached her just about at the same time. Billy grabbed her from behind, pinning her arms back. Lovella flung him off, kicking like a mule, yelling "Fuck-heads! You scum-sucking hypocrites!" One usher snagged her by the hair and the other took her feet. She shrieked and struggled as they carried her toward the road. I followed, glancing back briefly. Barbara Daggett was obscured by the mourners who'd stood up for a better look, but I saw that

Marilyn Smith was loving every trashy minute of Lovella's performance.

By the time I reached Lovella, she was lying in the front seat of Billy Polo's Chevrolet, hands covering her face as she wept. The doors were open on both sides of the car and Billy knelt by her head, shushing and soothing her, smoothing her rain-tangled hair. The two ushers exchanged a look, apparently satisfied that she was under control at that point. Billy bristled at their intrusion.

"I got her, man. Just bug off. She's cool."

Coral came around the car and stood behind him, holding the umbrella. She seemed embarrassed by Billy's behavior, uncomfortable in the presence of Lovella's excess. The three of them formed an odd unit and I got the distinct impression that the connection between them was more recent than Billy'd led me to believe.

The graveside service, I gathered, was drawing to a close. From the tent came the thin, discordant voices of the mourners as they joined in an a cappella hymn. Lovella's sobs had taken on the intensity of a child's— artless, unself-conscious. Was she truly grieving for Daggett or was something else going on?

"What's the story, Billy?" I said.

"No story," he said gruffly.

"Something's going on. How'd she find out about his death? From you?"

Billy laid his face against her hair, ignoring me.

Coral shifted her gaze to mine. "He doesn't know anything."

"How about you, Coral? You want to talk about it?"

Billy shot her a warning look and she shook her head.

Murmurs and activity from the tent. The crowd was breaking up and people were beginning to move toward us.

"Watch your head. I'm closing the car doors," Billy said to Lovella. He shut the door on the driver's side and moved around the front to catch the door on the passenger side. He paused with his hand on the handle, waiting for her to pull her knees up to make clearance. Idly, he surveyed the mourners still huddled under the cover of the tent. As the crowd shifted, I saw his gaze flicker. "Who's that?"

He was looking at a small group formed by Ramona Westfall, Tony, and the Smiths. The three adults were talking while Tony, his hands in his pockets, passed his shoe over the rung of a folding chair, scraping the mud from the sole. Barbara Daggett was just behind him, in conversation with someone else. I identified everyone by name. I thought Wayne was the one who seemed to hold his attention, but I wasn't positive. It might have been Marilyn.

"How come the Westfalls showed up for this?"

"Maybe the same reason you did."

"You don't know why I came," he said. He was agitated, jingling the car keys, his gaze drifting back to the mourners.

"Maybe you'll tell me one of these days."

His smirk said don't count on it. He signaled to Coral and she got in the back seat. He got in the car and started it, pulling out then without a backward glance.

18

Barbara Daggett invited me back to her mother's house after the funeral, but I declined. I couldn't handle another emotional circus act. After I've spent a certain amount of time in the company of others, I need an intermission anyway. I retreated to my office and sat there with the lights out. It was only 4:00, but dark clouds were massing again as though for attack. I slipped my shoes off and put my feet up, clutching my jacket around me for warmth. John Daggett was in the ground now and the world was moving on. I wondered what would happen if we left it at that. I didn't think Barbara Daggett gave a damn about seeing justice done, whatever that consisted of. I hadn't come up with much. I thought I was on the right track, but I wasn't sure I really wanted an answer to the question Daggett's death had posed. Maybe it was better to forget this one, turn it under again like top soil, worms and all. The cops didn't consider it a homicide anyway and I knew I could talk Barbara Daggett out of pursuing the point. What was there to be gained? I wasn't in the business of avenging Daggett's death. Then what was I uneasy about? It was the only time in recent memory that I'd wanted to drop a case. Usually I'm dogged, but this time I wanted out. I think I could have talked myself into it if nothing else had occurred. As it happened, my phone rang about ten minutes later, nudging me into action again. I took my feet off the desk for form's sake and picked up on the first ring. "Millhone."

A young-sounding man said hesitantly: "Is this the office or an answering service?"

"The office."

"Is this Kinsey Millhone?"

"Yes. Can I help you?"

"Yeah, well my boss gave me this number. Mr. Donagle at the Spindrift Motel? He said you had some questions about Friday night. I think maybe I saw that guy you were asking about."

I reached for a lined yellow pad and a pen. "Great. I appreciate your getting in touch. Could you tell me your name first?"

"Paul Fisk," he said. "I read in the paper some guy drowned and it just sure seemed like an odd coincidence, but I didn't know if I should say anything or not."

"You saw him Friday night?"

"Well, I think it was him. This was about quarter of

two, something like that. I'm on night desk and sometimes I step outside for some air, just to keep myself awake." He paused and I could hear him shift gears. "This is confidential, isn't it?"

"Of course. Strictly between us. Why? Did your girlfriend stop by or something like that?"

His laugh was nervous. "Naw, sometimes I smoke a little weed is all. Place gets boring at two A.M., so that's how I get through. Get loaded and watch old black-and-white movies on this little TV I got. I hope you don't have a problem with that."

"Hey, it's your business, not mine. How long have you worked at the Spindrift?"

"Just since March. It's not a great job, but I don't want to get fired. I'm trying to get myself out of debt and I need the bucks."

"I hear you," I said. "Tell me about Friday night."

"Well, I was on the porch and this drunk went by. It was raining pretty hard so I didn't get a real good look at him at the time, but when I saw the news, the age and stuff seemed pretty close."

"Did you see the picture of him by any chance?"

"Just a glimpse on TV, but I wasn't paying much attention so I couldn't say for sure it was him. I guess I should have called the cops, but I didn't have anything much to report and I was afraid it'd come out about the . . . about that other stuff."

"What was he doing, the drunk?"

"Nothing much. It was him and this girl. She had

him by the arm. You know, kind of propped up. They were laughing like crazy, wandering all over the place on account of his being so screwed up. Alcohol'll do that, you know. Bad stuff. Not like weed," he said.

I bypassed the sales pitch. "What about the woman? Did you get a good look at her?"

"Not really. Not to describe."

"What about hair, clothing, things like that?"

"I noticed some. She had these real spiky heels and a raincoat, a skirt, and let's see . . . a shirt with this sweater over it. Like, what do you call 'em, preppies wear."

"A crewneck?"

"Yeah. Same color green as the skirt."

"You saw all that in the dark?"

"It's not that dark there," he said. "There's a street-light right out front. The two of them fell down in a heap they were laughing so hard. She got up first and kind of looked down to see if her stockings were torn. He just lay there in a puddle on his back till she helped him up."

"Did they see you?"

"I don't think so. I was standing in the shadows of this overhang, keeping out of the wet. I never saw 'em look my way."

"What happened after the fall?"

"They just went on toward the marina."

"Did you hear them say anything?"

"Not really. It sounded like she was teasing him

about falling down, but other than that nothing in particular."

"Could they have had a car?"

"I don't think so. Anyway, not that I saw."

"What if they'd parked it in that municipal lot across the street?"

"I guess they could have, but I don't know why they'd walk to the marina in weather like that. Seems like if they had a car it'd be easier to drive and then park it down there."

"Unless he was too drunk. He'd had his driver's license yanked too."

"She could have driven. She was half sober at least."

"You've got a point there," I said. "What about public transportation? Could they have come by bus or cab?"

"I guess, except the buses don't run that late. A cab maybe. That'd make sense."

I was jotting down information as he gave it to me. "This is great. What's your home phone in case I need to get in touch?"

He gave me the number and then said, "I usually work eleven to seven on weekdays."

I made a quick note. "Do you think you'd recognize the girl if you saw her again?"

"I don't know. Probably. Do you know who she is?"

"Not yet. I'm working on that."

"Well, I wish you luck. You think this'll help?"

"I hope so. Thanks for calling. I really appreciate it."

"Sure thing, and if you catch up with her, let me know. Maybe you can do like a police lineup or something like that."

"Great and thanks."

He clicked off and I finished making notes, adding this information to what I had. Dinah had spotted Daggett and the girl at 2:15 and Paul Fisk's sighting placed them right on Cabana thirty minutes before. I wondered where they'd been before that. If they'd arrived by cab, had she taken one home from the marina afterward? I didn't get it. Most killers don't take taxis to and from. It isn't good criminal etiquette.

I hauled out the telephone book and turned to the Yellow Pages to look up cab companies. Fortunately, Santa Teresa is a small town and there aren't that many. Aside from a couple of airport and touring services, there were six listed. I dialed each in turn, patiently explaining who I was and inquiring about a 2:00 A.M. Saturday fare with a Cabana Boulevard drop off. I was also asking about a pickup anywhere in that vicinity sometime between 3:00 and 6:00 A.M. According to the morgue attendant, the watch Daggett had been wearing was frozen at 2:37, but anybody could have jimmied that, breaking the watch to pinpoint the time, then attaching it to his wrist before he was dumped. If she'd left the boat and swum ashore or rowed to the wharf and abandoned it there, it was still going to take her a little time to organize herself for the cab ride home.

All the previous week's trip sheets, of course, had been filed and there were some heavy sighs and grumblings all around at the notion of having to look them up. Ron Coachella, the dispatcher for Tip Top, was the only cheerful soul in the lot, primarily because he'd done a records search for me once before with good results. I couldn't talk anyone into doing the file check right then, so I left my name and number and a promise that I'd call again. "Whoopee-do," said one.

While I was talking, I'd been doodling on the legal pad, running my pencil around idly so that the line formed a maze. I circled the note about the green skirt. Hadn't that old bum pulled a pair of spike heels and a green skirt out of a trash bin at the beach? I remembered his shoving discarded clothing into one of the plastic bags he kept in his shopping cart. Hers? Surely she hadn't made her way home in the buff. She did have the raincoat, but I wondered if she might have had a change of clothes stashed somewhere too. She'd sure gone to a lot of trouble if she were setting Daggett up. This didn't look like an impulsive act, done in the heat of the moment. Had she had help? Someone who picked her up afterward? If the cab companies didn't come up with a record of a fare, I'd have to consider the possibility of an accomplice.

In the meantime, I thought I'd better head down to the beach and look for my scruffy drifter friend. I'd seen him that morning near the public restrooms when I did my run. I tore the sheet off the legal pad and folded it, shoving it in my pocket as I grabbed up my handbag, locked the office, and headed down the back stairs to my car.

It was now nearly quarter to five, getting chillier by the minute, but at least it was dry temporarily. I cruised along Cabana, peering from my car window. There weren't many people at the beach. A couple of power walkers. A guy with a dog. The boulevard seemed deserted. I doubled back, heading toward my place, passing the wharf on the left and the string of motels across the street. Just beyond the boat launch and kiddie pool, I pulled up at a stoplight, scanning the park on the opposite corner. I could see the band shell where bums sometimes took refuge, but I didn't see any squatters. Where were all the transients?

I circled back, passing the train station. It occurred to me that this was probably the bums' dinner hour. I cut over another block and a half and sure enough, there they were—fifty or so on a quick count, lined up outside the Redemption Mission. The fellow I was looking for was near the end of the line, along with his pal. There was no sign of their shopping carts, which I thought of as a matched set of movable metal luggage, the derelict's Louis Vuitton. I slowed, looking for a place to park.

The neighborhood is characterized by light industry, factory outlets, welding shops, and quonset huts where auto body repair work is done. I found a parking spot in front of a place that made custom surfboards. I pulled in, watching in my rearview mirror until the group outside the mission had shuffled in. I locked the car then and crossed the street.

The Redemption Mission looks like it's made out of papier-mâché, a two-story oblong of fakey-looking field-stone, with ivy clinging to one end. The roofline is as crenellated as a castle's, the "moat" a wide band of asphalt paving. City fire codes apparently necessitated the addition of fire escapes that angle down the building now on all sides, looking somehow more perilous than the possibility of fire. The property is considered prime real estate and I wondered who would house the poor if the bed space were bought out from under them. For most of the year, the climate in this part of California is mild enough to allow the drifters to sleep outdoors, which they seem to prefer. Seasonally, however, there are weeks of rain . . . even occasionally someone with a butcher knife intent on slitting their throats. The mission offers safe sleeping for the night, three hot meals a day, and a place to roll cigarettes out of the wind.

I picked up cooking odors as I approached—bulk hamburger with chili seasoning. As usual, I couldn't remember eating lunch and here it was nearly dinnertime again. The sign outside indicated prayer services at 7:00 every night and Hot Showers & Shaves on Mondays, Wednesdays, and Saturdays. I stepped inside. The walls were painted glossy beige on top and shoe brown below. Hand-lettered signs pointed me to the dining room and chapel on the left. I followed the low murmur of conversation and the clatter of silverware.

On the right, through a doorway, I spotted the dining room—long metal folding tables covered with paper, metal folding chairs filled with men. Nobody paid any attention to me. I could see serving plates stacked high with soft white bread, bowls of applesauce sprinkled with cinnamon, salads of iceberg lettuce that glistened with bottled dressing. The table seated twenty, already bent to their evening meal of chili served over elbow macaroni. Another fifteen or twenty men sat obediently in the "chapel" to my left, which consisted of a lectern, an old upright piano, orange molded plastic chairs, and an imposing cross on the wall.

The scruffy drifter I was looking for sat in the back row with his friend. Slogans everywhere assured me that Jesus cared, and that certainly seemed true here. What impressed me most was the fact that Redemption Mission (according to the wall signs) was supported by private donations, with little or no connection to the government.

"May I help you?"

The man who'd approached me was in his sixties, heavyset, clean-shaven, wearing a red short-sleeved cotton shirt and baggy pants. He had one normal arm and one that ended at the elbow in a twist of flesh like the curled top of a Mr. Softee ice cream cone. I wanted to introduce myself, shaking hands, but the stump was on the right and I didn't have the nerve. I took out a business card instead, handing it to him.

"I wonder if I might have a word with one of your clients?"

His beefy brow furrowed. "What's this about?"

"Well, I think he retrieved some articles I'm looking for from a trash can at the beach. I want to find out if he still has them in his cart. It will only take a minute."

"You see him in here?"

I indicated the one who interested me.

"You'll have to talk to the both of them," the man said. "Delphi's the fellow you want, but he don't talk. His buddy does all the talking. His name is Clare. I'll bring them out if you'll wait out there in the corridor. They got their shopping carts on the back patio. I'd go easy about them carts. They get a might possessive of their treasures sometimes."

I thanked him and retraced my steps, lingering in the entranceway until Delphi and Clare appeared. Delphi had shed some of his overcoats, but he wore the same dark watch cap and his skin had the same dusky red tone. His friend Clare was tall and gaunt with a very pink tongue that crept out of his mouth through the gap left by his missing front teeth. His hair was a silky white, rather sparse, his arms long and stringy, hands huge. Delphi made no eye contact at all, but Clare turned out to have some residual charm, left over perhaps from the days before he started to drink.

I explained who I was and what I was looking for. I

saw Delphi look at Clare with the haunted subservience of a dog accustomed to being hit. Clare may
have been the only human being in the world who
didn't frighten or abuse him and he evidently de-
pended on Clare to handle interactions of this kind.

"Yep. I know the ones. High heels in black suede.
Green wool skirt. Delphi here was pleased. Usually it's
slim pickin's around that bin. Aluminum cans is about
the best you can hope for, but he got lucky, I guess."

"Does he still have the items?"

The tongue crept out with a crafty life of its own, so
pink it looked like Clare had been sucking red hots. "I
can ask," he said.

"Would you do that?"

Clare turned to Delphi. "What do you think, Delphi? Shall we give this little gal what she wants? Up to
you."

Delphi gave no evidence whatever of hearing, ab-
sorbing, or assenting. Clare waited a decent interval.

"Now that's tough," Clare said to me. "That was his
best day and he likes that green skirt."

"I could reimburse him," I said tentatively. I didn't
want to insult these guys.

Out came the tongue, like some shy creature peering from its lair. Delphi's hearing seemed to improve.
He shifted slightly. I left Clare to translate this movement into dollars and cents.

"A twenty might cover it," Clare said at length.

I only had a twenty on me, but I took it out of the

zippered compartment in my black handbag. I offered it to Delphi. Clare interceded. "Hold that until we've done our business. Let's step outside."

I filed after them along a short corridor to a back exit that opened on a small concrete patio surrounded on three sides by an openwork fence made of lathing. Someone had "landscaped" the entire area in annuals planted in coffee cans and big industrial-sized containers that had held green beans and applesauce. Delphi stood by, looking on anxiously, while Clare pawed through one of the shopping carts. He seemed to know exactly where the shoes and skirt were located, whisking them out in no time flat. He passed them over to me and I handed him the twenty. It felt somehow like an illicit drug sale and I had visions of them buying a jug of Mad Dog 20-20 after I'd left. Clare held the bill up for Delphi to inspect, then he glanced at me.

"Don't you worry. We'll put this in the collection plate," Clare said. "Delphi and me have give up drink." I thought Clare seemed happier about it than Delphi did.

19

My dinner that night was cheese and crackers, with a side of chili peppers just to keep my mouth awake. I'd changed out of my all-purpose dress into a tee shirt, jeans, and fuzzy slippers. I ate sitting at my desk, with a Diet Pepsi on the rocks. I studied the skirt and shoes. I tried the right shoe on. Too wide for me. The back of the heel was scuffed, the toe narrowing to a bunion-producing point. The manufacturer's name on the inner sole had been blurred by sweat. A pair of Odor-eaters wouldn't have been out of line here. The skirt was a bit more informative, size 8, a brand I'd seen at the Village Store and the Post & Rail. Even the lining was in good shape, though wrinkled in a manner that suggested a recent soaking. I touched my tongue to the fabric. Salt. I checked the inseam pockets, which were empty. No cleaner's marks. I thought about the women connected, even peripherally, with Daggett's death. The skirt might fit any one of them, except for

Barbara Daggett maybe, who was big-boned and didn't seem like the type for the preppy look, especially in green. Ramona Westfall was a good candidate. Marilyn Smith, perhaps. Lovella Daggett or Billy's sister, Coral, could probably both wear an 8, but the style seemed wrong . . . unless the outfit had been lifted from a Salvation Army donation box. Maybe in the morning I'd stop by a couple of clothing stores and see if any of the salesclerks recognized the skirt. Fat chance, I thought. A better plan would be to show it, along with the shoes, to all five women and see if anyone would admit ownership. Unlikely under the circumstances. Too bad I couldn't do a little breaking and entering. The matching green sweater might come to light in someone's dresser drawer.

I padded into the kitchen and rinsed my plate. Eating alone is one of the few drawbacks to single life. I've read those articles that claim you should prepare food just as carefully for yourself as you would for company. Which is why I do cheese and crackers. I don't cook. My notion of setting an elegant table is you don't leave the knife sticking out of the mayonnaise far. Since I usually work while I eat, there isn't any point in candlelight. If I'm not working, I have *Time* magazine propped up against a stack of files and I read it back to front as I munch, starting with the sections on books and cinema, losing interest by the time I reach Economy & Business.

At 9:02, my phone rang. It was the night dispatcher

for Tip Top Cab Company, a fellow who identified himself as Chuck. I could hear the two-way radio squawking in the background.

"I got this note from Ron says to call you," said he. "He pulled the trip sheets for last Friday night and said to give you the information you were asking about, but I'm not really sure what you want."

I filled him in and waited briefly while he ran his eye down the sheet. "Oh yeah. I guess this is it. He's got it circled right here. It was my fare. That's probably why he asked me to call. Friday night, one twenty-three . . . well, you'd call that early Saturday. I dropped a couple off at State and Cabana. Man and a woman. I figured they were booked into a motel down there."

"I've heard the man was drunk."

"Oh yeah, very. Looked like she'd been drinking too, but not like him. He was a mess. I mean, this guy smelled to high heaven. Stunk up the whole back seat and I got a pretty fair tolerance for that kind of thing."

"What about her? Can you tell me anything?"

"Can't help you on that. It was late and dark and raining to beat the band. I just took 'em where they said."

"Did you talk to them?"

"Nope. I'm not the kind of cabbie engages in small talk with a fare. Most people aren't interested and I get sick of repeating myself. Politics, weather, baseball scores. It's all bull. They don't want to talk to me and I don't want to talk to them. I mean, if they ask me something I'm polite, don't get me wrong, but I can't manufacture chitchat to save my neck."

"What about the two of them? They talk to each other?"

"Who knows? I tuned 'em out."

God, this was no help at all. "You remember anything else?"

"Not offhand. I'll give it some thought, but it wasn't any big deal. Sorry I can't be a help."

"Well, at least you've verified a hunch of mine and I appreciate that. Thanks for your time."

"No problem."

"Oh, one more thing. Where'd the fare originate?"

"Now *that* I got. You know that sleazeball bar on Milagro? That place. I picked 'em up at the Hub."

I sat and stared at the phone for a moment after he hung up. I felt like I was running a reel of film backward, frame by frame. Daggett left the Hub Friday night in the company of a blonde. They apparently had a lot of drinks, a lot of laughs, staggered around in the rain together, fell down, and picked themselves up again. And little by little, block by block, she was steering him toward the marina, herding him toward the boat, guiding him out into the harbor on the last short ride of his life. She must have had a heart of stone and steadier nerves than mine.

I made some quick notes and tossed the index cards in the top drawer of my desk. I kicked off my slippers and laced up my tennies, then pulled on a sweatshirt. I snatched up the skirt and shoes, my handbag, and car keys and locked up, heading out to the VW. I'd start with Coral first. Maybe she'd know if Lovella was still in town. I was remembering now the fragment of conversation I'd overheard the night I eavesdropped on Billy and Coral. She'd been talking to Billy then about some woman. I couldn't remember exactly what she'd said, but I did remember that. Maybe Coral had seen the woman I was looking for.

When I reached the trailer park, I found the trailer dimly lighted, as if someone had gone out and left a lamp burning to keep the burglars at bay. Billy's Chevrolet was in the carport, the hood cold to the touch. I knocked on the door. After a moment, I heard footsteps bumping toward the front.

"Yeah?" Billy's muffled voice came through the door.

"It's Kinsey," I said. "Is Coral here?"

"Uh-uh. She's at work."

"Can I talk to you?"

He hesitated. "About what?"

"Friday night. It won't take long."

There was a pause. "Wait a sec. Let me throw some clothes on."

Moments later, he opened the door and let me in. He had pulled on a pair of jeans. Aside from that, he was barefoot and naked to the waist. His dark hair was tousled. He looked like he hadn't worked out recently, but his arms and chest were still well developed, overlaid by a fine mat of dark hair.

The trailer was disordered—newspapers, magazines, dinner dishes for two still out on the table, the counters covered with canned goods, cracker boxes, bags of flour, sugar, and corn meal. There wasn't a clear surface anywhere and no place to sit. The air was dense, smelling faintly of fresh cigarette smoke.

"Sorry to disturb you," I said. He looked like he'd been screwing his brains out and I wondered who was in the bedroom. "You have company?"

He glanced toward the rear, his dimples surfacing. "No, I don't. Why, are you interested?"

I smiled and shook my head, at the same time caught up in a flash fantasy of me and Billy Polo tangled up in sheets that smelled like him, musky and warm. His skin exuded a masculine perfume that conjured up images of all the trashy things we might do if the barriers went down. I kept my expression neutral, but I could feel my face tint with pink. "I have some questions I was hoping Coral might help me with."

"So you said. Try the Hub. She'll be there till closing time."

I laid the skirt and shoes across the television set, which was the only bare surface I could find. "Do you know if these are hers?"

He glanced at the items, too canny to bite. "Where'd you get 'em?"

"A friend of a friend. I thought you might know whose they were."

"I thought this was supposed to be about Friday night."

"It is. I talked to a cabbie who picked Daggett up at the Hub Friday night and dropped him off down near the wharf."

"I'll bite. So what?"

"A blonde was with him. The cabbie took them both. I figure she met him at the Hub, so I thought Coral might have had a look at her."

Billy knew something. I could see it in his face. He was processing the information, trying to decide what it meant.

I was getting impatient. "Goddamn it, Billy, level with me!"

"I am!"

"No, you're not. You've been lying to me since the first time you ever opened your mouth."

"I have not," he said hotly. "Name one thing."

"Let's start with Doug Polokowski. What's your re-lation to him? Brother?"

He was silent. I stared at him, waiting him out.

"Half-brother," he said grudgingly.

"Go on."

His tone of voice dropped, apparently with embar-rassment. "My mom and dad split up, but they were still legally married when she got pregnant by some-body else. I was ten and I hated the whole idea. I started gettin' in trouble right about then so I spent half my time in Juvenile Hall anyway, which suited me just fine. She finally had me declared a whaddyou call 'em. . . ."

"An out-of-control minor?"

"Yeah, one of them. Big deal. I didn't give a fat rat's ass. Let her dump us. Let her have a bunch more kids. She didn't have any more sense than that, then to hell with her."

"So you and Doug were never close?"

"Hardly. I used to see him now and then when I'd come home but we didn't have much of a relationship."

"What about you and your mother?"

"We're okay. I got over it some. After Doug got killed, we did better. Sometimes it happens that way."

"But you must have known Daggett was responsible."

"Sure I knew. Of course I did. Mom wrote and told me he was bein' sent up to San Luis. At first, I thought I'd get even with him. For her sake, if nothin' else. But it didn't work out like that. He was too pathetic. Know what I mean? Hell, I ended up almost feeling sorry for him. I despised him for the whiny little fucker that he was, but I couldn't leave him alone. It's like I had to torment him. I liked to watch him squirm, which maybe makes me weird but it don't make me a killer. I never murdered anybody in my life."

"What about Coral? Where was she in all this?"

"Hey, you ask her."

"Could she have been the one with Daggett that

night? It sounds like Lovella to me, but I can't be sure."

"Why ask me? I wasn't there."

"Did Coral mention it?"

"I don't want to talk about this," he said, irritably.

"Come on. You talked to Daggett Thursday night. Did he mention this woman?"

"We didn't talk about women," Billy said. He began to snap the fingers of his right hand against his left palm, making a soft, hollow pop. I could feel myself going into a terrier pup mode, worrying the issue like a rawhide bone, knotted on both ends.

"He must have known who she was," I said. "She didn't just materialize out of the blue. She set him up. She knew what she was doing. It must have been a very carefully thought-out plan."

The popping sound stopped and Billy's tone took on a crafty note. "Maybe she was connected to the guys who wanted their money back," he said.

I looked at him with interest. That really hadn't occurred to me, but it didn't sound bad. "Did you tip them off?"

"Listen, babe, I'm not a killer and I'm not a snitch. If Daggett had a beef with somebody, that was his lookout, you know?"

"Then what's the debate? I don't understand what you're holding back."

He sighed and ran a hand through his hair. "Lay off, okay? I don't know nothin' else so just leave it alone."

"Come on, Billy. What's the rest of it?" I snapped.

"Oh, shit. It wasn't Thursday," he blurted out. "I met Daggett Tuesday night and that's when he asked me to help him out."

"So he could hide from the guys at San Luis," I said, making sure I was following.

"Well, yeah. I mean, they'd called him Monday morning and that's why he'd hightailed it up here. We talked on the phone late Monday. He was drunk. I didn't feel like putting myself out. I'd just got home and I was bushed so I said I'd meet him the next night."

"At the Hub?"

"Right."

"Which is what you did," I said, easing him along.

"Sure, we met and talked some. He was already in a panic so I kind of fanned the flames, just twitting him. There's no harm in that."

"Why lie about it? Why didn't you tell me this to begin with?" I was crowding him, but I thought it was time to persist.

"It didn't look right somehow. I didn't want my name tied to his. Thursday night sounded better. Like I wasn't all that hot to talk to him. You know, like I didn't rush right out. I can't explain it any better than that."

It was just lame enough to make sense to me. I said, "All right. I'll buy it for now. Then what?"

"That's all it was. That's the last I saw of him. He

came in again Friday night and Coral spotted him, so she called me, but by the time I got there, he'd left."

"With the woman?"

"Yeah, right."

"So Coral did see her."

"Sure, but she didn't know who she was. She thought it was some babe hittin' on him, like a whore, something like that. The chick was buyin' him all these drinks and Daggett was lappin' 'em up. Coral got kind of worried. Not that either of us really gave a shit, but you know how it is. You don't want to see a guy get taken, even if you don't like him much."

"Especially if you've heard he's got thirty thousand dollars on him, right?" I said.

"It wasn't thirty. You said so yourself. It was twenty-five." Billy was apparently feeling churlish now that he'd opened up. "Anyway, what are you goin' on and on about? I told you everything I know."

"What about Coral? If you lied, maybe she's been lying too."

"She wouldn't do that."

"What'd she say when you got there?"

The look on Billy's face altered slightly and I thought I'd hit on something. I just didn't know what. My mind leapt ahead. "Did Coral *follow* them?" I asked.

"Of course not."

"What'd she say then?"

"Coral wasn't feeling so hot," he replied, uneasily.

"So she'd what, gone home?"

"Not really. She was coming down with this cold and she'd taken a cold cap. She was feeling zonked so she went back in the office and lay down on the couch. The bartender thought she'd left. I get there and I'm pissed because I can't find her, I can't find Daggett. I don't know what's goin' on. I hang around for a while and then I come back here, thinking she's home. Only she's not. It was a fuck-up, that's all. She was at the Hub the whole time."

"What time did she get home?"

"I don't know. Late. Three o'clock. She had to wait till the owner closed out the register and then he gave her a lift partway so she had to walk six blocks in the rain. She's been sick as a dog ever since."

I stared at him, blinking, while the wheels went round and round. I was picturing her at the wharf with Daggett and the fit was nice.

"Why look at me like that?" he said.

"Let me say this. I'm just thinking out loud," I said. "It could have been Coral, couldn't it? The blonde who left the Hub with him? That's what's been worrying you all this time."

"No, uh-uh. No way," he said. His eyes had settled on me with fascination. He didn't like the line I was taking, but he'd probably thought about it himself.

"You only have her word for the fact that this other woman even exists," I said.

"The cabbie saw her."

"But it could have been Coral. She might have been the one buying Daggett all those drinks. He knew who she was and he trusted her too, because of you. She could have called the cab and then left with him. Maybe the reason the bartender thought she was gone was because he saw her leave."

"Get the hell out of here," Billy whispered.

His face had darkened and I saw his muscles tense. I'd been so caught up in my own speculation I hadn't been paying attention to the effect on him. I picked up the skirt and shoes, keeping an eye on him while I edged toward the door. He leaned over and opened it for me abruptly.

I had barely cleared the steps when the door slammed behind me hard. He shoved the curtain aside, staring at me belligerently as I backed out of the carport. The minute the curtain dropped, I cut around to the trailer window where I'd spied on him before. The louvers were closed, but the curtain on that side gaped open enough to allow me a truncated view.

Billy had sunk down on the couch with his head in his hands. He looked up. The woman who'd been in the back bedroom had now emerged and she leaned against the wall while she lit another cigarette. I could see a portion of her heavy thighs and the hem of a shortie nightgown in pale yellow nylon. Like a drowning man, Billy reached for her and pulled her closed, burying his face between her breasts. Lovella. He began to nuzzle at her nipples through the nylon top, making wet spots. She stared down at him with that look new mothers have when they suckle an infant in public. Lazily, she leaned over and stubbed out her cigarette on a dinner plate, then wound her fingers into his hair. He grabbed her at the knees and lowered her to the floor, pushing her gown up around her waist. Down, down, down, he went.

I headed over to the Hub.

20

It looked like another slow night at the Hub. The rain had picked up again and business was off. The roof was leaking in two places and someone had put out galvanized pails to catch the drips . . . one on the bar, one by the ladies' room. The place, at its best, was populated by neighborhood drinkers—old women with fat ankles in heavy sweaters who started at 2:00 in the afternoon and consumed beer steadily until closing time, men with nasal voices and grating laughs whose noses were bulbous and sunburned from alcohol. The pool players were usually young Mexicans who smoked until their teeth turned yellow and squabbled among themselves like pups. That night the pool room was deserted and the green felt tabletops seemed to glow as though lighted from within. I counted four customers in all and one was asleep with his head on his arms. The jukebox was suffering from some mechanical quirk that gave the music a warbling, underwater quality.

I approached the bar, where Coral was perched on a high-backed stool with a Naugahyde top. She was wearing a Western-cut shirt with a silver thread running through the brown plaid, tight jeans rolled up at the ankles, and heels with short white socks. She must have recognized me from the funeral because when I asked if I could talk to her, she hopped down without a word and went around to the other side of the bar.

"You want something to drink?"

"A wine spritzer. Thanks," I said.

She poured a spritzer for me and pulled a draft beer for herself. We took a booth at the back so she could keep her eye on the clientele in case someone needed service. Up close, her hair looked so bushy and dry I worried about spontaneous combustion. Her makeup was too harsh for her fair coloring and her front teeth were decayed around the edges, as if she'd been eating Oreo cookies. Her cold must have been at its worst. Her forehead was lined and her eyes half squinted, like a magazine ad for sinus medication. Her nose was so stopped up she was forced to breathe through her mouth. In spite of all that, she managed to smoke, lighting up a Virginia Slim the minute we sat down.

"You should be home in bed," I said, and then wondered why I'd suggested such a thing. Billy and Lovella were currently back there groveling around on the floor, probably causing the trailer to thump on its foundations. Who could sleep with that stuff going on?

Coral put her cigarette down and took out a Kleenex to blow her nose. I've always wondered where people learn their nose-blowing techniques. She favored the double-digit method, placing a tissue over her hands, sticking the knuckles on both index fingers up her nostrils, rotating them vigorously after each honk. I kept my eyes averted until she was done, wondering idly if she was aware of Lovella's current whereabouts.

"What's the story on Lovella? She seemed distraught at the funeral."

Coral paused in her endeavors and looked at me. Belatedly, I realized she probably didn't know what the word distraught meant. I could see her put the definition together.

"She's fine. She had no idea they weren't legally married to each other. That's why she fell apart. Freaked her out." She gave her nose a final Roto-rooting and took up her cigarette again with a sniff.

"You'd think she'd be relieved," I said. "From what I hear, he beat the shit out of her."

"Not at first. She was crazy about him when he first got out. Still is, actually."

"That's probably why she called him the world's biggest asshole at the funeral," I remarked.

Coral looked at me for a moment and then shrugged noncommittally. She was smarter than Billy, but not by much. I had the same feeling here that I'd had with him. I was tapping into a matter they'd hoped to bury, but I didn't know enough to pursue the point.

I tried fishing. "I thought Lovella and Billy had a thing at one time."

"Years ago. When she was seventeen. Doesn't count for shit."

"She told me Billy set her up with Daggett."

"Yeah, more or less. He talked to Daggett about her and Daggett wrote and asked if they could be pen pals."

"Too bad he never mentioned his wife," I said. "I do want to talk to Lovella, so when you see her please tell her to get in touch." I gave her a business card with my office number on it, which she acknowledged with a shrug.

"I won't see Lovella," she said.

"That's what you think," said I.

Coral's attention strayed to the bartender who was holding a finger aloft. "Hang on."

She crossed to the bar where she picked up a couple of mixed drinks and delivered them to the one other table that was occupied. I tried to picture her flipping Daggett backward out of a rowboat, but I couldn't quite make it stick. She fit the description, but there was something missing.

When she got back to the booth, I held up the high heels. "These yours?"

"I don't wear suede," she said flatly.

I loved it. Like suede was against her personal dress code. "What about the skirt?"

She took a final drag of the cigarette and crushed it in the metal ashtray, blowing out a mouthful of smoke. "Nope. Whose is it?"

"I think the blonde who killed Daggett wore it Friday night. Billy says she picked him up in here."

Belatedly, she focused on the skirt. "Yeah, that's right. I saw her," she said, as if cued.

"Does this look like the skirt she wore?"

"It could be."

"You know who she is?"

"Uh-uh."

"I don't mean to be rude about this, Coral, but I could use a little help. We're talking murder."

"I've been all tore up about it too," she said, bored.

"Don't you give a shit about any of this?"

"Are you kidding? Why should I care about Daggett? He was scum."

"What about the blonde? Do you remember anything about her?"

Coral shook another cigarette out of the pack. "Why don't you give it a rest, kid. You don't have the right to ask us any of this shit. You're not a cop."

"I can ask anything I want," I said, mildly. "I can't force you to answer, but I can always ask."

She stirred with agitation, shifting in her seat.

"Know what? I don't like you," she said. "People like you make me sick."

"Oh really. People like what?"

She took her time extracting a paper match from a packet, scratching the tip across the striking area until it flared. She lit her cigarette. The match made a tiny tinkling sound when she dropped it in the ashtray. She rested her chin on her palm and smiled at me unpleasantly. I wanted her to get her teeth fixed so she'd be prettier. "I bet you've had it real easy, haven't you?" she said, her voice heavy with sarcasm.

"Extremely."

"Nice white-collar middle-class home. The whole mommy-hubby trip. Bet you had little brothers and sisters. Nice little fluffy white dog . . ."

"This is amazing," I said.

"Two cars. Maybe a cleaning woman once a week. I never went to college. I never had a daddy giving me all the advantages."

"Well, that explains it then," I said. "I did meet your mom, you know. She looks like someone who's worked hard all her life. Too bad you don't appreciate the effort she made in your behalf."

"What effort? She works in a supermarket checkout line," Coral said.

"Oh, I see. You think she should do something classy like you."

"I'm sure not going to do *this* for life, if that's what you think."

"What happened to your father? Where was he in all this?"

"Who knows? He bugged out a long time ago."

"Leaving her with kids to raise by herself?"

"Skip it. I don't even know why I brought it up. Maybe you should get to the point and let me get back to work."

"Tell me about Doug."

"None of your business." She slid out of the booth. "Time's up," she said, and walked away. God, and here I was being friendly.

I picked up the shoes and skirt and dropped a couple of bucks on the table. I moved to the entranceway, pausing in the shelter of the doorway before I stepped out into the rain. It was 10:17 and there was no traffic on Milagro. The street was shiny black and the rain, as it struck the pavement, made a noise like bacon sizzling in a pan. A mist drifted up from the manhole covers that dotted the block, and the gutters gushed in a widening stream where water boiled back out of the storm drains.

I was restless, not ready to pack it in for the night. I thought about stopping by Rosie's, but it would probably look just like the Hub—smoky, drab, depressing. At least the air outside, though chilly, had the sweet, flowery scent of wet concrete. I started the car and did a U-turn, heading toward the beach, my windshield stippled with rain.

At Cabana, I turned right, driving along the boulevard. On my left, even without a moon visible, the surf churned with a dull gray glow, folding back on itself with a thundering monotony. Out in the ocean, I could see the lights on the oil derricks winking through the mist. I'd pulled up at a stoplight when I heard a car horn toot behind me. I checked my rearview mirror. A little red Honda was pulling over into the lane to my right. It was Jonah, apparently heading home just as I was. He made a cranking motion. I leaned over and rolled the window down on the passenger side.

"Can I buy you a drink?"

"Sure. Where?"

He pointed at the Crow's Nest to his right, a restaurant with exterior lights still burning. The light changed and he took off. I followed, pulling into the lot behind him. We parked side by side. He got out first, hunching against the rain while he opened an umbrella and came around to my door. We huddled together and puddle hopped our way to the front entrance. He held the door and I ducked inside, holding it for him then while he lowered the umbrella and gave it a quick shake.

The interior of the Crow's Nest was done in a half-hearted nautical theme which consisted primarily of fishing nets and rigging draped along the rafters and mariner's charts sealed into the table tops under a half-inch of polyurethane. The restaurant section was closed, but the bar seemed to be doing all right. I could see maybe ten tables occupied. The level of conversation was low and the lighting was discreet, augmented by fat round jars where candles glowed through orange glass. Jonah steered us past a small dance floor toward a table in the corner. The place had an aura of edgy excitement. We were protected by the weather, drawn together like the random souls stranded in an airport between flights.

The waitress appeared and Jonah glanced at me.

"You decide," I said.

"Two margaritas. Cuervo Gold, Grand Marnier, shaken, no salt," he said. She nodded and moved off.

"Very impressive," I said.

"I thought you'd like that. What brings you out?"

"Daggett, of course." I filled him in, realizing as I summed it up that I'd had just about as much of Billy Polo and his ilk as I could take for one night.

"Let's don't talk about him," I said when I was done. "Tell me what you're working on."

"Hey, no way. I'm here to relax."

The waitress brought our drinks and we paused briefly while she dipped neatly, knees together, and placed a cocktail napkin in front of each of us, along with our drinks. She was dressed like a boatswain except that her high-cut white pants were spandex and her buns hung out the back. I wondered how long uniforms like that would last if the night manager was required to squeeze his hairy fanny into one.

When the waitress left, Jonah touched his glass to mine. "To rainy nights," he said. We drank. The tequila had a little "wow" effect as it went down and I had to pat myself on the chest. Jonah smiled, enjoying my discomfiture.

"What brings you out so late?" I asked.

"Catching up on paperwork. Also, avoiding the house. Camilla's sister came down from Idaho for a week. The two of them are probably drinking wine and carving me up like a roast."

"Her sister doesn't like you, I take it."

"She thinks I'm a dud. Camilla came from money. Deirdre doesn't think either one of them should take up with guys on salary, for God's sake. And a cop? It's all too bourgeois. God, I gotta watch myself here. All I do is complain about life on the home front. I'm beginning to sound like Dempsey."

I smiled. Lieutenant Dempsey had worked Narcotics for years, a miserably married man whose days were spent complaining about his lot. His wife had finally died and he'd turned around and married a woman just like her. He'd taken early retirement and the two of them had gone off in an RV. His postcards to the department were amusing, but left people uncomfortable, like a stand-up comic making mean-spirited jokes at a spouse's expense.

Conversation dwindled. The background music was a tape of old Johnny Mathis tunes and the lyrics suggested an era when falling in love wasn't complicated by herpes, fear of AIDS, multiple marriages, spousal support, feminism, the sexual revolution, the Bomb, the Pill, approval of one's therapist, or the specter of children on alternate weekends.

Jonah was looking good. The combination of shadow and candlelight washed the lines out of his face, and heightened the blue of his eyes. His hair looked very dark and the rain had made it look silkier. He wore a white shirt, opened at the neck, sleeves rolled up, his forearms crosshatched with dark hair. There's usually a current running between us, generated I suppose by whatever primal urges keep the human race reproducing itself. Most of the time, the chemistry is kept in check by a bone-deep caution on my part, ambivalence about his marital status, by circumstance, by his own uneasiness, by the knowledge on both our parts that once certain lines are crossed, there's no going back and no way to predict the consequences.

We ordered a second round of drinks, and then a third. We slow danced, not saying a word. Jonah smelled of soap and his jaw line was smooth and sometimes he hummed with a rumbling I hadn't heard since I sat on my father's lap as a very young child, listening to him read to me before I knew what words meant. I thought about Billy Polo lowering Lovella to the trailer floor. The image was haunting because it spoke so eloquently of his need. I was always such a stoic, so careful not to make mistakes. Sometimes I wonder what the difference is between being cautious and being dead. I thought about rain and how nice it is to sink down on clean sheets. I pulled my head back and Jonah looked down at me quizzically.

"This is all Billy Polo's fault," I said.

He smiled. "What is?"

I studied him for a moment. "What would Camilla do if you didn't come home tonight?"

His smile faded and his eyes got that look. "She's the one who's talking about an open relationship," he said.

I laughed. "I'll bet that applies to her, not you."

"Not anymore," he said.

His kiss seemed familiar.

We left soon afterward.

21

I drove to the office at 9:00. The rain clouds were hunched above the mountains moving north, while above, the sky was the blue white of bleached denim. The city seemed to be in sharp focus, as if seen through new prescription lenses. I opened the French doors and stood on the balcony, raising my arms and doing one of those little butt wiggles so favored by the football set. *That* for you, Camilla Robb, I thought, and then I laughed and went and had a look at myself in the mirror, mugging shamelessly. Amazing Grace. I looked just like myself. Where tears erase the self, good sex transforms and I was feeling energized.

I put the coffee on and got to work, typing up my case notes, detailing the conversations I'd had with Billy and Coral. Cops and private eyes are always caught up in paperwork. Written records have to be kept of everything, with events set out so that anyone who comes along afterward will have a clear and comprehensive résumé of the investigation to that point. Since a private eye also bills for services, I have to keep track of my hours and expenses, submitting statements periodically so I can make sure I get paid. I prefer fieldwork; I suspect we all do. If I'd wanted to spend my days in an office, I'd have studied to be an underwriter for the insurance company next door. Their work seems boring 80 percent of the time while mine only bores me about one hour out of every ten.

At 9:30, I touched base with Barbara Daggett by phone, giving her a verbal update to match the written account I was putting in the mail to her. The duplication of effort wasn't really necessary, but I did it anyway. What the hell, it was her money. She was entitled to the best service she could get. After that, I did some filing, then locked up again, taking the green skirt and heels with me down the back stairs to my car, heading out to Marilyn Smith's. I was beginning to feel like the prince in search of Cinderella, shoe in hand.

I took the highway north, driving in the newly washed air. Colgate is only a fifteen-minute drive, but it gave me a chance to think about events of the night before. Jonah had turned out to be a clown in bed . . . funny and inventive. We'd behaved like bad kids, eating snacks, telling ghost stories, returning now and then to a lovemaking which was, at the same time, intense and comfortable. I wondered if I'd know him again. He was so generous and affectionate, so amazed at being with someone who didn't criticize or withhold, who didn't withdraw from his touch as though from a slug's. I couldn't imagine where we'd go from here and I didn't want to start worrying. I'm capable of screwing things up by trying to solve all the problems in advance instead of simply taking care of issues as they surface.

I missed my off-ramp, of course. I caught sight of it as I sped by, cursing good-naturedly as I took the next exit and circled back.

By the time I reached Wayne and Marilyn Smith's house, it was nearly 10:00. The bicycles that had been parked on the porch were gone. The orange trees, though nearly leafless with age, still carried the aura of ripe fruit, a faint perfume spilling out of the surrounding groves. I parked my car in the gravel drive behind a compact station wagon I assumed belonged to her. A peek into the rear, as I passed, revealed a gummy detritus of fast-food containers, softball equipment, school papers, and dog hair.

I cranked the bell. The entrance hall was deserted, but a golden retriever bounded toward the front door, toenails ticking against the bare floors as it skittered to a stop, barking joyfully. The dog's entire body waggled like a fish on a hook.

"Can I help you?"

Startled, I glanced to my right. Marilyn Smith was standing at the bottom of the porch steps in a tee shirt, drenched jeans, and a straw hat. She wore goatskin gardening gloves and bright yellow plastic clogs that were spattered with mud. When she realized it was me, her expression changed from pleasant inquiry to a barely disguised distaste.

"I'm working in the garden," she said, as if I hadn't guessed. "If you want to talk you'll have to come out there."

I followed her across the rain-saturated lawn. She tapped a muddy trowel against her thigh, distractedly.

"I saw you at the funeral," I remarked.

"Wayne insisted," she said tersely, then looked over her shoulder at me. "Who was the drunk woman? I liked her."

"Lovella Daggett. She thought she was married to him, but it turned out the warranty hadn't run out on his first wife."

When we reached the vegetable patch, she waded between two dripping rows of vines. The garden was in its winter phase—broccoli, cauliflower, dark squashes tucked into a spray of wide leaves. She'd been weeding. I could see the trampled-looking spikes scattered here and there. Farther down the row, there was evidence that the earth had been turned, heavy clods piled up near a shallow excavation site.

"Too wet for weeding, isn't it?"

"The soil here has a high clay content. Once it dries out, it's impossible," she said.

She shucked the gardening gloves and began to tear widths from an old pillow case, tying back the masses of sweet pea plants that had drooped in the rain. The strips of white rag contrasted brightly with the lime green of the plants. I held up the skirt and shoes I'd brought.

"Recognize these?"

She scarcely looked at the articles, but the chilly smile appeared. "Is that what the killer wore?"

"Could be."

"You've made progress since I saw you last. Three days ago, you weren't even certain it was murder."

"That's how I earn my pay," I said.

"Maybe Lovella killed him when she found out he was a bigamist."

"Always possible," I said, "though you still haven't said for sure where you were that night."

"Oh, but I did. I was here. Wayne was at the office and neither of us has corroborating witnesses." She was using that bantering tone again, mild and mocking.

"I'd like to talk to him."

"Make an appointment. He's in the book. Go down to the office. The Granger Building on State."

"Marilyn, I'm not your enemy."

"You are if I killed him," she replied.

"Ah, yes. In that case, I would be."

She tore off another strip of pillow case, the width of cotton dangling from her hand like something limp with death. "Sounds like you have suspects. Too bad you're short on proof."

"But I do have someone who saw her and that should help, don't you think? This is just preliminary work, narrowing the field," I said. It was bullshit, of course. I wasn't sure the motel clerk could identify anybody in the dark.

Her smile dimmed by a watt. "I don't want to talk to you anymore," she whispered.

I raised my hands, as if she'd pulled a gun. "I'm gone," I said, "but I have to warn you, I'm persistent. You'll find it unsettling, I suspect."

I kept my eyes on her as I moved away. I'd seen the muddy hoe she was using and I thought it best not to turn my back.

I cruised by the Westfalls on my way into town. I was going to have to show the skirt to Barbara Daggett at some point, but the Close was on my way. The low fieldstone wall surrounding the place was still a dark gray from the passing rain. I drove through the gates and parked along the road as I had before, pulling over into dense ivy. By day, the eight Victorian houses were enveloped in shade, sunlight scarcely penetrating the branches of the trees. I locked the car and picked my way up the path to the front steps. In the yard, the trunks of the live oak were frosted with a fungus as green as the oxidized copper on a roof. Tall palms punctuated the corners of the house. The air felt cool and moist in the wake of the storm.

The front door was ajar. The view from the hallway was a straight shot through to the kitchen and I could see that the back door was open too, the screen door unlatched. A portable radio sat on the counter and music blasted out, the *1812 Overture*. I rang the bell, but the sound was lost against the booming of cannons as the last movement rose to a thunder pitch.

I left the front porch and walked around to the back, peering in. Like the rest of the house, the kitchen had been redone, the owners opting here to modernize, though the Victorian character had been retained. There was a small floral print paper on the walls, lots of wicker, oak, and fern. The cabinet doors had been replaced with leaded glass, but the appliances were all strictly up-to-date.

There was no one in the room. A door on the left was open, the oblong of shadow suggesting that the basement stairs must be located just beyond. Two brown grocery bags sat on the kitchen table and it looked like someone had been interrupted in the course of unloading them. There was an electric percolator plugged into the outlet on the stove. While I was watching, the ready-light went on. Belatedly, I picked up the smell of hot coffee.

The music ended and the FM announcer made his concluding remarks about the piece, then introduced a Brahms concerto in E minor. I knocked on the frame of the screen door, hoping someone would hear me before the music started up again. Ramona appeared from the depths of the basement. She was wearing a six-gore wool skirt in a muted gray plaid, with a line of dark maroon running through it. Her pullover sweater was dark maroon, with a white blouse under it, the collar pinned sedately at the throat by an antique brooch. For effect, I decided not to mention the heels and wool skirt I'd brought.

"Tony?" she said. "Oh, it's you."

She had an armload of ragged blue bath towels which she dumped on a chair. "I thought I heard someone knock. I couldn't see who it was through the screen." She turned the radio off as she passed and then she opened the screen door to admit me.

"Tony's bringing groceries in from the garage. We just got back from the market. Have a seat. Would you like a cup of coffee? The pot's fresh."

"Yes, please. That's nice." I moved the pile of rags out of the chair and sat down, putting the skirt and shoes on the table in front of me. I saw her eyes stray to them, but she made no comment.

"Isn't this a school day for him?" I asked.

"They're giving the sophomores some sort of academic placement tests. He finished early so they let him go. He's got an appointment with his therapist shortly anyway."

I watched her move about the kitchen, fetching cups and saucers. She had one of those hairstyles that settle into perfect shape with a flick of the head. I butcher my own at six-week intervals with a pair of nail scissors and a two-way mirror, causing salon stylists to pale when they see me. "Who *did* that to you?" they always ask. I wanted perfect waves like hers, but I didn't think I could achieve the effect.

Ramona poured two cups of coffee. "There's something I probably should have mentioned before," she said. She took a ceramic pitcher from the cupboard and filled it with milk, realizing then that I was waiting for her to continue. Her smile was thin. "John Daggett called here Monday night, asking to talk to Tony. I took his number, but Ferrin and I decided it wasn't a good idea. It might not matter much at this point, but I thought you should be aware."

"What made you think of it?"

She hesitated. "I came across the number on the pad by the phone. I'd forgotten all about it."

I could feel a tingle at the back of my neck—that clammy feeling you get when your body overloads on sugar. Something was off here, but I wasn't sure what it was.

"Why bring it up now?" I asked.

"I thought you were tracking his activities early in the week."

"I wasn't aware that I'd told you that."

Her cheeks tinted. "Marilyn Smith called me. She mentioned it."

"How'd Daggett know where to reach you? When I talked to him on Saturday, he had no idea where Tony was and he certainly didn't have your name or number."

"I don't know how he got it," she said. "What difference does it make?"

"How do I know you didn't make a date to meet him Friday night?"

"Why would I do that?" she said.

I stared at her. A millisecond later she realized what I was getting at.

"But I was here Friday night."

"I haven't heard that verified so far."

"That's ridiculous! Ask Tony. He knows I was here. You can check it out yourself."

"I intend to," I said.

Tony thumped up the wooden porch steps, armed with two more grocery bags, his attention diverted as he groped for the screen door handle, missing twice. "Aunt Ramona, can you give me a hand with this?"

She crossed to the door and held it open. Tony spotted me and the green skirt at just about the same time and I saw his gaze jump to his aunt's face quizzically. Her expression was neutral, but she busied herself right away, pushing canned goods aside so he could set one bag on the tabletop. The second bag she took herself and placed on the counter. She sorted through and lifted out a carton of ice cream. "I better get this put away," she murmured. She crossed to the freezer.

"What are you doing here?" Tony said to me.

"I was curious how you were feeling. Your aunt mentioned that you had a migraine Monday night."

"I feel okay."

"What'd you think about the funeral?"

"Bunch of freaks," he said.

"Let's get these unloaded, dear," his aunt said. The two of them began to put groceries away while I sipped my coffee. I couldn't tell if she was deliberately distracting him or not, but that was the effect.

"You need some help?" I asked.

"We can manage," she murmured.

"Who was that lady who went nuts?" Tony asked. Lovella had made a big impression on everyone.

Ramona held up a soft drink in a big plastic bottle. "Stick this in the refrigerator while you're there," she said.

She released the bottle an instant before he'd gotten a good grip on it and he had to scramble to catch it before it toppled to the floor. Had she done that deliberately? He was waiting for my reply so I gave him a brief rendition of the tale. It was gossip, in some ways, but he was as animated as I'd seen him and I hoped to keep his attention.

"I don't mean to interrupt, but Tony does have homework to take care of. Finish your coffee, of course," she said. Her tone suggested that I suck it right down and scram.

"I'm due back at the office anyway," I said, getting up. I looked at Tony. "Could you walk me to my car?"

He glanced at Ramona, whose gaze dropped away from his. She didn't protest. He ducked his head in assent.

He held the door for me while I gathered the skirt

and shoes and turned back to her. "I nearly forgot. Are these yours, by any chance?"

"I'm sure not," she said to me, and then to him, "Don't be long."

He looked like he was on the verge of saying something, but he shrugged instead. He followed me out on the porch and down the steps. I led the way as we circled the house. The path to the street was paved with stepping-stones spaced oddly, so that I had to watch my feet to gauge the distances.

"I have a question," I said as we reached the car.

He was watching me warily by then, interested but on guard.

"I was curious about the migraine you had Friday night. Do you remember how long that one lasted?"

"Friday night?" His voice had a croak in it from surprise.

"That's right. Didn't you have a migraine that night?"

"I guess."

"Think back," I said. "Take your time."

He seemed uncomfortable, casting about for some visual clue. I'd seen him do this before, reading body language so he could adjust his response to whatever was expected of him. I waited in silence, letting his anxiety accumulate.

"I think that's the day I got one. When I came home from school," he said, "but then it cleared."

"What time was that?"

"Real late. After midnight. Maybe two . . . two-thirty, something like that."

"How'd you happen to notice the time?"

"Aunt Ramona made me a couple of sandwiches in the kitchen. It was a real bad headache and I'd been throwing up for hours so I never had dinner. I was starving. I must have looked at the kitchen clock."

"What kind of sandwiches?"

"What?"

"I was wondering what kind she made."

His gaze hung on mine. The seconds ticked away. "Meatloaf," he said.

"Thanks," I said. "That helps."

I opened the VW on the driver's side, tossing skirt and shoes on the passenger seat as I got in. His version was roughly the same as his aunt's, but I could have sworn the "meatloaf" was a wild guess.

I started the car and did a U-turn, heading toward the gates. I caught a glimpse of him in the rearview mirror, already moving toward the house.

22

It's a fact of life that when a case won't break, you have to go through the motions anyway, stirring up the waters, rattling all the cages at the zoo. To that end, on my way into town I did a long detour that included a stop at the trailer park, in hopes that Lovella would still be there. It was obvious to me, as I'm not a fool, that toting a green wool skirt and a pair of black suede heels all over town was a pointless enterprise. No one was going to claim them and if someone did, so what? The articles proved nothing. No one was going to break down sobbing and confess at the mere sight of them. The pop quiz was simply my way of putting them all on notice, making the rounds one more time to announce that I was still on the job and making progress, however insignificant it might appear.

I knocked at the trailer door, but got no response. I jotted a note on the back of a business card, indicating that Lovella should call. I tucked it in the doorjam, went back to my car, and headed for town.

Wayne Smith's office was located on the seventh floor of the Granger Building in downtown Santa Teresa. Aside from the clock tower on the courthouse, the Granger is just about the only structure on State Street that's more than two stories high. Part of the charm of the downtown area is its low-slung look. The flavor, for the most part, is Spanish. Even the trash containers are faced with stucco and rimmed with decorative tile. The telephone booths look like small adobe huts and if you can ignore the fact that the bums use them for urinals, the effect is quaint. There are flowering shrubs along the walk, jacaranda trees, and palms. Low ornamental stucco walls widen in places to form benches for weary shoppers. Everything is clean, well kept, pleasing to the eye.

The Granger Building looks just like hundreds of office buildings constructed in the twenties—yellow brick, symmetrical narrow windows banded with granite friezes, topped by a steeply pitched roof with matching gables. Along the roofline, just below the cornice, there are decorative marble torches affixed to the wall with inexplicable half shells mounted underneath. The style is an anomaly in this town, falling as it does between the Spanish, the Victorian, and the pointless. Still, the building is a landmark, housing a movie theater, a jeweler's, and seven stories of office space.

I checked the wall directory in the marble foyer for Wayne Smith's suite number, which turned out to be 702. Two elevators serviced the building and one was out of order, the doors standing open, the housing mechanism in plain view. It's not a good idea to scrutinize such things. When you see how elevators actually work, you realize how improbable the whole scheme is . . . raising and lowering a roomful of people on a few long wires. Ridiculous.

A fellow in coveralls stood there, mopping his face with a red bandanna.

"How's it going?" I asked, while I waited for the other elevator doors to open.

He shook his head. "Always something, isn't it? Last week it was that one wouldn't work."

The doors slid open and I stepped in, pressing seven. The doors closed and nothing happened for a while. Finally, with a jolt, the elevator began its ascent, stopping at the seventh floor. There was another interminable delay. I pressed the "DOOR OPEN" button. No dice. I tried to guess how long I could survive on just that one ratty piece of chewing gum at the bottom of my handbag. I banged the button with the flat of my hand and the doors slid open.

The corridor was narrow and dimly illuminated, as there was only one exterior window, located at the far end of the hall. Four dark, wood-paneled doors opened off each side, with the names of the professional tenants in gold-leaf lettering that looked as if it had been there since the building went up. There was no activity that I could perceive, no sounds, no muffled telephones ringing. Wayne Smith, C.P.A., was the first door on the right. I pictured a receptionist in a small waiting area, so I simply turned the knob and walked in without knocking. There was only one large room, tawny daylight filtering in through drawn window shades. Wayne Smith was lying on the floor with his legs propped up on the seat of his swivel chair. He turned and looked at me.

"Oh sorry! I thought there'd be a waiting room," I said. "Are you okay?"

"Sure. Come on in," he said. "I was resting my back." He removed his legs from the chair, apparently in some pain. He rolled over on his side and eased himself into an upright position, wincing as he did. "You're Kinsey Millhone. Marilyn pointed you out at the funeral yesterday."

I watched him, wondering if I should lend him a hand. "What'd you do to yourself?"

"My back went out on me. Hurts like a son of a bitch," he said. Once he was on his feet, he dug a fist into the small of his back, twisting one shoulder slightly as if to ease a cramp. He had a runner's body— lean, stringy muscles, narrow through the chest. He looked older than his wife, maybe late forties while I pegged her in her early thirties. His hair was light, worn in a crewcut, like something out of a 1950s high school annual. I wondered if he'd been in the military at some point. The hairstyle suggested that he was hung up in the past, his persona fixed perhaps by some significant event. His eyes were pale and his face was very lined. He moved to the windows and raised all three shades. The room became unbearably bright.

"Have a seat," he said.

I had a choice between a daybed and a molded plastic chair with a bucket seat. I took the chair, doing a surreptitious visual survey while he lowered himself into his swivel chair as though into a steaming sitz bath. He had six metal bookcases that looked like they were made of Erector sets, loosely bolted and sagging slightly from the weight of all the manuals. Brown accordion file cases were stacked up everywhere, his desktop virtually invisible. Correspondence was piled on the floor near his chair, government pamphlets and tax law updates stacked on the window sill. This was not a man you'd want to depend on if you were facing an I.R.S. audit. He looked like the sort who might put you there.

"I just talked to Marilyn. She said you came by the house. We're puzzled by your interest in us."

"Barbara Daggett hired me to investigate her father's death. I'm interested in everyone."

"But why talk to us? We haven't seen the man in years."

"He didn't get in touch last week?"

"Why would he do that?"

"He was looking for Tony Gahan. I thought he might have tried to get a line on him through you."

The phone rang and he reached for it, conducting a business-related conversation while I studied him. He wore chinos, just a wee bit too short, and his socks were the clinging nylon sort that probably went up to his knees. He switched to his good-bye tone, trying to close out his conversation. "Uh-huh, uh-huh. Okay, great. That's fine. We'll do that. I got the forms right here. Deadline is the end of the month. Swell."

He hung up with an exasperated shake of his head.

"Anyway," he said, as a way of getting back to the subject at hand.

"Yeah, right. Anyway," I said, "I don't suppose you remember where you were Friday night."

"I was here, doing quarterly reports."

"And Marilyn was home with the kids?"

He sat and stared at me, a smile flickering off and on. "Are you implying that we might have had a hand in John Daggett's death?"

"Someone did," I said.

He laughed, running a hand across his crewcut as if checking to see if he needed a trim. "Miss Millhone, you've got a hell of a nerve," he said. "The newscast said it was an accident."

I smiled. "The cops still think so. I disagree. I think a lot of people wanted Daggett dead. You and Marilyn are among them."

"But we wouldn't do a thing like that. You can't be serious. I despised the man, no doubt about that, but we're not going to go out and track a man down and kill him. Good God."

I kept my tone light. "But you did have the motive and you had the opportunity."

"You can't hang anything on that. We're decent people. We don't even get parking tickets. John Daggett must have had a lot of enemies."

I shrugged by way of agreement. "The Westfalls," I said. "Billy Polo and his sister, Coral. Apparently, some prison thugs."

"What about that woman who set up such a howl at the funeral?" he said. "She looked like a pretty good candidate to me."

"I've talked to her."

"Well, you better go back and talk to her again. You're wasting time with us. Nobody's going to be arrested on the basis of 'motive' and 'opportunity.'"

"Then you don't have anything to worry about."

He shook his head, his skepticism evident. "Well. I can see you have your work cut out for you. I'd appreciate it if you'd lay off Marilyn in this. She's had trouble enough."

"I gathered as much." I got up. "Thanks for your time. I hope I won't have to bother you again." I moved toward the door.

"I hope so too."

"You know, if you did kill him, or if you know who killed him, I'll find out. Another few days and I'm going to the cops anyway. They'll scrutinize that alibi of yours like you wouldn't believe."

He held his hands out, palms up. "We're innocent until proven otherwise," he said, smiling boyishly.

23

Waiting for the elevator, I replayed the conversation, trying to figure out what I'd missed. On the surface, there was nothing wrong with his response, but I felt irritated and uneasy, maybe just because I wasn't getting anyplace. I banged on the DOWN button. "Come on," I said. The elevator door opened partway. Impatiently, I shoved it back and got on. The doors closed and the elevator descended one floor before it stopped again. The doors opened. Tony Gahan was standing in the corridor, a shopping bag in hand. He seemed as surprised to see me as I was to see him.

"What are you doing here?" he said. He got on the elevator and we descended.

"I had to see someone upstairs," I said. "What about you?"

"A shrink appointment. He's been out of town and now his return flight was delayed. His secretary's supposed to pick him up in an hour so she said to come back at five."

We reached the lobby.

"How are you getting home? Need a ride?" I asked.

He shook his head. "I'm going to hang around down here." He gestured vaguely at the video arcade across the street where some high school kids were horsing around.

"See you later then," I said.

We parted company and I returned to the parking lot behind the building. I got in my car and circled the four blocks to the lot behind my office where I parked. For the time being, I left the skirt and shoes in the backseat.

There were no messages on my answering machine, but the mail was in and I sorted through that, wondering what else to do with myself. Actually, I realized I was exhausted, the emotional charge from Jonah having drained away. I'm not used to drinking that much, for starters, and I tend, being single, to get a lot more sleep. He'd left at 5:00, before it was light, and I'd managed maybe an hour's worth of shut-eye before I'd finally gotten up, jogged, showered, and fixed myself a bite to eat.

I tilted back in my swivel chair and propped my feet up on the desk, hoping no one would begrudge me a snooze. The next time I was aware of anything, the clock hands had dissolved magically from 12:10 to 2:50

and my head was pounding. I staggered to my feet and trotted down the hall to the ladies' room. I peed, washed my hands and face, rinsed my mouth out, and stared at myself in the mirror. My hair was mashed flat in the back and standing straight up everywhere else. The flourescent light in the room made my skin look sickly. Was this the consequence of illicit sex with a married man? "Well, I soitonly hope so," I said. I ducked my head under the faucet and then dried my hair with eight rounds of hot air from a wall-mounted machine that had been installed (the sign said) to help protect me from the dangers of diseases that might be transmitted through paper towel litter. Idly, I wondered what diseases they were worried about. Typhus? Diphtheria?

I could hear my office phone from halfway down the hall and I started to run. I snagged it on the sixth ring, snatching up the receiver with a winded hello.

"This is Lovella," the glum voice said. "I got this note to call you."

I took a deep breath, inventing as I went along. "Right," I said. "I thought we should touch base. We really haven't talked since I saw you in L.A." I sidled around my desk and sat down, still trying to catch my breath.

"I'm mad at you, Kinsey," she said. "Why didn't you tell me you had Daggett's money?"

"To what end? I had a cashier's check, but it wasn't made out to you. So why mention it?"

"Because I'm standing around telling you I'm married to a guy who'd just as soon kill me as look at me and you're telling me to call the rape crisis center, some bullshit like that. And all the time, Daggett had thousands of dollars."

"But he stole the money. Didn't Billy tell you that?"

"I don't care where it came from. I'd just like to have a little something for myself. Now he's dead and she gets everything."

"Who, Essie?"

"Her and that daughter."

"Oh come on, Lovella. He couldn't have left them enough to worry about."

"More than he left me," she said. "If I'd known about the money, I might have talked him out of some."

"Yeah, right. As generous as he was," I said drily. "If you'd gotten your hands on it, you might be dead now instead of him. Unless Billy's been lying to me about the punks from San Luis who were after him." I'd never really taken that story seriously, but maybe it was time I did.

She was silent. I could practically hear her shifting gears. "All I know is I think you're a shit and he was too."

"I'm sorry you feel that way, Lovella. John hired me, and my first loyalty was to him . . . misguided, as it turned out, but that's where I was coming from. You want to vent a little more on the subject before we turn to something else?"

"Yeah. I should have got the money, not someone else. I was the one who got banged around. I still got two cracked ribs and an eye looks like it's all sunk in on one side from the bruise."

"Is that why you freaked out at the funeral?"

Her tone of voice became tempered with sheepishness. "I'm sorry I did that, but I couldn't help myself. I'd been sittin' in some bar drinkin' Bloody Marys since ten o'clock and I guess I got outta hand. But it bugged me, all that Bible talk. Daggett never went to church a day in his life and it didn't seem right. And that old fat-ass claimed she was married to him? I couldn't believe my eyes. She looked like a bulldog."

I had to laugh. "Maybe he didn't marry her for her looks," I said.

"Well, I hope not."

"When did you see him last?"

"At the funeral home, where else?"

"Before that, I mean."

"Day he left L.A.," she said. "Week ago Monday. I never saw him after he took off."

"I thought maybe you hopped a bus on Thursday after I left."

"Well, I didn't."

"But you could have, couldn't you?"

"What for? I didn't even know where he went."

"But Billy did. You could have come up to Coral's last week. You might have met him at the Hub Friday night and bought him a couple of drinks."

Her laugh was sour. "You can't pin that on me. If that was me, how come Coral didn't recognize me, huh?"

"For all I know, she did. You're friends. Maybe she just kept her mouth shut."

"Why would she do that?"

"Maybe she wanted to help you out."

"Coral doesn't even like me. She thinks I'm a slut so why would she help me?"

"She might've had reasons of her own."

"I didn't kill him, Kinsey, if that's what you're getting at."

"That's what everyone says. You're all wide-eyed and innocent. Daggett was murdered and nobody's guilty. Amazing."

"You don't have to take my word for it. Ask Billy. Once he gets back, he can tell you who it was for sure, anyway."

"Oh hey, sounds great. How's he going to manage that?"

There was a pause, as if she'd said something she really wasn't authorized to say. "He thought he recognized somebody at the funeral and then he figured out where he'd seen 'em before," she said reluctantly.

I blinked at the telephone receiver. In a quick flash, I remembered Billy's staring at the little group formed by the Westfalls, Barbara Daggett, and the Smiths. "I don't understand. What's he up to?"

"He set up a meeting," she said. "He wants to find

out if his theory's right and then he said he'd call you."

"He's going to *meet* with her?"

"That's what I said, isn't it?"

"He shouldn't be doing that by himself. Why didn't he notify the police?"

"Because he doesn't want to make a fool of himself in front of them. Suppose he's wrong? He doesn't have any proof, anyway. Just a hunch is all and even that's not a hundred percent."

"Do you have any idea who he was talking about?"

"Uh-uh. He wouldn't tell, but he was pretty happy with himself. He said we might get some money after all."

Oh God, I thought, not blackmail. I could feel my heart sink. Billy Polo wasn't smart enough to pull that off. He'd blow it like he did every other crime he tried. "Where's the meeting taking place?"

"What makes you ask?" she said, turning cagey.

"Because I want to go!"

"I don't think I should tell."

"Lovella, don't do this to me."

"Well, he didn't say I could."

"You've told me this much. Why not the rest? He could be in trouble."

She hesitated, mulling it over. "Down at the beach somewhere. He's not dumb, you know. He made sure it was public. He figured in broad daylight, there wouldn't be any problem, especially with other people around."

"Which beach?"

"What if he gets mad at me?"

"I'll square it with him myself," I said. "I will *swear* I forced the information out of you."

"He's not going to like it if you show up and spoil everything."

"I won't spoil it. I'll lurk in the background and make sure he's okay. That's all I'm talking about."

Silence. She was so slow I thought I'd scream. "Look at it this way," I said. "He might be happy for the help. What if he needs backup?"

"Billy wouldn't need back up from a *woman*."

I closed my eyes, trying to keep my temper in check. "Just give me a hint, Lovella, or I'll come over to the trailer and rip your heart out by the roots." That, she heard.

"You better never tell him I told," she warned.

"Cross my heart and hope to die. Now come on."

"I think it's that parking lot near the boat launch. . . ."

I banged the phone down and snagged my handbag. I locked the office in haste and ran down the hall, going down the back stairs two and three at a time. I'd had to park my car at the far end of the lot and once I got to the pay booth, there were three other cars in front of mine. "Come on, come on," I murmured, banging on the steering wheel.

Finally, it was my turn. I showed the attendant my parking permit and shot through the gate as soon as the bar went up.

Chapel is one way, heading up from the beach, so I had to turn right, take a left, and hit the one-way street going down again. I caught the light wrong at 101 so that delayed me. I didn't want to miss this one. I didn't want to show up two minutes late and miss the only chance I might have. I pictured a citizen's arrest . . . me and Billy Polo saving the day.

The light turned green and I crossed the highway. Two blocks more and I reached Cabana where I took a right turn. The entrance to the lot I wanted was all the way around the bend near Santa Teresa City College. I got a ticket from the machine and threaded my way along the perimeter of the lot. I scanned the parked cars, hoping for a glimpse of Billy's white Chevy. The marina was on my right, the sun reflecting starkly from the white sails of a stately boat as it glided out of the harbor. The boat launch itself was at the very end of the parking lot, through a second parking gate. I pulled a second ticket and the arm went up. I found a slot and left my car, proceeding on foot.

Four joggers passed me. There were people on the boat dock, people on the walk, people by the snack shop and the public restrooms. I broke into a trot, searching the landscape ahead of me for some sign of Billy or the blonde. I heard three hollow pops in quick succession dead ahead. I ran. No one else was reacting, but I could have sworn it was the sound of shots.

I reached the boat launch, where the parking lot slants down into the water. There was no one in sight.

No one running, no one leaving the scene in haste. The air was still, the water lapping softly at the asphalt. Two pontoon piers extend into the water about thirty feet, but both were empty, no boats or pedestrians in sight. I did a three-sixty turn, surveying every foot of the area. And then I spotted him. He was lying on his side by a boat trailer, one arm caught under him awkwardly. He struggled, gasping, and turned himself over on his back. I crossed the macadam rapidly.

A man in cutoffs had come out of a snack shop and he peered at me as I went past. "Is that guy okay?"

"Call the cops. Get an ambulance," I snapped.

I knelt beside Billy, angling so he could see me. "It's me," I said. "Don't panic. You'll be fine. We'll have help here in a second."

Billy's eyes strayed to mine. His face was gray and there was a widening puddle of quite red blood spreading out under him. I took his hand and held it. A crowd was beginning to collect, people running from all directions. I could hear them buzzing at my back.

Somebody handed me a beach towel. "You want to cover him with this?"

I grabbed the towel. I let go of him long enough to unbutton his shirt, opening it so I could see what I was dealing with. There was a hole in his belly. He must have been shot from behind, because what I was looking at was an exit wound, ragged, welling with blood. The slug must have severed the abdominal aorta. A coil of his lower intestine was visible, gray and glistening, bulging through the hole. I could feel my hands start to shake, but I kept my expression neutral. He was watching me, trying to read my face. I made a pad of the towel, pressing it against the wound to staunch the flow of blood.

He groaned, breathing rapidly. He had one hand resting on his chest and his fingers fluttered. I took his hand again, squeezing hard.

He tilted his head. "Where's . . . my leg? I can't feel nothin' down there."

I glanced down at his right knee. The pantleg looked like it had caught on a nail. Blood and bone seemed to blossom through the tear.

"Don't sweat it. They can fix that. You'll be fine," I said. I didn't mention the blood soaking through the towel. I thought he probably knew about that.

"I'm gut-shot."

"I know. Relax. It's not bad. The ambulance is on its way."

The hand I held was icy, his fingers pale. There were questions I should have asked, but I didn't. I couldn't. You don't intrude on someone's dying with a bullshit interrogation like you're some kind of pro. This was just me and him and nothing else entered into it.

I studied his face, sending love through my eyes, willing him to live. His hair looked curlier than I remembered it. With my free hand, I moved it away from his forehead. Sweat beaded on his upper lip.

"I'm goin' . . . I can feel myself goin' out . . ." He

clutched my hand convulsively, bucking against a surge of pain.

"Take it easy. You'll be fine."

He began to hyperventilate and then his struggle subsided. I could see the life drain away, see it all fade—color, energy, awareness, pain. Death comes in a gathering cloud that settles like a veil. Billy Polo sighed, his gaze still pinned on my face. His hand relaxed in mine, but I held on.

24

I sat on the curb near the snack shop and stared at the asphalt. The proprietor had brought me a can of Coke and I held the cold metal against my temple. I felt sick, but there wasn't anything wrong with me. Lieutenant Feldman had appeared and he was hunkered over Billy's body, talking to the lab guys, who were bagging his hands. The ambulance had backed around and waited with its doors open, as if to shield the body from the public view. Two black-and-whites were parked nearby, radios providing a squawking counterpoint to the murmurs of the gathering crowd. Violent death is a spectator sport and I could hear them trading comments about the way the final quarter had been played. They weren't being cruel, just curious. Maybe it was good for them to see how grotesque homicide really is.

The beat officers, Gutierrez and Pettigrew, had arrived within minutes of Billy's demise and they'd radioed for the CSI unit. The two of them would probably drive over to the trailer park to break the news to Coral and Lovella. I felt I should ride along, but I couldn't bring myself to volunteer yet. I'd go, but for the moment, I was having trouble coping with the fact of Billy's death. It had happened so fast. It was so irrevocable. I found it hard to accept that we couldn't rewind the tape and play the last fifteen minutes differently. I would arrive earlier. I would warn him off and he could walk away unharmed. He'd tell me his theory and then I'd buy him the beer I'd promised him that first night at the Hub.

Feldman appeared. I found myself staring at his pantlegs, unable to look up. He lit a cigarette and came down to my level, perching on the curb. I hugged my knees, feeling numb. I barely know the man, but what I've seen of him I've always liked. He looks like a cross between a Jew and an Indian—a large flat face, high cheekbones, a big hooked nose. He's a big man, probably forty-five, with a cop haircut, cop clothes, a deep rumbling voice. "You want to bring me up to speed on this?" he said.

It was the act of opening my mouth to speak that brought the tears. I held myself in check, willing them back. I shook my head, struggling with the nearly overwhelming rush of regret. He handed me a handkerchief and I pressed it to my eyes, then folded it, addressing my remarks to the oblong of white cotton. There was an "F" embroidered in one corner with a thread coming loose.

"Sorry," I murmured.

"That's okay. Take your time."

"He was such a screw-up," I said. "I guess that's what gets me. He thought he was so smart and so tough."

I paused. "I guess you never know which people will affect your life," I said.

"He never said who shot him?"

I shook my head. "I didn't ask. I didn't want the last minutes of his life taken up with that stuff. I'm sorry."

"Well, he might not have said anyway. What was the setup?"

I started talking, saying anything that came to mind. He let me ramble till I finally took control of myself and began to lay it out systematically. After hundreds of reports, I know the drill. I cited chapter and verse while he nodded, making notes in a battered black notebook.

When I finished, he tucked his ballpoint pen away and shoved the notebook back into the inside pocket of his suitcoat. He got up and I rose with him, automatically.

"What next?" I asked.

"Actually, I got Daggett's file sitting on my desk," he said. "Robb told me you tagged it a homicide and I thought I'd take a look. We had a double killing, one of those execution-style shootings, up on the Bluffs late yesterday and we've had to put a lot of manpower on that one, so I haven't had a chance as yet. It'd help if you came down to the station and talked to Lieutenant Dolan yourself."

"Let me see Billy's sister first," I said. "This is the second brother she's lost in the whole Daggett mess."

"You don't think there's any chance she's the one who plugged him?"

I shook my head. "I thought she might connect to Daggett's death, but I can't picture her involved in this. Unless I'm missing something big. For one thing, he wouldn't have to meet her out in public like this. It was someone at the funeral, I'm almost sure."

"Make a list and we'll take it from there," he said.

I nodded. "I can also stop by the office and make some copies of my file reports. And Lovella may know more than she's told us so far." It felt good, turning everything over to him. He could have it all. Essie and Lovella and the Smiths.

Pettigrew approached, holding a small plastic Ziploc bag by one corner. In it were three empty brass casings. "We found these over by that pickup truck. We're sealing off the whole parking lot until the guys have a chance to go over it."

I said, "You might check the trash bins. That's where I found the skirt and shoes after Daggett was killed."

Feldman nodded, then gave the shells a cursory look. "Thirty-twos," he remarked.

I felt a cold arrow shoot up my spine. My mouth

went dry. "My thirty-two was stolen from my car a few days ago," I said. "Gutierrez took the report."

"A lot of thirty-twos around, but we'll keep that in mind," Feldman said to me, and then to Pettigrew, "Let's hustle these folk out of here. And be polite."

Pettigrew moved away and Feldman turned to study me. "Are you all right?"

I nodded, wishing I could sit down again, afraid once I did I'd be stuck.

"Anything you want to add before I let you go?"

I closed my eyes for a moment, thinking back. I know the snapping sound a .32 makes when fired and the shots I'd heard weren't like that. "The shots," I said. "They sounded odd to me. Hollow. More like a pop than a bang."

"A silencer?"

"I've never heard one except on TV," I said, sheepishly.

"I'll have the lab take a look at the slugs, though I don't know where anybody'd get a silencer in this town." He made another quick note in his book.

"You can probably order one from the back of a magazine," I said.

"Ain't that the truth."

The photographer was snapping pictures and I could see Feldman's gaze flick in that direction. "Let me tend to this guy. He's new. I want to make sure he covers everything I need."

He excused himself and crossed to Billy's body

where he engaged in a conversation with the forensic photographer, using gestures to describe the various angles he wanted.

Maria Gutierrez came up to me. "We're going out to the trailer park. Gerry said you might want to come."

"I'll follow in my car," I said. "You know where it is?"

"We know the park. We can meet you there if you want."

"I'm going to see if Billy's car is here in the lot. I'll be along shortly, but don't wait on my account."

"Right," she said.

I watched them pull out and then I worked my way through the lot, checking the vehicles in the area adjacent to the boat launch. I spotted the Chevy three rows from the entrance, tucked between two RV's. The temporary sticker was still on the windshield. The windows were down. I stuck my head in without touching anything. The car looked clean to me. Nothing in the front seat. Nothing in the back. I went around to the passenger window and peered in, checking the floorboards from that side. I don't even know what I was hoping for. A hint, some suggestion of where we might go from here. It looked as if Feldman might initiate a formal investigation after all, and glad as I was to turn it over to him, I still couldn't quite let go.

I stopped by my car and picked up the skirt and shoes, which I handed over to Lieutenant Feldman. I told him where to find Billy's car and then I finally got back in mine and took off. In my heart, I knew I'd been stalling to allow Pettigrew and Gutierrez a chance to deliver the news of Billy's death. That has to be the worst moment in anybody's life, finding two uniformed cops at your door, their expressions somber, voices grave.

By the time I got to the trailer park, the word had apparently spread. By some telepathic process, people were collecting in twos and threes, all staring at the trailer uncomfortably, chatting in low tones. The trailer door was closed and I heard nothing as I approached, but my appearance had generated conversation at my back.

A fellow stepped forward. "You a family friend? Because she's had bad news. I wasn't sure if you were aware," he said.

"I was there," I said. "She knows me. How long ago did the officers leave?"

"Two minutes. They were real good about it . . . talked to her a long time, making sure she was all right. I'm Fritzy Roderick. I manage the park," he said, offering me his hand.

"Kinsey Millhone," I said. "Is anybody with her now?"

"I don't believe so, and we haven't heard a peep. We were just talking among ourselves here . . . the neighbors and all . . . wondering if someone ought to sit with her."

"Is Lovella in there?"

"I don't know the name. Is she a relative?"

"Billy's ex-girlfriend," I said. "Let me see if I can find out what's going on. If she needs anything, I'll let you know."

"I'd appreciate that. We'd like to help any way we can."

I knocked at the trailer door, uncertain what to expect. Coral opened it a crack and when she saw it was me, she let me in. Her eyes were reddened, but she seemed in control. She sat down on a kitchen chair and picked up her cigarette, giving the ash a flick. I sat down on the banquette.

"I'm sorry about Billy," I said.

She glanced at me briefly. "Did he know?"

"I think so. When I found him, he was already in shock and fading fast. I don't think he suffered much if that's what you're asking."

"I'll have to tell Mom. The two cops who came said they'd do it, but I said no." Her voice trailed off, hoarse from grief or the head cold. "He always knew he'd die young, you know? Like when we'd see old people on the street, crippled or feeble. He said he'd never end up like them. I used to beg him to straighten up his act, but he had to do everything his way." She lapsed into silence.

"Where's Lovella?"

"I don't know," Coral said. "The trailer was empty when I got here."

"Coral, I wish you'd fill me in. I need to know what

was going on. Billy told me three different versions of the same tale."

"Why look at me? I don't know anything."

"But you know more than I do."

"That wouldn't take much."

"Level with me. Please. Billy's dead now. There's nothing left to protect. Is there?"

She stared at the floor for a moment and then she sighed and stubbed out her cigarette. She got up and started clearing the table, running water in the tiny stainless steel kitchen sink. She squirted in Ivory Liquid, dropping silverware and plates into the mounting suds, talking in a low monotone as she worked. "Billy was already up at San Luis when Daggett got there. Daggett had no idea Doug was related to us, so Billy struck up an acquaintance. We were both of us bitter as hell."

"Billy told me he and Doug were never close."

"Bullshit. He just told you that so you wouldn't suspect him. The three of us were always thick as thieves."

"So you did intend to kill him," I said.

"I don't know. We just wanted to make him pay. We wanted to punish him. We figured we'd find a way once we got close. Then Daggett's cellmate died and he got all that money."

"And you thought that would compensate?"

"Not me. I knew I'd never be happy till the day

Daggett died, but I couldn't do it myself. I mean, kill someone in cold blood. Billy was the one who said the money would help. We couldn't bring Doug back, but at least we'd have something. He always knew Daggett lifted the cash, but he didn't think he'd get away with it. Daggett gets out of prison and sure enough, he's home free. He starts throwin' money around. Lovella calls Billy and we decide to go for it."

"So the guys up at San Luis never did figure it out," I said.

"Nope. Once Billy saw Daggett was in the clear, we decided to rip him off."

"And Lovella was part of it?"

Coral nodded, rinsing a plate, which she placed in the dish rack. "They got married the same week he got out, which suited us just fine. We figured if she didn't talk him out of it, she could steal it. . . ."

"And failing that, what?"

"We never meant to kill anyone," she said. "We just wanted the money. We didn't have much time anyway because he'd already spent part of it. He went through five grand before we could bat an eye and we knew if we didn't move fast, he'd blow the whole wad."

"You didn't realize he intended to give the rest of it to Tony Gahan?"

"Of course not," she said with energy. "Billy couldn't believe it when you told him about that. We thought most of it was still around somewhere. We thought we could still get our hands on it."

I watched her face, trying to compute the information she was giving me. "You mean you set Daggett up with Lovella so you could con him out of twenty-five thousand bucks?"

"That's right," she said.

"You were splitting it three ways! That's a little over eight grand apiece."

"So?"

"Coral, eight grand is nothing."

"Bullshit, it's nothing! Do you know what I could do with eight grand? How much do you have? Do you have eight grand?"

"No."

"So, all right. Don't tell me it's nothing."

"All right. It's a fortune," I said. "What went wrong?"

"Nothing at first. Billy called him up and said the guys at San Luis heard about the money and they wanted it back. He told Daggett they were coming after him, so that's when Daggett split."

"How'd you know he'd hightail it up here?"

"Billy told Daggett he'd help him out," she said with a shrug. "And then when Daggett got into town, Billy started working on him, trying to get him to fork it over to us. He said he'd act as a go-between, smooth it all over and get him off the hook."

"He'd already given it to me at that point, right?"

"Sure, but we didn't know that. He acted like he still had it handy. He acted like he might turn it over to Billy, but that was all crap. Of course, he was drunk all the time by then."

"So he was conning you while you conned him."

"He was just stringing us along!" she said indignantly. "Billy met him Tuesday night and Daggett was real cagey. Said he needed time to get his hands on it. He said he'd bring it in Thursday night, so Billy met him at the Hub again, only Daggett said he needed one more day. Billy really laid into him. He said these guys were getting very pissed and might kill Daggett anyway, whether he gave 'em the money or not. Daggett got real nervous and swore he'd have it the next night, which was Friday."

"The night he died."

"Right. I was working that night, and I was supposed to keep an eye on him, which I did. Billy decided to come late, just to make him sweat, and before I knew what was happening this woman showed up and started buying him drinks. You know the rest."

"Billy told me you took some kind of cold cap and crashed in the back room. Was that true?"

"I was just laying low," she said. "When I saw Daggett leave, I knew Billy'd have a fit. I already felt bad enough without putting up with his bullshit."

"And Billy finally figured out who she was?"

"I don't know. I guess. I wasn't here this morning, so I don't know what he was up to."

"Look. I have to go down to the police station and tell Lieutenant Dolan what's been going on. If Lovella comes back, please tell her it's urgent that she get in touch. Will you do that?"

Coral wedged the last clean dish against the pile in the rack. She filled a glass with water and poured it over the lot of them, rinsing off the few remaining suds. She turned to look at me with a gaze that chilled. "Do you think she killed Billy?"

"I don't know."

"Will you tell me if you find out it's her?"

"Coral, if she did it, she's dangerous. I don't want you in the middle of this."

"But will you tell me?"

I hesitated. "Yes."

"Thank you."

25

I had a brief chat with the manager of the trailer park. I gave him my card and asked him to call me if Lovella came back. I didn't really trust Coral to do it. The last I saw of him, he was tapping at her door. I got in my car and headed over to the police station. I asked for Lieutenant Dolan at the desk, but he and Feldman were in a section meeting. The clerk buzzed Jonah for me and he came as far as the locked door, admitting me into the corridor beyond. Both of us were circumspect—pleasant, noncommittal. No one observing us could have guessed that mere hours ago, we'd been cavorting stark naked on my Wonder Woman sheets.

"What happened when you got home?" I asked.

"Nothing. Everybody was asleep," he said. "We have something in the lab you might want to see." He moved down the hall to the right and I followed. He looked back at me. "Feldman had the guys check the trash bins at your suggestion. We think we found the silencer."

"You did?" I said, startled.

He opened the half-door into the crime lab, holding it for me as I passed in front of him. The lab tech was out, but I could see Billy's bloody shirt, tagged, on the counter, along with an object I couldn't at first identify.

"What's that," I said. "Is *that* it?" What I was looking at was a large plastic soft drink bottle, painted black, lying on its side with a hole visible in the bottom.

"A disposable silencer. Handmade. A sound suppressor, in effect. It's been wiped clean of prints," Jonah said.

"I don't understand how it works."

"I had to have Krueger explain it to me. The bottle's filled with rags. Take a look. The barrel of the gun is usually wrapped with tape and the bottle affixed to it with a one-inch hose clamp. The soda bottle has a reinforced bottom, but it's only effective for a few shots because the noise level increases each time as the exit hole gets larger. Obviously, the device works best at close range."

"God, Jonah. How do people know about these things? I never heard of it."

He picked up a paperbound booklet from the counter behind me, flipping through it carelessly so I could see. Every page was filled with diagrams and photographs, illustrating how disposable silencers could be made out of common household objects. "This is from a gun shop down in Los Angeles," he said. "You ought to see what you can do with a length of window screen or a pile of old bottle caps."

"Jesus."

Lieutenant Becker stuck his head in the door. "Line one for you," he said to Jonah and then disappeared. Jonah glanced at the lab phone, but the call hadn't been transferred.

"Let me take this and I'll be right back," Jonah said. "Hang on."

"Right," I murmured. I leaned toward the silencer, trying to remember where I'd seen something similar. Through the hole in the bottom, I caught a glimpse of the blue terrycloth filling the interior. When I realized what it was, my mental process clicked in, and the interior machinery fired up. I knew.

I straightened up and crossed to the door, checking the corridor, which was empty. I headed for my car. I could still see Ramona Westfall coming up the basement stairs with an armload of ragged blue bath towels, which she'd dumped on the chair. The plastic bottle had been filled with a soft drink which she nearly dropped as she passed it to Tony to refrigerate.

I stopped by the office long enough to try the Westfall's number. The phone rang four times and then the machine clicked in.

"Hello. This is Ramona Westfall. Neither Ferrin nor I can come to the phone right now, but if you'll leave your name, telephone number, and a brief message, we'll get back to you as soon as possible. Thank you." I hung up at the sound of the tone.

I checked my watch. It was 4:45. I had no idea where Ramona was, but Tony had a 5:00 appointment just a few blocks away. If I could intercept him, I could lean on him some about her alibi since he represented the only confirmation she had. How had she pulled it off? He had to be on heavy medication for the migraine, so she might have slipped out while he was sleeping, adjusting the kitchen clock when she got back so she'd be covered for the time of Daggett's death. Once she was home again, Tony had wakened—she'd probably made sure of that so she'd have someone to corroborate the time. She'd fixed the sandwiches, chatting pleasantly while he ate, and as soon as he went back to bed, she changed the clock again. Or maybe it wasn't even as complicated as that. Maybe the watch Daggett wore had been set for 2:37 and then submerged. She could have killed him earlier and been home by 2:00. Tony may have realized what she'd done and tried to shield her when he understood how close my investigation was bringing me. It was also possible that he was in cahoots with her, but I hoped that wasn't the case.

I locked my office and went down the front stairs, trotting up State Street on foot. The Granger Building was only three blocks up and it made more sense than hopping in my car and driving all the way around to the parking lot behind the building. Tony might still be hanging out at the arcade across the street. I had to get him before she had a chance to intercept. I didn't want him going home. She had to realize things were getting hot, especially since I'd shown up at the house with the shoes and skirt. All I needed from him was an indication I was on the right track and then I'd call Feldman. I thought about the Close, which I knew would be gloomy with the gathering twilight. I didn't want to go back there unless I had to.

I checked the arcade. Tony was at the rear, on the right-hand side, playing a video game. He was concentrating fully and I didn't think he was aware of me. I waited, watching small creatures being blasted off the screen. His scores weren't that good and I was tempted to have a try at it myself. The creatures suddenly froze into place, random weapons firing off here and there without regard to his manipulations. He looked up. "Oh hi."

"I need to talk to you," I said.

His eyes moved to the clock. "I got an appointment in five minutes. Can it wait?"

"I'll walk you over. We can talk on the way."

He picked up his package and we moved out to the street. The fading afternoon sun seemed bright after the darkness of the arcade. Even so, the fog was rolling in, November twilight beginning to descend. I punched the button at the crosswalk and we waited for the light to change. "Last Friday . . . the night Daggett died, do you remember where your uncle was?"

"Sure. Milwaukee, on a business trip."

"Are you on medication for the migraines?"

"Well, yeah. Tylenol with codeine. Compazine if I'm throwing up. How come?"

"Is it possible your aunt went out while you slept?"

"No. I don't know. I don't understand what you're getting at," he said.

I thought he was stalling, but I kept my mouth shut. We'd reached the Granger Building and Tony moved into the lobby ahead of me.

The elevator that had been out of order was now in operation, but the other one was immobilized, doors open, the housing visible, two sawhorses in front of the opening with a warning sign.

Tony was watching me warily. "Did she say she went out?"

"She claims she was home with you."

"So?"

"Come on, Tony. You're the only alibi she has. If you were zonked on medication, how do you know where she was?"

He pressed the elevator button.

The doors opened and we got on. The doors closed without incident and we went up to six. I checked his face as we stepped into the hallway. He was clearly conflicted, but I didn't want to press just yet. We headed down the corridor toward the suite his psychiatrist apparently occupied.

"Is there anything you want to talk about?" I asked.

"No," he said, his voice breaking with indignation. "You're crazy if you think she had anything to do with it."

"Maybe you can explain that to Feldman. He's in charge of the case."

"I'm not talking to the cops about her," Tony said. He tried the office door and found it locked. "Shit, he's not here."

There was a note taped to the door. He reached up to snatch the piece of paper, turning the movement into an abrupt shove. Next thing I knew, I was on my hands and knees and he'd taken off. He banged on the elevator button and then veered right. I was up and running when I heard the door leading to the stairway slam back against the wall. I ran, banging into the stairwell only seconds after he did. He was already heading up.

"Tony! Come on. Don't do this."

He was moving fast, his footsteps scratching on the concrete stairs. His labored breathing echoed against the walls as he went up. I don't keep fit for nothin', folks. He had youth on me, but I was in good shape. I flung my bag aside and grabbed the rail, starting up after him, mounting the steps two at a time. I peered upward as I ran, trying to catch sight of him. He reached the seventh floor and kept on going. How many floors did this building have?

"Tony. Goddamn it! Wait up! What are you doing?"

I heard another door bang up there. I stepped up my pace.

I reached the landing at the top. The elevator repairman had apparently left the door to the attic unlocked and Tony had shot through the gap, slamming the door behind him. I snatched the handle, half expecting to find it locked. The door flew open and I pushed through, pausing on the threshold. The space was dim and hot and dry, largely empty except for a small door opening off to my right where the elevator brake, sheave, and drive motors were located. I ducked my head into the cramped space briefly, but it appeared to be empty. I pulled out and peered around. The roof was another twenty feet up, the rafters steeply pitched, timbers forming a ninety-degree angle where they met.

Silence. I could see a square of light on the floor and I looked up. A wooden ladder was affixed to the wall to my right. At the top, a trap door was open and waning daylight filtered down. I scanned the attic. There was an electrical panel sitting on some boxes. It looked like some kind of old light board from the theater on the ground floor. For some reason, there was a massive papier-mâché bird standing to one side . . . a blue jay, wearing a painted business suit. Wooden chairs were stacked, seat to seat, to my left.

"Tony?"

I put a hand on one of the ladder rungs. He might well be hiding somewhere, waiting for me to head up to the roof so he could ease out and down the steps again. I started up, climbing maybe ten feet so I could survey the attic from a better vantage point. There was no movement, no sound of breathing. I looked up again and started climbing cautiously. I'm not afraid of heights, but I'm not fond of them either. Still, the ladder seemed secure and I couldn't figure out where else he might be.

When I got to the top, I pulled myself into a sitting position and peered around. The trap came out in a small alcove, hidden behind an ornamental pediment, with a matching pediment halfway down the length of the roof. From the ground, the two of them had always looked strictly decorative, but I could see now that one disguised a brace of air vents. There was only a very narrow walkway around the perimeter of the roof, protected by a short parapet. The steep pitch of the roof would make navigating hazardous.

I peered down into the attic, hoping to see Tony dart out of hiding and into the stairwell. There was no sign of him up here, unless he'd eased around to the far side. Gingerly, I got to my feet, positioning myself between the nearly vertical roofline on my left and the ankle-high parapet on my right. I was actually walking in a metal rain gutter that popped and creaked under my weight. I didn't like the sound. It suggested that any minute now the metal would buckle, toppling me off the side.

I glanced down eight floors to the street, which

didn't seem that far away. The buildings across from me were two stories high and lent a comforting illusion of proximity, but pedestrians still seemed dwarfed by the height. The streetlights had come on, and the traffic below was thinning. To my right, half a block away, the bell tower at the Axminster Theater was lighted from within, the arches bathed in tawny gold and warm blue. The drop had to be eighty feet. I tried to remember the velocity of a falling object. Something-something per foot per second was as close as I could come, but I knew the end result would be an incredible splat. I paused where I was and raised my voice. "Tony!"

I caught a flash of movement out of the corner of my eye and my heart flew into my throat. The plastic bag he'd been carrying was eddying downward, floating lazily. Coming from where? I peered over the parapet. I could see one of the niches that cut into the wall just below the cornice molding. The frieze that banded the building had always looked like marble from the street, but I could see now that it was molded plaster, the niche itself down about four feet and to the left. A half shell extended out maybe fifteen inches at the bottom edge and it held what was probably meant to be some sort of lamp with a torch flame, all molded plaster like the frieze. Tony was sitting there, his face turned up to mine. He'd climbed over the edge and he was now perched in the shallow ornamental niche, his arm locked around the torch, legs dangling. He'd taken a wig out of the bag he carried, donning it, looking up at me with a curious light in his eyes.

I was looking at the blonde who'd killed Daggett.

For a moment, we stared at each other, saying nothing. He had the cocky look of a ten-year-old defying his mom, but under the bravado I sensed a kid who was hoping someone would step in and save him from himself.

I put a hand on the pediment to steady myself. "You coming up or shall I come down?" I kept my tone matter-of-fact, but my mouth was dry.

"I'll be going down in a minute."

"Maybe we could talk about that," I said.

"It's too late," he said, smiling impishly. "I'm poised for flight."

"Will you wait there until I reach you?"

"No grabbing," he warned.

"I won't grab."

My palms were damp and I wiped them on my jeans.

I squatted, turning to face the roof, extending a foot tentatively down along the frieze. I glanced down, trying to find some purchase. Garlands of pineapple, grapes, and fig leaves formed a bas relief design that wound across the face of the building. "How'd you do this?" I asked.

"I didn't think about it. I just did it. You don't have to come down. It won't help."

"I just don't want to talk to you hanging over the edge," I said, lying through my teeth. I was hoping to get close enough to nab him, ignoring visions of grappling with him at that height. I steadied myself, tucking a toe into the shallow crevice formed by a curling vine. The niche was only four feet away. At ground level, I wouldn't have given it a thought.

I sensed that he was watching me, but I didn't dare look. I held onto the parapet, lowering my left foot.

He said, "You're not going to talk me out of this."

"I just want to hear your side of it," I said.

"Okay."

"You won't try to kill me, will you?" I asked.

"Why would I? You never did anything to me."

"I'm glad you recognize that. Now I feel really confident." I heard him laugh lightly at my tone.

I've seen magazine pictures of a man who can climb a vertical cliff face in a pair of tennis shoes, holding himself with the tips of his fingers tucked into small cracks that he discovers as he ascends. This has always seemed like a ludicrous pursuit and I usually flip to an article that makes more sense. The sight of the photographs makes me hyperventilate, especially the ones taken from his vantage point, staring down into some yawning crevasse. Maybe, if the truth be known, I'm more anxious about heights than I let on.

I allowed my right foot to inch down again as far as the lip of the niche. I found a handhold, down and to the right. Felt like a pineapple, but I wasn't sure. Pinning my safety to a phony piece of fruit. I had to be nuts.

The hardest part was actually letting go of the coping once my foot was resting safely in the recess. I had to bend my knees, turning slightly to the right, sinking little by little until I could take a seat. Tony, ever gallant, actually gave me a hand, steadying me until I eased down next to him. I'm not a brave soul. I'm really not. I just didn't want him flying off the side of that building while I looked on. I locked my left arm around the torch, just below his, holding onto my wrist with my right hand. I could feel sweat trickle down my sides.

"I hate this," I said. I was winded, not from effort but from apprehension.

"It's not bad. Just don't look down."

Of course I did. The minute he said that I had an irresistible desire to peek. I was hoping somebody would spot us, like they always do on TV. Then the cops would come with nets and the fire engines would arrive and somebody would talk him out of this. I'm an organism of the earth, a Taurus. I was never born of air, of water, or of fire. I'm a creature of gravity and I could feel the ground whisper. The same thing happens to me in old hotels when I'm staying on the twenty-second floor. I open a window and want to fling myself out.

"Oh, Jesus. This is such a bad idea," I said.

"For you maybe. Not for me."

I tried to think back to my short life as a cop and the standard procedure for dealing with potential suicides.

Stall for time was the first rule. I didn't recall any-thing about hanging your ass off the side of a building, but here I was. I said, "What's the story, babe. You want to tell me what's been going on?"

"There's not much to it. Daggett called the house on Monday. Aunt Ramona made a note of the number so I called him back. I dreamed about killing him. I couldn't wait. I had fantasies for months, every night before I went to sleep. I wanted to catch him with a wire around his neck and twist till it bit into his wind-pipe and his tongue bugged out. It doesn't take that long. I forget what that's called now . . ."

"Garroting," I supplied.

"Yeah, I would have liked that, but then I figured it was better if it looked like an accident because that way I could get away with it."

"Why'd he call?"

"I don't know," Tony said uncomfortably. "He was drunk and blubbering, said he was sorry and wanted to make it up to me for what he did. I go, 'Fine. Why don't we meet and talk?' And he goes, 'It would mean so much to me, son.'" Tony was acting out the parts, using a quavering falsetto for Daggett. "So then I tell him I'll meet him the next night at this bar he's calling from, the Hub, which didn't give me much time to put together this getup."

"Was that Ramona's skirt?"

"Nah, I got it at the Salvation Army thrift store for a

buck. The sweater was another fifty cents and the shoes were two bucks."

"Where'd the sweater go?"

"I tossed it in another trash can a block away from the first. I thought it would all end up at the dump."

"What about the wig?"

"That was Aunt Ramona's from years ago. She didn't even know it was gone."

"Why'd you keep it?"

"I don't know. I was going to put it back in her closet where I got it, in case I needed it again. I had it on at the beach, but then I remembered Billy already knew who I was." He broke off, obviously confused. "I might have told my shrink about the whole thing if he'd been here. Anyway, the wig's expensive. This is real hair."

"The color's nice too," I said. I mean, where else could I go with this? Even Tony recognized the absurdity and he flashed me a look.

"You're humoring me, right?"

"Of course I'm humoring you!" I snapped. "I didn't come down here so we could have an argument."

He did a half shrug, smiling sheepishly.

I said, "Did you actually meet him there Tuesday night?"

"Not really. I went. I had it all worked out by then, only when I walk in, he's sittin' at this table talking to some guy. Turned out to be Billy Polo, but I didn't know it at the time. Billy was sitting in this booth with his back to the door. I saw Daggett, but I didn't realize he had company till I was right there in front of him. I veer off the minute I spot Billy, but by then he's had a good look at me. I'm not worried. I figure I'll never see him again anyway. I hang around for a while but they're really into it. I can tell Billy's leaning all over him and isn't likely to let up so I take a hike and go home."

"Was this one of the nights you had a migraine?"

"Yeah," he said. "I mean, some are real and some are fake, but I have to have a pattern, know what I mean? So I can come and go as I please."

"How'd you get down to the Hub, by cab?"

"My bike. The night I killed him, I rode down and left it at the marina and then I called a cab from a pay phone and took it over to the Hub."

"How'd you know he'd show up?"

"Because he called again and I said I'd be there."

"He never twigged to the fact that you'd showed up the first time in drag?"

"How was he going to know? He hadn't seen me since way before the trial. I was twelve, thirteen, something like that, a fat boy back then. I figured even if he guessed, I'd do it anyway, kill his ass . . . and once he was dead, who would know?"

"What went wrong?"

His brow furrowed. "I don't know. Well, I do. The plan went fine. It was something else." His eyes met mine and he looked every bit of fifteen, the blonde wig adding softness and dimension to a face that was nearly formless with youth. I could see how he'd pass as a woman, slim, with a clear complexion, sweet smile on his wide mouth. He looked down at the street and for a moment I thought he meant to swing out into space.

"When I was eight, I had these pet mice," he said. "Really sweet. I kept 'em in this cage with a wheel and a water bottle hanging upside down. Mom didn't think I'd take care of 'em but I did. I'd cut up strips of paper in the bottom of the cage so they could nest. Anyway, the girl mouse had these babies. They couldn't have been as long as this." He was indicating the end of his little finger. "Bald," he went on. "Just little bitty old things. We had to go out of town one weekend and when we got back the cat had tried to get in the cage. Knocked it off the desk and everything. The mice were gone. Probably the cat got 'em except for this one that had been laying in all these paper shreds. Well, the water had spilled so the paper was damp and the little thing must have had pneumonia or something because it was panting, like it couldn't breathe good. I tried to keep it warm. I watched it for hours and it just kept getting worse and worse so I decided I better . . . you know, do away with it. So it wouldn't suffer anymore."

He leaned forward, swinging his feet back and forth.

"Don't do that," I murmured anxiously. "Finish the story. I want to know what happened next."

He looked over at me then, his tone of voice mild. "I

tossed it in the toilet. That's the only way I could think of to kill it. I couldn't crush it, so I just figured I'd flush it away. The little thing was half dead anyway and I thought I'd be doing it a favor, putting it out of its misery. But before I could do it, that little tiny hairless baby started struggling. You could tell it was in a total panic, trying to get out of there, like it knew what was happening . . ." He paused, dashing at his eyes. "Daggett did that and now I can't get away from the look on his face, you know? I see it all day long. He knew. Which was fine with me. I wanted that. I wanted him to know it was me and his life wasn't worth two cents. I just didn't think he'd care. He was a drunk and a bum and he killed all those people. He should have died. He shoulda been glad to go. I was putting him out of his misery, you know? So why'd he have to make it so hard?"

He fell silent and then he let out a deep breath. "Anyway, that's how that went. I can't sleep anymore. I dream about that stuff. Makes me sick."

"What about Billy? I assume he figured it out when he saw you at the funeral."

"Yeah. That was weird. He didn't give a shit about Daggett, but he felt like he should get part of the money if he kept his mouth shut. I would have given him all of it, but I didn't believe him. You should have seen him. Swaggering around, making all these threats. I figured he'd start bragging one night about what he knew and there I'd be."

The edge of the niche was beginning to cut into my rear end. I was hanging on so tightly that my arm was getting numb, but I didn't dare ease up. I couldn't figure out how to get us out of this, but I knew I'd better start talking fast.

"I killed a man once," I said. I meant to say more, but that's all I could get out. I clamped my teeth together, trying to force the feelings back down where I'd been keeping them. It surprised me that after all this time, it was still so painful to think about.

"On purpose?"

I shook my head. "Self-defense, but dead is dead."

His smile was sweet. "You can always come with me."

"Don't say that. I'm not going to jump and I don't want you to either. You're fifteen years old. There are lots of other ways out."

"I don't think so."

"Your parents have money. They could hire Melvin Belli if they wanted to."

"My parents are dead."

"Well, the Westfalls, then. You know what I mean."

"But Kinsey, I murdered two people and it's first degree because I looked it up. How'm I gonna get away with that?"

"The way half the killers in this country do," I said with energy. "Hell, if Ted Bundy's still alive, why shouldn't you be?"

"Who's he?"

"Never mind. Someone who did a lot worse than you."

He thought for a moment. "I don't think it would work. I hurt too bad and I don't see the point."

"There isn't a point. That's the part you invent."

"Could you do me a favor."

"All right. What's that?"

"Could you tell my aunt I said good-bye? I meant to write her a note, but I didn't have a chance."

"Goddamn it, Tony! Don't do this. She's had enough pain."

"I know," he said, "but she's got my Uncle Ferrin and they'll be okay. They never really knew what to do with me anyway."

"Oh, I see. You've got this all worked out."

"Well, yeah, I do. I've been reading up on this stuff and it's no big deal. Kids kill themselves all the time."

I hung my head, almost incapable of framing a response. "Tony, listen," I said finally. "What you're talking about is dumb and it doesn't make any sense. Do you have any idea how crummy life seemed when I was your age? I cried all the time and I felt like shit. I was ugly. I was skinny. I was lonely. I was mad. I never thought I'd pull out of it, but I did. Life is hard. Life hurts. So what? You tough it out. You get through and then you'll feel good again, I swear to God."

He tilted his head, watching me intently. "I don't think so. Not for me. I'm in too deep. I can't bear any more. It's too much."

"Tony, there are days when none of us can bear it, but the good comes around again. Happiness is seasonal, like anything else. Wait it out. There are people who love you. People who can help."

He shook his head. "I can't do that. It's kind of like I made a deal with myself to go through with this. She'll understand."

I could feel my temper snapping. "You want me to tell her that? You took a flying leap because you made a fucking *deal* with yourself?" His face clouded with uncertainty. I pressed on in a softer tone. "You want me to tell her we sat up here like this and I couldn't talk you out of it? I can't let you do it. You'll break her heart."

He looked down at his lap, his eyes remote, face coloring up the way boys do in lieu of tears. "It doesn't have anything to do with her. Tell her it was me and she did just great. I love her a lot, but it's my life, you know?"

I was silent for a moment, trying to figure out where to go next.

His face brightened and he held up an index finger. "I nearly forgot. I have a present for you." He shifted, letting go of the torch with a move that made me snatch at him instinctively. He laughed at that. "Take it easy. I'm just reaching in the waistband of my jeans."

I looked to see what he'd produced. My .32 lay across his palm. He held his hand out so I could take it, realizing belatedly that I couldn't free up a hand to reach for it.

"That's okay. I'll put it right here," he said kindly. He set it in the niche, behind the ornamental torch I was clinging to.

"How'd you get it?" Stalling, stalling.

"Same way I did everything else. I used my head. You put your home address on that business card you gave Aunt Ramona, so I rode over on my bike and waited till you got home. I was going to introduce myself, you know, and act like this real polite kid with good manners and a nifty haircut and stuff like that. Real innocent. I wasn't sure how much you knew and I thought maybe I could steer you off. I saw the car and you almost stopped, but then you took off again. I had to pedal my ass off to keep up with you and then you parked at the beach and I saw a chance to go through your stuff."

"You killed Billy with that?"

"Yeah. It was handy and I needed something quick."

"How'd you know about disposable silencers?"

"Some kid at school. I can make a pipe bomb too," he said. Then he sighed. "I gotta go soon. Time's nearly up."

I glanced down at the street. It was really getting dark up here, but the sidewalk was bright, the arcade across the way lit up like a movie house. Two people on the far side of the street had spotted us, but I could tell they hadn't figured out what was going on. A stunt? A movie being shot? I looked at Tony, but he didn't seem to be aware. My heart began to bang again and it made my chest feel tight and hot.

"I'm getting tired," I said casually. "I may go back up, but I need some help. Can you give me a hand?"

"Sure," he said. And then he paused, his whole body alert. "This isn't a trick, is it?"

"No," I said, but I could hear my voice shake and the lie cut my tongue like a razor blade. I've always lied with ease and grace, with ingenuity and conviction and I couldn't get this one out. I saw him make a move. I grabbed him, hanging on for dear life, but all he had to do was give his arm a quick twist and my hand came loose. I reached again, but it was too late. I saw him push out, lifting off. For a moment, he seemed to hover there, like a leaf, and then he disappeared from my line of sight. I didn't look down again after that.

I thought I heard a siren wailing, but the sound was mine.

Epilogue

I billed Barbara Daggett for $1,040.00, which she paid by return mail. It's nearly Christmas now and I haven't slept well for six weeks. I've thought a lot about Daggett and I've changed my mind about one thing. I suspect he knew what was going on. From a distance, Tony might have passed for a woman, but up close, he looked exactly what he was ... a young kid playing dress-up, smart beyond his years, but not wise enough by half. I don't think Daggett was fooled. Why he went along with the game, I'm not sure. If he believed what Billy'd told him, he must have figured he was dead either way. Maybe he felt he owed Tony that last sacrifice. I'll never know, but it makes more sense to me that way. Some debts of the human soul are so enormous only life itself is sufficient forfeit. Perhaps in this case, all of the accounts are now paid in full ... except mine.

—Respectfully submitted,
Kinsey Millhone